What We Carry

What We Carry

♦ *A NOVEL* ♦

KALYN FOGARTY

alcove
press

Copyright © 2021 by Kalyn Fogarty

All rights reserved.

Published in the United States by Alcove Press, an imprint of The Quick Brown Fox & Company LLC.

Alcove Press and its logo are trademarks of The Quick Brown Fox & Company LLC.

Library of Congress Catalog-in-Publication data available upon request.

ISBN (paperback): 978-1-64385-847-0
ISBN (ebook): 978-1-64385-848-7

Cover illustration by Celeste Knudsen

Printed in the United States.

www.alcovepress.com

Alcove Press
34 West 27th St., 10th Floor
New York, NY 10001

First Edition: August 2021

10 9 8 7 6 5 4 3 2 1

To Kevin and my girls, Hayden and Hunter.
It's what we carry together that's everything.

Angel Baby Fogarty, 10.13.17.
Carried in my heart, always.

◆ 1 ◆

CASSIDY

May 22

HOPE SLIPPED AWAY AS my water broke all over the emergency room floor. I steadied myself against Owen, clutching his shoulder with all my strength, afraid I too might slip away if I didn't catch hold of something solid, something strong.

"I think my water just broke," I said to no one in particular. My voice echoed in my ear, unfamiliar and hollow. I was suddenly unsure if I'd even spoken aloud. Perhaps it was some other woman saying those words, feeling the warm wetness seep through *her* yoga pants, soak into *her* sneakers. I opened and closed my mouth, testing the hinges of my jaw. A shallow moan escaped my lips, and I snapped it closed once again. Owen pulled me closer as though he might consume my pain and fear through osmosis. His touch anchored me in the moment, my fears confirmed. This was happening, and it was happening to *me*.

In the movies, these scenes always played out in slow motion. People rushed around, their lips and feet moving, but I didn't hear a sound. The world was starkly in focus but somehow blurry and removed all at once. I was trapped in a moment I'd replay for the rest of my life, not realizing it was merely seconds for everyone else. I'd always assumed it was some Hollywood camera trick, an illusion designed to magnify the drama. As I stood in the ER with my own tragedy dripping around my ankles, I realized the movies were closer to reality than I'd ever cared to be.

"I'm making a mess," I whispered. Owen and a nurse were talking about me as if I weren't right beside them. The nurse frowned and nodded in my direction. I could only stare blankly back. Her black hair was pulled back severely in a bun, secured with a velvet scrunchie. The skin around her eyes was stretched so tight I wondered if such a style gave her a headache. Her forehead was already so high and her brow so stern it erased any softness from her expression. She'd look nicer with her hair loose around her shoulders.

She looked away from me and back to Owen, who gave her the information I was too distracted to share.

"I'm sorry I'm such a mess," I said, louder this time. Both Owen and the nurse turned toward me. An orderly appeared out of nowhere and placed a hand on my elbow, helping me into a wheelchair.

"Don't you even worry about it, Cassidy," the nurse said. I noticed her name tag read *Patti* and the *i* was dotted with a heart sticker. Maybe she wasn't as hard as her hair suggested. "Someone will take care of it. Let's just worry about taking care of you, mama," she said as she grabbed the handles of the chair and pushed me quickly toward the double doors of the elevator.

I bit my tongue against the surge of rage that arose, bubbling up to the surface, desperate to escape my throat. No doubt Patti was simply doing as she was trained, offering kind words and comfort to a nervous patient. Following protocol. *Mama.* The word taunted me. *Mama.* It repeated itself over and over in my head as we ascended the three floors toward the maternity ward. *Mama.*

I wasn't anyone's mama anymore.

✦ 2 ✦

CASSIDY

Before
October 13

"COME ON IN," I said, opening the door a little wider for Rosie to scoot through. Like the obedient dog she was, she'd been waiting patiently in the hallway with one ear cocked in my direction until I gave her the okay to tag along. "We're basically the same," I murmured as she padded in and made herself comfortable on the bathmat. I remembered how surprised I'd been at the similarities between human and dog estrus cycles. I'd never fully grasped my own fertility until I learned about animal cycles in vet school, despite the many anatomy and physiology classes I'd been forced to take along the way. Only recently had I realized how little women were educated about their own bodies.

Rosie rested her soft muzzle on her paws and looked up at me with inquisitive eyes. I'd been talking to the dog more and more since she'd become my coconspirator in Operation Make Baby Morgan. "Well, not you," I laughed. "No babies for you." Rosie cocked one ear toward the sound of my voice as if she were contemplating a response. Trying not to glance at the stick perched precariously on the corner of the sink, I replayed the facts and figures related to my rising and falling hormone levels, a soothing biological mantra that always calmed my impatient mind. It's just science, I reminded myself. Science was my jam. Science was my life. The stick loomed ominously in my periphery as the timer on my phone ticked off the minutes. Ninety more seconds to go.

To keep my restless hands occupied, I picked up the box and tried to focus on the small writing on the back. The instructions were simple enough, but the promise plastered on the front was far less clear. *Results five days before your missed period.* How could one know for sure the date of something that, by definition, would be missed? From my extensive—bordering on obsessive—research of the trying-to-conceive (TTC) blogs, I knew some women claimed to get their positive result as soon as seven days early. On the flip side, there were women who didn't get their plus sign until a week after the fact. Some women had a consistent twenty-eight-day cycle and ovulated on day twelve like clockwork. If only I were so lucky. Instead, I varied from month to month. At the suggestion of a cyberfriend, I'd started an herbal supplement and begun rubbing progesterone cream on my wrists every night, which helped to regulate things a bit. Since setting out on this TTC journey eight months ago, I'd come to realize I knew much more about an animal's cycle than my own. This revelation had caused me to throw myself into learning everything there was to know about my body, as if I were back in vet school studying for finals. No detail was too trivial or gross for me. I needed to know it all.

Rosie whimpered. She knew me better than my husband. "I know, I know," I muttered, resisting the urge to peek. Twelve more seconds. "I said I would wait longer this month." Rosie closed her eyes and looked away. Apparently she'd had enough of this too.

Female fertility was fundamentally a math equation, and I'd always succeeded at math. It had taken some trial and error with the ovulation strips, but I'd finally figured out I ovulated early in my cycle. All those months of doing the deed too late in my cycle made me cringe. So many wasted opportunities. The big "O" held new meaning when you were trying to conceive. I'd quickly recognized Owen didn't have the same gung ho attitude for "ovulation" as for its sexy counterpart, so I'd learned to shut my mouth against all the baby-making banter and readjusted our calendar accordingly. Some new lingerie and red wine didn't hurt, either.

By my precise calculations, I could get a positive pregnancy test by day eighteen of my cycle. That happened to be today. All signs pointed toward positive this month. I could feel it. There was no such thing as oversharing when it came to fertility tracking, and it had thrilled me to report to my online support group two days ago that I'd seen a little blood, which had to be a sure sign of the elusive implantation bleeding. Only the most vigilant of moms-to-be on the support groups noticed it. I'd horrified poor Owen when I called him into the bathroom to confirm my suspicion. He nearly tripped over his own shoes as he ran from the room after I showed him the small brown spots. Each month he acted like I was conducting some elaborate science experiment when, really, I was securing our future. God forbid he had to examine a little blood without getting all squeamish. Just one of the many differences between a man and a woman.

My phone alarm buzzed, and I grabbed it before it fell into the sink. Rosie stood from her spot and moved next to my knee, rubbing her soft red coat against me. I scratched the top of her head as though she were a talisman of good fortune and silently wished for luck. I didn't want much, just a baby.

A single horizontal line. My chest tightened with the familiar force of disappointment. Rosie stared up at me and I nudged her away with my knee, ignoring the small look of hurt in her big brown eyes. I held the stick up closer to the vanity light, twisting it side to side and willing a second line to appear. The overhead light was dull; that was the problem. This was *the* month. It had to be. I squinted, every fiber of my being hoping for at least a faint pink line, but even in the bright glare of the mirror light, it was negative.

I dropped the test in the trash and braced both hands on the counter, staring at myself in the mirror. My high school boyfriend had once told me sad looked pretty on me. Brushing my fingertips across my cheeks, which were flushed a peachy pink, I had to concur that my reflection wasn't entirely unpleasant. My green eyes glittered with tears that would never fall. Sad *did* look pretty on me. But I wished I were crying ugly tears of joy, my face twisted and contorted with happiness.

"Come on, Rosie," I said. Perking up, having forgotten I'd pushed her away only moments before, she followed me into the living room. She jumped up next to me on the couch and curled into my hip as I stroked her muzzle and started the second phase of my monthly ritual.

Every month I'd promised myself I wouldn't test early—but I always did. I'd vowed not to test every day—but I couldn't resist. I'd tell myself everything would be okay, there was always next month—but waiting thirty more days seemed impossible. Eight months. Eight cycles. Zero pregnancies. Thirty early-detection tests at $13.99 a pop; countless cheapie ovulation and pregnancy test strips bought in bulk online and discarded daily. Every one of them had shown only one line. Negative, negative, negative. Picking up the remote, I flipped through Netflix, settling on something I'd seen countless times. *I won't test tomorrow*, I vowed. It wasn't the truth, but it was the lie I had to tell myself to get through the day, the week, the month. Rosie lifted her head and licked my hand before settling back to rest. She knew as well as I did we'd be back in the bathroom tomorrow, but she was telling me everything would be okay. *It's all okay. Everything's okay.*

◆ 3 ◆

CASSIDY

May 22

"**Y**OU SEEM BETTER NOW," Owen murmured. He hovered beside my bed, one hand rubbing my shoulder and the other clenching and unclenching in time with my heart rate monitor. He kept looking at the machines as if he understood what the numbers meant. "Are you still in pain?" His eyes searched my face, looking for any sign of hope. I wished I could give it to him, but I'd left it in the lobby, spilled on the floor.

Less than an hour ago the cramping had been so bad I'd thought I was dying. Since our twenty-week ultrasound was scheduled for this afternoon, Owen had already been on his way home when I called him. We'd been looking forward to this scan for weeks, since we'd finally find out the sex of our baby. One minute I was getting dressed, daydreaming about what names we might choose for a girl versus a boy; the next, pain knocked me to my knees and I barely had the strength to crawl down the stairs to find my phone.

"Cass?" Owen lifted his brow. I shrugged and patted the space next to me on the hospital bed. His nervous energy was making me crazy.

"It's better since we got into the waiting room," I said, refusing to acknowledge out loud what was so obvious to me, if not to Owen. The pain had lessened after my water broke. I didn't need a veterinary degree to know it couldn't be a coincidence.

Owen sat, but his entire body thrummed with pent-up nerves. He looked down at me expectantly, and I wanted to scream but mustered a weak smile instead. How could I be mad at him for relying on me to help him with all the medical jargon? He was out of his element, and the least I could do was calm his fears.

Before I could say anything else, a young nurse in hot-pink scrubs marched into the room, tennis sneakers squeaking on the white floors.

"Hi, Mr. and Mrs. Morgan, my name is Liv, and I'll be asking a couple questions before the doctor gets in," she said, settling herself on the stool in the corner of the room. I missed Patti with an *i* and her stern hair already. It took incredible self-control, but I resisted the urge to correct the *Mrs.* to *Doctor*. I knew it irritated Owen when I did that; he always insisted it made me sound pompous. However, *he* hadn't spent almost a decade working his ass off for those letters after his name.

With her pen and clipboard ready, Liv started asking me a list of prepared questions. I wondered how many times she'd witnessed women experiencing their worst nightmare while she checked boxes and filled in the forms. *Describe the pain. Any bleeding in the first trimester? Any changes to your diet or routine?* I closed my eyes, the dull throbbing in my womb a mere echo of the discomfort I'd felt earlier. Placing my hand over the ever-so-slightly rounded mound of my stomach, I started answering.

As we finished, a faint glimmer of something almost like hope lodged itself in my mind. Nothing else about my pregnancy was out of the ordinary; maybe, just maybe, this was a fluke. Owen squeezed my shoulder, and I realized it was already too late for him. He wanted to believe things were okay.

Liv capped her pen and smiled again. I'd misjudged her when she strode into the room with her swinging ponytail and pink, glossy lips. Her face was unreadable, a perfect mask. "We'll send you up for an ultrasound, and then the doctor will see you." Liv stood, placing the file on the table. "Hang in there, sweetie," she said. Just when I was starting to like her, she called me sweetie. Owen caught me rolling my eyes as she left. I knew I should've insisted on *Doctor*.

He let go of my hand and started pacing around the room like a caged lion once more. Stopping as he passed my file, he let one hand hover above it like he might try to sneak a peek inside, but he decided against it and continued to stalk the perimeter.

"Please sit down," I asked, trying to keep my voice from rising. "You're making me nuts."

"Sorry." He took a seat on the nurse's stool. "It's good they're doing an ultrasound, right? They wouldn't do that if something was wrong with the baby." He said it as confidently as he could, but I heard the hint of a question in his voice. I loved him for trying to be strong, but I knew him too well to be fooled by his bravado.

Still, I wished for once I was the one being comforted. For our entire relationship I'd been the calm and rational one in a crisis. I was the one you called when things got rough and you needed a steady hand and dry eyes. How many pet owners had I consoled after their beloved animal was euthanized? How many times had I calmly explained to a client what such an illness meant to their pet's life expectancy? It was no wonder Owen was looking to me now, expecting me to soothe his fears and tell him just what he needed to hear.

"Maybe," I managed, the only word I could muster that wasn't a sarcastic retort. He looked at me, his eyes already wet with tears on the brink of falling. It was too soon for crying. "I'm sure it will be fine," I added, my voice betraying all the doubt I felt. I didn't have the power to change what was happening, but I had the power to make Owen feel better a little bit longer. And that was better than nothing.

◆ 4 ◆

OWEN

Before
November 11

OPENING MY OWN CONTRACTING company had gone against all the wisdom bestowed on me during my middle-class, midwestern upbringing. How many times had Dad uttered the phrase *slow and steady wins the race* or Mom told me to *play it safe*? I'd never doubted their belief in me, but I sensed their fear of failure and change was greater than any dreams they might have imagined for me—or themselves, for that matter. Dad always expected I'd attend State and play ball—*like he did*. He assumed I'd find a decent-paying job I liked well enough to make a career out of—*like he did*. I'd start a family here in Kansas where I'd be a respectable, hardworking father who provided—*like he did*. Declining the baseball scholarship and attending a private college in Boston was the first time I'd ever stood up against their modest expectations.

Since then, I'd been reinventing myself from the corn-fed Kansas boy everyone saw at first glance into something new and improved. I still subscribed to *slow and steady wins the race*, but I'd decided I wanted bigger and better things from life than I'd ever get by playing it safe.

For four years I'd struggled to keep the business in the black, scraping by each fiscal period with a bit more profit than the one before. Certainly not what I'd hoped to gain by leaving my comfortable position as foreman at a contracting company that catered to the upper echelons of suburbanites north of Boston. Although sorry to see me go, my boss had been supportive when I'd told him I intended to start my own company specializing in landscape architecture along with the standard home renovations that were the bread and butter of his own operation. Since then my business had been steady but not yet booming. Without a booming business, I couldn't afford to hire the extra workers I needed to get the business booming. It was a perpetual struggle I needed to power past. All I needed was my big break, that one account that might push Morgan Contracting and Landscape Art into the major leagues. Without *putting the cart before the horse*—another of my dad's favorite expressions—I thought today might be that big day.

Pulling into our gravel driveway, I let the truck idle in park while Tom Petty finished singing my favorite song. Our stately old saltbox stood tall and proud against a perfect blue sky, an example of why autumn in the northeast was better than autumn anywhere else. When my mom called to lament that I lived so far away, I'd tell her I'd traded the monotonous plains of yellow cornfields for rolling mountains and multicolored leaves. Though there was plenty of beauty in my home state, there wasn't a more picturesque place than here in the center of New England, especially in the fall.

Rosie darted across the yard and dropped her tennis ball next to my truck as she patiently waited for me to greet her. My wife rounded the corner a few seconds behind her, smiling and squinting into the sunlight. Cutting the engine, I stepped down from my big diesel truck. Rosie immediately snatched her ball back, teasing it near my outstretched palm.

"There's my beautiful ginger girl," I said, scratching the curly hairs between her ears before she ran back to

Cassidy. "I missed my pretty ladies." I followed the dog and pecked a kiss on Cass's cheek.

"You're home early," she said, frowning. "Everything okay?"

I smiled, barely able to hide my excitement. I had planned on drawing out the suspense, but who was I kidding? Surprises had never really been my thing. My mom claimed she could tell I was lying from miles away just by the look in my eye. Some things never changed.

"Better than okay," I said, causing her to cock her head and raise a brow at me, eyes twinkling. "I won the bid over at Bourne Mansion." When I'd gotten the news this morning, I'd wanted to scream and shout it from the rooftops but settled for a quick meeting over coffee and doughnuts with my crew. Although I appreciated their grunts of congratulations and pats on the back, I was eager to tell the one person in the world I knew would jump for joy with me.

"Oh my god!" she cried, throwing her arms around my neck and hugging me tight. This was why I couldn't tell her over the phone or drag out the suspense. I wanted to see the pure joy on her face as I gave her the good news, her excitement a mirror of my own. For months she'd listened as I hammered out the proposal for revamping the landscaping surrounding the famous grounds. My mind had been so consumed with the project it was all I thought about, all I dreamed about. It was a mammoth job, the biggest my company had ever bid on. It required an exclusive contract and hiring a team of men to get the work done. Although it was a giant undertaking, the payout would be worth all the time and pressure. Most importantly, it would help build my company's reputation.

"We need to celebrate," she insisted, standing on her tiptoes and kissing me on the lips. Rosie danced around our ankles, eager to get in on the action. "I'll call and make reservations at Sarentino's." She led me into the house.

Cassidy headed toward the small kitchen table and started scrolling through her phone. In the den, the television blared and I rolled my eyes. Cassidy would leave every light and television in the house on if left unchecked. It was one of the few things we'd ever argued about since we'd begun dating almost ten years ago. Maybe turning things off saved only a few dollars a month, but that was a few dollars we wouldn't have otherwise.

The den looked more like a kindergarten classroom than a living space inhabited by two grown adults. Three bins, overflowing with every crafting material known to man were tipped on their sides, spilling markers and construction paper everywhere. A hot-glue gun was stuck to a piece of cardboard beside two tubes of red and green glitter—both closed, I was pleasantly surprised to notice.

I leaned over to pick up one of the projects Cassidy must have been working on before I got home. A Santa Claus, made of clay and an obscene amount of glitter, with the words *Congratulations, Grandpa!* written in Cassidy's neat script across a banner below Santa's boots. I turned the figurine in my hand and saw there was a ribbon attached to the top. A Christmas ornament.

"Seven thirty is perfect, thank you," Cassidy said from the kitchen. I picked up another ornament, this one of Mrs. Claus. *Congratulations, Grandma!* it read. I put the ornaments back down and clicked the television off. Cleary my wife was more talented in the secret-keeping department than I was. Good things occurred in threes, my mom always said, and I was giddy with excitement. Wondering what the third charm might be, I headed back into the kitchen, smiling at Cassidy. How long would she wait to tell me the news?

"I'm sooo craving their rigatoni," Cassidy said, looking up at me from the table.

"Is there anything else you're craving?" I asked, as visions of pickles and ice cream danced in my head.

Cassidy laughed, but I saw a small look of panic cross her face. Overcome with guilt, I realized I was ruining her surprise. Her eyes darted toward the den and then back to me. She hadn't been expecting me home until much later, which would have given her plenty of time to clean up and hide the ornaments until she was ready.

Biting her lip, she looked on the verge of tears. "I can explain," she stammered. I followed as she rushed to the den, nearly knocking over her chair in the process. "It's nothing," she muttered, falling to her knees to shove the markers back into the bins. "I was just preparing."

"Cass, you don't have to explain," I said, confused about where this conversation had gone wrong. "This is amazing news." I was unable to hide the question in my tone. It *was* amazing news—wasn't it?

Cassidy looked up at me and scowled. "I know I say it every month, but this time it's different," she said, still tossing markers into a bag. I watched her scoop everything else up and close the container. When I reached out my hands to help her up, she flinched and clutched the ornaments tighter to her chest. Still clueless, I waited, desperate for an explanation. "I have all the symptoms, and we did everything right last month. A woman can tell," she added, shrugging her shoulders. "I can feel it."

My heart fell as I sank onto the edge of the couch. New month, same story. For the better part of the last year, Cassidy had scheduled sex so it coincided with her monthly cycle. Some months she was better at hiding her motive than others, but I always played along. At first, I looked at it like I was winning either way, but the pressure to perform had made it nearly impossible to feel the same level of passion we'd once had. Spontaneity had become a thing of the past after she informed me I needed to save my swimmers for game day. I tried to ignore the idea that she was only going through the motions, telling myself she wanted a baby but she also wanted me. She thought it went unnoticed when she pulled up the tracking app on her phone and checked off a box after we did the deed.

Like clockwork, ten days later she would complain about some obscure pains and insist she was nauseous, convincing herself she was pregnant. She would take a pregnancy test and I wouldn't hear anything about it until the next time we needed to schedule our special monthly meetings. This was the first time I'd seen anything that might lead me to believe there was more to her phantom symptoms.

"You took a test?" I asked, knowing the answer but afraid to hear her response. She'd started making gifts. This time must be different. Otherwise, this was crazy, and Cassidy wasn't crazy. In fact, she was the most sensible woman I'd ever met. There must be an explanation. She refused to meet my gaze and just sat there, holding the stupid ornaments.

"Cass," I repeated, my face growing hot. "Don't you think it's a little presumptuous to be making gifts for our parents until we know for sure?" I tried to keep the accusatory tone out of my voice but failed. I didn't want to embarrass her, but what the hell was she doing?

Cassidy lifted her green eyes at me, wrought with shame and contempt. "I just wanted to get started on things," she said, tossing both ornaments into the only open container. "Whatever. If we don't need them this year, we will eventually," she said, her voice high and on the verge of hysteria. Her lip trembled and she looked close to bursting into tears. Maybe she was pregnant. It would take a huge hormonal imbalance for Cassidy to cry over a minor argument. She looked miserable, and I didn't have a clue how to comfort her. The stress of getting pregnant was breaking her.

I sighed. Today should be about celebrating the bright future we'd always dreamed of. Hadn't we always wanted to wait until we were settled and successful in our careers before having a baby? There would be plenty of time to start our family. We were both young and healthy. Maybe this was the key to it all, some small blessing in disguise. I knew how to lift the incredible pressure off her slight shoulders.

"I think we should wait," I said, confident I'd figured out the way to make Cassidy happy again. There was no rush. We had a lot left to do before we started the next phase of our life.

Cassidy rolled her eyes as she pushed herself to her feet. "Fine, I'll wait until I get the positive test. Should be any day now," she said.

I shook my head. She wasn't understanding me. "No, I mean we should wait to have a baby," I whispered. This was all my fault. She'd thrown herself into making a baby because she thought it was what I wanted, and it wasn't in her nature to do things half-assed. "Let's stop trying for a while and focus on each other. We don't have to rush," I said, standing and reaching for her elbow. She flexed against me and I loosened my touch, unsure. "I want a baby made from love."

Retracting as if slapped, she froze. Wishing I could rephrase, I tried to backtrack, but stumbled to find the words. What I'd meant to say was I didn't want to schedule sex anymore. I didn't want to worry about ovulation and discharge and all the other words I cringed at each month. What I meant to say was good things happened when you weren't looking for them. Unable to get the words out, I withered under her scornful gaze and said nothing at all.

Cassidy nodded once and allowed me to pull her into a hug she didn't reciprocate. The confidence I'd felt earlier abandoned me as I held her limp body against my own. "Are you okay?" Maybe I'd misread the situation. Was she sad or relieved?

"I'm good," she said, her forced smile not touching her eyes. "Let me finish cleaning up."

With her back turned, I refrained from asking her again if she was okay, knowing it would only irritate her. Sometimes Cassidy needed space to regroup and recharge. I'd learned that lesson the hard way over the years. Pushing her was pointless; she was an immovable force.

I headed back through the kitchen to the hallway bathroom to wash my hands, still covered in dirt and debris from the fire pit I'd built this morning. As I turned on the faucet, I knocked a plastic stick into the sink. Picking it up between my thumb and forefinger, momentarily grossed out at where it had been, I squinted at the small window in the center. Negative. My heart sank a little lower. Setting it back on its perch next to the soap, I turned the water off and backed out of the room. I'd just wash my hands upstairs.

♦ 5 ♦

CASSIDY

May 22

THE TRUTH WAS HIDDEN somewhere in the words the technician didn't say. Even after my water broke and the cramping stopped, I'd allowed a sliver of hope to wedge itself into my brain. Even after the ultrasound was silent, I reasoned that maybe the volume was turned off. Maybe the absence of a heartbeat was a mistake and not the silent sound of my own heart breaking into a million pieces. Through all of this, I kept my thoughts to myself, resisting the urge to ask questions and insert useless medical facts learned from Google and veterinary school.

Owen watched the screen, the black-and-white static alien to him, nothing more than an abstract visual of the baby inside me. The technician left us to wait for the OB/GYN on call tonight. The five-minute wait felt like an eternity, but it wasn't long enough. At least in this limbo there was some chance my baby was alive.

The doctor walked in and, like a vacuum, sucked all the air from the room. I recognized the look on her face. Wasn't I adept at that same look? Owen and she exchanged names and some pleasantries, but I barely heard. I couldn't stop looking at her face.

"I'm sorry, the baby has no heartbeat," the doctor said, her voice echoing in the compact exam room.

No preamble, no placations. No one had invented a better way to deliver bad news. The walls closed in around me. A machine wailed, the keening so loud I gripped my hands against my ears, desperate to quiet the sound. It took Owen shushing me and rocking me against his chest before I realized the horrible noise was coming from somewhere deep inside my soul.

"We'll leave you for a few moments," the doctor said, head bowed to her chest. "A nurse will be in shortly to prepare you for what comes next." She backed out of the room, the technician right behind her.

"I'm so sorry," Owen whispered against my ear, his breath hot and wet and alive. I tried to pull away, but he hugged my stiff body against him, digging his hands into my shaking back. The air was too thick, and I dry-heaved against his shoulder, choking for oxygen. I ripped myself away, but not before seeing his handsome face a mess of tears. He'd never hidden his feelings well, and this was no exception. But beneath the sadness, I saw pity in his blue eyes. A wave of anger flared to the surface. Anger, so much easier than anguish, settled into my core. How much easier to be mad at the way Owen looked at me then to let it break me down. I rejected his pity.

Wiping the tears from my cheek with the back of my hand, I steeled myself against the agony threatening to overwhelm me. I took a few deep breaths, tearing myself from Owen's gaze and grasped for the last semblance of reason I had left.

I avoided hysteria by resorting back to science, something that made sense. "Something was wrong with the fetus," I said, unable to call it a baby any longer, knowing I'd break if I uttered the word. "This was nature's way of balancing the scales." My voice was brittle and unyielding, like the biology textbook I'd recited from memory. Owen pulled back, shocked. Slapping him would have been kinder. "It wouldn't have been healthy," I reasoned, shaking my head back and forth, over and over. "It's better this way." I looked up at Owen, daring him to argue. His shoulders sagged as one last tear fell from his eyes. Before he could take my hand, I pulled it beneath the covers, folding it across my lifeless belly. Looking away, I pinched the exposed skin, relishing the sharp pain.

♦ 6 ♦

CASSIDY

I'D ALWAYS BEEN A creature of habit. My mom had loved to tell anyone who'd listen how I ate only oatmeal for breakfast or how my hair was always crazy in the morning because I showered only at night and refused to brush my hair before bed. There were so many unflattering anecdotes she loved to embarrass me with that I'd lost track of them, even though they used to infuriate me. But the joke was on her. My daily rituals led to productive days, which wasn't embarrassing at all.

Despite her gross exaggerations (I did in fact eat things other than oatmeal and my hair never looked *that* bad), all her little stories only showed how I preferred routine and order. God forbid I didn't crave chaos and uncertainty, the recipe for my mom's specific brand of "creativity" she insisted I lacked. What she called artistic, I called undisciplined. Tomato, tomato, right?

For eight months my morning routine had comprised a predictable chain of events. My alarm went off at 6:45 AM. Before anything else, even using the bathroom, I took my basal body temperature, since you garnered the most exact reading upon waking. While waiting the ninety seconds, I scrolled to one of three apps on my phone dedicated to fertility tracking. Here I'd record my temperature and any other data pertinent to making a baby—usually whether Owen and I had made love the night before or if I'd observed any discharge or abnormalities. After noticing Owen sigh and roll over the few times I'd recorded the deed the night of, I'd decided to dedicate my first waking moments to data collection. My alarm would sound again at 7:00 AM, so I spent the last few minutes browsing the TTC blogs and forums I'd bookmarked before jumping up from bed to prepare for work.

Old habits died hard. As if I were one of Pavlov's dogs, my hand still reached for my bedside drawer to grab the thermometer as soon as the alarm sounded, even after we'd decided to take a break. By day three, I knew something had to be done. It took a few swipes of my angry thumb to delete the apps and throwing the thermometer in the trash to kill the habit.

Over two months had passed, and I was still unsure about waiting. After the initial flare of anger, I'd fluctuated between relief and resentment, with daily doses of sadness. Confusion had reigned supreme. *A baby out of love*, he'd said. What did this mean? Was Owen so oblivious he thought babies floated from the heavens on the beak of a stork? Maybe he thought that because two people loved each other and wanted a baby, one just magically appeared nine months later. Perhaps only women knew how much more went into having a baby.

Consumed by my obsession to make a baby, I'd neglected to think beyond conception and pregnancy. Relieved of my former routine, I now had plenty of time to focus on broader concerns. Suddenly, creating a baby was only the first of many obstacles that I'd never considered but now kept me up at night. Who'd watch the baby while we worked? Breast or bottle? Did we have enough money saved? Were we even cut out to be parents? The less time I focused on ovulation and conception, the more preoccupied I became with the magnitude of raising a human for eighteen years and beyond. At two in the morning, my eyes wide open and staring at the ceiling fan, conception seemed the easiest part in the equation. Unfortunately, I couldn't even get that right.

It was then, during the witching hours of the night, that other thoughts crept into my head. My life had rolled along on a very specific track, one I'd set upon at full speed with no room for doubt. First stop was a top college and veterinary school. *Check.* My education had landed me my dream career, and my hard work ensured that I was successful. *Check.* I'd met and married the man of my dreams; a healthy mixture of luck and timing had led me to Owen. Our mutual love and respect made our relationship survive and thrive. *Check.* A family was next. We had both assumed we'd know when the time was right to have children. Now we'd been married for over five years, with stable jobs and a nice home. The only thing missing from our perfect life was those children. At two in the morning, sleep a distant joke, I wondered *why* we wanted them. Lying awake, I was unable to answer that question. Conception seemed so much more straightforward than motherhood. As night brightened into day, I let the question slip away, tucking it back where it belonged. Off my track.

Some days it was refreshing to live without planning around the days of my cycle, but my pesky internal clock refused to let me off the hook. The ebb and flow of Aunt Flow reminded us women of our empty wombs, a red river that signaled different things to different women. To some, it was a harsh mockery: *Try again next month.* To others it was a symbol of freedom—another month safe. Even though I no longer compulsively checked my apps, the promise of blood made it impossible to ignore my biological clock ticking down. So, while the burden had been lessened, a weight still sank to the pit of my stomach every twenty-odd days, and my heart was heavy with all that I carried.

In an effort to *focus on us*, Owen surprised me with a weekend getaway to our favorite ski resort in New Hampshire. Initially I was irritated at his presumptuous gesture, aided by the help of my boss. Turned out a spontaneous weekend away was exactly what we needed to clear our heads and find our way back to each other at a time when we felt further apart than ever. While I packed my duffel bag, I resisted the urge to slip the ovulation strips (still tucked safely behind the tampons in the medicine cabinet) into the front pocket and slid in a pair of black lace undies instead.

★   ★   ★

Three inches of snow had fallen overnight, and the bright winter sun reflected sharply off the untouched surface, making the parking lot sparkle. The sun was only for display today, its rays shining down nothing but bitter white cold.

Fumbling in my purse for my keys and sunglasses, I shivered against the chill. My body still loosened up from yoga, I jogged the rest of the way to my 4Runner, eager to hop inside. As I reached the door, a wave of light-headedness forced me to lean my forehead against the window to steady myself against the weakness in my knees. Once I'd heaved myself into the driver's seat, my hands shook as I placed them on the steering wheel, leaving a trail of sweaty fingerprints on the leather. Skipping breakfast had been a mistake. My heart rate steadied and I breathed in, relishing the cool air in the car after the stuffy humidity of my Bikram class. This was my punishment for forcing myself out of bed for a seven AM yoga class. Only crazy people did such things.

As I pulled out of the slippery lot, my phone rang. The familiar notes of "Free Fallin'" caused me to involuntarily smile.

"Hey, babe," I said, connecting to the Bluetooth. I hated Bluetooth—the echo annoyed me—but Owen had insisted I use it after my second run-in with a cop for talking while driving. My voice reverberated over the speakers, and I cringed. I've never liked the sound of my own voice. "What's going on?"

This was a rare weekend where we were both off from work. Despite not having any active jobs, Owen had been busy on his computer when I left for class. Usually his business slowed in the dead of winter, but it had been steady since he won the Bourne bid and he'd even been able to turn down customers, a luxury he'd never imagined. Assuming he'd be preoccupied until lunchtime, I'd planned on treating myself to a mani-pedi and maybe even a massage. Checking the clock, I hoped whatever he was calling about would leave time for the self-care I so desperately needed.

"You home soon?" Owen asked, his deep voice playful over the stereo. "I have a surprise for you."

I hated surprises and Owen hated keeping secrets, so it was no wonder he was calling to warn me. Chuckling, I flicked the blinker with my left hand. "I'm almost home," I said, turning onto our block. The snow was wet and heavy, sticking to the massive oaks lining both sides of Foxlea Road. Big wooded lots and wide, quiet streets were a few of the reasons we'd chosen this area of Lynn. The school district was another huge factor, but I pushed the flood of anxiety revolving around this issue to the back of my mind as I pulled in beside Owen's truck.

I took a moment to appreciate the splendor of the big farmhouse I called home. The bright black shutters on our old saltbox, painted a traditional barn red, framed the long windows like a set of eyelashes. It always looked as though the house were smiling.

"Home," I said, turning off the ignition. "Thanks for shoveling the driveway, by the way." Ending the phone call, I pressed my other hand to my mouth as a surge of nausea rose to the back of my throat. I swallowed it back and grabbed my purse, eager to get inside. I hoped Owen's surprise involved breakfast. Some pancakes and bacon sounded perfect right about now.

★ ★ ★

"What's all this?" I pointed to all the papers covering our small butcher-block island. Owen sidled up to the edge and perched on one of the antique stools I'd found at a yard sale last spring. Anticipation was killing him, and he patted the seat next to him, eager to show me whatever it was he had in store for me.

"Oh, just a little something I've been busy working on," he said, smoothing out a large scroll of parchment paper. Leaning over, I planted a kiss on his cheek, causing him to scrunch his nose. "You're all wet and gross," he moaned, wiping his cheek with the back of his hand.

I shrugged and peeled off my coat. It stuck to my sweaty arms and fell in a wet heap to the floor. "Well, I did just spend ninety minutes in a hundred-degree room." I sniffed my armpits and cringed. "I need a shower and food, ASAP." My stomach growled to reiterate the point.

"I promise I'll make you breakfast, but first I want you to look at this," he said, gesturing shyly at the papers in front of him, the dimple in his right cheek prominent as he bit the corner of his lip and lifted one eyebrow at me. He always looked so handsome when inspired. Following his gaze, I studied the complicated drawings and diagrams. It was a floor plan—I could decipher as much—but that was the extent of my understanding.

"We've always talked about making the kitchen bigger," he started, looking around our cramped space. It retained its original layout, a U-shaped room with a formal wall separating the dining room on one side and a small butler's pantry and tiny powder room off the other. While shopping for houses, we'd imagined buying a modern home with a trendy open-concept floor plan. After touring what felt like a million houses, we'd stumbled across this gorgeous old saltbox colonial built in 1854. Between the wide plank floors, high-beamed ceilings, and one-of-a-kind built-ins, we were smitten. We made an offer that same day. Soon we were envisioning ways to update the rambling layout while maintaining its authentic farmhouse roots. We decided to renovate slowly, one room at a time, but life kept getting in the way. Five years later and the house was exactly the same as when we'd bought it, creaky stairways and all.

Owen's blue eyes bored holes in my side, so I studied the plans a little closer. The blueprints were a puzzle to my untrained eye, but I'd picked up a few basics over the years. It was hard to live with Owen without getting an earful about architecture every once in a while.

Turing my head side to side, I oriented myself on the paper and realized it was a blueprint of our kitchen. The shapes and scribbles came into focus. "Is that another room?" I asked, pointing to what might be an extension off one side.

He nodded excitedly. "I'll knock down the wall between the dining room and kitchen and extend the exterior wall in both directions. It would open up the space so we'd have room for an actual island," he said, tapping our makeshift butcher block on wheels for emphasis. "The rest of the space could be a sun-room or an office, whatever we want it to be." He pulled another sheet of paper out from beneath the plans. "Then I'd redo the back patio, adding a pergola over on this side . . ." He stopped, brow furrowed, as he let out a hurried breath. "You hate it?" Looking at me, his face fell.

Shaking my head, I tried to smile, but bile rose in my throat again. The drawings swam before my eyes, and I pushed back from the island, scattering the blueprints every which way.

I made it to the toilet just in time to see last night's dinner come back up. Owen rapped on the door, and I let

out a weak moan. "I'm okay," I said, wiping my mouth
with a tissue before flushing. "Just overdid it this morning
on an empty stomach." I could hear Owen just outside the
door, unsure if he should come in and help or leave me be.
"I'm okay, promise." His footsteps backed away from the
door.

As I turned on the faucet, it hit me. Doing the math
in my head, I counted back the days since my last period.
I might not have the app on my phone, but I was unable
to delete my innate knowledge of my body. My hands
shook as I rummaged in the closet to find one of the tests
I'd buried behind the decorative soaps and towels. Guilt
washed over me as I peed on the stick and tucked it back
into the closet, too scared to wait for the result.

"Much better," I said, closing the bathroom door and
walking back to stand behind Owen. Wrapping my arms
around his neck, I forced a smile. "Tell me more about
this beautiful kitchen you're making for me," I whispered
in his ear. His body relaxed at my touch, and another stab
of guilt lodged itself in my chest. "Better yet, why don't
you tell me all about it as you make me some eggs." My
jaw ached from holding a smile for so long. An imaginary
clock ticked down in my head.

Rosie padded into the room, looking up at me expectantly. *Thirty more seconds*, a voice somewhere deep inside
reminded me. Ignoring it, I grabbed the eggs from the
fridge and busied myself helping Owen make breakfast.
Rosie watched me, sensing my anxiety. She knew me too
well.

◆ 7 ◆

CASSIDY

May 22

THE ANESTHESIOLOGIST ASKED IF I wanted something to ease the pain. Without hesitation, I said yes. What I didn't tell him was that the contractions were nothing compared to the constriction in my chest and the relentless pounding in my head. I only hoped the drugs might help those too.

You're having a miscarriage. In case the lack of a heartbeat wasn't evidence enough, the doctor was required to make it clear that our baby was dead. *Miscarriage. Mis-carry.* Such a peculiar word. To miscarry implied I'd carried my baby badly, or mistakenly. As far as I remembered, I'd done everything right. I'd taken my prenatal vitamins, even though the extra folic acid and iron made me sick. I'd avoided alcohol, sushi, and soft cheeses, even though I loved all three. At work, I'd relied on a technician to take the X-rays, even though I knew I took better images. I ate healthy and exercised, gaining the perfect amount of weight in my first few months. Like every good pregnant woman, I was a regular pincushion for blood tests, and each one had come back negative for abnormalities.

I'd carried my baby well.

Dr. Weinstein, the anesthesiologist, chatted away as he bent over the side of my bed. Not sure if he was talking to me or the nurses, I absently nodded but looked away as he pushed a plunger full of something promising to take away my pain into my IV. The nurses laughed as he joked about the Red Sox, but I couldn't muster a smile. I'd always been a football fan anyway.

Almost instantly the drugs warmed my body, sweet relief coiling into my veins and spreading toward my limbs. The doctor asked me something, but his voice was muted, like he was talking underwater. He seemed pleased with the result and floated backward out of the room. From the corner the television flashed its blue glare into the darkness, casting the room under a strobe light effect. Party in room 4B.

On my left, Owen sat in the uncomfortable pink chair and tried to grab my hand, but my strength was slipping from me. Mumbling, I explained my body was like liquid lava, bubbly and hot and oozing, but my tongue was stuck to the roof of my mouth and my lips were glued to my teeth. The pounding in my head subsided, replaced by the steady whoosh of my heartbeat, growing louder with every beat. *Lub-dub. Lub-DUB. LUB-DUB.*

"My heart," I whispered, closing my eyes to better hear the sound. Owen leaned toward me, his jaw clenched against the tears he held back.

He stroked my cheek, wiping away tears I hadn't realized I'd cried. "I know," he murmured, reaching over the bed and pulling me into a rib-crushing embrace. He squeezed harder, his cheek against my chest, as though he might hug me tight enough to keep my heart from breaking into a thousand pieces, but he was too late. I was already broken.

"I hear it," I said, taking his hand from under my heart and placing it on top of my stomach. "Is it the heartbeat?" I asked, pushing his hand harder against my belly, desperate for him to feel it. The sound I heard was much too fast to be my own heart. I tried to lift my head from the pillow to check the monitors, but it was too heavy; I was stuck. Panic crept to the surface. I needed a doctor. Someone needed to check on my baby. His heart was beating. They'd missed it before, but I heard it now. *Lub-dub. Lub-DUB. LUB-DUB.*

Owen stood and tried to hold me down on the bed, his hands pushing on either shoulder, but I bucked against his palms. The drugs made me weak, but not too weak to fight for my baby. He grabbed for the buzzer to call the nurse, but I ripped it from his hands. "Cass, you need to lay back," he pleaded with me, his face crumbling in despair. We both looked toward the doorway, but no one heard our struggle. It was just us. "The baby doesn't have a heartbeat anymore," he whispered, his lip quivering as he sniffed back the sadness in his own voice.

My head was filled with marbles, each banging against one another as I shook it viciously at him, furious that he didn't hear it, didn't believe me. "I hear it." I clutched my belly. "I *feel* it," I insisted. *LUB-DUB.* Why couldn't he hear it? The machines blipped louder and faster and I closed my eyes, each beep drilling a hole into my brain.

Finally, a nurse rushed in, beckoned by the sound of the machines. Owen let out a relieved sigh. "How's it going in here?" Her voice was low and raspy, like she'd just smoked a pack of cigarettes. Worry creased her already lined forehead as she looked back and forth between us.

Owen didn't look at me. "I think she needs more of whatever the doctor gave her," he said, his voice breaking. "She thinks the baby's still alive." As soon as the words were uttered, he began sobbing. "Please, give her something." The nurse nodded and hurried from the room.

When I opened my eyes—had it been seconds? minutes?—the doctor was back. Dr. Weinstein leaned over my bedside once again and plunged more of the liquid lava into my system. His brown eyes softened behind his dark-rimmed glasses. "Get some rest; you'll be all right." Slowly his voice faded away, and the whooshing became quieter and quieter until it was gone.

Before I could say thank-you, darkness overcame me.

★   ★   ★

The entire process took less than an hour. Along with a little more sedation, Dr. Weinstein administered Pitocin, a drug that induced uterine contractions. The machine showed them coming fast and furious, but I felt nothing. Owen sat by my side the entire time, his face pale and drawn as he watched me push our baby into the world. I didn't yell. I didn't cry. I stayed as silent as our baby.

Dr. Mandini, the doctor on call tonight, explained to us what was happening each step of the way. I turned my head into the pillow, intent on blocking out her voice and thankful for the drugs that let me slip in and out of the room at will. Poor Owen didn't have the luxury of sedation. By the time our baby was delivered, he'd run out of tears. All that remained were two salty streaks running down either cheek.

"Is it over?" Owen asked. My ears perked to the answer I'd been waiting for.

"She just has to deliver the placenta," the doctor answered. Turning my head back to the wall, I let my body do the rest. Later I might marvel at the efficiency of the human body, but in this moment I hated it. Closing my eyes, I willed myself to go somewhere else. Owen squeezed my hand when the doctor finally called it.

"What now?" he asked, still holding my hand.

A nurse stood at the foot of the bed, the doctor already gone. "We can bring him in here for you to say goodbye," she offered. *He.*

"It was a boy?" I asked, the words stilted and slow, the first I'd spoken in hours. Earlier in the day we'd been excited to learn the sex of the baby. I'd never imagined this was how we'd find out. Filled with a sudden rage, I wanted to scream at the nurse, at Owen, at anyone who'd listen. This wasn't how it was supposed to happen. This wasn't fair.

"He was a boy," Owen murmured. He stumbled backward into the chair before his legs gave out. Dropping his head into his hands, he cried so hard his shoulders shook with each sob. It seemed he hadn't run out of tears after all. "Yes, we'd like to see him, please," he said, polite even in his agony.

A few minutes later the nurse returned and placed my son in the palms of my hands. His eyes were closed, a small fluttering of black lashes laid against his cheeks. I studied his perfect button nose and pouted lips. A blue hat covered his head. Someone had wrapped a white layette made from satin and lace around his body like a shroud. If I hadn't known better, I would have thought he was only sleeping. But he was too cold. Too blue.

"I'll leave you alone for a few minutes. Some parents like to take a picture to remember," the nurse added. "Just buzz me when you're ready."

My son was both bigger and smaller than I'd imagined. One app had likened a twenty-week-old fetus to a banana, but he was nothing like a fruit. My baby was seven inches long and weighed twelve ounces. A hint of straight and stern eyebrows framed his closed eyes. Eyebrows like his daddy's. With my fingertips, I stroked his small hands, ten perfectly formed fingers closed over each other as if in prayer. Owen reached down and grazed his own finger across our baby's smooth forehead, gently pushing back the hat to reveal reddish-blond hair so soft it was like touching a whisper.

"Do you want me to take a picture?" Owen asked, reaching into his pocket for his phone.

It took me a moment to answer. I couldn't bring myself to take my eyes off my baby. I memorized his face. Holding him closer to my heart, I wished I could put him back inside me.

"No," I said at last. "I'll always remember him." Lifting him to my mouth, I kissed his porcelain cheek, my lips burning against the cool expanse. "I don't need a picture."

Owen nodded, and I moved over to let him sit next to me on the narrow hospital bed. When I passed him into Owen's big hands, he looked even smaller. Owen cradled him in his callused palm, his thumb stroking his shrouded shoulder. "Me neither," he agreed, reaching over and kissing me on the forehead. We lay together in silence for a few more minutes, neither of us sure how to say good-bye.

◆ 8 ◆

OWEN

I'D KNOWN BETTER THAN to trust the damn groundhog, but here I was, fooled again. In my defense, the last ten days had been tropical for March in New England, with temperatures near fifty degrees midday and never dipping below freezing at night. Dad always swore March roared in like a lion and out like a lamb, but this year's gentle start had been a ruse and we might roar our way right into April.

To make matters worse, I'd woken up to Cassidy's phone ringing with the first of what would surely be many emergency calls. Even though I was still uncertain exactly what it means when a horse colicked, I was fairly certain that whoever coined the phrase *healthy as a horse* had never met one. From my experience as a veterinarian's husband, those enormous animals got a tummy ache at the drop of a hat, and something as simple as the weather was always a factor.

Cass had kissed my forehead before tiptoeing downstairs early this morning. Careful not to wake me, she didn't even turn on the light as she threw on her work clothes in the pitch-blackness of dawn. I waited until I heard the familiar sound of her SUV tires crunching over gravel as she reversed out of the drive before jumping out of bed. It was never clear how long she'd be out on calls, but I figured I had at least two hours. While brushing my teeth, I was plagued with a wave of doubt but convinced myself waiting wasn't an option.

I'd gone over my schedule in painstaking detail and determined I could spare the manpower right now. The weather was always a gamble, but I hoped to finish the exterior renovation before March turned on me again. The sudden drop in temperature gave me a second's pause, but the forecast promised a few more days of lamb weather before the lion roared his ugly head. Better to start now than risk pushing it to the back burner, where it would stay for the next five years.

Despite the chill in the air, it was a beautiful day to be working outside. The sky was that special shade of blue you only saw when the air was a little too cold and the sun was huge and bright but still too far away to warm you. A few of my guys had offered to help, but since we were heading into the busy season, I needed them rested and eager. Today was only setting up; the real construction wouldn't start until Monday.

Bob Seger's raspy voice singing through my earbuds quieted the anxious voice nagging in the back of my head. For the hundredth time, I reminded myself that Cassidy would love the renovation. Sure, it had been a while since we'd discussed it, but she'd been sincerely excited when I showed her the blueprints a month or so back. With all the craziness of doctor's appointments and morning sickness, it was normal to be distracted. That didn't mean she'd changed her mind. *Distracted*, that was it. The kitchen would be off-limits for a few weeks, but she'd never complained about ordering takeout before. Apprehension swirled in my gut, despite my careful planning. Cassidy hated surprises, but this was a happy surprise, right?

★ ★ ★

"Owen!" she yelled again, annoyance and cold painting each cheek a rosy pink. Cassidy stood in front of me, hands on her hips, lips pressed together in a thin line. Clearly, she'd been screaming my name for some time. Pulling my earphones out, I wiped my hair out of my face with a gloved hand.

"Morning, babe," I said, giving her my best million-dollar smile. She didn't look amused. Her eyes flitted around the yard, taking inventory of the sawhorses and tools strewn around the patio.

She opened her mouth like she might yell again but closed it and pinched the bridge of her nose with two fingers, a clear signal she was fighting a headache. Since she'd found out she was pregnant, her migraines had gotten worse. *Hormones,* she'd explained. "You okay?" I asked, hopeful it was the morning sickness causing her distress.

"Well, no, not really," she said, shaking her head. "But that's beside the point. What are you doing?" she asked.

I pushed the goggles back from my face and used them to hold my shaggy curls out of my eyes. Cassidy's eyes softened, igniting a flicker of hope inside me. "I thought I'd get started on the addition," I answered, pulling off my gloves and setting them on the makeshift workbench before handing her the rolled-up piece of paper from my back pocket. She looked it over, but her face remained unreadable. "Remember?" She nodded, still unimpressed. The paper folded back up into itself as she handed it back to me. Not the reaction I'd hoped for.

She sighed, and my stomach dropped. A husband learned his wife's sounds, and I knew what that sigh meant. "Do you really think *now* is the best time to start this?"

Clenching my teeth, I bit back the quick-tempered response that rose to my tongue. I hated that tone. She usually reserved it for her mother, but I'd been on the receiving end enough times to recognize it at once.

"Now is the *perfect* time to start. We've been talking about doing this for ages," I said, standing a little straighter. "And we could use the extra space with the baby coming."

Cassidy sighed again and dropped her chin to her chest, rolling her neck from side to side. "Can we talk about this inside? I'm freezing," she said, bouncing on the balls of her feet. Neither of us moved toward the door. If I followed her inside, it was all over. Sensing my hesitation, she continued, "This is just too much to take on right now. You have the Bourne job coming up, and I'm exhausted. I can't deal with your guys ripping apart my kitchen too." She blew on her hands and waited for me to respond, but I stayed silent.

"Plus, we need to save money now. Who knows what I'm going to do about work once the baby's here." Childcare had always been a point of contention between us, even though I was fully aware that Cassidy intended to continue working full-time after children. She loved her job, and it paid well. Still, she acted as though no one in the history of parenthood had made such an arrangement work. Eventually we'd stopped discussing it. I guess we both hoped it would work itself out when the time came.

"There will never be a good time to do it," I argued, hoping my voice didn't reveal the desperation I felt. Did she really think I hadn't thought of all this, that I'd woken up one morning and decided to bust holes in our walls with no forethought? Looking at her expressionless face, I thought maybe she did think so little of me. "I will always have a job that gets in the way. You're pregnant now, but it won't be any easier once the baby's born."

I'd already lost her. She looked toward the house, not listening to a word I was saying. I might as well be talking to the sawhorse. This argument was over before it started.

"I get what you're saying," she said, stepping toward me with her green eyes shining. "I'm just so overwhelmed." Cassidy rarely let the curtain fall back from her carefully guarded emotions. Either her sudden vulnerability was an act, or pregnancy hormones had softened her. No matter. I wasn't the guy who'd keep fighting until my pregnant wife cried.

"You won't have to do anything. I'll handle it all." Arguing at this point was useless, but I had to give it one last shot. She looked up at me, biting her lip. I sighed my own particular sigh, the sigh of defeat. "But if you really want to wait, I guess we can plan for after the Bourne job . . ."

Instantly her face changed, and relief spread across it in a smile. "I think that's best," she said, wrapping her arms around my neck and kissing my cheek, rough with week- end stubble. "Thank you for listening to me."

Pulling from her embrace, I flipped the goggles back down over my face to shield myself from her gaze. "Get warm. I'm going to clean up, then head to the office to finish up some paperwork," I said, bending and picking up a piece of wood before throwing it onto the makeshift table, causing a hammer to fall to the grass.

She cocked her head as though she might argue but thought better of it. Cassidy always knew to quit while she was ahead. "Okay, I'll see you for lunch?" she asked, furrowing her brow.

"Sure," I said, managing a thin smile that seemed to satisfy her. As she headed back toward the house, I popped my earbuds back in and let the Moody Blues croon. My shoulders sagged as I looked around the yard, then started picking up the tools scattered in the grass. Disappointment replaced my anxiety, and I wasn't sure which was worse. Again I was stuck waiting for the right time to be the right time. Seemed like it would always be not quite right.

My mind distracted, the saw I held slipped from my grasp and landed squarely on my other thumb. Pain, quick and hot, seared through my body, and I cursed out loud. The pain faded to a warm throb as I stood there staring at our unfinished patio, letting the tears fall inside my goggles.

♦ 9 ♦

CASSIDY

OWEN TAPS THE STEERING wheel in time with the radio, and it's driving me crazy. Normally, I'd be singing along. He's even changed the station to an old-school country tune he knows I like, even though he despises country music. This small kindness keeps me from snapping at him to stop. *Just stop.* Not just the tapping but the furtive glances he shoots in my direction as though he's scared I might open the door and throw myself into traffic.

I stroke my empty stomach, trying to remember how it felt yesterday when my son was still inside me. It should feel different, but it doesn't. I push and prod my slightly soft midsection, but it feels exactly the same as yesterday and the day before that and the day before that. It isn't fair. Maybe I'd feel better if there was physical proof my baby is gone. A gaping hole, blood and guts spewing every which way, or a jagged scar seems appropriate. Instead, my stomach is the same rounded mound, only now it's empty.

My baby had only just began kicking before he was gone forever. I think back to the first time I felt it, just a gentle tap from the inside, a little nudge that might've been mistaken for gas or indigestion. Since he was still so small, the kicks were sporadic. Some days I was hardly aware he moved at all. Now I wish I'd memorized each little punch, held my hand against my stomach to feel the tiny weight of each push.

Ironically, I feel every twinge and pull now that he's gone—my uterus contracting back to its normal size, according to the discharge papers. Biting back tears, I hate myself for ignoring the expanding glory of my body as it was happening. I took the miracle of pregnancy for granted and even complained about the discomfort it caused me. Feeling my womb deflate is a special form of torture.

Owen glances at me again. Thankfully, he's stopped tapping. We should talk about it, but I let the radio fill the silence between us instead. I don't know what comes next. Maybe I should Google *what to do the afternoon after losing your child.* I'm sure someone on the internet has written an article on it.

Ignoring his scrutiny, I stare out the window. In the last thirty-six hours, it's rained, and the trees still glisten with dew. Everything is green, so alive and earthy. Unlike me. I close my eyes and rest my temple against the cool window, shutting out the bright spring sun.

The test was positive. No doubt as to whether it was an evaporation line or an actual pink line this time. It was bright and stark against the white window. With shaking hands, I'd peed on the expensive digital test I'd saved for such a time. I didn't even have to wait the full three minutes. PREGNANT popped up almost instantly. Tears stung the corners of my eyes. I'd been waiting for this for so long that I should have been overjoyed. Still, I couldn't shake the sinking feeling in the pit of my stomach. I wrapped both tests in tissue and shoved them to the back of the towel shelf. Out of sight, out of mind.

We hit a pothole and I bite my tongue, the hot copper taste of blood filling my mouth. "Did this happen because we didn't want him?" I whisper, my voice raw and cracked from disuse.

Owen grips the wheel tighter with both hands. "Of course we wanted him," he says, trying to catch my eye, but I continue staring straight ahead. "What are you talking about?"

I was afraid to tell Owen about the test. We were finally in a good place, making plans for the future and acting more like ourselves than we had in years. He'd asked me to wait and here we were, not even three months since having that conversation, and I was pregnant. He wouldn't believe me if I said it hadn't been part of some grand plan the whole time. I wasn't even sure I believed me.

"Nothing," I mutter. It's a crazy thought. We wanted a baby. We always wanted a baby. Until we wanted to wait. "Maybe we didn't want him enough," I say, finally turning toward him. If only our son knew how much I wanted him now. I want him more than I've ever wanted anything in my entire life. Maybe this is the problem. Maybe I want him more now that he's gone.

Without signaling, Owen pulls the car over to the shoulder of the road. "Don't," he says, taking my limp hand in his. He shakes it, like he's trying to shake the life back into me. "We wanted him, and we loved him." He looks at me, blue eyes watering. "This isn't our fault," he says firmly. I shake my head, wanting it to be the truth.

"Are you mad?" I asked. For a split second something flashed across his face, but it was gone before I could define it. He lifted me off my feet, hugging me close.

"Mad? Why would I be mad?" he said, mouth against my ear. "This is everything we ever wanted." I leaned into his chest and listened to his heart as it fluttered wildly. I'd dreamed about this moment, obsessed over it, planned for it. Why was I so scared?

"Cass," he says, and my attention snaps back toward him. "This isn't your fault."

A million *what-if*s and *could've/should've*s run through my mind. Was it the wine I drank before I knew I was pregnant? Did I push too hard at work? Should I have stopped drinking coffee? Selfishly I insisted on still drinking my one cup a day, despite the potential risks. I failed our son in one big way or many little ways, and there's nothing I can do to fix it now.

"I don't understand why this happened," I moan. "It's not fair."

Owen sighs. "No, it's not." He turns to me and strokes my cheek. "But everything . . ."

I jerk my head up and pull away from him. "Don't," I say, shaking my head. "I don't want to hear it from you too. I hate that fucking expression." I pick at a loose thread on the sleeve of my gray sweater. It unravels, and I pull harder. "*Everything happens for a reason*," I mock. "What the hell does that even mean?"

Owen settles back behind the wheel, refusing to engage. He puts the truck back in gear, and the tick of the turn signal fills the car. "I don't know, Cass." He pulls onto the road. "It's just something people say."

"It's bullshit," I mutter. The thread of the sweater loosens up other threads. Soon the entire thing will come undone. It's my favorite; now it's ruined.

★   ★   ★

It's been seven years and I still haven't gotten my wedding dress cleaned and preserved. After the wedding, I meant to take it to the dry cleaner in town but kept forgetting. It hung in the dining room for two weeks before Owen dragged it up the two flights of stairs to the old attic. A compulsive neat freak, he couldn't stomach seeing it hanging there day after day. When I finally noticed it was missing, he promised to retrieve it whenever I was ready to take it to the cleaners. It's been collecting dust ever since.

I left the hospital without a baby, but I got a care package instead. Along with the extra-absorbent maxi pads and mesh panties meant to curb the bleeding, the nurses sent home a piece of the "bereavement gown" my baby had been buried in. Stapled to the gown was a business card with the name and number of the woman who donated shrouds to the hospital. Laying the satin fabric on my knee, I pull my laptop out, and a quick Google search finds a Facebook business page for *Angel Gowns*. Under the ABOUT ME heading, I learn she uses donated wedding dresses to supply hospitals with gowns meant for stillborn babies. Her most recent status update indicates she's in need of dresses. A few more clicks and I'm private messaging the woman. To my relief, there's a donation box on her front porch. I can drop my dress without having to speak to anyone, and better yet, she's only fifteen minutes away.

Owen comes in as I'm closing the computer and sets a bowl of chicken soup on the side table. My stomach growls, but the thought of food makes me nauseous.

"Eat," he says, holding his own bowl on his lap and blowing on it. "You haven't eaten in days," he says, as though I don't already know.

"I told you," I repeat, staring at him defiantly. "I'm not hungry."

He slurps his soup, and I cringe at the sound. Listening to people eat is irritating when I'm in a pleasant mood. Now it fills with me with a near murderous rage. "I want to donate my wedding dress to the company that made the burial gown." I speak loudly, hoping to drown out the sound of the gulping. "Can you bring it downstairs when you're done?"

He nods, wiping his mouth. "I think that's an amazing idea," he says, putting the spoon down. I feel my shoulders ease a little. "Of course I'll get it down for you."

I cock my head at him and raise my brow. "I want to donate it today," I say, daring him to argue. "I told the woman I'd drop it this afternoon."

Owen opens his mouth, confused. "Cass, can't it wait a few days? We *just* got home. I think you should rest," he sputters.

I stand, the blanket falling in a puddle to the rug. "I'll get it myself," I say. "I thought you'd be happy to get rid of the dress; you complained about it enough," I hiss.

He frowns, wounded. I just look away. "Cass, sit down. I'll get it for you." He stands to follow me.

"No, it's fine." I take the full bowl of soup and head to the kitchen with him on my heels. "I need to do this now."

He stops me as I stand in front of the sink and wraps his arms around me. I pull away, desperate to escape his embrace, but he holds me tighter. I throw my head back and catch him in the nose, but he's undeterred. "Shhh," he whispers in my ear, shushing me like I'm a child having a tantrum. As I struggle harder, the bowl clatters into the sink, sending soup everywhere. "Shhh," he whispers again.

"Stop it," I growl, trying to claw his arms off mine, but he's too strong. He spins me around and I stiffen my back, pulling away but I'm stuck between Owen and the sink. "Let me go," I mumble.

"No," he says, entwining his hands behind my shoulders. "I won't."

I curse at him under my breath, the fight leaving me. A deep whimper escapes my mouth, and I crumple like a rag doll into his arms.

"Why?" I ask again. "Why did this happen?"

Owen hugs me tighter, and I lean my forehead against his shoulder. My body heaves with dry sobs. He rubs my back and lets me shudder against him. I scream into his chest, spit soaking through his shirt and mixing with our tears.

"I'll get the dress and take you wherever you want to go," he murmurs, rubbing his hand over my hair, and I nod, swallowing the lump in my throat. "I love you."

I close my eyes and let him hold me. My mind races with all the things I should say, but don't. There's no reason to donate the dress today, and Owen's right, I should rest. I knew he'd protest my request, but I asked anyway. I wanted the fight. Lashing out felt good, and part of me wishes Owen fought back. But he agrees to my crazy whim because that's Owen, and he loves me. He'd do anything to ease my pain—anything. Without a doubt in my mind, I know he'll be an amazing father. Blinking back the hot tears bubbling from my eyes, I wish I had as much confidence that I'll be a good mother.

◆ 10 ◆

JOAN

After
May 23

CASSIDY DIDN'T LEARN TO talk, she learned to argue. For example, thirty odd years ago we sat at this very table with a pack of crayons and a coloring book and she haughtily declared I was coloring the sky wrong. When I said the sky was blue, she informed me it was actually purple. This was the start of a lifetime of contrary views. Once I mentioned that she looked lovely in yellow dresses and with her hair pulled back. From that day forward, she kept her wild mane loose and untamed and refused to wear anything besides jeans. She avoided the color yellow completely until some boyfriend convinced her it looked nice on her (well, duh). When she was thirteen, I encouraged her to explore the arts. Some of her sketches (mostly of horses and animals) were so promising. To spite me, she abandoned her pencils and dedicated her focus to studying science and math. We couldn't even share an after-dinner snack. If I was in the mood for something sweet, she wanted something salty. Which is the perfect word to describe my firstborn daughter—*salty*. Thankfully, she was a gifted student who kept out of trouble. I always worried she'd develop a drug habit or an affinity for bad boys as a sort of teenage rebellion. Instead, she mostly ignored me. Not sure which was worse.

"Why hasn't she called?" I ask. Jack lifts his eyes from the crossword puzzle perched on his knee but doesn't move from his easy-boy recliner. While I've been running around all morning like a chicken with her head cut off, he's been sitting here, mindlessly filling in the boxes and asking for help with clues every so often. This normally irritates me, but it's much easier maneuvering around the kitchen without him hovering at my shoulder trying to "help." For this occasion, I haven't even asked his opinion. I found a recipe for some good old-fashioned comfort food promising to bring family together and warm the soul all on my own.

He raises a brow and drops his pencil to the side table. I wince as he cracks his knuckles, one of his worst habits. "I don't know, Joanie. I'm sure she's just taking it easy," he says, glancing toward the kitchen. "Sure smells good in there."

No surprise he's sticking up for Cassidy. Rolling my eyes, I flitter back to check on the bread machine. Claire, my youngest, gave it as a gift a few years ago, but this is my first time using it. With all the low-carb, no-carb diets phasing in and out, I've been hesitant to serve bread with dinner anymore, afraid of committing some modern faux pas. Maybe cauliflower bread would be a cool substitute. Everything seems made of cauliflower nowadays.

My sourdough is rising properly. Well, it's rising, anyway. There's still twenty minutes left, but the warm, yeasty smell fills the kitchen, mixing pleasantly with the garlic and onions in the stew. Pleased with myself, I stare at the phone on the wall, willing it to ring. It stays stubbornly silent, just like my daughter.

"She's infuriating," I proclaim, standing in front of the brick fireplace. A framed picture of Cassidy and Claire as adolescents sits front and center. Cassidy was fourteen, the age when daughters naturally pull away from their mothers. Since Cassidy had started that phase a decade earlier, fourteen was just another rough year among many. Claire was only eleven, still my baby girl, but eager to please her antagonistic big sister. The picture captures a harmonious moment, but it's only a brief snapshot of a brutal day that began with Cassidy refusing to wear the matching outfits I'd set out for her and Claire. Once Claire realized her big sister thought it was dorky, she adamantly refused as well. Resigned, I let them choose their own clothes. We proceeded to fight about everything, from where to take the picture to how to stand and smile. Eventually I snapped one picture of them smiling with their arms around each other. I'm pretty sure one of us was in tears at every point during that nightmare of a photo shoot.

Heaving himself back to an upright position, Jack settles me with one of his long looks, one that usually puts me in my place. "You can't be mad at her today," he chastises. "I'm sure she'll call you as soon as she can."

I shrug, but I'm skeptical. Most likely she'll call Jack before reluctantly agreeing to talk to me. The chances of her calling me outright are slim to none. I pull my phone out of my back pocket to check the screen, even though it's set to vibrate. Nothing. No calls or texts. At this point I'll settle for one of her short, rude text messages. Something's better than nothing.

"Maybe you should call her," I suggest, sitting on the plaid couch across from Jack. "I'm sure she wouldn't mind hearing from you." I can't hide the bitterness in my voice. "I just don't understand that girl," I say, shaking my head. "A girl needs her mom at a time like this."

Jack nods slowly, stuck between us like he so often ends up. Quick to defend Cassidy's tantrums and acts of defiance since childhood, Jack remains loyal to her moody ways, even now. Sometimes he stands up for me, eager to soften the blows between his two stubborn women, but the scales have always been tipped in Cassie's favor. There are times when I'm careless with my words, especially when stressed, and I'm thankful he's always been there to translate what I mean but can't verbalize. Still, I wish he'd stand firmly on my side—just once—even if I'm being irrational or harsh.

"Please, Jack," I plead. "I need to grieve too. I want to be there for her."

He bites his lip but nods once in agreement. Surprised, I refrain from outright gloating, though I can't help a slight smile. "But let me do the talking, all right?" he says, taking out his own phone. He waits for me to agree before dialing her number. Eagerly I nod my head, but I cross my fingers behind my back.

"Put her on speakerphone." Glaring at me, he lifts a finger to his lips and beckons me to be quiet. Satisfied I'll remain silent, he hits speakerphone and sets the phone on the side table between us.

It rings and rings, and just as I fear she's screening the call and sending us to voice mail, she answers. "Hi, Dad," she says, her voice raspy, as if she's been crying. Although a normal response, it's still shocking. Cassidy never cries. Even as a baby she let us know we upset her in other ways.

"Hi, sweetie, how are you doing?" he says, his voice soft and soothing. I sit on the edge of the couch, waiting with bated breath.

A pause. "I'm okay. Upset, obviously," she stammers before clearing her throat. "We're just trying to make sense of it." Another long pause. It takes all my willpower not to speak up. God, how do Jack and Cassidy ever have phone conversations?

"Take all the time you need. Your mother and I are here if you need us," Jack says. Sensing the conversation is already ending, I wave my hands and point toward the kitchen. Why isn't he inviting her over for dinner? Do I really have to spell it all out for him? I curse at myself for not giving him a list of talking points before asking him to make the call. I'm not sure what I expected. He's never been much for small talk.

Jack squints at me and shrugs, puzzled as to why I'm swinging my hands around wildly. I lean back on the couch in frustration before pointing at the kitchen and mouthing *invite them over* as clearly as I can. Exasperated, I grab the phone from the table before he can say good-bye and hit the speaker button again. Pressing the phone to my ear, I scurry to the kitchen.

"Joan," he scolds, standing to follow me. Casting a quick glance over my shoulder, I shrug and give him my best innocent look. He glares at me, his thick eyebrows a stern line across his forehead.

"Cassidy," I murmur. Despite the distance between us, I sense her tension, right through the phone line. The subtle exhalation followed by pregnant silence. "We are just so sick over what happened," I say, ignoring her lack of response. Picking up the ladle, I stir the stew. It's thickening up nicely and smells exactly like I hoped, warm and inviting. *Good Housekeeping* was right, just the meal to cure the blues.

"Thanks." Her voice is hard, not thankful at all. My hand stutters and stew spills over the side of the pot, sizzling on the burner. I replay my words, unsure what I've said that makes her sound so angry.

Placing the lid back on the pot, I trudge on, determined to get through to her. "What I mean is, we'd love to have you and Owen over for dinner." Smiling into the phone, I wait for her reply. The moment stretches on. "I really think we need to grieve together," I add, remembering a bit of advice I heard on *Oprah*, or maybe it was *Dr. Phil*. Whoever it was told the audience how important it is to mourn the loss of a family member together and how isolating oneself is detrimental not only to the grieving process but also to your health in general.

"This was our grandchild, and we're mourning too." My voice cracks, but I suppress my tears. Even though this baby is gone, we considered him a grandchild just as if he were alive and well.

Cassidy snorts into the phone. "You would make this all about you," she says. If she were standing in front of me, she'd be rolling her eyes. I can see it clearly in my mind's eye. "Unbelievable. Can I speak to Dad again, please?"

I'm speechless. Again I'm at a loss as to where things went wrong. I've only ever wanted to support my daughter, and here she is, throwing it in my face and accusing me of being selfish. *Me.* I look around the kitchen at the overflowing sink full of dishes, the mess of ingredients on the counter, the bubbling stew. My eyes settle on the red light flashing on the bread machine. I missed the timer. Rushing to the counter, I see the once-golden crust has turned a dark brown and is spilling from beneath the lid. Ruined.

Unplugging the machine, I switch the phone to my other ear. "No, you may not speak to your dad again. You can come over and eat the dinner I've spent all day cooking and talk to me and your father together," I grumble, eliciting another look from Jack. "You need to be with family today." Silence over the line. "Cass, you there?"

A sigh. "Yes, Mom, I'm here," she says. "I'm not feeling up to leaving the house today. I just delivered my dead baby and want to curl up on my couch and not *talk it out* with family right now. Say 'bye to dad for me." She hangs up.

I hold the silent phone to my ear for a moment before setting it down on the table. Jack looks at me with concern, and I shake my hand at him, heat rising to my cheeks. It was so typical of her to lash out when I was only trying to help. Cassidy has always twisted my words and turned even the most innocent statement into a criticism I never intended. Half the time I keep my mouth shut for fear of having my head chewed off. But I couldn't keep my mouth shut about this. That would have been heartless.

"What did she say?" Jack dares to ask. "She coming over?"

I let out a frustrated groan. I'm not sure who's more maddening, Jack or my daughter. They're both so purposefully obtuse, it makes me want to scream.

"No, Jack, she's not coming over," I say. "Your daughter was clear she has no intention of spending any time with us today. Like always, she's got it all figured out herself." I bite back the hysterical tears I feel boiling to the surface. A cup of lavender tea and a cool compress will ease my nerves. Inhaling through my nose, I relax my shoulders and purse my lips, keeping my jaw relaxed like my yoga instructor taught me. As I exhale through my mouth, some tension melts away.

"I just don't understand why she's always so hard on me," I lament. "Not just today, but every time we have a conversation, it ends with her talking down to me like I'm nothing," I say, sniffling. I'm not one for self-pity, but sometimes a mother feels abused by her daughters. Enough is enough already. If only I'd had sons.

Jack licks his lips, a surefire sign he is about to dig in and offer some pearls of wisdom. I'd be more annoyed if they weren't often spot-on. I married the man for a reason. I brace myself for some hard truth.

"Joanie, you never say what you mean when you're talking to Cassie," he starts, rubbing his mouth with the back of his hand before continuing. "Take right now, for instance. You've been worried sick about her for the last twenty-four hours, cooking up a storm and preparing to have her over and take care of her like she was a baby girl again," he says.

Nodding in agreement, I'm glad he understands where I'm coming from. If only Cassidy weren't so bullheaded.

"I've watched you pace around this house so many times, I'm surprised there isn't a divot in the rug from those slippers."

I nod again, but my relief is replaced with irritation as his face changes. I sense a *but*.

"But then you get on the phone and you don't say any of that. You change, and I'm not sure how to describe it, but you do. Suddenly you're bringing up this, that, and the other thing, and none of them are what you ought to be saying. Then she talks back like she always does, and you get all flustered and you dig yourself deeper down the hole you've dug, and neither one of you gets anything good from the talk."

Inhale deeply and slowly through your nose, I remind myself. I can't help but purse my lips as I exhale loudly, scowling at Jack. So typical. He understands me, but he's taking Cassidy's side. Like always.

"I do not get flustered," I argue, feeling a little flustered now, but I'll be damned if I let him know that. "She just refuses to listen. I don't know why it's so hard for her to come over here," I mutter. "I never have this problem with Claire," I insist, knowing it's not fair to compare the two girls. Claire's always been my steady child. Where Cassidy wanted to argue and fight, Claire wanted to keep the peace. Claire's never been a pushover, but she's diplomatic about picking her battles, even more so now that she's a mom herself. It must take the patience of a saint to raise a house with three young boys, and Claire makes it look easy. Cassidy could learn a thing or two from her little sister, if you ask me. Which she never does.

Jack looks at me, one side of his mouth lifting in a knowing smile. "Maybe we let her have a pass this one time," he whispers. "She's been through the ringer, and I doubt she meant to hurt your feelings. Why don't we take some stew over to their place tomorrow instead?"

I shrug halfheartedly. As much as it kills me to admit it, he's right. I can't imagine the heartache Cassidy is suffering. If I could take her pain away and make it my own, I would. If only I could say as much to her without sticking my foot in my mouth. Somehow I just never get it right. I've always tried too hard or not hard enough, never mastering the perfect motherly amount some women are naturally gifted with. If only I could be more like Jack. In Cassidy's eyes, Jack can do no wrong. Sometimes I've hated him for it, but mostly it's a blessing. I'm not sure what would have become of us if Jack hadn't been around to soften our hard edges.

"Fine," I agree, letting out one last deep breath. He holds out his arms and I fall into his embrace, snuggling deeper into his big bear hug. Laying my cheek against his broad chest, I let him comfort me, the way only Jack can.

◆ 11 ◆

CASSIDY

After
May 29

MY FIRST DAY BACK at work is a blur of well-wishes and platitudes, depending on whether the client has heard the bad news or not. Hoping a little mindless shopping might erase the torture of each overly sympathetic face, I take the long way home and end up drawn to the giant red dot like a moth to a flame. Now I wonder if I should've cut my losses for the day. Gritting my teeth, I push my cart around a woman parked sideways across the aisle, brushing against her purse and eliciting an angry stare. I bite my tongue and stroll deeper into the store. No sympathetic faces here, just a lot of self-involved jerks.

You look amazing! Absolutely glowing! Cherish this time; it's over in the blink of an eye! Mrs. Kennedy clearly hadn't heard that my glow had been extinguished, although her last little nugget was on point. It *was* all over in the blink of an eye.

I'm so sorry, Doc. At least you know you kids can get pregnant; that's half the battle. This one irritated me a bit more than the others, especially after hearing it so frequently from members of our own family. Owen reminded me the intention was good, but still. Too soon. Yes, I can get pregnant. But that doesn't bring my baby back or offer any explanation as to why this tragedy happened. What good is being able to get pregnant if I can't stay pregnant?

Another text pings, my phone a relentless source of "comfort" in the wake of my loss. I don't bother pulling it out of my purse. I can guess what it says. Some message meant to ease the discomfort and guilt someone has over having healthy children, for not being broken themselves. It always ends the same—*you don't have to respond, I just wanted you to know I'm thinking about you.* Usually a few heart emojis are stuck to the end for good measure. It makes me evaluate all the benign but hollow texts I've sent over the years. The ones I sent in hopes of warding off my own bad luck, hoping karma would one day reward me for my kindness. The truth is, they don't want my response and I don't plan on giving one.

★ ★ ★

"Shit!" I mutter, the front tire of my cart hitting a paper towel display and scattering a few across the tile. Throwing two rolls into the cart, I quickly turn the corner, hoping no one saw.

Everything happens for a reason. By far my least favorite and the most common of the bunch. It's thrown around all the time to explain the inexplicable, often followed by a tale of heartbreaking loss and resilience, promising that some exceptional thing will come from this shitty situation. I'm not a heartless person, but I wish they'd shut the fuck up. Nothing good is coming from losing my baby. Maybe someday I'll feel differently, but right now it's just a terrible thing that happened. No greater meaning need be discerned. Promising that everything happens for a reason only eases the discomfort of the person making the promise.

Like magic, I end up in the baby section. People joke that you don't know what you need when you walk into Target—Target *tells* you what you need. This has always applied to me. Somehow a quick trip for laundry detergent inevitably ends with me spending hundreds of dollars on stuff I didn't realize I needed . . . until Target told me so. Looking up at the ceiling, I wonder what cosmic prank the universe is playing on me but stroll down the infant aisle as though pulled by an invisible force.

Standing in front of a clothing display, I feel like a fraud invading a space reserved for mommies and mommies-to-be. I flip through a rack of onesies, my heart tugging painfully as I finger one with a tiny dinosaur on the front. A shelf lined with stuffed animals floats above the display, a blue *It's a boy!* teddy bear sitting in the center. Without thinking, I snatch the bear and toss it into the cart, glancing around furtively to see if anyone caught me, the fake mom, buying toys for a baby who doesn't exist. The blood rushes to my head and I backtrack, adding the dino onesie and some socks into the cart. I see a bib with *Mama's Boy* emblazoned across the front and throw it atop my growing pile. My body tingles and my heart races. This must be what shoplifters experience when they slip a tube of lipstick into their pocket, unseen.

A woman pushes her stroller into the aisle space next to me, startling me from my sneak shopping. Her baby is about six months old and wears an enormous pink bow. It's hard not to stare at her cute and gummy smile, those chubby cheeks and little toes that she keeps grabbing at while giggling in my direction.

"I'm expecting a son," I hear myself say to this stranger. Her hand pauses on a frilly dress as she glances at me without making eye contact. Using her free hand, she pulls the stroller a little closer to her hip. I'm aware I'm holding my flat stomach and nodding my head manically, but I can't stop myself. I've no control of my actions. Sensing something is off, the other mom smiles without showing her teeth and makes her way down the aisle. As they turn the corner, the baby cries. It starts as a quiet whimper but turns into a full-blown wail once they're out of sight, the baby also sensing something's amiss.

The baby's cry echoes in my brain, triggering some primal instinct of my own. I clutch my hand across my chest, afraid I'm having an acute heart attack in the middle of Target. For a brief second I'm embarrassed someone will find me collapsed next to my cart of fraudulent baby goods and debate pushing it out of reach. Pain spreads across my chest again, but I realize it's not a cardiac event. It's worse. My boobs, already bigger from the pregnancy, swell and harden beneath my palm. A tingling around my nipples turns into a sharp pulling and tightening that radiates toward my armpits. The wailing seems to get louder, even though I know that's impossible. The baby is long gone by now, probably halfway to the checkout line if the look on her mother's face was any indicator. My shirt stretches uncomfortably across my chest. A vision of The Hulk ripping through his civilian clothes comes to mind. *My milk is coming in.* The rational, scientific part of my brain comes to the rescue, struggling to quell the panic rising inside me. Glancing down, I see two large wet spots circling either nipple. Pain and mortification fight the logical part of my psyche and come out victorious.

Looking around for someplace to hide, I see a sign for MATERNITY. Another cosmic sign I'll meditate on later. Grabbing a sweatshirt from the closest rack, I push my cart to the dressing room.

"How many, miss?" the cheery attendant asks, her smile too wide and happy for my current disposition.

"One," I snarl, clutching the hoodie to my chest and pulling my cart behind me. "Can I leave this here?" I ask, eager for the woman to open a room so I can have my moment of shame in solitude.

The woman eyes my cart full of baby paraphernalia and notices my stained shirt. She nods sympathetically. "Oh, honey, it's happened to us all," she says, shooting me a grandmotherly look over her shoulder as she unlocks a room. She holds it open as I scurry inside, afraid my face will melt off I'm so ashamed.

"After my first, whenever I heard a baby cry, my milk would let right out and I'd be a soaking mess," she says, her kind eyes wrinkling at the corners as she loses herself in a memory. "Mine are all up and grown now, but I remember when they were little. It's so hard to leave them, isn't it?" She shakes her head, bringing herself back to the present. "You take all the time you need in here," she says before finally closing the door. I let my breath out in a whoosh and sit on the plastic seat, avoiding my reflection in the fluorescent-lit mirror.

A light tap on the door. "Cabbage leaves," the woman says without waiting for my permission. "Little trick to ease the pain when those milk machines fill in. They work miracles," she adds. "Oh! And there are some nursing pads in the formula aisle." Each little piece of advice is like a bullet to my heart.

Glancing up, I see a disheveled woman staring back at me in the mirror. Her hair is loose from its clip and sticks out on either side, and her mascara is smudged under one eye. This woman looks haggard and sad. *Desperate.* I don't recognize her. Some other woman has taken over my body.

Exhaustion hits me like a truck. My breasts ache, but the worst of the pain has already spilled inside my bra and down the front of my shirt. Even my boobs are crying now. Pulling the new sweatshirt over my head, I ignore the rest of my hair that falls loose from the clip. I stare at myself a moment longer in the mirror and almost laugh at the ironic slogan on my chest—LITERALLY PREGNANT. Ripping the price tag from the sleeve, I stuff it in my pocket so I can pay for this forty-dollar monstrosity at the register.

Sparing myself one last glance in the mirror, I lift my chin and try to tame my wild hair. Peeking out of the dressing room, I say a silent prayer of thanks that the attendant is busy somewhere else. I don't think I can stand any more unwarranted advice about my boobs. Rushing to my cart, I wheel my embarrassing stash away from maternity toward the grocery section of the superstore. Before heading for the self-service register, I make a detour to the vegetables and grab a head of cabbage, just in case. Like every other time I've checked out at Target, I marvel at the amount of money I've spent and curse the store for insisting I *need* every last item.

★ ★ ★

The bright glare of the truck's headlights warns of Owen's arrival just a moment before the familiar crunch of gravel travels in through the open window. For a brief second they illuminate the nursery, a spotlight first on the diaper-changing station (still in its cardboard box), then the crib (missing the mattress), and settling on the half-finished forest mural on the wall opposite the window. Owen helped me paint after agreeing upon a camping theme for the room. It was a unisex nod to our mutual love of the outdoors.

The headlights fade as the truck door slams and darkness descends on the nursery. It doesn't matter; I can describe the room with my eyes closed. In the back corner is a little tent filled with stuffed animals and toys, a perfect hideaway for a little boy or girl. I imagined my child snuggled in his tent with his favorite book, pretending he was holed away in a magical forest. The hazy purple moonlight filters in from outside and the tent casts a long shadow across the room, like an arrow pointing toward me.

Rosie studies me, her inquisitive eyes soft and unblinking and her nose resting on her paws. We've been sitting together on the thick carpet for so long I've lost track of time. The room went from dim to dark quite a while ago. Resting on my lap is a blue box labeled *Baby*

Box. A gift from my mother, it's supposed to hold all the special "firsts" you're meant to collect and cherish—the hospital receiving blanket, first tooth, first lock of hair. My baby won't have any firsts, so I'm improvising. I've folded up the T. rex onesie I bought and placed it beside a pair of blue socks and the teddy bear. The burial gown made from some stranger's wedding dress is draped in the corner over a silver rattle. Maybe the woman who wore this white dress lost a baby herself and donated it on the day she left him at the hospital. It comforts me to think I'm a member of a secret club of bereaved mothers shrouding the children of those who come after us.

As I stroke the soft fur of the teddy bear, my gaze circles the dark nursery. I had plenty of things to add to the box right here in this room, but none belonged. Everything in the room is from *before*. *Before* miscarriage and death were blips on my radar and my only concern was which mobile to buy and which sheet set matched the theme of the room. Sometimes I complained about all the trivial stuff needed to prepare for a baby. My registry was a source of anxiety as I tried to discern which items were essential versus wastes of money. Diaper Genie or regular trash can? Swing or rocker? What I wouldn't give for those worries now.

I hear Owen's footsteps climbing the staircase an instant before the hallway light flicks on, a ray of yellow light sneaking under the crack of the door. Rosie lifts her head and wags her tail but doesn't get up. She looks at me, waiting.

"Cass?" Owen calls, the floorboards in the hall creaking and moaning as he makes his way toward the nursery door. Everything in the big old house is swelling. We've skipped right past spring and straight to the heat and humidity usually saved for August.

Holding my breath, I clutch the baby box closer to my body, pressing the cool cabbage leaves tucked inside my bra closer to my chest, their presence another reminder of all that I've lost. Rosie stays by my side even though she stares at the door, eager to greet Owen. She's always favored me slightly. Owen once joked that she loved me more, and even though I denied it, it's true. Like humans, dogs can't help but have favorites. She inches a little closer to me, nudging my bare feet with her cool wet nose.

The doorknob twists and I brace myself. Owen pushes the door open, his silhouette dark against the bright hallway. Blinking back the hot tears streaming down my cheeks, I turn my face toward the wall. He hesitates in the doorway, letting me compose myself.

"Are you okay?" he asks, one foot poised to step inside the mausoleum that is our baby's room, the other foot safely in the hall. "Want me to order dinner?"

No, I'm not okay. I don't know if I'll ever be okay. Please don't leave me. Hug me. Hold me. Cry with me. I don't say any of these things. I'm afraid to lay them out in the open where they might take on a life of their own. At least, with them trapped inside my heart, I can save Owen from their anguish.

I shrug, keeping the box pressed against my chest to cover the ugly words strewn across the sweatshirt I'm still wearing. "I just want to be alone a few minutes," I whisper, gulping back the lump in the back of my throat. *Don't go.* Closing my eyes, I pray he reads my mind and throws open the door and falls to the floor to cry over this pathetic box with me. But it's wishful thinking. He'll close the door and give me some time alone because that's what I've always demanded of him.

"Okay," he says, but I know he's torn. It's my own fault. I've punished him too many times for pushing back when I asked for space. He's learned his lesson over the years. "I'll order Chinese food," he says, holding the door open a second longer, giving me one last chance to change my mind. "Come down when you're ready." He pulls the door shut with a click, leaving me and Rosie enveloped in the heavy darkness. His footsteps retreat down the hall and fade away down the stairs, leaving the room thick and alive with silence. The quietness thrums in my ears like a live wire. Pulsating. *Da-dum. Da-dum. Da-dum.*

◆ 12 ◆

OWEN

After
June 2

SHE THINKS I DON'T hear her crying, but I do. Each night I lay down next to her, and even though we're only inches apart, we might as well be miles. I close my eyes, but it's only the start of my nightly vigil as I wait for her silent sobs to start, the ones she tries so hard to muffle against her pillow and dampen beneath our comforter.

She assumes I'm asleep, but since we lost our son, everything's changed. Our nightly ritual has fallen apart. We used to go to bed together, but not anymore. Now I leave her alone on the couch, sipping a cup of herbal tea and staring at a novel. She barely notices when I leave the room. *Before* she would've begged me to wait while she finished one more chapter—which always turned into three. I'd wait a million pages for her now if only she'd ask. But she doesn't ask, and I don't stay.

Alone, I trudge up the narrow staircase to our bedroom and fall into our queen-sized bed, where I watch some stupid TV show for thirty minutes before shutting it down, enveloping the room in silence. Later she'll slide into bed without a word, careful not to let even a toe brush up against my leg. I'm wide awake, but I feign sleep, hoping she might whisper something to me across the divide. *Good night. I love you.* Anything.

The space between us is just a sliver of cool sheets, but it feels like a bottomless chasm. Words fail me every night as she climbs under the covers and rolls to her side, creeping closer to the edge of the bed, farther away from me. Her slight body shakes as she cries herself to sleep. It's like sleeping in an earthquake, each tiny shudder shifting the seismic plates of our union further apart. I used to have the words. I'd make her talk to me in the safety of the darkness. Sometime, somewhere, the words disappeared.

In the morning we pretend everything's normal. It's been just over a week since the miscarriage, but the days are long and every minute pulls and stretches us apart. I never imagined ten years unraveling in ten days, but here we are. How many good mornings will we waste by neglecting to say good-night? Ten more? A hundred? Maybe we won't make it that far before we fall so far apart there's nothing left.

Cassidy moves around the house like a ghost of her former self. On the outside, not much has changed. Even at almost five months pregnant she'd barely gained any weight, so her body doesn't reveal the pain she feels inside. Her stomach had just started to round but never "popped." At the time, she'd been thrilled to fit into her prepregnancy clothes. I wonder if she misses the slight tightness in her jeans now that it's gone. Cassidy thought those weekly bump pictures everyone posted were corny. I should've forced her to let me take them.

"Have a good day at work," I say as she grabs her to-go mug.

She hesitates, one eye on the door. Stepping back toward me, she brushes a dry kiss on my cheek before muttering for me to have a good one too. The door slams behind her, and my stomach churns. Popping an antacid with my morning coffee is my new normal.

The Bourne project is a welcome distraction, keeping me occupied ten long hours a day. While at work I can pretend things are fine at home. I'm fine, Cassidy is fine. We're both just fine—it's what I tell anyone who asks. Maybe if I repeat it often enough, it'll be true.

Days turn into more days, and those will keep turning into more. The sun comes up, the sun goes down. We lost a baby and the world kept spinning. Work keeps working and life keeps living. But I'm stuck and her nightly tears are proof she's stuck, too. Talking about it would help us, but we've both been struck silent. A therapist might help, but I'm too scared to mention the idea. She'll shut me down, and I can't bear her closing me out any more than she already has. So, I'm giving it time and space. Maybe it'll heal our wounds enough for her to let me back in.

I caught her crying in the kitchen yesterday. *Before* I would've run to her, held her in my arms, and told her everything would be okay. But I'm broken. I've lost my nerve. I don't know if I can make things right this time. I've never lied to her, and the thought of promising something I can't deliver breaks my heart all over again. Instead, I try to do other things for her. I do the grocery shopping. I bring home dinner. I do the laundry and feed the dog. My goal is to take care of all the little details in hopes the big ones will take care of themselves.

My parents call to check in and I lie, tell them we're fine. They promise to visit soon, answering my lie with a lie of their own. Although I know they're sad for us, sympathy and grief aren't in their wheelhouse. Stoic, midwestern stock, their answer would be to get back on the horse and have another one. I'm not sure either of us is ready to hear the wisdom in such a statement.

Tonight she's on an emergency call and I'm sitting alone at the kitchen table eating leftover spaghetti and meatballs. Finding a half-empty bottle of red wine on the counter, I pour myself a generous glass even though I prefer beer.

I'm drawn to a framed picture from our engagement shoot centered on the side table. In it we're sitting intertwined like lovestruck teenagers while Rosie, still a puppy, lies on the grass before us. Cass's chestnut hair was longer then. Mine was shorter and I was clean-shaven. In this picture I gaze at my beautiful fiancée like I'm the happiest man in the world. We were so in love, we didn't have to force the cheesy poses. Our love was easy to capture, shot after shot.

Where are those kids now? What I'd give for even one moment of such radiant bliss in our lives today. Sipping my wine, I wipe a smudge from the corner of the glass before placing it back on the table.

Minutes tick by slowly. Finishing the last of the wine, I retrieve another dusty bottle from the shelf. Glass in hand, I study the pictures hanging in the hallway, finding it difficult to reconcile the me in those photos with the man I am today. I refuse to believe that in ten days we've grown so different from the couple we once were that we can't get back.

As the wine settles into my bloodstream, it loosens up my thoughts. *It's been a bit longer than ten days, and you know it.* I refill my empty glass, almost draining the second bottle. Perhaps the alcohol is right. Maybe we've been drifting toward this point for some time now. This catastrophe just sped up the process.

Rosie rushes to the door a moment before it clicks open. Cassidy pushes into the foyer, soaked to the bone and dripping on the mat. *When did it start raining?* She crouches to pet Rosie before noticing me standing in the hallway. Frowning, she shrugs off her rain jacket.

"Hey," I say, my tongue thick in my mouth.

She kicks off her boots and nudges them closer to the door. "You're up late," she answers, not meeting my eyes.

Not hostile, but not friendly. She doesn't move to kiss or embrace me, just stands awkwardly in the entrance as though she's waiting for me to get out of her way. Though she's wearing her raincoat, her jeans and shirt are soaked through. She's probably eager to get out of her clothes and into something warm and dry, but I'm stuck in place, drinking her in. Purple circles fan both eyes, made worse by the mascara starting to smudge after a wet sixteen-hour workday. Her hair hangs heavy and damp, a wildfire extinguished by the elements.

"What?" she sighs, her shoulders sagging under the weight of the day and all the days before.

Maybe it's the wine talking, but I'm emboldened. I miss my wife. Just one touch. Something before she's too far out of reach.

Placing my wineglass on the desk in the foyer, I take the leap, crossing the room in two steps and pulling her into my arms, her damp shirt sticking to my chest. She squirms in my embrace, stiffening both arms to her sides and pushing against me with her shoulders. Rosie sits on the doormat, watching us with interest. I think she's rooting for me.

"Stop," she yells, "I'm soaking wet!" She jerks her head away from my chest. I pull her tighter. "Let. Me. Go."

I don't. I hold her tight and let loose everything I've been holding back. Before I can stop, I'm sobbing into her hair, my tears more raindrops soaking into her curls. My knees give out and I fall to the ground in front of her, still holding on, pulling against the back of her thighs and resting my cheek against her flat stomach. My body trembles and heaves. She stands stiff and tall, unwavering.

She doesn't flinch, and I keep crying, my body purging itself of the pain it's tried to hide. I don't know how long we remain like this, maybe only a minute, maybe much longer. Cassidy doesn't move a muscle. Just lets me release.

"I'm sorry," I whimper. "I'm sorry for everything." I sniff back the tears, pulling myself together.

I look up and she's staring down the hall, her face vacant. I wonder if she's heard me.

"Cass," I whisper, desperate for her to respond. "I'm sorry," I repeat.

Running her cold hand through my hair, she lets it rest for a quick second on the back of my neck. Every nerve in my body lights up at this simple touch. But it's gone as quickly as it came.

"Me too," she whispers before gently pushing her way out of my loosened embrace and heading toward the kitchen. Rosie whines in my direction, then follows Cassidy into the other room, leaving me alone once more.

◆ 13 ◆

CASSIDY

*After
June 6*

THE TOILET SEAT IN my sister's house is always up. One of the many perils of living in a house full of boys, she always says. Knowing I'm fighting a losing battle, I set it back down, wondering how she keeps up with all the mess. From the outside, Claire's large, modern home on the elm-lined cul-de-sac looks neat and peaceful, almost a cookie-cutter image of the other futuristic-looking houses neighboring it. Aside from her chic style and fashionable furniture, the inside of the house is anything but serene most hours of the day. Upon entering, you're bombarded with the crashes and clatters of three little boys weaving their way through the rooms. Claire must constantly trail behind them, picking up the destruction left in their wake.

"How are you feeling?" Claire asks as she fills two mugs with steaming coffee and slides one across the island toward me. She pushes the cream and honey in my direction after adding some of each to her own cup. Different though we may be, we take our coffee the same peculiar way.

Before I can answer, Claire's youngest son, Matt, or "Little Matty" as everyone calls him, runs around the corner, nearly knocking himself out on the edge of the kitchen table. Another inch taller and he'd be flat on his back right now.

"Mommmmmmmmy!" he wails, his face beet red and his strawberry-blond hair disheveled. He's wearing only a diaper, and I wonder if he started the day with clothes and lost them along the way or if he prefers the freedom. Claire's wild child, he throws himself around her thigh, burying his grubby face in the expensive Lycra of her yoga pants. Just two years old, he's going through a clingy stage and learning some new phrases. "Want you, Mama," he says, his lower lip trembling. Eyeing my sister, I'm amazed at her patience. From what I've witnessed, his newfound speech mostly involves needing something from his mommy. *Feed me. Pick me up. Give me a toy.*

Steve bursts into the room with their middle son squirming and giggling under one arm. "Where's my babe?" he asks before nodding a quick hello in my direction. "Sorry about that. I swear, I look away for *one* minute and he's gone," he says, shaking his head good-naturedly. He sets Shane down, and my nephew immediately runs back toward the den without so much as a glance in my direction. "How you doing, sis?" Steve asks, kissing me on the cheek now that his hands are free. "Glad to have you at the circus." Before I can answer, he's scooping Matty up from the floor, leaving us in relative quiet.

"As you were saying," Claire continues, sipping her coffee and smirking at me, "better talk quick. I give it five minutes before Little Matty escapes Steve's ever-so-watchful supervision again." She's teasing, but I don't doubt it for a second. Steve's a great dad, the fun and attentive weekend warrior every little boy craves. Always eager to get down and dirty with his boys, he loves to roughhouse and play, but I sense he prefers to leave most of the "boring" parenting duties to Claire. The feminist in me wants to resent him for this, but he's a hard guy not to like. Plus,

Claire loves her life as a stay-at-home mom and kicks ass at it. *To each their own.*

"I'm okay," I say, eliciting a frown from my sister. "Well, as good as I can be," I admit, withering beneath her shrewd gaze.

"Cut the bullshit, Cass." Adding a little more honey to her cup, she sips and nods approvingly. "Talk to me. How's Owen doing? You guys working through it?" Somehow Claire manages the cooking, cleaning, and chauffeuring, all the while maintaining a beautiful home and keeping up her killer body. As a result, she's always a little strapped for time and cuts straight to the chase. Normally I appreciate her ability to weed through the nonsense, but more so when it's directed at someone else. It's a little uncomfortable feeling the weight of her focused intensity aimed at such a personal aspect of my life. Although we're close, we generally stick to lighter conversation—where to get the best yoga pants, what shows to stream on Netflix, and anything having to do with our mother. Pinching the bridge of my nose and rubbing gently, I fear a migraine is brewing.

"He's fine. Giving me some space," I murmur as she lifts one eyebrow. Claire's never hidden her disapproval of our problem-solving tactics. When I first told her how Owen and I preferred to let a little time and space come between our disagreements, she laughed and offered to help find me a divorce lawyer in a few years.

"Space?" She snorts, rolling her eyes dramatically. "Space is literally the last thing either of you needs." Looking at me seriously, she frowns. "This happened to both of you. You know that, right?" Guilt washes over me, and I turn away so she can't see the color rising to my cheeks. Typical Claire, seeing through my crap within five minutes and hitting the nail right on the head. I've told her multiple times she should've been a therapist. She insists she is. She's a mom.

Owen and I both lost a son. Still, I can't help but feel like the loss is a little more mine than his. My body swelled and changed as he moved inside me. My breasts engorged and eventually leaked. My body held him inside before pushing him out before his time. My body mis-carried our son. He mourns the loss, but I wonder if he's mourning this baby or the idea of a baby. Even though he'll never admit it, I know in his heart he believes we'll just have another.

He didn't even want this one. The thought creeps into my head now like it does late at night when I'm staring up at the ceiling through tear-bleary eyes, unable to sleep while Owen snores beside me. Somehow my mind makes its way back to that stupid conversation where Owen made the unilateral decision for us to wait to have a baby. He got what he wanted.

"What?" Claire asks, refilling my coffee.

Color rises to my cheeks and I shake away the nagging feeling of blame. Guilt shades everything lately. "Nothing," I mutter. Sensing Claire won't be satisfied with this, I pick my words carefully. "I wonder why we lost the baby and if it was something I did or didn't do," I say, biting my cheek to hold back the tears that are precariously close to falling. "I wonder if the baby knew we didn't want him."

Unable to hide her shock, Claire sets her mug down too hard, coffee spilling onto the marble. "You guys were trying for months!" she exclaims. As far as she knew, this was the case. For months I moaned and complained about our struggle to conceive, but I never told her Owen asked me to put things on hold.

Backtracking, the flush on my face creeps down my neck and across my chest. Expressing my emotions has never been easy for me. "No, we were," I say, taking a deep breath. "But we'd decided to take a little break on trying, and of course, that's when we got pregnant. Maybe the timing was off and my body sensed it."

"Bullshit," she says, waving her hand. "Are you serious? You know things always happen when you least expect them. Look at Derek," she reminds me, referring to her first son. Claire got pregnant almost immediately after graduating college. Even though everyone assumed she'd marry Steve eventually, they'd planned to wait a few years for the wedding and then a few more for children. The plan was fast-tracked once she got that positive pregnancy test. I vividly remember her sobbing into the phone, telling me the news even before she told Steve. Claire knows a thing or two about bad timing. "Stop being so . . . you. Not everything has some concrete reason. Shit happens. Bad shit, good shit. You just have to roll with it. There's not always some higher meaning or explanation. Sometimes things simply happen, and you move on."

Curbing my desire to stick my tongue out at her or flip her off, I make myself busy shredding a paper napkin. Maybe she understands bad timing, but our situations are far from the same. Even though motherhood came earlier than expected for Claire, she's always been steadfast in her desire to have children. It's no surprise that she has three perfect sons and lives in a perfect home in the perfect school district with her perfect husband. Claire never grappled with the decision to stay home and care for the kids; it was a given. Steve offered to hire a live-in nanny, but Claire refused. Conception, birth, and motherhood have all come naturally to Claire. She makes mothering look easy. She doesn't get that it's not like that for everyone.

Once upon a time Claire had a future that didn't revolve around playdates and soccer practice. Excelling right out of college, she was on track to move up the corporate ladder at a top marketing firm in Boston. Blindsided by her pregnancy and quick marriage, she put her career on hold. The company promised to keep her application on file, but she never went back. At first I thought she was waiting until Derek was old enough for day care, but the months turned into years and then she was pregnant again . . . and again . . . and even the quiet mentions of freelance work became fewer and further between. I still wonder if she regrets this path now. Looking around her warm home, filled with love and laughter, it appears not.

Having dedicated my youth to my education and my adulthood to my career, it's hard to imagine a version of my life where I'd give it all up. I love my job, but sometimes I dream of a life that doesn't revolve around sick animals who get sickest during the wee hours of the morning or on weekends. Maybe then I'd have time to finish decorating my house or get my nails done. Maybe then I'd have time for a baby.

"Earth to Cassidy," my sister says, tapping the counter with her manicured nails. "Seriously, you need to stop beating yourself up over it and share the load."

I shrug, sipping my coffee while my thoughts spiral. Even Claire's coffee is better than mine. Eyeing the expensive and complicated stainless-steel espresso maker in the kitchen's corner, I realize I wouldn't even know how to turn it on. Most days I settle for the Dunkin' Donuts drive-through and let Owen fend for himself. Claire probably has a fresh latte waiting on the counter for Steve every morning. Just another reminder of how I'm failing in my marriage.

"So, I should stop my whining and move on?" I ask, unable to hide the bitterness in my voice.

Claire sighs. "No. That's the opposite of what I'm saying, and you know it." Before she can elaborate, we're interrupted by the pitter-patter of little feet running into the kitchen. Her oldest pops his head around the counter and smiles at me. "I'm saying you need to talk to someone, and if you can't talk to me or Owen, maybe you should talk to a professional," she hisses, plastering a fake smile on her face and pulling Derek in for a hug. At almost eight years old, he grimaces and pretends to pull away from her embrace as though he's too old for such displays of affection. He betrays himself, leaning in a second too long.

I lift my brows and nod. "You would suggest this," I say, letting out a dry laugh. My sister the "woke" one. Next she'll be telling me about some essential oil or herbal supplement that might help. "Mom tell you to say that?"

Claire ruffles Derek's hair and ignores me. "Hey, talk to your Aunt Cassie for a minute, hon," she says. "I'm gonna go check and make sure your dad hasn't lost the other two."

She hustles off toward the den, which has become suspiciously quiet, leaving me and my nephew facing off awkwardly in the kitchen. He turns his small but rather adult face up at me.

The pregnancy books don't prepare you for how to talk to a first grader—or maybe he's a second grader? I literally know nothing about kids except what days of the month they can be made.

"What grade are you in?" I ask, desperate to break the uncomfortable silence.

He looks at his feet and fiddles with the cuffs of his shirt. "I'm going into third grade," he answers, not looking up. "I'm seven and a half," he adds for good measure. I remember always insisting on adding the all-important *half* to both my age and height when I was little.

"You're tall for seven and a half," I say, although I've no idea if this is true, just another thing I liked to hear when I was a kid. Being told I was smart for my age was my all-time favorite.

He puffs out his chest ever so slightly and lifts his chin toward me. "Thanks. I'm the tallest in my class," he says with obvious pride. "Dad's tall, so mom says I'll take after him and not her." He looks me up and down, furrowing his brow in sincere seriousness. "You're short like Mom is," he says, and laughs shyly. "But that's okay, since you're a girl."

This is the longest conversation I've ever had with Derek, and I'm charmed by his earnestness, so like his mother's. "You'll probably be taller than me by the time you're in the fourth grade," I guess, earning a wide grin revealing two missing teeth.

"You know what?" he says, his green eyes boring into my own. "You would've been a really good mom." His eyes flick toward the doorway. "Mom and Dad told me I was going to have a cousin, but he went to heaven instead." It isn't a question, just a simple statement.

Not wanting to break down in front of my poor nephew, I swallow the tickle at the back of my throat. "You're right. I had a baby, but he went to heaven already," I say, my voice shaking. Not sure what he knows about death, I tread lightly. "Hopefully someday I'll have another one who will grow up to be your new cousin," I say. None of the books prepare you for how to talk to a child about miscarriage, that's for certain.

He looks at me with his mossy-colored eyes, almost the same gray-green as my own. "Okay," he says, squeezing my hand. "Could you make it a girl cousin? We have enough boys around here already."

I laugh, and just like that the spell is broken. Derek pulls his hand away, eager to get back to the TV in the other room. "I'll do my best," I say, gesturing toward the door. "Go find your mom for me." Though he's too polite to run away without permission, I see the relief on his face when he's allowed to escape back to something more fun than his sad aunt.

He scurries away and I sit alone at the counter, my coffee cold. *You would've been a good mom.* Turning the words around in my head, I lock them away for later. From the mouths of babes.

◆ 14 ◆

CASSIDY

After
June 8

HORSES RARELY MATE THE old-fashioned way outside in the wild anymore. Ever since they transformed from a beast of burden to a domesticated animal—one often considered extremely valuable for its athletic prowess— more civilized methods of breeding these expensive creatures have been used to protect the investments of all parties involved. Artificial insemination is the dominant technique employed now.

Live coverage, when stallion and mare join together to do the dirty, is saved for farm horses and the accidental pet whose owner didn't realize it might not be wise to stable an ungelded colt next to a female horse. Like teenagers, stallions will find a way, whether they have to jump a fence or knock down a barn door to get there. The risk of injury is quite high when you mix two fifteen-hundred-pound beasts with raging hormones and minds of their own.

People assume the brawny stallion is the one that should be feared, but in my experience, it's the opposite. I've had to treat quite a few stallions for lacerations and bites after their wanton advances were met with the sharp teeth and strong hind hooves of a mare not in the mood. Never underestimate a mare in heat. It's for this reason AI is preferred.

As I pet Kitty on the rump, she swings her long neck around and fixes her light-brown eyes on me. I swear I see the same hope and frustration I'm feeling mirrored back at me. A surly redheaded mare standing just over 15.3 hands, what she lacks in height she makes up for in whippet-like speed and agility and a fiery personality to match. With a pedigree a mile long, she was one of the Lombardos' prized racing mares until an unfortunate tendon injury on a muddy track stopped her promising career when she was only three years old. When rehabbing the filly back to racing wasn't an option, the Lombardos switched gears and prepared Kitty for the next phase of her life—motherhood. Unfortunately, the road to producing a foal has been anything but straightforward. After three failed rounds of artificial insemination, the owners made the risky decision to attempt live cover in May.

Kitty let the stallion, Atlanta Gold, know exactly how she felt about his advances by landing a few blows on his wide-set shoulders and heavy flank. Thankfully, her steel shoes had been removed and no serious damage was done to the world-class stallion. If anything, he seemed more attracted to the chestnut temptress after being dealt a few warning kicks. Eventually the deed was done, and we waited two long weeks only to be disappointed once again.

With a final plunge of the syringe attached to the long pipette, I hold the instrument in place for thirty more seconds before withdrawing it and rewarding Kitty with another light pet on the side. Always an exemplary patient, she stood like a lady inside the breeding chute for forty minutes while I tranquilized her, poked her, and ultra-sounded her before I even started the insemination process. Even though she's an old pro at the procedure by now, it doesn't make it any less unpleasant.

"So, how long until we know if this takes?" Joe Lombardo asks, watching me as I wipe down my instruments.

We've been over the protocol multiple times, but I repeat the drill again. I know better than anyone how reassuring facts and figures can be, especially when you're helpless to do anything besides wait. Sitting idly on the sidelines is difficult for someone like Joe, who makes his living working hard and literally taking the reins. Considering the hefty price of each of these failed attempts must make it even harder.

"I'll come back in two weeks and check whether the egg was fertilized. If not, we should be able to catch her next estrus cycle and start again," I say, noting the way his weathered face falls. "I'm hoping this time it took," I add. "The HCG injection we administered gave us a much better idea of when she ovulated, so I am optimistic we're in the proper window this time."

After all the failed attempts, we opted to utilize human chorionic gonadotropin—HCG—which induces ovulation thirty-six hours after injection. Guided by an initial ultrasound, we confirmed Kitty's ovaries were ready and determined insemination would occur as planned. Since each vial of Atlanta Gold's semen costs over $5,000, this nonexistent foal has already cost a significant sum. Apparently, this would be mere pennies if the foal ended up selling at auction for the same price as others in this famous bloodline. Million-dollar babies are not unheard of in the racing industry.

"Fingers crossed," Joe says. "Feel bad prodding the little lady so much." He takes a mint from his pocket and lets her nibble it from his outstretched palm. "When can we take her home?"

I study her for a moment, noting the color of her gums and the brightness in her eyes. The minimal amount of tranquilizer I gave earlier has almost worn off. Another thirty minutes and she'll be her feisty self. Some say motherhood softens edgy mares, but I hope she keeps her spark and passes it on to her foals. "Let's just put her in one of the clinic stalls while we go over some paperwork in the front office. By the time that's done, she'll be good to go."

Our technician scurries to unhook Kitty from the chute and leads the mare off to a stall before I can ask. Smiling to myself, I remember being an eager intern not that long ago and make a mental note to acknowledge her work ethic later. Good technicians are hard to find.

Joe spares one last glance at Kitty before following me down the rubber-matted hallway toward the front office. Only a few more minutes of paperwork stand between me and home, and relief settles over my body. It's been a long day and every fiber in my body is yearning to rest, to lay my head down and close out the world. I imagine Kitty feels the same way.

★ ★ ★

Grief is a lonely pursuit. Work, normally my reprieve, hasn't been doing the trick lately. Usually I enjoy the long drives between calls, but now it's just more time stuck alone with only my thoughts for company, unable to escape the crushing weight of sorrow. Instead of listening to the radio or a podcast like usual, I mentally prepare what mask I must wear at the next appointment. Sometimes this means fake smiling my way through small talk at routine check-ups; other times it means acting appropriately stoic while delivering bad news. By the end of the day, I'm exhausted from all the effort spent pretending to be something else.

No one tells you how long it takes to get over a loss. I'm reminded of some common advice offered concerning breakups. Supposedly it takes just as long as the relationship lasted to get over a breakup, so if you dated for a year, it will take a year to move on. Can I apply this theory to my miscarriage and assume it'll take one day for every day I was pregnant? I lost my baby 17 days ago, and he was inside me for 136. Do I have another 119 days to go before I'm ready to move on? Perhaps the pain will always remain but lessen a little more every day until I hardly remember the feeling of my son moving inside me, the grief a mere echo reverberating in my heart every once in a while. Maybe someday a new baby will grow in his place, pushing out the pain and filling it with joy instead. Maybe it hurts this bad forever.

Some days I'm surprised to remember what joy feels like. I find myself laughing, and sometimes the smile even reaches my eyes. But grief always worms its way back in and reminds me that every moment of happiness is a betrayal of my son and I end up choking on the treachery of my laughter, horrified I'm forgetting all I've lost. Grief taunts me with its cruel condemnations. A *real* mother mourns her child forever. A *real* mother cries over a future that'll never be. A *real* mother doesn't laugh or have fun or make love. Whenever life tempts me into living, these thoughts creep back in, convincing me to crawl back into the darkness. In the dark it's easy to punish myself for wanting to move on, for wanting to work, for wanting something as primal as my own husband. A real mother only wants her child back, the grief whispers, reminding me of the worst parts of myself, the *wanting* parts.

Instead of drowning in grief, I drown myself in work. Pushing the chastising voice away, I fill my schedule and push myself so hard I fall into bed each night too exhausted to hear the wounds grief tries to inflict. It's not healthy to run from your problems, but it's easier. Unfortunately, I can't run while trapped in the metal fortress of my SUV. No amount of loud music or unnecessary phone calls can save me from myself and the nagging insistence to *remember*.

Leaning my head against the headrest, I let my shoulders sag into the soft leather seats. I can't wait to get home, but I dread the drive. I should stop at the grocery store, but the thought of even a few more minutes in the car is unbearable. I'll call Owen to pick up something. Lately we've been eating too much takeout, but he doesn't seem to mind. I think he's eager to get out of the house and away from me.

At some point it starts to rain, light sideways drizzle at first, but the droplets get heavier and faster as I take the exit ramp and merge onto the long stretch of two-lane road between the clinic and home. My finger hesitates below the wiper switch as my eyes lose focus on the road through the blurry haze of raindrops on the windshield. It's coming down hard, one of those late-spring storms that brings out all the flowers tomorrow. The road is narrow and windy up ahead, the speed limit dropping quickly from forty-five miles per hour to twenty-five and often catching drivers unaware. But it's as familiar to me as the back of my hand. I can drive this road in my sleep. Dim headlights coming at me cast a foggy yellow light into the car, blinding me. I close my eyes for a second. Two seconds. Three. I let it all go.

Not today, a small voice from *before* scolds, and I blink back the surge of panic washing over me as I lose control of the wheel, tires hitting a patch of water as the SUV glides a few feet toward the edge of the road before traction control kicks in and jerks me forward so that my chest hits the steering wheel. I flick the wipers on full blast and the steady whoosh fills the silent car, beating in time with my racing heart. Letting out the breath I've been holding, I turn the radio on. Gripping the wheel firmly at ten and two, I focus on the dark road in front of me. Only a few more miles and then I'll be home.

◆ 15 ◆

CASSIDY

After
June 15

"CASSIDY?" A VOICE BOUNCES off the cereal boxes and lands in my ear like it's been whispered directly behind me. Lifting my gaze from the wide variety of oatmeal I've been debating, I search for the person calling my name. "Is that you?" High-pitched and tinged with a thick Boston accent, the voice is distinctly familiar. A few customers shift to make room for the woman weaving her way down the busy aisle. I throw a box of apple-cinnamon oatmeal packets and a container of steel-cut in the cart. Nothing like having a multitude of breakfast options.

Recognition hits a moment before I see her face. Janice Topping, all five foot nothing of her, is on a mission, and no one and nothing will get in her way. Proving this point, she maneuvers another customer's cart from her path and shoots a pointed glare at the woman for good measure.

For a split second I contemplate ditching my cart and bolting to the nearest entrance. The doors aren't far. I'm only in aisle four. As Janice comes into view, I see running is pointless. Decked out in full athleisure wear and donning a pair of sparkling white Nikes, I'm pretty sure she'd embark on a high-speed chase to get to me. Using my cart as a shield, I brace for the upcoming onslaught.

"Janice!" I exclaim in as exuberant a voice as I can muster, hoping it's been long enough she won't sense the false ring of my tone. "It's so nice to see you!" I plaster a smile on my face as I take inventory of my old friend. Janice might be dressed for the gym, but her full face of makeup and perfectly coiffed hair suggest her Lululemon is more decorative than functional. Rubbing a hand through my hair, I try to smooth back a few errant strands. In my rush to hit the market, I threw my curls into a messy bun and left my face painfully bare, not even bothering to swipe a quick layer of mascara over my pale lashes. Washed-out and haggard is not how I would have wanted to look when I bumped into the prom queen.

"Oh, hon, come here." She abandons her cart, nearly tripping over a display of cornflakes in her efforts to pull me into a hug. Her smothering embrace lasts a little too long and smells overwhelmingly like citrus-and-coconut shampoo.

News travels fast down the grapevine. Even though Janice and I drifted apart after high school, our mothers remain close friends and talk almost daily. I'm sure my mom couldn't wait to tell Mrs. Topping what happened. From there, the news probably spread like wildfire. My mom's friends thrive on gossip, and something as juicy and tragic as a miscarriage would have been headline news for at least a week.

Teardrops, comically fat, pool in her eyes. I resist the urge to roll my eyes and gag myself with a spoon, as we used to say. "How are you doing?" I ask, managing a sad smile. Her lower lip trembles and I clench my jaw, biting my tongue.

"No, how are *you* doing?" She draws out each word, each one louder than the last. A few other store patrons linger. I wonder if they're my mom's friends too. They have the look of eavesdropping busybodies.

Janice tilts her head, pouting at me. In school, she was one of the stars of the drama club. I'm pretty sure she always got the lead because of her big voice and ability to exaggerate every emotion as opposed to any discernible acting skills. Her ability to make a spectacle and draw attention is in full effect this morning.

Eager for this interaction to end, I take a step back. "I'm fine," I say, and she scowls. "Hanging in there," I add. She reaches her hands toward mine and grabs them, gripping tightly. Hers are cold and dry.

"I can't imagine what you're going through," she says, shaking her head. "It's just so terrible for you." She pulls one icy hand away to wipe a tear from her cheek. "Your mom told my mom everything." She cries in earnest now, her narrow shoulders shaking. My own skin crawls and my heart races in response.

Desperate to escape the stares of the other shoppers, I choke back my growing irritation and summon a thin smile. "It's been tough, but we're getting through it." Lying is so much easier than the uncomfortable truth.

If Janice were a friend, I might confide that things suck and I don't know if they'll ever get better. But she's not a friend, and I wish she'd say good-bye now instead of awkwardly standing in front of me offering up her overdramatic condolences. Does she think this makes me feel better? It's like she wants me to comfort her because *my* miscarriage has made *her* upset. I'm about one hiccup away from slapping her.

She sniffles. "You know, I'm always here if you need anything. We were so close in high school. I miss you," she adds, brown eyes sparkling. I get a cruel spark of pleasure when I notice her eyeliner smudging.

The worst part is, I can't tell if she's sincere. In high school, she fed off pain and suffering. Other people's misery sustained her sense of superiority. One minute she'd be offering a shoulder to cry on, the next wielding those secrets like weapons to suit her needs. Mean-girl culture is real, and I'm guilty of my share of bad behavior too. It was eat or be eaten in high school, and Janice was always full. I've long since moved past this phase, but something in her deep-brown eyes makes me wonder if she has.

"Thanks, that's very sweet," I say, glancing at my watch. "I should get going. I have to work later this afternoon . . ."

Janice nods but shifts closer, effectively blocking my exit. For such a tiny person, she is still quite the impenetrable figure. "God only gives you what you can handle," she whispers, her lips a thin line as she casts her eyes down as if in prayer. Her forehead is perfectly immobile, untouched by lines and wrinkles, lending her an air of confused youthfulness. A normal forehead should be creased. I'm fascinated by her marble head, unable to look away.

"What's so funny?" Janice asks. Confused, I look blankly back at her. A look of sharp anger passes over her features before turning to disgust. "You laughed." Hands on her hips, she dares me to disagree. *Shit.* I must've chuckled while contemplating her statue-like skin. All traces of her earlier sympathy disappear. "Some things just never change, do they?" she spits.

I lift my own brow, untouched by Botox and very expressive.

"Don't give me that look," she growls, finally lowering her voice. I imagine the old biddies nearby leaning in to hear us. "Ever since you graduated, you thought you were better than everyone. What gives you the right to stand there and laugh at me when I'm only doing what any good Christian would do?" she hisses. "Your mom was right. You really aren't meant for this," she adds, eyes glinting with a specific mean-girl twinkle.

Somewhere in the last five minutes I entered the twilight zone and Janice jumped from tearful condolences to calling me an ungrateful heathen. The proper thing to do is try to steer this train wreck back on track so I'm not cast as a monster when this story inevitably gets back to my mother and her friends. But I'm feeling distinctly unproper. Time to derail this train once and for all.

"All right then, it was *so* great to see you," I say, hoping she'll step aside and we can avoid any more hostile words getting launched about. But I'll have no such luck. Janice always has to have the last word.

"Just leave," she stammers, loudly again. The other customers don't bother hiding their intrigue at the young women battling in the cereal aisle. "I was only making sure you were okay, but you've never cared about anyone besides yourself, so I'm not sure why I bothered." Her hands are balled into fists at her sides and her cheeks are red and splotchy beneath her heavy foundation. Shooting daggers at me, she goes in for the kill. "You would've made a horrible mother anyway."

"Well, thanks for that," I murmur, the blood draining from my face. I use the handle of the cart to steady myself and lift my chin. "You made me feel much better." I hip-bump her cart as I push past, and a few boxes of Cheerios fall to the floor. Petty, but I don't care. Somehow she's always made me stoop to her level.

I refuse to spare even one glance back. Without missing a beat, I round the corner and grab my purse, letting the cart roll aimlessly into the center of the main speedway until it eventually stops in front of a tomato sauce display. Fighting back tears, I hurry from the store. I'll just order pizza later.

★　★　★

"I just don't understand why you're mad at me for telling my *best friend*," my mom moans, her tone incredulous. She's been ranting for ten minutes now, uninterrupted.

She pauses to take a breath, and I jump in. "What I don't understand is how you already know what happened," I say, shaking my head. "It literally *just* happened,"

I mutter. In a moment of poor judgment, I called to explain my side of the story, lest she hear it from one of her friends later. Clearly the grapevine moves faster than my own phone skills. "Janice and I aren't friends, Mom. I don't want her knowing my very personal business."

My mother's sigh is loud and obnoxious over the speaker. I can picture the exact face accompanying that heavy exhalation. "I didn't tell Janice your business," she says, matter-of-factly. "I told Janice's mother, who shared it with her daughter. I don't see anything wrong with her offering you comfort. You used to be so close."

Opening my mouth wide in a silent scream, I flip both middle fingers at the phone. "We aren't close anymore. She told me God gave me what I could handle and then burst into tears." The more I think about it, the angrier I get. "She started crying, and then what was I supposed to do? Comfort her? Tell her everything happens for a reason and she'll get over my miscarriage someday?"

Silence hums over the speaker, and I wonder if I've lost the connection. Worse things could happen. But then Mom sighs again, adding a little disappointed groan to the end to further emphasize her displeasure with me.

"What? Please tell me again how I've upset you."

"Oh, stop it," she snaps. "Stop being so damned sensitive. Sometimes people just want to see how you're doing. It's not always with some ulterior motive. It's called being human, Cassidy. Humans bond over shared experiences. Janice was only trying to make you feel better."

Pinching my nose with my thumb and forefinger, I count to three before answering, but my anger still burns hot. "Are you fucking kidding me? She most certainly failed at making me feel better, if that was her intention. She's still the same bitch she was in high school."

"Enough," my mom barks, warning me I've pushed too far. "Janice and her mother are good people. They don't deserve to be called names just for trying to be nice to you."

My anger deflates as I recognize defeat. This phone call was a mistake from the start. Some irrational part of me hoped my mom might have my back, but as soon as I snapped at Janice, it stopped being about me. Now word will get around that Joan's daughter is an ungrateful girl, and my mom will lose the group's sympathy and all the attention that garners. No matter how I feel, I've embarrassed her in front of her friends, so I'm the one in the wrong. End of story.

"Okay, Mom. Sorry. Next time I'll take Janice for coffee so she can cry over my unborn fetus until she's feeling better."

She huffs, and I hear a chair screeching back over the wood floor. She must be at the kitchen table. "An apology would suffice," she says, ignoring the sarcasm leaking from my every word.

"Sure, I'll call her now and apologize. But for what, exactly? For miscarrying and making our reunion awkward? For not breaking down and hugging it out?" She keeps her mouth shut for once. "I've got to go." I hit end before she reprimands me again for bad behavior.

Without looking, I shift into reverse and back out of the spot, only to hear screeching tires followed by an angry blast of a horn. A man in a silver minivan yells a few four-letter expletives in my direction through his open window. Pulling back into the space, I cut the engine. The other driver lays on his horn again for good measure.

"*Fuck!*" I yell, banging both hands on the steering wheel. Catching sight of myself in the mirror, I see the same unrecognizable women I saw in the Target dressing room. My hair is loose from the clip, and a halo of strawberry-blond frizz frames my pale face. Through the passenger window I watch Janice walk toward a black Range Rover two aisles over, and I slouch in my seat. "Fuck."

Something inside snaps, and tears fall hot and quick down my cheeks. If only my mom and Janice were seeing me now. People like them hoped I'd break so they could prop me back up again. That's what would make them feel better.

◆ 16 ◆

CLAIRE

After
June 16

STEVE REFERS TO MY office as the "command center." It's not much more than a small room tucked neatly off the kitchen; some might call it a butler's pantry. Considering our kitchen has more room than we'll ever need, we converted the extra space into a catchall for paying bills, keeping a family calendar, and storing the assorted odds and ends that otherwise accumulated on the kitchen counter. I'm the only one who ever uses it. Steve enters on the odd occasion when he's unable to locate his wife and children and needs to refer to my obsessively organized calendar. Most of the time he doesn't bother to look and shoots me a quick text, thus saving him the time and trouble of decoding my "complicated" system.

The command center revolves around a giant whiteboard centered on the far wall, carefully drawn up to form a calendar. I painstakingly rework the dates the night before the start of each new month. Each family member has a dedicated marker color and coordinating Post-it to mark appointments, meetings, playdates, and other notes relevant to our daily lives. Steve is blue, I'm pink, Derek is green, Shane is purple, and Matty is red. Inside every square is a space with our name followed by a blank appointment line to be filled out in my neat script as we go. Even our cleaning lady, Marge, and babysitter, Sofia, have their own colors—orange and yellow, respectively.

For instance, June 16:

Steve: Happy hour with coworkers. Home late.
Claire: Pilates 5:30 am. Grocery shopping 10 am. Read first
4 chapters of book club choice. Schedule appt to remove IUD
ASAP. Dinner salmon, asparagus, and roasted potatoes.
Derek: Soccer in the park 3:30 pm. Start on summer reading
list.
Shane: Story time at library 12:15 pm, Park playdate w/
Ryder 3:30 pm.
Matty: Park playdate w/ Sidney 3:30 pm. *Mom's name is
Gemma.

I look over the day's schedule and, with a satisfactory swoop, erase Pilates from my list. Holding the eraser to the board, I also erase the reminder to make an appointment to remove my IUD. I'll reschedule that for a few months from now, just to be safe.

Maybe I never held court in front of a boardroom, wielding a laser pointer at perfectly prepared PowerPoint slides and impressing a roomful of colleagues with my creative genius. But here, in my command center, I'm CEO, CFO, and head of operations. I'm also in charge of maintenance, janitorial, and culinary services. I'm a regular one-woman circus. Everything that happens under my roof happens under my careful and precise supervision. There are days I long to discuss something other than Transformers or Mickey Mouse Clubhouse, but I have book club and Pilates. The grass is always greener . . . they say, so when I yearn to trade packing lunches and helping with homework for presentations and conference calls, I remind myself of all the blessings in my life. Most days I wouldn't trade my life as a stay-at- home mom for all the money in the world. My days are so busy I rarely have time to contemplate what I'm missing or compare the cost. In my heart I know this is where I'm meant to be.

Taking a sip of coffee, I settle at the vintage secretary desk I restored and painted myself. I grab a fresh piece of stationery—peach, with my name scrawled across the top in cursive, a Mother's Day gift from Steve and the boys—and hastily jot down the grocery list. It's staggering how much my four men eat in a week. Someone's always eating something. Keeping the pantry and fridge stocked is a constant battle. Thankfully, only Shane is picky. The other three eat anything and ask for seconds.

My phone buzzes, vibrating toward me and flashing *Mom* with every sound. It's already 9:47 AM. Although the market is only a five-minute drive and shopping shouldn't take more than forty-five minutes, I know picking up means I risk running behind schedule all day. *Buzz. Buzz.* Debating my options, I bounce back and forth between hitting ignore and biting the bullet and answering now.

"Hey, Mom," I say, deciding not to delay the inevitable. Sofia's here this morning, so I should be able to squeeze everything in if I keep this call relatively short. Plus, I blew Mom off yesterday and will never hear the end of it if I dare ignore her again.

"Oh good, you're home," she answers, thinly veiled exasperation in her voice. Even though she's glued to her smartphone 24-7, she still assumes one must be "home" to answer.

"Yup, just drinking some coffee before heading out on some errands," I say, hoping she catches the hint.

"Have you talked to your sister?" she asks, not bothering to hide her frustration. I don't worry about responding, since she'll fill me in whether I like it or not. "I can't deal with her attitude anymore, Claire. Yesterday she ran into her old friend from high school, Janice—you remember her—who asked how she was doing. Cassidy ended up yelling at the poor girl, causing a whole scene and making her feel terrible," she says, clearing her throat before continuing. "I'm still close with Janice's mother, so of course I told her about Cass' little problem. She must've told her daughter, and the sweet girl offered her condolences to Cassidy, who couldn't just graciously accept," she exclaims, voice rising. I click the volume down button a few times. "No, she had to make it a whole *thing*. Then she calls me and starts yelling at me for sharing the news with my friend. Like I'm the bad guy in all this. To make it even worse, she *hung up* on me and hasn't returned any of my calls or texts since yesterday."

Jesus. Really wish Cassidy had given me a heads-up on this one. Usually she let me know when she's engaged in a battle with our mother. Last time she sent me a text with a few eye-rolling and fire emojis, warning me to expect a call, since I've always been the middleman in their eternal showdown. Cassidy's radio silence leads me to believe she's more upset than normal, a few emojis not enough to express her hurt feelings.

"I haven't heard from her in a few days," I admit.

I know what comes next. Mom will belabor all the ways Cassidy has wronged her, not only yesterday but in the last twenty years. If I try to cut her off, she'll accuse me of always taking my sister's side—which is false, since I never take sides. It's why I'm the perfect middleman. The only way to end this conversation and get on with my day is to hear her out.

"What did she say?" I ask, settling into my familiar role. Lifting my mug, I wish I had something stronger than coffee in my cup this morning.

★ ★ ★

It was Christmas 1992—Cassidy was seven and I was four—when Mom made one of her most memorable mothering blunders. Eager to open our last presents under the tree, I ripped open the wrapping and was delighted to find a Cabbage Patch Kid. Cassidy unveiled a rock tumbler kit and some rocks. To this day, Cassidy still gives Mom shit about the "worst" gift ever and Mom bemoans how ungrateful a daughter Cassidy was.

To be fair, both of them tell the story wrong. Cassidy forgets to mention she was a major science nerd and Mom neglects to admit she had no idea what to buy her geeky daughter. Even though I was only four, I remember Cass forcing me to dig in the dirt with her every chance we had. Being the younger child, I had very little say in our game choices. I was just happy to be included and gladly followed her around the yard, insisting we were looking for T. rex bones or buried treasure. So, Mom's gift might have seemed like a weird choice for a little girl, but it wasn't completely farfetched. I truly believe Mom thought Cassidy would love it.

My present was perfect. My doll came with a real birth certificate and a couple outfits. Her name was Olive and she had brown hair made of yarn that was tied up in two matching ponytails, the same way I liked to wear my own hair. Much to Cassidy's annoyance, I brought that doll everywhere. Again, I was only four, so my memory of this story is based as much on what I've been told over the years as on actual recollection, but from what I understand, Cassidy was insanely jealous she didn't get a Cabbage Patch Kid since she had secretly coveted one for some time.

A few days or weeks after Christmas (it always changes), we were in her room playing with her new rock tumbler set. Come to find out, it was actually a really cool toy once you figured out how to use it. It took normal rocks and buffed and polished them until they shone like gemstones. I was given the task of polishing the rocks while Cassidy did the more fun job of fashioning the finished product into jewelry using fasteners and loops of string.

It was all going well until something got stuck in the machine and the motor ground to a halt midway through a rock working its way through the tumbling system. Cassidy brushed me aside, her deft little hands working to free the rock, but it wouldn't budge. She wedged a pair of scissors inside the mechanism and tried to shimmy it out but only got it jammed worse. In a fit of frustration, she tried banging the whole thing against the table, hoping to dislodge the pesky rock. Nothing.

"You've ruined it!" she yelled at me. I'm sure I started crying and pleading for forgiveness. Honestly, I was too young to be playing with motorized machines, but that's a parenting issue for another day. Cassidy banished me from the room, where she remained sulking over her broken rock tumbler, alternately banging it against the table and stabbing the rock with the scissors to no avail. In my hurry to escape my sister's wrath, I forgot to grab Olive.

About an hour later she came out of her room and started watching TV like nothing had happened. Thrilled that she wasn't mad anymore, I snuggled up with her, eager to win back her favor. She suggested I go get Olive from our room so we could have a tea party. I was sure it was my lucky day, since Cassidy never wanted to play fun things like house or kitchen, even though I always asked. I ran from the room to get my doll before she changed her mind.

My blood-curdling scream awakened our mother from her nap. She came running and found Cassidy watching cartoons, completely nonplussed by my incessant wailing from the other side of the house. When asked where her sister was, she simply shrugged, forcing Mom to find me herself.

I was on my bed sobbing over the massacred hair of my precious Olive. Using the same scissors that couldn't fix her machine, Cassidy had given my doll an impromptu haircut, shearing off half of either ponytail. Poor Olive looked like she'd made a pass through the rock tumbler herself. Bits and pieces of brown yarn littered the floor. When I saw my mom, I held up my butchered doll and squealed in agony. My beautiful Olive was ruined.

Yanking the doll from my hands and snatching the scissors from my pillow, Mom stormed back into the living room to confront Cassidy, who only tilted her head innocently as though amused by the situation unfolding. I'm pretty sure I stood behind the couch, whimpering.

"Did you do this?" she yelled, shaking the doll, which caused more yarn to tumble from her mangled head.

"Yes," Cassidy said.

Shocked at the easy confession, my mother was flustered. I'm sure she expected a denial, or at least an excuse. "Why?" she asked, beckoning for me to come out from my hiding place. I crept to her side, thumb in my mouth. It's likely I'm projecting my adult emotions onto the little girl in this memory, but I imagine I was torn between wanting my mother to punish my sister and not wanting to be the cause of my sister's punishment. If Cassidy got into trouble, she'd blame me and I'd have no one to play with. But she ruined my doll, so my heart and mind were at odds.

"She broke my toy and I hate that doll," she said unapologetically. "It's stupid and ugly and it looks better now," she sputtered. She saw me crying behind my mom's legs and sighed, a hint of remorse clouding her mossy eyes. "C'mon, Claire, dolls are for babies anyway. I'll play with you outside later."

I sniffled and tried to control my sadness and confusion over why my big sister had chopped off my doll's hair. Mom made Cassidy apologize formally, so I received a reluctant, "I'm sorry." Four-year-old me was eager to accept it if it meant Cassidy wouldn't hate me anymore. Later she fulfilled her promise, inviting me to build a snowman in what was left of the previous week's snowstorm.

After that day I left Olive behind, playing with her only when I was by myself. A few days (or weeks) later, I came home to find Olive's hair trimmed equally on both sides. A blue ribbon was tied into either short ponytail. She did look better with short hair, I told Cassidy. My sister hugged me (which she never did) and dragged me into the living room to play some nerdy game with her. I left Olive sitting safely on my bed.

★ ★ ★

"I'll call her and let you know what she says, I promise." Resting the back of my head against the edge of the chair, I catch sight of the clock. 10:52 AM. So much for grocery shopping before the library.

"Well, I'm not speaking to her until I get an apology. It's simply unacceptable how she's been treating me." Her voice wobbles. She can't cry. I'll never get off the phone if she starts sobbing.

"I understand," I say quickly, hopeful that she'll mistake it for agreement. "Mom, I have to run now. Sofia needs help getting the boys ready. I'll call her soon, I promise," I reiterate.

She sighs, undoubtedly annoyed that I'm rushing her off the phone even though it's been well over an hour. "Give those beautiful boys kisses from Grandma," she says instead, her voice changing. And just like that, she makes it harder to be mad at her.

"I will. Love you," I say, hanging up before the call can linger any longer.

Letting the phone fall to the desk, I rest my head in my hands and gently massage my temples. I've been mediating the fights between my mom and sister for so long, but they still bother me. Steve constantly cautions me against inserting myself into their battles, but he doesn't understand. This is our dynamic.

Cassidy insists Mom likes me better because we're so similar. This insinuation would insult me if I didn't know better. She doesn't say it to be hurtful. But Cassidy sees only what Cassidy sees. Growing up, Mom never let us forget how she gave up her promising career as an artist to stay home and raise us. Mom once had dreams of curating an art house or painting her own exhibit. It was never clear exactly what she gave up, only that it involved her art and that the dream ended with us children. She blamed marrying young and having kids for stalling her "otherlife," as she referred to it. For example: *In my otherlife, I would be a famous artist in Boston or New York.* Once Cassidy and I were grown, she began painting in earnest, and she's actually quite talented. It was just easier for her to use her status as a stay-at-home mother as an excuse for not prioritizing her dreams than it was to explore why she romanticized her *otherlife*.

Cassidy and I are simply products of our upbringing. Cassidy leaned hard into the idea of motherhood standing in the way of career and was determined not to make the same mistakes as Mom by studying hard and ensuring that her career would always come first. Mom thought Cassidy shoved her brilliance in her face, but I believe straight As and a scholarship were Cassidy's misguided attempt at making Mom proud. Instead of binding them, it served only to create more distance between them. Naturally combative, they butted heads constantly. No matter what Mom might say, Cassidy found fault. If pushed to succeed, Cass was mad at her for pushing. If Mom warned her she was pushing herself too hard, Cassidy was angry that she didn't support her. Cassidy was aiming to live the *otherlife*, but it only bred resentment and jealousy.

Mom gravitated toward me because I was easier. I was smart without being obsessive. Popular and pretty, I was an all-around normal teenage girl. I made sense to Mom. Even though I went off to college, I ended up pregnant and married very young, just like her. To everyone's surprise, I left the workplace to raise my first baby, then the next two, and never went back. This makes Mom proud and irritates my sister. I let them think whatever they want. Truth is, I leaned even harder against my upbringing than Cassidy. I saw the emotional turmoil holding the weight of my mother's disappointment put on us, and I swore never to put such guilt on the shoulders of my own children. I had the *otherlife*, and I chose this one. Never will my children fear I want something *more* or something *other*. I pick my family every day. I saw my mother's shortcomings and vowed to be better not for her, but for myself and my children. In my opinion, it's the *onlylife*.

◆ 17 ◆

OWEN

After
July 4

I'M ALMOST SORRY THIS job is ending. *Almost*. Bourne Mansion has consumed all my time and energy for months now. I ended up needing far more guys than projected and we almost ran over budget not once, but three times. By some stroke of luck—and luck it must have been, since I can't take credit for smart planning—we finished on time and came in just *under* budget. The board of trustees was shocked and thrilled at this good news.

When I bid on the project last year, I never imagined I'd win. Although I was confident in my qualifications, my résumé wasn't nearly as impressive as those of the competing companies. Once the exhilaration of winning the job wore off, I quickly came to understand why I won. Even though my work is impeccable, the board was most impressed by my price point. If I wasn't the best choice, I was certainly the cheapest.

In my inexperience, I failed to take into account some of the more obscure building codes and federal ordinances placed on such a famous piece of public property and ended up spending many hours researching the various codes and double-checking them with lawyers. Some unexpected pushback from the community resulted in more research and time spent creating a "sustainable" design that changed my original land grading and storm management solutions. It was no wonder the more experienced companies were more expensive. Most came in at almost double my estimate. Ultimately it was a lot more work than I'd bargained for, but we got it done.

Standing here with the mansion behind me and Revere Beach stretching across the horizon in front of me, it all feels worth it. All the blood, sweat, and tears my crew and I have spilled are built into every stone wall, fountain, and veranda on the property. Before we started, the grounds were a mess, acres of sprawling, untended lawns and overgrown gardens with walkways that crumbled beneath your feet and led nowhere. The marshlands abutting the back property line lent a dank air of despair to the entire place, the tall grass and murky waters threatening to close in on the once-majestic park. With some careful planting and a new drainage system, we reclaimed the land. Now the marshes serve as a beautiful boundary, blending seamlessly with rolling turf and sustainable gardens.

Gracing the center of it all is the fourteen-bedroom brick mansion, power-washed and painted back to its former glory. After touring the house, all cleaned and restored, you can walk outside into the walled garden. Where there was once a large cement block, cracked and overgrown with weeds, there's now a cobblestone patio with pathways leading to four different flowered gardens, each more magical than the last.

As long as the town approves everything, the house will be open to the public next month. My part in the process is finished. Soon the grounds will be filled with families picnicking on the lawns and enjoying the serenity that such a beautiful piece of history allows.

In my dreams, Cassidy is standing here with me today, celebrating the conclusion of all my hard work and ready to settle down for a picnic of our own. We'd pop a bottle of champagne and toast to better things to come. In reality, she doesn't even know I'm finished. I used to tell her everything. Now it's hard to tell her anything at all.

Every night I ask her about her day. It's what you do when you love someone. You ask the question, even when you're tired or cranky and don't care to hear about another lame or sick horse. You ask anyway. In response, the old Cassidy asked about my day. Maybe she only pretended to care about retention walls and patio pavers, but it didn't matter. Her curiosity and sincere belief in me urged me to work harder, bid on bigger projects. I'd never have considered putting the company up for this job if it hadn't been for her insistent confidence in my abilities.

One day she stopped asking, even before we lost the baby. Other questions stole its place. What did I want for dinner? Did I need anything from Target? Trivial questions that were both boring and necessary. Every once in a while, I offered up my day just to bask in the familiar intensity of her attention, but it wasn't the same. The response was forced, like I was grasping at something just out of reach.

For a little while we talked only about babies. *How to make a baby*—something I'd thought was pretty straightforward. I was wrong. *When to make a baby*—I'm not an idiot; I know there's a special time each month. What I didn't realize was that my life would soon revolve around a four-day window. *What I should eat to make a baby*—oysters, oranges, and lots of nuts. I laughed at the last suggestion, prompting an exaggerated eye roll. *What I should wear to make a baby*—loose pants! And although she never outright said this last one, she strongly suggested what I should be *thinking* about to make a baby. *Babies.* How, when, and why to make them.

Baby talk drove us both insane. Cass worried herself into a state of exhaustion and disappointment so deep it got harder to recover each month. Sex with my wife had always been one of the greatest joys of my life, but it was very unsexy watching her record the session on her phone while lying with a pillow under her ass and her legs pointed toward the ceiling. If only she'd rolled over to cuddle or talk instead of dropping her legs and falling asleep. She didn't even bother kissing me good-night. My job was done. Eventually I recoiled when she dimmed the lights and reached across the sheets, knowing she was doing it for one reason only and that reason wasn't me.

I'd always seen a baby in our future. I'd never guessed it would be so hard. I'm not blind to the struggle some couples have conceiving, and I respect the families with the tenacity required to undergo IVF and other fertility treatments. In my heart, I know Cassidy and I would go to the moon and back to start a family if necessary. Our doctor warned that it could take up to a year before we fell pregnant. When it didn't happen the first month, she took it as a sign of failure, and failure wasn't something she was familiar with. We needed a break before it broke us. Somewhere in all the baby talk, we lost *us*, the most critical factor in the process. Fast-forward to losing the baby she tried so hard for, and there's barely anything left. Of her. Of us.

Now we don't talk at all. Our beautiful old house is dark when I pull up after work. Some nights she opts to stay out on call late into the evening. Summer is her busiest season, but I know Dr. Ford isn't forcing her to stack her schedule. She's pushing herself too hard, choosing to see one more horse after hours or catching up on billing, a job she could easily pass on to the office secretary. When she's home, she's shut in our son's nursery or sitting on the couch staring blankly at a novel. Black smudges live under her eyes and her cheeks are hollow. She barely bothers brushing her hair.

But I'm too scared to say anything. I'm locked out. Her grief is untouchable, although I wish I could take it from her shoulders and carry it myself. Sometimes I sit with her, but she flinches when I touch her and shrinks further into herself. Each time she pulls away, I feel my grasp on her loosening. I'm afraid I'm losing her. On the lonelier nights, I fear she's already gone.

★　★　★

Dusk settles over the Atlantic, but the temperature doesn't drop with the sun. Even the breeze rolling in off the water can't cool the heavy and oppressive air. Sitting in my truck with the AC running and the windows down (a colossal waste of energy, my dad would lecture), I let my mind wander. Instead of heading home, I drive the quarter mile down the road to the best spot overlooking Revere Beach. I've never enjoyed the salt and sand on my skin, but I love watching the water and looking out over the endless horizon, listening to the waves break to shore. Before moving east, I'd never seen a coastline, and the novelty of the ocean hasn't worn off yet. Learning to swim in lakes and pools, I've always been a strong swimmer, but something about the ocean unnerved me and I'm still hesitant to do more than dip my toes in the frothy waves along the shore. I can't get used to the power and movement of the water, the feeling of being dragged into and under its mass. It's not fear that keeps me from straying too far from the shoreline so much as respect. I prefer to admire the ocean's strength and beauty from a distance.

Kids play along the beach, some building sand castles, others chasing siblings and friends in and out of the shallow waves. Watching from chairs or reclined on beach towels, tired parents shield their eyes from the last remaining rays of light, no doubt counting down the minutes before they can pack the kiddos up and head into some air conditioning. The comforting sounds of summer—yelling children and squawking sea gulls—blend with the soothing rhythm of the waves and overshadow the light traffic whizzing down North Shore Drive, cars packed with families heading to the famous Kelly's Roast Beef or the soft-serve ice cream shop on the corner.

All the happy families make me think about my own mom and dad back home. It's still early evening in Kansas, but Mom prefers to eat supper early. I imagine she's at the kitchen sink washing the old blue plates with the farm scene on them, the same plates we had in the house when I was a kid. These were the everyday set, the ones she placed our turkey sandwiches on—sliced diagonally—with a side of chips or raisins for lunch. She used the fancy wedding china only for holidays and company. It used to be just the three of us, and now it's only two. It must get lonely in the big old farmhouse.

July in Kansas isn't all that different from July here. Hot and humid in Revere, it's probably the same at my parents' house. It might even be hotter in the Midwest, where there's no sweet relief from a cool ocean breeze. People here assume Kansas is either blue skies over rolling cornfields or gray and on the verge of a tornado. In reality, it's the same as anywhere else. This disappointed me when I first moved to Boston, expecting some drastic climate change. But summers are hot and winters are cold both here and there. The leaves are much prettier on the East Coast, though.

Dad's probably in his studio building furniture. It seems like boring work, but I've seen how intricate each piece is. I learned to appreciate how something functional could also be a thing of extreme beauty. Tables were my inspiration for getting into design work. As I grew older, I asked Dad why he didn't sell the pieces he made. Each was time-consuming, especially since he was a slow and methodical worker who created only after he was finished grading papers and handling the household chores. He never really answered, just shrugged and said he made them for my mother. This made little sense to me at the time, since someone was always bumping a shin against an extra table or chair in our already crowded house. I get it now. Making tables made him happy. Selling tables might not have.

By now Mom's finished drying the dishes. She's put them in the cupboard, where they'll be taken back down tomorrow for breakfast. On the stove, a kettle whistles. She'll make herself a cup of tea and sip it out on the porch while she reads one of her mystery books as the sun goes down. Our front porch faces the western horizon, and the view at sunset can't be beat. You can literally see for hundreds of miles. Classical music spills softly from the old radio perched in the open kitchen window. There's no air conditioning in the house. Dad prefers to catch a cross breeze.

Later tonight, both will settle down together to watch a show. Cassidy and I gifted them with a Netflix subscription, but I'm pretty sure they prefer network television. Mom claims she likes the commercials, says it keeps her up to date on new products she might need. She's a coupon-clipping, old-fashioned lady stuck in her ways. Dad's a little more modern, but only by an inch. He can use a few apps and manages to text, even though he still signs his name to each message as if it were an email. By ten o'clock (Kansas time), Mom will head upstairs to wash her face and set her hair. Dad will lock up the house before reading a few pages from one of the hardcover biographies he keeps beside his recliner. He prefers Civil War–era generals but reads widely.

What would they do if their world fell to pieces? Like most kids, I didn't pay much attention to my parents growing up. As long as they picked me up from baseball and drove me to the movies, I was content. I knew their jobs and schedules, but I didn't ask about their lives. They were "Mom and Dad." My friends often complained about crummy parents who fought or were getting divorced. In comparison, mine seemed stable. With no gauge as to what made a good marriage, I thought theirs was perfect. They rarely fought. They provided well for me. They seemed to love each other, always kissing good-bye and good-night. Most importantly, they're still together forty years later, an eternity by today's standards.

How would they handle losing a child? Growing up an only child, I often wished for a sibling. From ages six to nine, I asked Santa Claus for a baby brother. The last time I wrote to the North Pole, I amended my previous year's wish and said I'd accept a little sister, even though nine-year-old me wasn't thrilled at the prospect of a girl in the house. I was so desperate for a playmate I would've taken whatever I could get. I don't remember what my parents told me to explain why Santa didn't leave a sibling under the tree. I remember the disappointment but not the reason. Eventually, I stopped asking. Did they not want more children? Looking back, it seems odd that my mom, the type who baked cookies and hand stitched my Halloween costumes, had only one child.

The sun's almost set over the horizon. Closing my eyes, I envision my childhood from a different perspective. Even now, I recognize that they were amazing parents. We went hiking and fishing each summer. They encouraged and supported my interests. They were there to guide me and catch me when I fell. But I can't remember what they did together not involving me. We went to dinner as a family. We watched movies as a family. Their life together revolved around me. Dad built furniture and Mom liked to read and knit, but these things they did on their own. What did they have together, as a married couple, not as parents?

Opening my eyes, I vow to call Dad tomorrow and ask some of these questions. The prospect of such an intimate conversation is intimidating but feels important. So important, I'm tempted to call now. I've always held their marriage up as the gold standard, and now I worry it might only be gold plated.

The sky is electrified by a burst of crisp white light that pops and dances in the shape of a star before falling delicately to the horizon. Another loud succession of bangs and booms follows, and a trail of red fireworks traces its way across the purple sky. The air is too thick for stars to shine through, but the fireworks sparkle against the velvet backdrop. I close the windows and blast the AC, turning the radio up high.

Looks like Cassidy and I won't be watching the fireworks on the beach this year. Another tradition forgotten. A few red-white-and-blue bursts stab across the sky, falling like tears into the ocean.

◆ 18 ◆

CASSIDY

After
July 12

"NAMASTE."
"*Namaste*," I murmur in chorus with the dozen other women in class. When I open my eyes, the air stirs as a few people rise from *Shevasana* to wipe and roll up their mats. I don't lift my head, preferring to remain horizontal a few extra minutes to allow my heart rate to steady and my body temperature to normalize while the room cools from a toasty 105 degrees back down to a more humane ninety or so.

Groaning, I shrug my way up onto my elbows and revel in the not entirely unpleasant wave of light-headedness swirling around my body as I reenter the real world again.

Tara is busy spritzing her hot-pink mat with a dose of lavender detox spray. Despite ninety minutes of intense sweating, she looks invigorated and ready to start class all over again. I wish I looked as radiant after yoga; I imagine I resemble a wet sheepdog in need of a bath. Tomorrow I'm sure I'll regret signing up for the advanced-flow class, since my muscles are aching in protest already, but I felt guilty canceling on Tara for the fourth time in a row. I thought I was still in relatively good shape after my brief pregnancy, but by my third downward dog I realized that even if my body hadn't changed much, my ab muscles sure remembered what happened.

"Coco Leaf or the Juicery?" Tara asks, gracefully hopping to her feet and stretching all five foot eight of her lithe body toward the ceiling.

"I could go for a burger and milk shake," I joke, provoking a jaunty eye roll from my devoutly low-carb-, low-fat-loving best friend. Model thin, even in college and grad school where we survived on pizza and beer, Tara sticks to a mostly vegetarian and decidedly boring diet. She jokes that she prefers to save her calories for alcohol, but deep down I know it stems from something less innocuous. We all have our demons. "Fine, I'll settle for something with a side of bacon," I add, my stomach growling loudly. Tara wrinkles her nose. "I hear bacon is very keto friendly."

She reaches out a perfectly manicured hand to help me up from the floor. "Well, we did just burn like five hundred calories," she says, weighing the consequences of indulging in a meal more substantial than a green smoothie. I can almost see the calorie cogs turning in her mind. "I suppose we could try Tuesdays," she offers, a compromise in the form of a better-than-diner type breakfast establishment catering to the Sunday brunch crowd and offering an assortment of twenty-dollar eggs Benedicts and four different types of hash.

I take comfort in how easily we fall back into our old routine. In the months following my pregnancy announcement, she pulled away, sending fewer texts and calling less often. At first I was hurt by the distance growing between us. Hurt, but not surprised. Tara was just being Tara. In her mind I'd broken the promise we made over a decade ago while drinking boxed wine in the dorm rooms of Tufts University, back before we had any idea what we truly wanted out of life. Tara is a throwback to a carefree time when I dreamed all the dreams without marriage or babies muddling things up. Somewhere along the way our paths forked, but Tara refuses to acknowledge the change.

She looks at me for a response and I smile and nod my head, tucking my mat under one arm and linking the other through hers. "Tuesdays sounds perfect," I say, feeling a second wind at the prospect of bacon. "That's the place with the Bloody Mary bar, right?"

★　★　★

Seated at a cozy corner booth at the retro-kitschy restaurant, we're surrounded by people enjoying their overpriced but undoubtedly delicious food and reveling in the hipster-cool atmosphere of the hot spot. Most of the tables are filled with twentysomething women, the "bruncher" crowd, but a few families with small children in tow are parked at bigger tables near the kitchen. One lovely couple feeds an infant sitting in a wooden high chair. The parents talk while the baby babbles, unconcerned that she's covered in sticky maple syrup. My heart aches and I pull my eyes from the infant long enough to take a long sip of my loaded Bloody Mary. Since the miscarriage, I haven't drunk much, and the vodka goes straight to my head.

"Come on, be honest," Tara says, catching my eye drifting back from the baby. "How much did you miss this?" she teases, sipping her own drink after maneuvering the straw from behind a strip of crispy bacon. She delicately lifts a jumbo shrimp from the rim of the glass and considers it before plopping it onto her napkin, wrinkling her pert little nose.

I swallow, the spicy liquid hitting my empty stomach. Tara toys with the strip of bacon before breaking off a small piece and shoving it into her mouth like a thief. I try to suppress a laugh.

"Just eat the whole thing." I pop half a piece into my own mouth and swallow deliberately. "Your scrawny ass will thank me." Tara's less-than-robust behind has tormented her since college. No amount of squatting or Pilates could change the fact that she resembles a twelve-year-old boy from the back, albeit a really tall one.

Sticking out her tongue, she nibbles a little more. "You can't tell me it doesn't feel good to be drinking," she repeats. "Your body is your own again," she adds, slurping her drink until all that's left is tomato-stained ice.

Exhaling, I smile through gritted teeth. *She means well,* I remind myself. After being married so long, it's tough putting myself in Tara's decidedly single shoes. Tara never pretended to want kids, content to live the life of the wild aunt swooping in to spoil her friends' kids before handing them back to their rightful owners. Men are a different story. Plenty of potential mates have come and gone, none lasting over six months except the One Who Got Away. Everyone thought Paul was *the one.* After a year of dating he took her on a romantic trip to Turks and Caicos, and we all predicted she'd come back engaged.

To our surprise, she came back ringless and the relationship fizzled shortly after. She insisted she didn't see herself with Paul long-term. Only I knew the real truth. Tara couldn't forgive Paul for not popping the question. He was devastated. A few months after their breakup, I messaged him on Facebook, and he confided that he'd bought Tara a ring a month before the doomed trip. Sensing she saw a proposal coming, he wanted to wait so she didn't feel the pressure to say yes. He probably dodged a bullet. His error in judgment only proved he wasn't the right man for Tara, who both expected and desired a showy display of affection. Either way, Tara decided he'd missed his chance, and we'll never know.

"Sure," I concede, more to keep the peace than anything else. "I missed the occasional cocktail," I admit. While pregnant I was jealous of Owen's weekend beers and Tara's Instagram story, which was flooded with trips to wineries and girls' nights out I wasn't invited to. After one failed attempt at hanging out, I realized being the sober girl in the bar wasn't fun at all. In fact, it was hardly bearable. She stopped asking me to come after that.

"Please," Tara snorts. "Occasional cocktail? Don't pretend you didn't take five tequila shots to pregame the shots you'd take at the bar!" She cocks her arched brow at me, daring me to disagree. I nod, recalling some barely remembered nights out with Tara. "Remember senior year when we vowed to never have kids?" she asks, still laughing, but with a hard note in her voice. "We planned on being career women who'd conquer the world."

Pushing my half-finished drink away, I suddenly don't feel like reminiscing. The tomato juice is too spicy, and I'm dizzy from the vodka. Drunk is different now.

Alcohol has loosened my lips in the worst of ways, and I'm not strong enough to resist the bait she dangles before me. I should let the comment die. But the vodka makes it impossible. "Well, we're both doctors, so I'd say we've done a pretty good job conquering shit," I say, only half joking.

She shrugs and looks around for the waitress, pointing at her drink and signaling for another. Maybe the waitress will bring some waters with this round. My mouth is dry and sour. "True. But that isn't enough anymore." The last few words in her statement tilt upward. Her habit of turning every sentence into a slight question has always been irritating, but it's even more annoying today.

"Are you asking me this or telling me?" I say, aware this is exactly how a certain professor used to address Tara whenever she made the mistake of talking to him in her singsong manner. Tara worshiped our microbiology professor to the point of blatant obsession. She claims she never slept with him, but the rumor was actively making the rounds by the end of senior year. Regardless, my comment hits the mark, and she's practically bristling across the table.

Tara flashes me a radiantly white smile, but there's no kindness behind her eyes. She might as well be baring her fangs at me. She shrugs and twirls a strand of icy-blond hair around her finger. Always the coolest girl in the room, Tara had the low-key stare down before she was out of diapers. Instantly I'm transported back to the first day of orientation our freshman year. I was the nerdy horse girl standing awkwardly in my boot-cut jeans and non–Abercrombie & Fitch sweater, surrounded by a group of peers infinitely cooler than me. At the front of the room the RA covered some basic floor rules, but only half the residents paid any attention. Instead we all eyed each other in the way only teenagers can—with equal amounts curiosity and disdain.

My eyes were drawn to a beautiful girl with impossibly long and tan legs sitting cross-legged on the couch to the right of the RA. Dressed in a pair of barely-there denim shorts and a baby tee with the ridiculous slogan *Trust Me, I'm a Doctor* plastered across the front, she looked straight out of the pages of a Hollister catalog.

This girl settled her bright-blue eyes in my direction and my cheeks flushed pink, but I couldn't look away. Rather than rolling her eyes or elbowing the pretty brunette sitting beside her, she tilted her delicate head and winked at me. Emboldened by her attention, I feigned boredom at the RA's speech, even though the goody two-shoes in me actually wanted to hear the rules. After we shared a smirk, my heart swelled with hope that I'd actually made a friend on campus. As soon as the RA finished her lecture, I hurried across the room before I lost my nerve or, worse, she forgot about me.

Despite our obvious differences, we bonded over our shared loved of *Grey's Anatomy* and frozen coffee drinks. Within a few minutes we'd determined we were both biology majors, and even though I was intent on veterinary medicine and Tara was leaning toward human medicine, we'd still share most of the same classes. Back then, Tara planned to focus on emergency medicine but admitted it was only because she loved a certain trauma doctor on our favorite show.

Fast-forward to sophomore year when Tara learned she could handle blood and guts on the TV screen but not so much in real life. Unfortunately, this lesson came at my expense. A drunken accident on the quad resulted in me slipping and busting my mouth open, painting the snow bright red. Tara promptly passed out at the sight and hit her own head. After this incident, she swiveled her career ambitions toward clinical psychology.

The waitress reappears with another drink for Tara and a notepad to take our order. My appetite is diminished by the bitter pit of resentment building in my stomach, but I order an omelet with a side of bacon anyway. The promise of food helps ease some of the tension at our table, but as we wait, I struggle to remember why we've remained friends at all. Like any longtime friends, we've had our share of difficulties but always found our way back to each other. Growing up often means growing apart, and we've had our share of that too. Still, I envisioned us weathering the storms of adulthood and calling each other BFF long into our old age. Even though I have a sister of my own, Tara's always been my confidante, and I know that Tara, an only child, considers me the sister she never had. Sisterhood is a bond transcending blood, and sisters are for life.

"How's Owen doing?" Tara asks. She plucks an olive off the toothpick and bites into it, grimacing.

I shrug. "Owen is Owen," I answer. One of the few topics I've learned to steer clear of is marriage.

Owen was a member of our friend group before we began dating, so when we made the leap into romance, I assumed Tara would be happy for us. Although supportive, she was quick to tease and acted as though it were some passing college phase that would undoubtedly end after graduation. Instead, Owen and I moved in together, and though we offered to find a place big enough to include Tara, I knew she'd never agree to a third-wheel arrangement. Her jokes faded, but the judgment sharpened. The night I invited her over to tell her "something important," she showed up at my door with wine and ice cream, assuming Owen and I had broken up. When I told her we were engaged, she threw her arms around me and gushed about the ring—but not before I saw a quick flash of dismay darken her pretty face. Always a wonderful actress, she recovered quickly and pretended to be happy for me. I almost believed it.

Tara's the psychologist in the group, but I don't need a degree to see she's jealous. Not jealous of me, but jealous that things didn't turn out *the way they should be.* Everyone assumed Tara would get married first. Men fell over themselves for the chance to spend time with her, and for good reason. She was stunning and brilliant, with a big personality to match. Tara just happened to fall for the guys more interested in *right now* instead of the *forever* Tara desperately wanted but so vehemently denied wanting.

Tara spits the olive onto her napkin and wrinkles her nose. "Whoever said your taste buds change as you age is wrong," she says, rinsing her mouth with water. "Seriously, I don't know why I keep trying to like those things." She sips some of her second Bloody. "I'm really a mimosa girl and should stick with what I like," she adds, her voice taking on a particular tone I can't ignore.

"What's that supposed to mean?" I ask, sighing and looking toward the kitchen. Food would make this so much better right now. I'm too old for these silly mind games. Tara used to make me feel young and alive. Now she exhausts me. "I take it you aren't actually talking about brunch drinks?"

She shrugs, tossing her hair over her shoulder with a flick of the wrist, a move she's perfected over the years.

"I'm just saying it's hard to teach an old dog new tricks."
Owen would get a kick out of hearing Tara use one of his
much-loved clichés. Might be the only thing the two have
in common.

Crossing my arms across my chest, I stare at Tara,
refusing to talk. I'll let her break first. Silence isn't something she's comfortable sitting in. Great at analyzing others, she hates being in the hot seat herself.

"Jesus, Cass, lighten up," she laughs, color rising in
both cheeks. "Let's just enjoy our drinks and freedom for a
while, since it's been ages since you could do either."

Typical Tara, able to strike where it hurts with a
seemingly offhand comment. Best friends are great—you
always have someone to share your secrets with. But they
are also dangerous. They know all your weaknesses and
exactly how to cut you.

"I'm so sorry I got pregnant and you lost a drinking
buddy," I sneer. Smiling, I pick up my own drink and take
a long sip, the watered-down tomato juice bitter in my
mouth. "I'm sorry I got married and you lost your wing
woman," I add. My straw hits the bottom and I wipe my
mouth, not taking my gaze from my best friend.

Unflappable, Tara just laughs and rolls her eyes. "I'm
only looking out for you, Cass. Seems like you've lost sight
of who you are the past few years. Just trying to remind
you."

Years? I recoil as though slapped, nearly spilling my
drink. I thought Tara was annoyed I'd been MIA while
pregnant. Clearly, my life choices have bothered her not
for weeks or months but *years*. My mind races to recall
the daily texts and weekly calls. Even though they were
less frequent while I was pregnant, I never failed to check
in on her or send her a funny meme or "like" her stupid
Instagram posts. Obviously, we don't talk for hours each
night like we did when we were nineteen, but I thought
we'd done a damn good job of fitting each other into

the complicated puzzle of our adult lives. Evidently, I'm mistaken.

Tara sighs and shrugs. "Never mind," she says, shaking her head as the waitress descends on us with two steaming plates of food. "Breakfast is served," she adds lamely.

"I'm not hungry," I say, refusing to let this go.

"You're always hungry," she insists, her brow softening.

She's not getting off the hook this time. Our dynamic can be toxic. Tara always gets the last word, and I always end up groveling for some sort of acceptance. Even now, I'm tempted to apologize to make this uncomfortable conversation go away. But it won't really go away, just be swept under the rug and left to fester.

"You can't just say shit like that and then eat a waffle and pretend it's all okay," I say, hating the pleading sound of my own voice. "Just tell me what you mean."

Putting her fork down, she considers me for a moment. She puckers her plump lips and studies me as though I'm one of her patients. It's unnerving sitting on the receiving end of her professional stare.

"Fine." All traces of Tara my best friend are replaced by Dr. Tara Clark, PhD in clinical child psychology. "Ironically enough, Cass, you *could* just eat a waffle right now and pretend everything was okay. In fact, that's exactly your problem," she starts, her voice low and heavy. "Things weren't perfect at home for a while. You constantly complained about your relationship, how Owen 'didn't understand you' and how hard it was to find a home and work balance," she says, voicing some of the grievances I'm guilty of sharing over the years. But that's what friends do. Complain about their significant others. Vent about coworkers. Share the stuff they can't share with anyone else. She continues, "So, instead of actually addressing these issues with your husband, you pretend they don't exist and decide the best way to fix all your marital problems is to have a baby," she says, her voice dripping with sarcasm. "Because we all know how often this works to save a marriage."

I attempt to hide the deep shame and anger I feel, but my fair skin has never been one to keep a secret. Tara's using my own words against me, and though I can argue they've been taken out of context, it's partly the truth, even if feels like a cheap shot. I love Owen and I love our life together. Most of the time. What marriage doesn't have its problems? Over a few drinks, I grumbled to my best friend, sometimes exaggerating things so Tara felt included, always aware I was lucky to be married while Tara remained forever single. Bragging about the good things in my marriage seemed cruel in the face of Tara's online dating horror stories. Complaining about Owen's lack of attention was both easier and kinder. Tara bitched about the jerk who ghosted her online and I unloaded some of my marital grievances. I didn't know we were keeping score.

I lean back in my chair and raise my brows, giving her permission to finish. She's just getting started.

"Unable to do anything half-assed, you put your heart and soul into making a baby, and when you didn't see instant results, you spiraled out of control." She perches on the edge of her seat and rests her chin on her clasped fingers. "Even Owen saw this, as aloof as he is. He saw the stress you were under, but it was too late. I know it's hard to admit, but maybe he was right all along. Maybe a baby wasn't the solution."

I want a baby out of love . . . Owen's voice, soft and with the best of intentions, echoes in my head, a phrase that will haunt me for the rest of my life. How I wish I never repeated those words to Tara.

"We both know you never wanted children," Tara says, reaching her hand across the table toward mine. I retract my arm so fast my fork flies across the table and lands with a loud and final clatter on the hardwood floor. A few other patrons look at us with curiosity.

"Just stop," I plead, my entire body on edge. "Just stop talking."

Tara pulls her hand back and brushes her bangs from her forehead. Shrugging, her face softening, she resembles my friend once more. "I'm sorry," she says, but she doesn't sound sorry at all. Her voice is smug and her eyes glitter with an *I told you so* twinkle. "I know it's hard to hear this stuff when you're so close to it."

A laugh erupts from somewhere deep in my chest, startling us both. "Please. You know nothing about marriage or babies or even being an actual grown-up," I hiss, the words flowing hot and free from a place I've kept locked inside for too long. "You've had what? *One* relationship that's lasted longer than a hot minute?" I'm satisfied to see the hurt flash across her face. "Don't project your shit onto me," I say, pushing my chair back and pulling a fifty from my purse. "Maybe stick to diagnosing kids with ADD and keep the fuck out of people's marriages," I add. "You can't even commit to a brunch drink, Tara. What makes you think you have any idea what it's like being me?" I throw the money on the table and turn on my heel without sparing my best friend another glance.

✦ 19 ✦

OWEN

After
July 21

NOT TO WAX POETIC, as my dad might say, but the sight of my wife's truck parked in the drive used to set my heart aflutter, like I was some lovestruck teenager with butterflies in my stomach. I regret taking even a single moment of that feeling for granted. Never in my wildest dreams did I imagine those butterflies would be replaced by the dark and stormy churning of doom that settles in the pit of my gut each time I come home now.

Today, like yesterday and all the days before, the house is cool and damp, like a dank cave. The kitchen holds the sweet smell of decay, and I wonder when the trash was last emptied. We used to alternate the chore. Whoever was up first emptied the canister and wheeled the big plastic can to the street. It falls to me alone now, although I can't recall the last time it was done. I think Monday. Today is Friday.

Pulling off my work boots, I slip into my house shoes, the ones I always leave by the door. My mother had a strict rule that no shoes were allowed in the house. Cassidy poked fun at my habit, insisting our house was far from spotless with a dog running amuck and a messy animal doctor traipsing in who knew what from barns. Old habits die hard.

Rosie is rustling around somewhere in the depths of the house, probably chewing a bone or playing with one of her many toys. Loyal to Cassidy, Rosie won't leave her side to greet me. I'm glad Cass has her company, but I miss the old days when both my girls met me in the foyer after a long day at work. I miss the kisses and the barely contained chaos as Rosie jumped around our waists, trying to get in on the action. I miss the sound of Cassidy's laughter and Rosie's excited barks. Any noise would be welcome now, anything to drown out the labored hum and buzz of the old AC cranked too high and still failing to keep the house cool enough in this brutal heat. Central air was an integral part of the big renovation but, like my marriage, is stuck on hold. Stalled until further notice.

Afraid Cassidy went back to work too soon, I called her boss to check in, ready to swoop in and save the day if he told me her work was suffering like everything else in her life. Looking back, I'm not sure what I really expected. What I *hoped* to hear would have hurt far less than the truth. I hoped Dr. Ford would confess she was quiet and distracted, incapable of performing at her normally high standard. Instead, he confirmed what I'd supposed all along. Cassidy was fine. Dr. Ford said she was her normal professional self, calm and unflappable, always charming with the customers and patient with the animals. Though I was relieved she could still find joy in the job she loved, John's words also left me desperately and insanely jealous. Cassidy was still Cassidy out in the world, just not with me.

Flicking on the lights above the small butcher-block island, I cringe at the ever-growing stack of unopened mail Cassidy refuses to address. When the hospital invoice arrived with the term MEDICAL ABORTION listed in bold as the cause of our two-day stay with a price tag of over three thousand dollars, she called the insurance company in a blind rage, ready for war. I was thankful her anger was aimed at something so deserving—who doesn't hate insurance companies?—but it was short-lived. Her fury was so hot, it burned out, and instead of finishing the fight, she gave up. After that, the envelopes sat untouched on the counter. FINAL NOTICE is stamped on the front of the latest bill, and I wonder how many have gone ignored. Adding it to the ever-growing list of things I need to do, I vow to handle it myself. On Monday. I'll take care of it Monday.

Cassidy coughs, startling me. Sitting in the tiny den off the foyer, she doesn't lift her head from her novel as I enter the room. Her eyes are fixed on one page, and even though she turns to the next, she's obviously only pretending to read.

"Babe?" I ask, hating myself for the despair in my voice. Hating Cassidy for putting it there. Even though it's almost ninety degrees outside and the AC is struggling, she's dressed against the cold in her favorite sweatshirt and the fleece pants I bought her in New Hampshire last winter. The blinds are closed against the still-bright day.

Cassidy glances up, looking like a petulant teenager. "Hey," she says, laying the book facedown on her lap.

My throat goes dry and my back stiffens. I'm not sure how much longer I can play this drawn-out game. I don't know any of the rules and she holds all the cards. Behind the sullen stare is my wife, the love of my life, and she's in so much pain. It's as though she's daring me to come closer just so she can shut me out. I imagine a rattlesnake, coiled and ready to strike. Like an idiot, I keep poking it.

Resisting the urge to answer her coolness with snark, I play it safe. "How was work?" I take the easy road, since the other paths are rocky and full of unknown terrors. "How's the colic?" I ask, hoping she'll take my olive branch and engage in something resembling a civil conversation.

"Foundering," she corrects. "It foundered, not colicked. I've told you that like fifteen times," she says, picking up her book. So much for the branch. She snapped it and stomped it into the ground.

Counting to five in my head, I will myself to let it go. It's been a long day. I'm over budget on a project and need to get things back on track before the job collapses around me. A cold beer and a few pleasant words with my wife are all I wanted. A hug or a kiss would be icing on the cake, but I'd settle for a simple touch on the arm at this point. Any physical contact is more than we've shared lately.

"Sorry, I get them confused," I say, shrugging. Tentatively, I perch on the edge of the ottoman. She pulls her legs away. Deciding to poke the snake, I rest my hand on her thigh, and she flinches but doesn't move. "You know, not all of us went to vet school," I add, aware I'm treading in dangerous territory.

She rolls her eyes and brings the book back up toward her chest. "Don't need to go to vet school to learn how to listen to your wife," she murmurs.

When I was growing up, my parents never argued. In hindsight, I realize this isn't as admirable as I once thought. Though they never yelled, they never talked much either. On the flip side, Cassidy's parents fought like cats and dogs. Cassidy told me how in the heat of the moment her mother once hurled a can of spaghetti sauce at her dad's head, luckily missing and sending it crashing through the kitchen window instead. She claimed they fought passionately but always ended up laughing and making up like nothing happened. In our own marriage, we aimed for middle ground. We talked. Gave each other space. Compromised. We thought we were being rational and mature. Now I wonder if we were using our upbringings as an excuse to be lazy with our own problems.

"Are you fucking kidding me?" The weight of the last two months crashes down on my tired shoulders all at once. I despise swearing. My midwestern manners don't coincide with yelling or curse words. But after weeks of snide comments and tiptoeing around like a prisoner in my own home, enough is enough. Pushed hard enough, even a Kansas boy like me will fight back.

Clearly Cassidy is taken by surprise. Her eyes widen, but only for a moment. Quickly the disbelief is replaced by anger. She's been itching for a reaction, poised for this fight.

"I guess you didn't hear me, again," she says, sitting up and cocking her head. "Seems to be the common theme here."

"You really want to do this, Cassidy?" I stand, afraid I might grab her by the shoulders and shake sense into her if I get too close. "Maybe I forget a few things here and there, but at least I make an effort to listen to you. Please, tell me *one* thing I've been doing these last few weeks, just one thing." I fold my arms across my chest and raise my brows. She glares at me, and I see a glint of hatred in her eyes. "Oh, wait. You wouldn't know a damn thing about what I'm doing because you haven't asked me. Not once."

She stares at me without moving.

"I move around like a ghost in this fucking house. I'm so afraid of making you upset, I sneak in and out like a thief in the night. We don't talk, and when you think to speak to me, it's never more than a few words I have to pull out of you one by one. You haven't asked me once how my day's been," I continue, trying to read her blank face. "You haven't touched me, not even a kiss good-bye in the morning," I add, the truth of the statement hitting me hard. We always kissed good-bye *before*. My heart hurts with every word I say out loud. All these little grievances have been adding up. Bottled up, the pain was easier to keep at bay. Now it's all out there and hurts all over again.

"Poor Owen. Do you feel neglected?" she sneers. "I'm so sorry I haven't been giving you enough attention as I deal with the crippling loss of our baby," she says, her voice cold and unyielding. "Do you even remember what happened? Remember how I was pregnant and instead of

leaving the hospital with a baby, I delivered a dead one
and went home empty-handed? I remember. I remember
all day, every day. Clearly there's a lot you wanted to talk
about in the last two months, but you sure haven't said one
word about *that*. So yes, I'm very sorry I don't give a flying fuck about the stupid bathroom you're redoing or the
backyard patio you designed, because my brain really can't
handle giving a fuck about anything right now."

My anger deflates. Like she intended, her words cut
straight to my broken heart, tearing what's left into jagged pieces. I didn't know it was possible to feel worse than
before, but I was wrong. Every day I've meant to talk
about what happened, but something always stops me.
Initially, she said she needed space. So, I gave her space.
I'm not sure when it happened, but the space turned into
distance, and then I didn't know how to get back to her.
She was so sad all the time, I feared bringing up the worst
day of our life would only make it worse. When she
stopped crying all the time, I dared hope it was getting
better. I was afraid talking about it would make her cry
again. After the tears dried up, everything else did too.
She turned to stone—hard, cold, and immovable. Nothing I said softened her. Again, fear kept me from talking
about the one thing we needed to talk about most. But
no one gives you a user manual for grief. I thought I was
doing the best I could to manage my own pain without
making hers worse. Turns out, it wasn't good enough.
Not by a long shot.

"That's not fair," I mutter. Her small body is stiff and
upright on the couch, her muscles flexed like she's on the
verge of flight.

Sitting down again, my shoulders hunching, I long to
hold her close, squeeze her tight until she's mine again,
whole again. I inch closer, but she pulls her legs beneath
her, positioning herself as far as possible from me on the
small love seat. "Hey," I whisper. "I'm not the enemy."

The unfamiliar glint in her eyes darkens. "I don't want to talk, Owen," she mumbles. Flipping her book right side up, she turns her gaze from me. I grab the novel and toss it across the room, knocking a framed photo of us hiking to the rug. Rosie lifts her head, alert and ready to come to Cassidy's aid. I take my wife's hands in my own. "Just leave me alone," she says, trying to wring them away. "Please," she pleads.

"No, we do this now." I squeeze her hands, but she doesn't squeeze back. The fight fades from her like a candle being snuffed, pissing me off even more. I can't fight for something that isn't there. "Talk to me. Fucking yell at me. Just stop pulling away," I beg.

She looks away and sighs. "I have nothing left." Any tears I thought I saw dry up. "It's too late. You don't understand what I'm going through," she says. "No one does."

Letting go of her lifeless hands, I stare into her beautiful green eyes, the ones I've loved for so long. There's none of her normal sparkle, and even the angry gleam is gone.

"I lost a baby too," I say, watching her carefully. Her jaw clenches and she lifts her chin. "I might not have carried him inside of me, but I held him too." Cassidy has the power to stop her tears at will, but I don't. My own flow freely, hot and angry, down my cheeks. "I loved him too."

I stand, leaving her alone in the dark.

◆ 20 ◆

CASSIDY

After
July 21

ALL THE AIR IN the room leaves with Owen. Suddenly the darkness is hot and oppressive, and I struggle to pull the Tufts sweatshirt over my head, tossing it in a ball to the floor, where it knocks over a half-empty glass of water. The weight of our fight settles over me, threatening to crush me. I'm overcome with an overwhelming desire to nap. Today is too much to bear, the promise of sweet oblivion so tempting. But I know sleep will be restless and shaky, not the dreamless sleep of the dead I crave when it all hurts too much.

Owen never leaves. Owen *stays*. He might give me space when I ask, but he always comes back to me. A firm believer in never going to bed angry, Owen has never let me off the hook. Over the years I've found this quality simultaneously annoying and endearing. He's always insisted on compromise, even as I hemmed and hawed, trying to "win" the argument, or worse, turned my back in stony silence. We never screamed or threw things. It always felt very adult, a far cry from my own chaotic upbringing. I still cringe thinking about my mother's irrational arguments and my dad's stubborn rebuttals. Something's different this time. This time he's turning his back on me.

"Fuck," I mutter to the empty room. The sound of muffled laughter floats down the stairs. It's not even eight PM and he's already in bed watching TV.

The prospect of a restless night's sleep on the couch isn't very alluring, but I'm not sure I'm welcome in our shared bed. Closing my eyes, I wish for the darkness to wash over me. Lately, sleep attacks at the most inconvenient times—while working, driving, or trying to hold a conversation midafternoon—but it always hovers just outside my grasp, beyond the deep-purple haze of my tightly closed lids when I crave it most.

Out of nowhere, my dad's quiet Yankee twang melts into my mind and warms me like an old flannel coat. *Dolly Pahh-ton, Cass. Just like that dahmn dahg.* He's a man of few words, but those he chooses to speak tend to be wise ones even stubborn mules like me can't ignore.

Dolly was my first experience with death. A ragtag yellow mutt Dad had brought home from the pound, she was my first real pet. Even though she'd been around before I could walk, she was mine as soon as I was old enough to follow her everywhere. Despite always looking a little worse for wear, Dolly seemed like she would live forever. I've no idea of her actual age, but she had to have been at least fifteen years old when she passed away the summer I turned six.

As a veterinarian, I know it's likely Dolly was dying slowly for years, the creeping death brought along by a cancer that sneaks into the bones of older dogs, especially big ones. Six-year-old me didn't understand this. One day Dad said Dolly was sick and needed to see the doggy doctor. Since I saw the doctor all the time, I thought nothing of it and watched them leave, content to play alone with my jump rope until Dolly came back and we could roam around the yard together. Claire was still a toddler and not nearly as much fun to play with.

After I waited forever, Daddy finally came back, but Dolly wasn't sitting in the passenger seat with her big head shoved out the window. When I rushed to the station wagon, Daddy caught me in his arms and explained how Dolly was too sick to come home and was going to an enormous field in the sky to chase rabbits, one of her favorite things to do. Not satisfied with this turn of events, I raged and screamed, blaming him for stealing my best friend. I didn't speak to him for three full days, an eternity for a six-year-old. What infuriated me most was that he didn't even seem sad. No one seemed to care at all. I didn't expect my mom to mind much—she was always complaining about how much hair Dolly left on the sofa—but I would have thought my dad would be upset. No one else seemed to love poor Dolly, and now she was gone. I hadn't even had a chance to say good-bye.

On the third day, I saw my dad sobbing. He was in the garage, tinkering with the lawn mower, the one that was always in some state of disrepair during my childhood. The side door was propped open with an old cooler filled with lukewarm Coors Light, all the ice having long since melted. I was outside playing with my toy horses and needed a milk crate to craft into a makeshift barn, so I ventured into my dad's inner sanctuary, stopping dead in my tracks when I heard the deep, guttural sound of my dad crying. At first, I was sure he was choking and almost turned on my heels to fetch my mom. Upon closer inspection, I realized he was in fact breathing and actually had tears streaming down his ruddy cheeks. Shocked by the sight, I was both horrified and fascinated to learn that adult men cry. I'd thought tears were reserved for little girls and mommies.

"Daddy?" I whispered, forgetting my vow to never speak to him again.

He looked up from the wrench and wiped a tear from his cheek before it could fall into his reddish beard. His eyes were glassy and wet. "Hey, Cassie-girl," he said, smiling and holding his arms out wide. Without hesitation, I ran right into them and allowed him to envelope me in the type of bear hug only daddies knew how to give.

"What's wrong?" I asked. "Did you hurt yourself fixing the chopper?" I reached for his hand, studying it carefully for some sort of cut or a trace of blood, some source of obvious pain that might explain the tears I saw on his face.

He spun me around on his knee so I faced him and touched his forehead to mine, leaning into me for a beat before sitting back and sighing. "I'm just sad about ol' Dolly Pahhton," he said, brushing a strand of hair off my sweaty face. "I loved that old dog." His voice was gruff and raspier than normal, like his words were cutting his throat.

"I didn't know," I murmured, my own lip starting to tremble. But at the same time, I did. My little-girl brain remembered all the times Dad had taken Dolly for car rides and let her lick his dinner plate, often leaving some big pieces of chicken or steak he'd probably wanted to eat himself. He would even cook an extra hotdog (or two) on the grill when we barbecued and sneak them to Dolly when Mom wasn't looking. Just because Dad had never said it in so many words didn't mean he had never loved Dolly.

"It's okay," he said, his smile deepening and reaching his eyes. "Everyone loves different." He picked me up and plopped me on the ground in front of him. "You can't guess at other people's pain, little one," he added, finding a screwdriver and tossing it from hand to hand. "People try, but it's something that belongs to each of us." He glanced at the clock and motioned toward the door. "Now go on out there and play for a little longer. I'll make us some grilled cheeses for lunch," he promised, his focus already drifting back to the engine in front of him. I scurried back outside, the anger at my dad forgotten. I didn't know it yet, but my overwhelming grief over Dolly had lightened, already turning from pain into fond memories.

Thinking about it now, I realize my dad must have been in his early thirties when Dolly died, but he'd seemed wise beyond his years. It's so easy to see your parents as "old" and forget they were once as young and scared as you. Dad probably didn't know how to deal with grief any more than I do, but he shared his with me, and that's what I remember now.

"Fuck," I mutter, opening my eyes.

★ ★ ★

Owen lies in our bed with the remote pointed toward the TV as if he might actually change it to something other than *30 Rock*. Guilty of watching the same four shows in rotation, we never look for something new, just start an old show from the beginning each time we've finished the last. Last I knew, I think we were on our sixth repeat of Tina and Alec's comic revelation and still laughing at every episode.

Standing in the doorway, I have a feeling I'm on the precipice of something major. Part of me wants to run back down the stairs, but my heart is screaming *now or never*. For months I've wallowed in my own pain, shutting Owen out and using the miscarriage as an excuse for every shitty thing I've said and done. Grief has been my shield and my crutch. Instead of trying to heal, I decided I didn't *want* to feel better. Moving on terrifies me. Letting Owen in, choosing my marriage and my future, requires letting go of the little bit of control my misery lends me.

"I'm no good at this," I say, one foot in the room, the other glued to the floor of the hallway, poised to bolt. The overhead fan swirls cool air around the room and goose bumps rise on my arms, each hair standing at attention as a second turns into two . . . three . . . four. Will we break together or break apart? Five seconds . . . Alec Baldwin laughs on-screen, and I brace for my retreat.

Owen closes his eyes, and my stomach drops. My fight-or-flight instinct shrieks for me to run back downstairs, to avoid confrontation at all costs.

"I know," he finally says, a ghost of a smile spreading across his face. Instantly the air feels lighter. I can breathe again.

Tentatively, I move toward the bed. He pulls back the white comforter and pats the mattress next to him. I'm across the room in three steps and fall into the cool sheets, into his arms, letting him hold me closer than I have in months. Since *before*. Since *before* the *before*.

"I need your help," I whisper against his chest, careful to keep my face hidden from view. Asking for help has never come easily, and I've carried this burden alone for so long I'm territorial about it. The pain is my punishment and reminder. Sharing it seems like the easy way out. Maybe I don't deserve such relief.

Not saying a word, he strokes my hair and rests his chin on top of my head. Leaning into him, I'm eager to be closer, greedy for his touch. "I need you too," he says, finally turning my chin up to look me in the eyes.

The pain is etched so plainly across his face. Convinced my hurt was worse, I ignored the signs all along. Owen's been suffering every day, needing me as much as I needed him. Instead of comforting each other, I abandoned him to indulge in my own misery. A fixer, Owen tried to be there for me, to be the strong one. I pushed him away. He tried to mend his own broken heart by fixing mine, and I refused him that minor comfort.

"I'm so . . ." I start, but before the apology can leave my lips, he gently touches his own mouth to mine, accepting the *sorry* with one soft kiss. He presses harder, releasing some of his pain, melding it with my own. Giving my mind a break, I let my body take control. My desire is primal, animal like in its urgency. We lose ourselves in each other and slowly find our way back together in a tangle of sheets.

◆ 21 ◆

CASSIDY

After
July 25

ICOMPLETED MY SURGICAL internship at Cummings Veterinary Medical Center, the same place I'd studied during my junior and senior clinical years of veterinary school. By this point in my training I was 95 percent sure I intended on practicing large-animal medicine in a private clinical setting, but I was still curious what it would be like to work in a big hospital. So, instead of heading out on my own after graduation, I signed up for another eight months of grueling—mostly unpaid—labor in a quest to learn more about large-animal surgery.

Three months into my rotation I was scheduled for the overnight shift and charged with monitoring all the hospital inpatients. These included two horses recovering from colic surgery, both stable and set to be discharged in the next seventy-two hours but still requiring IV fluids, vital updates, and routine checks. In an isolated ward of the hospital, a stallion—minus his two prized possessions—was recovering after castration. We perform most neutering procedures as outpatient services, but this was an incredibly valuable show horse and the owners were worried about the potential risks of infection. Since we were in the area, they requested we retrieve and freeze several vials of his best swimmers before cutting off the source forever. To this day, that stallion was the most beautiful creature I've ever seen. Sadly, the spark I saw in his eye when he was admitted was diminished when he left us a few days later.

The most memorable horses of my internship, and maybe my entire career, were two mares who both went into labor at the start of my overnight shift. Elektra and Iris were healthy mares who were spending the last weeks of pregnancy in the hospital as case studies. Since Tufts was a teaching hospital, it offered this mutually beneficial service to local horse owners. The mares were available to students for learning purposes and the owners could rest easy knowing their horses were in the care of professionals at a heavily discounted price. We referred to this part of the hospital as the "Mom Shed." Usually the Mom Shed was a straightforward part of night check. Not this fateful night.

It had been a freakishly hot and humid week in western Massachusetts, with temperatures in the high nineties and air thicker than pea soup. Out of nowhere a cold front swept through the low mountains and valleys nearby, and the temps plummeted overnight. Any good veterinarian knew this was a recipe for disaster in horses who were sensitive to even the slightest change in barometric pressure.

Warned by the head veterinarian to be ready for some potential emergency colics—the most common ailment in response to weather change—the other overnight intern and I prepared the surgical suite. The staff vet had neglected to mention how subtle weather shifts might also kick-start labor in a pregnant mare. By midnight, both mares were in active labor. This in itself wasn't reason to panic, since most mares labor naturally without intervention, so the nurses and I monitored the horses over the stall cameras and checked in person every half hour. At first, things seemed fine. Both mares were progressing well on their own.

When the clock struck midnight, things took a turn for the worse. Suddenly, Iris's vitals crashed and she was in respiratory distress, showing signs of not only a complicated labor but also colic. In the stall next to Iris, Elektra's vitals were strong, but labor had slowed. Upon examination, we found her foal was in the breech position. By one in the morning, we'd roused the head surgeon and two staff vets from their beds to help with the disaster unfolding in the Mom Shed. By two in the morning, both deliveries were hanging in the balance, the fates of the mares and foals uncertain.

By three in the morning it was all over. Iris had delivered a premature but healthy foal. However, her colic symptoms had progressed so far that both her uterus and stomach had flipped, requiring immediate invasive surgery. She died on the table without ever meeting her baby.

In the next stall over, Elektra struggled with her breech birth, and despite our best attempts to aid it, the foal had been without oxygen too long and was delivered perfectly intact, but stillborn.

In stall A was a mare whose baby lay still and blue in the straw beside her, its long legs folded up in the half-broken sac. I'll never forget the sadness in Elektra's eyes as she desperately licked the afterbirth from her baby's face, first gently and then with more forceful nudging, as she tried to rouse him to his feet to nurse. In stall B, a foal not even twenty minutes old stood on wobbly legs, glancing around for her mother, every instinct in her body telling her it was time to feed.

A mother who'd lost her baby and an orphan seeking reassurance within thirty feet of each other—it seemed obvious what should be done. But things are never so black-and-white. Owners needed to be called and insurance forms filled out and processed. Medical charts required thorough updating and signing off by the properly authorized staff. After what felt like hours of back-and-forth on the phone, what only seemed natural was finally allowed to take place.

I led Elektra into the filly's stall. We named her Lily, an ode to her beautiful mother. A tech stood near the filly's head, urging her toward the mare. Lily balked at first, still shy, since she'd interacted only with the strange two-legged animals since birth. Carefully I allowed Elektra to walk up next to the foal, letting their noses touch. They'd warned me to keep a tight grip on the mare's halter in case she rejected the foal and attempted to harm it, but the warnings were unnecessary. Elektra gravitated toward Lily instantly, wrapping her long neck around the baby's cheek and pulling her close. She stepped forward, helping the filly find her teats, and the foal latched on as if it were meant to be.

Overcome with exhaustion and exultation, I wrapped my own arms around the technician, both of us aware that we bore witness to something both precious and miraculous. The tragic night had spawned something beautiful from the wreckage. In an instant, the mare and foal started to heal each other.

Lost in memories of the past, I nestle closer to Rosie. My tears burn down my cheeks, a steady stream I fear might never end. Today was another hard day at work. Thankfully the patients were all healthy, but pretending I was okay was more difficult than normal. A clueless customer asked where I was registered, oblivious that I was no longer pregnant despite my lack of a bump. I smiled and told her Amazon because it was easier than explaining the truth. I see her only a few times a year, so I can't blame her for not knowing, but it stung just the same.

Owen is still at work, catching up on some invoicing we desperately need. He offered to bring home pizza, correctly assuming I haven't grocery shopped or cooked again. A pang of guilt hits me, but I shrug it off. Cooking is the least of my concerns.

All I can think about is the look in Elektra's eyes the moment she understood her baby was dead. No words can describe that pain, because it's not meant to exist. It's unnatural. I close my own eyes and try to envision something else, something magical. The pure love and relief I witnessed when Elektra saw Lily for the first time and claimed her as her own comes to mind. Motherhood isn't something you can always choose and plan for. But once it's there, in your soul and in your bones, it's there for good.

"I need a baby," I whisper. Rosie doesn't stir, and the dark room answers back with nothing but heavy silence.

◆ 22 ◆

OWEN

"WHERE DOES IT HURT the worst?" Cassidy asks, her eyes wandering around the small room.

Black-and-white sketches of skulls and roses are plastered along one wall. The other is covered in Polaroids of intricate arm sleeves and full back tattoos scattered among drawings of portraits so lifelike they look like photos themselves. No denying the artist is talented. Let's just hope he's also gentle with the very aggressive-looking needle gun he's holding up to my arm.

Jimmy, the artist in question, chuckles as he applies a generous amount of rubbing alcohol to a wad of cotton. "Everyone hurts different," he answers, catching my eye and holding it for a second. Cassidy looks at me and grimaces.

Although the room is decorated in a mix between hipster punk and nineties grunge, the instruments gleam and the chairs and tables are covered with exam paper like at a doctor's office. Everything smells vaguely of disinfectant despite the incense burning on the front desk.

I lie back on the chair, and the paper crinkles beneath me. The alcohol hits my skin and I draw in a quick breath, waiting for the needle pinch to follow in the same spot. *Everyone hurts different.* Not only talented but also wise.

I know this tattoo will hurt. But I'm hoping it'll also be cathartic, like so many people claim. Why else would someone ask to be stabbed three thousand times per second by a little needle and pay for the pleasure?

"You're doing great," Cassidy says. She's straddling a chair next to us, chin resting on her crossed forearms. I'm glad I lost the coin toss and had to go first. I'd much rather get it over with. I'm afraid if I watched Cassidy suffer, I'd be too chicken to offer up my own arm.

"You should consider warming the alcohol," I tease, eliciting a brief nod and grunt from Jimmy, who busies himself attaching daggers to his gun.

With growing horror, I watch as he dips the needle tip into the ink and lets the engine run once, the whirring hiss of the gun enough to make my stomach clench.

"Here we go," Jimmy says as he descends upon the sensitive skin of my bicep.

After the initial shock, the quick back-and-forth stroke of the needle becomes rhythmic and soothing. Predictable pain, immediate and sharp. I get lost trying to envision which part of the design each pinch makes. We decided on using our son's handprints, actual size, copied from the inkblot given to us by the hospital. The date of his passing will be etched in script underneath. Cassidy chose to tattoo her rib cage. *Closer to her heart*, she said. Since I've always worn my heart on my sleeve, I chose my arm, for all the world to see.

"Does it hurt?" Cassidy asks, breaking the silence. Afraid talking might cause some unnecessary vibrations to ruin the steady flow of endorphins running through my system, I gently shake my head once.

"Almost done," Jimmy murmurs. I should be relieved, but I wish he'd keep going. People aren't kidding when they say tattoos are addictive.

Jimmy finishes and I stand in front of the mirror. Two perfect little hands, about the size of a quarter, forever imprinted on me. "It's great, bud," I say. My heart tightens and I resist the urge to hug my tattoo artist. Cassidy held those hands in her body; I had only those few precious moments in the hospital. Now a piece of him will always be with me. I pat Jimmy on the back, and he nods solemnly. Beneath the eyebrow rings and tattoos, I can tell he's a sensitive guy.

"Your turn," I say, tapping the chair as Cassidy hops in. Even though she'd never admit it, she looks a little pale. "No backing out now."

"We're in it together," she says, leaning forward and pecking me on the lips. She drops to her side and lifts her shirt. "Do your worst, Jimmy," she jokes, relinquishing herself to the pain.

★ ★ ★

"Margaritas or ice cream?" Cassidy asks as we walk hand in hand down Main Street. Dusk settles around us, a brilliant sunset fading into magenta shadows. The air is warm, but there's a slight crispness in the breeze, a gentle reminder that summer will eventually turn to fall. For now, the days remain long and autumn patiently waits her turn.

Lifting our conjoined hands, I kiss her wrist. She smells like lavender. "Both?" I venture, unable to make such a tough decision. My heart swells with happiness. How amazing it feels knowing that our only responsibility is to decide between two such sweet things.

"Tequila-flavored ice cream?" she wonders aloud. "Now *that* I could get behind . . ."

I laugh, cherishing this moment. It wasn't so long ago I feared we might never laugh together again. "Not exactly what I had in mind, but it has a certain adult appeal," I agree.

We walk in companionable silence for a block, both lost in our own thoughts. As so often happens to long-married couples, I sense a shift in her mood before she opens her mouth.

"Do you feel guilty?" she asks, her voice small and serious.

Cassidy obsessed over this concept for months. Plagued with doubt and guilt, she constantly questioned why this happened and whether either of us might have done something to change the outcome. My answer was always the same, but it did little to ease her conscience. While I regret failing Cassidy and failing to protect our family, she's worried over all the ways she might have done things differently, taking the full weight of the miscarriage as hers alone. But I carry the burden too. She might have carried him inside her body, but I hold my love for him—and her—in my heart and soul. He was the best parts of both of us, and it's what we carry *together* that's everything.

"It wasn't your fault," I say again. Our doctor has assured her many times of this, but it's never enough. "It wasn't anyone's fault. We did nothing wrong."

She shakes her head, brows furrowing. "No, I know that," she says, though I wonder if she truly believes it yet. She sighs, biting her lip. "I mean, guilty about this." She gestures around to nothing in particular. "Walking down the street laughing and joking about ice cream and booze. Guilty for feeling happy?"

I stop and pull her to face me. Pain is written across her face, little wrinkles in the creases where they never used to be. Cassidy always looked young for her age, often getting carded at bars and mistaken for a college student into her early thirties. She looks older now. The lines around her eyes a little deeper, the hollows beneath darker. Grief has chipped away at her youth but has been unable to lay claim to it all. Thankfully, her green eyes have regained some of the sparkle that dimmed in the weeks after the loss.

"We will never forget this baby," I say. After months of saying the wrong thing or, worse, saying nothing at all, I'm painfully aware of each word. "We can't stop living because we miss him. We can't not laugh or enjoy things because he's gone." My eyes blur with tears, and she blinks back her own. "At some point, grieving turns to remembrance, and that's okay." My mom told me this when my grandpa died. She promised it might hurt for a long time, but I'd have happy memories for even longer.

Considering this, she nods. "I like that." Her smile lights up her entire face. When we first started dating, I did anything I could to get that smile pointed in my direction, her energy radiating outward and warming everything it touched. "Did you just make that up?"

"Wish I could take credit," I say. Slowly the world comes back into focus. Cars move past us at full speed again and people brush by on the sidewalk. "It's nice, though, right?"

Reaching up on her tiptoes, she kisses me softly, then deeper. "I love you." She settles back on her heels and takes my hand, tugging me toward the crosswalk. "I also love Ben & Jerry's." The WALK sign flashes, and we jog toward the ice cream parlor, still holding hands.

♦ 23 ♦

JOAN

After
August 9

A BULL IN A china shop. That's how I'd describe my elder daughter whenever she bothers to visit. Always one to make an entrance, she stomps through the front door and clomps down the hall as if wearing steel-toed boots. Come to think of it, it wouldn't surprise me if that's what she actually wore. Since she sometimes comes straight from some barn, she often has mud and manure still caked to her heels and refuses to leave her shoes at the door like a civilized human being. I hear her coming from a mile away, her lumbering gait causing my knickknacks to shiver and shimmy closer to the edge of the dresser. I swear she tries to make them fall just so she can poke fun at my love of porcelain birds. Not that it bothers me. I love my little birdies, and no amount of teasing can change that. There's over a hundred scattered about the house.

"Cassidy, is that you?" I call out from the kitchen where I'm drying the last of the lunch dishes.

Hostile energy hits me before she even enters the room. I brace against the swirl of red and yellow energy vying for attention, her aura at odds with itself. Every person has an aura surrounding them. Most have only one color, shifting with their moods. Some have two, the energies melting together like cotton candy. Cassidy's battle each other, refusing to blend. Such a fight can end with the aura turning black, the negative of all colors.

Today she's red and yellow. Together these could meld to a vibrant orange—the color of vitality and joy—but her colors stay stubbornly separate. Since her soul is restless, the positive attributes of red—courage and strength—give way to less favorable qualities—irritability and a fiery temperament. Yellow auras are analytical and intelligent, two adjectives that aptly describe my brilliant daughter. But when unsettled, a yellow aura is tempestuous and hypercritical of themselves and others. This is shaping up to be a *lovely* visit.

"Who else would it be?" she asks, brushing a quick kiss on my cheek. "Better hope I'm not an armed robber," she jokes. "Here to steal all your tchotchkes."

I refrain from rolling my eyes. Cassidy triggers my inner teenager, and I promised Jack I wouldn't antagonize her. This agreement came after a rather heated argument where I insisted *she* always provoked *me*. In the end, I reluctantly agreed to cut her some slack, but obviously she wasn't going to make this an easy task.

"Tea?" I ask, pulling the kettle from the burner before it can swoon.

She shrugs and settles herself into one of the wicker chairs at the breakfast table. "Sure, thanks."

When Claire visits, things are effortless. I don't need to ask how she takes her tea, since I already know. Claire and I never stumble around awkwardly looking for bits of conversation, since we just pick up where we left off last time or, better yet, talk about the boys. Full of pink energy, Claire is all softness and love for others. If anything, she gives too much of herself, sacrificing her own needs for her family.

"How's Owen?" I ask, setting a cup of English breakfast tea before her. In the center of the table, I've laid out the sugar, honey, and milk. She grabs for the honey, just like her sister.

She shrugs again, and I feel a nerve in my eye tic. "He's good," she says, blowing on the mug before taking a sip and wincing before putting it back down.

Fine. Good. Better. It's worse than pulling teeth. Whenever I call on her, she's always fine. When I ask about work, it's always busy. Owen's always good. The house is always great. She never elaborates and instead asks me equally mundane questions. How's dad? *Good.* How's my latest painting? *Almost finished.* How's the garden? *Growing.* We quickly run out of topics and start all over again during the next stilted call.

"What?" she asks, looking at me like I'm a crazy person. I must've made a noise. Sometimes that happens lately, my inner filter lost somewhere in the last twenty years.

"Nothing," I snap. *I will not fight, I will not fight,* I remind myself.

"What's wrong?" she sighs. Something in her tone catches me off guard, and I see red. Her aura consumes me. Usually I hate words like *triggered*, thrown around by this new generation as an excuse for bad behavior, but it applies now. I'm triggered.

Hot tears cloud my eyes. Cassidy claims I use tears as weapons, but she's wrong. I can't control them like that. Not everyone can wield their emotions like a sword.

"I just don't understand how you haven't come to visit me sooner," I murmur, my lip quivering. "I'm your mother, Cassidy. Girls need their moms in times like this, and you've barely even spoken to me on the phone." I wish I could stop the whimpering tone in my voice. Watching her carefully, I note the calculating tilt of her head as she studies my face. I'm unsure how to act under this scrutiny.

"No, Mom, let's be real. *You* needed *me*," she says, toying with her steaming mug of tea but not drinking. "You wanted me to run over here so you could 'help' me, but really you just wanted to be wanted."

My hand flutters to my chest, and she scowls.

"It's never about me, or Claire, or Dad. It's always about you," she continues, her voice like a dagger through my heart. She gains strength with each word, drawing power from wounding me. "You want to tell yourself you fixed me and that I couldn't have survived without you," she hisses, finally taking a deep breath and fixing me with a hard stare. "But I don't need you, and I'm completely fine. Thanks again for asking."

Sitting back in my own wicker chair, I look out the bay window and across our backyard, anywhere but at her angry face. I used to sit here and watch the girls play in the yard. Sometimes I'd sketch, but usually I was too distracted. There was always some chore that needed tending, and anything I got on the paper I'd end up throwing out later.

As the girls got older, I'd sit here and try to help with their homework. Cassidy raced through her own and then assisted Claire while I pretended I wasn't completely confused by algebra and biology. We rarely ate at this table, saving our meals for the more formal dining room or trays in front of the television. This table was meant for sitting and talking. How many times have I sat here trying to talk with Cassidy and ended up unable to find the words?

I turn back to face her. "What?" she asks, the defiant tone of her teen years echoing in my ears. Funny how something as simple as the sound of one's voice can send you hurtling back through time.

Senior year of high school was fraught with bickering and fighting between Cassidy and me. We'd always butted heads, but now that she was on the verge of spreading her wings, we were at odds more than ever. The day she found the envelope from Tufts University lying in a stack of mail on this very table, her face lit up and all traces of the moody seventeen-year-old girl evaporated. She ripped open the thick package and squealed with pure joy, literally jumping up and down with excitement. I'm not a genius, but even I knew a big fat envelope meant they'd accepted her. The moment I brought it in from the mailbox, I'd started adding up tuition, room and board, books, travel expenses. Tufts wasn't a cheap school, and although Cassidy was a gifted student, it was unlikely she'd get a full scholarship. Jack and I had a modest college fund saved. A state university tuition amount. The rest would have to be in loans, and after reading how young adults were putting themselves into serious debt paying for astronomical college expenses, I knew I had to help Cassidy make the right choice for her future.

Once she settled down at the table, reading and rereading the acceptance letter, I took the seat across from her. I congratulated her, I'm sure I did. The first words out of my mouth would've been how proud we were of such an amazing accomplishment. I'm certain I said those things. But then I told her she should consider all her options. She'd been accepted into the honors program at UMass Amherst and based on merit received a full academic scholarship. Attending UMass and then investing in grad school was the practical thing to do. She'd mentioned veterinary school a few times, but I always assumed she'd go away and change her major fifteen times like everyone else. She listened to my guidance, her eyes growing a shade darker. When I finished, she stood and left the room and didn't speak to me for a week. During that time, she accepted Tuft's offer of admittance and applied for the appropriate financial aid. She never asked us for a dime.

"Are you there?" Cassidy asks again, a slight edge of concern tingeing her voice.

"I'm here." I sigh, shaking my head against the memory. It's one of a hundred other times where my best intentions fell short and blew up in my face. "I just only ever want you to be happy," I mumble. It's all I ever wanted for my girls. Everything came easily for Cassidy. Except happiness.

She lets out an abrupt laugh. "Yes, you always loved to say that to us," she says, bringing her sister back into the conversation even though it's like comparing apples and oranges. *"Just be happy,"* she mimicked, her voice a high falsetto meant to sound like me. "Everything you ever did, you did for us. You gave up your own happiness for ours, right, Mom?"

Each word is like a slap across the face. True, in the throes of parenthood, I uttered these phrases. Back in another lifetime I was a promising art student. I was taking courses at the community college but planned to transfer to an art school in Boston after two years. One professor told me I had raw talent, and that was enough for me. I dreamed of having my own exhibit or working at a gallery and painting on the side. But all that was some otherlife. In this life, I met Jack. We got pregnant. Marriage followed. I dropped out of school so he could finish. Another baby came along. I did what I had to do. I was a young mother with dreams beyond diapers and strollers, but that's what I was dealt, and it was my job to curate some happiness in this life—if not for myself, then for my daughters.

"You know I was happy raising you and your sister." A statement. I don't dare pose it as a question.

Motherhood grew on me. It wasn't the path I chose, but I did the best I could with the circumstances dealt to me. As I watched my older daughter throw herself into her studies and excel at every turn, I was both proud and terrified. Her single-minded focus could be derailed at any moment, and she was grossly unprepared. Like I'd once been. She had no contingency plan. She went straight from undergrad into veterinary school and then internships and private practice. I'm thankful she met Owen and he was able to jump aboard her fast-moving train without slowing her down. But she didn't leave room for error. It was my job to prepare her for the tricks and traps life might throw at her. Maybe if I nudged her the right way, she'd create space in her life for things outside her narrow focus.

"You were happy when you were happy, and you resented it the rest of the time," she says, leaning back and letting her shoulders fall. "As soon as we were out of the house, you didn't waste any time turning our room into your studio. It was like you'd been waiting twenty years for your actual life to start."

"Oh, Cassidy, grow up," I snap, suddenly infuriated by her righteous indignation, as strong now as ever. "I loved being your mother, but I am also a person who has interests and a life of my own. You should know that better than anyone." She looks down, biting her tongue. I'm sure she has a smart comeback, but she keeps her mouth closed for once. "I'm not the villain in your story."

But oh, how many times she's cast me as the evil queen in the fairy-tale version of her life. She tells everyone I "hated" her wedding venue. In fact, I thought her choice of a simple barn for the ceremony and reception was lovely. However, I'd hoped she'd choose a barn that wasn't used to store actual hay, considering I have a ghastly allergic reaction to the stuff. Of course, this was spun as me making the wedding all about me. Regardless, she booked the barn and I survived the ceremony with a Claritin, Benadryl, and eye drop cocktail that still didn't prevent me from breaking out in small red hives by the end of the night.

"I never said you were the villain." She sighs, finally meeting my eyes. She looks older, tired. I blink and her lovely face is transformed back to the baby-faced toddler she once was, all red curls and rosy cheeks. A daughter is always a daughter, no matter her age. "I just wanted to make sure you were okay."

I bite my lip, unsure if I should reach my hand across the table and take hers in my own. If she were Claire, I wouldn't hesitate. Instead, I run my fingers through my graying hair. "I'm okay," I assure her, nodding my head. My glasses slip to the edge of my nose, and I nudge them back with my knuckle. "I'm better now that I've seen you."

Cassidy smiles sadly. I know better than to wait for any tears to fall. Tough as nails, she hardly ever cries. She didn't even shed a tear when she broke her arm falling off some wild pony when she was nine. This trait she inherited from her father, which makes me smile.

"Me too," she whispers, taking a sip of her cooling tea. It's possible she's just saying it to make me feel better, but I hope there's some truth to it.

We sit quietly, enjoying a rare moment of contentment. The silence is broken by the slap of the screen side door leading into the house from the patio. The familiar tap-tap of Jack's boots, heel first, then toe, two times on either side, fills the house. He lumbers down the hall toward us, his sizable frame too tall for the low ceilings of the old farmhouse, a house constructed in a different era and made for smaller people.

"How're my gals?" he says, his booming voice warming up the kitchen. Catching my watery eyes, he winks, and my heart melts. "How about some eggs?" he asks, opening the fridge and taking out the ingredients for his famous scramble before either of us can answer. According to Jack, a hearty breakfast can fix just about anything.

Setting the carton down, he kisses Cassidy on the cheek. "Cassie-girl, that baby boy of yours is up in heaven now," he whispers. Cassidy leans her head against his side. "He's gone, but he's still in here," he says, tapping his chest once. He stands and takes the eggs to the counter and starts cracking them over the trash.

In the old days, I was jealous of how Jack always knew what to say. Not anymore. After thirty-five years of marriage, I've learned it's okay to let the other pick up the slack when we're lacking. Another woman might've learned this sooner, but I've never been a quick study. All that matters now is that Cassidy came home and is leaving here feeling just a little bit better than fine.

♦ 24 ♦

CASSIDY

After
August 15

ZIPPERING UP MY PREPREGNANCY jeans, now loose
around the waist, I hurry to escape the harsh fluores-
cent lighting of the exam room. According to the scale,
I've shed twice the number of pounds I gained during my
brief pregnancy. Under different circumstances, this unexpected weight loss would thrill me. Now, I just wish for
a belt. Satisfied I've left nothing behind, I make my way
down the long hallway toward Dr. Julian's office, where
both Owen and the maternal-fetal medicine doctor are
waiting.

Before sitting, I peck a kiss on Owen's cheek. He's sitting ramrod straight, his hands folded at his knee, long legs
twisted awkwardly to fit between the chair and desk. I'm
reminded of a schoolboy waiting to be reprimanded by the
principal. Dr Julian sits across from us with a pen in hand,
my file open before her. Smiling, she glances quickly at
the clock. Since she's one of the best fetal medicine spe-
cialists in the area, I've no doubt her time is extremely
valuable. We're lucky to have gotten an appointment on
such brief notice.

"So, your exam looked good," Dr. Julian begins, skipping straight to the point. From the start, I've appreciated

her direct approach. Nothing worse than a chatty OB/ GYN insisting on small talk while staring into your nether regions. "Your regular OB sent over all your files, and after looking them over, I've no reason to think you'd be a high-risk patient except for the miscarriage itself," she says, flipping to a new page. It's difficult to see what she's staring at when the words are upside-down, but it looks like my hospital discharge papers.

"An autopsy of the fetus was performed, but there were no conclusive findings suggesting a genetic deformity," she says. Owen squeezes my hand but keeps his focus on the doctor, his face pale and tightly drawn. "Combined with the previous genetic screenings also coming back negative, it's unlikely the miscarriage stemmed from one of the typical anomalies."

My chest tightens at the implication of this statement. Owen looks back and forth between us, unsure what to make of the words. Slipping my shaky hand from his grasp, I lean forward in my chair.

"So, you're saying I'm the problem?" I ask, voice trembling despite my best effort to remain calm. For months I've held on to hope that there's a reasonable and natural explanation for why my son didn't survive, one involving a genetic abnormality that made my baby unsuitable for life. The alternative has plagued me with shame and guilt, haunting my dreams. It sits on the periphery of my everyday thoughts, mocking me, accusing me. If it wasn't the baby, it's me.

Dr. Julian shakes her head. "From my exam, I don't see any reason to suspect you're the problem. More to the point, you did nothing to cause this miscarriage." Her eyes are kind and sympathetic, her voice confident. I've no doubt she's said these same words over and over to grieving mothers. "Up until the loss, everything showed you were a completely healthy pregnant woman that did everything right. Unfortunately, these things just happen sometimes," she says, echoing the same thing my sister and so many others have told me. Usually I'd take comfort in an expert reassuring me, but I'm still unsatisfied. I want a rational explanation based on factual, hard data. Some *cause* that produced such a catastrophic *effect*.

Biting back tears, I let Owen place a protective arm around my shoulder, resisting my initial urge to shrug him away. "There has to be a reason. It was a second-trimester loss," I say. Hours' worth of research races through my desperate mind. "These aren't common. There has to be an explanation." A foolish part of me wishes the doctor would just make something up. How can I figure out the solution when I'm not even sure what the problem is?

Dr. Julian closes my file and clasps her long fingers together. I imagine those hands catching babies, screaming with life. Her wedding ring glimmers in the light. I always take my own ring off at work, afraid of losing it at a barn. I wonder if she wears hers while delivering babies.

"You're not wrong," she says, carefully measuring her words. I sense a slight midwestern twang and note a diploma from Northwestern University hanging proudly on the wall behind her head. Boston accents are so prevalent here that outsiders stick out like sore thumbs. "Second-term losses aren't as frequent as first, but far more common than you'd think," she says, stating a fact I've come across in my own studies. "You were referred to me since after a late-term loss your subsequent pregnancies will be labeled as high risk and monitored more closely than your first, especially since we don't have a concrete diagnosis for why you miscarried." Her sensible explanation and plan offer me a slight sense of relief. She's here to help, and when we decide to have another baby, she will help keep him safe, despite the risks.

"Is it okay to try again?" I ask, careful not to look at Owen. Since the loss we haven't talked about another baby. Every time I want to bring it up, I stop myself, ashamed to even think of another child while still mourning the first. Of course, we both want to try again. I'm just unsure of the proper timeline.

"Is it safe for Cassidy?" he asks, his voice deep and startling, surprising both the doctor and me. Until now, he's been the silent and supportive partner. "It seems soon," he adds. "Is her body ready?" Uncertainty clouds his voice and worry furrows his brow.

"I've already gotten my period," I add, but am quickly interrupted by Dr. Julian.

"Listen," she says, laying her palms flat on the desk in front of her. "I've helped a lot of couples through some pretty tough times." Looking from Owen to me, she continues. "You're young and healthy and your body is physically healed. Our hearts take a little longer to mend." Out of the corner of my eye, I see Owen nod in agreement. He shares a look with the doctor, and I suddenly feel like the two of them are ganging up on me. "You'll both know when it's time to start again. I can't make that decision for you. My job is to make sure that when you get pregnant again, we do everything to help you hold that pregnancy to term."

Nodding, I'm afraid I'll say something I'll regret if I speak. Lashing out in anger will only show both of them that my heart and head aren't ready yet.

"In the meantime, we'll run some blood panels that test for anomalies in your system that may have affected the pregnancy. Usually they don't run these tests until after three consecutive pregnancy losses, but I find the results can be useful sooner. We should have results in three to five days."

Three consecutive losses. Why would anyone wait until a woman lost three babies before running a test that might help? Making a mental note to research this test, I can't imagine there's any good reason behind the protocol besides saving the insurance companies some money.

Dr. Julian stands from her desk, ending our meeting. Owen rises and offers to help me up, but I push my chair back and stand on my own.

"Thank you so much for your time," I say, reaching out to shake her cool hand.

"You're very welcome," she says, holding my hand between both of hers a moment longer. "I hope to see you back here in a few months," she adds sincerely. Any frostiness I felt toward her melts away, and I murmur another thank-you.

Owen follows me out of the office and back to the parking lot, jogging to catch up with me. He starts the truck but doesn't pull out. Staring out the passenger window, I refuse to speak.

"Cassidy, are we going to talk about this?"

I let out a little snort. "What is there to talk about, Owen?" I mutter, still looking out the window. It's a hot and soggy day. Heavy gray clouds hang in the sky, promising an afternoon storm. "You want to wait a little longer. *Make a baby out of love*," I say, the edge in my voice razor-sharp. "I get it. No need to talk."

As he shifts the car into reverse, the first few raindrops splatter the windshield. "You don't get anything," he mumbles, pointing us toward home.

★ ★ ★

Statistics was the only class I didn't ace in college. Asking for help has always been tough for me, and I was scared that my peers—all supercompetitive premed students like me—would judge me for my apparent weakness if I admitted my struggle. About halfway through the semester I realized I'd never get an A and that even a B might be impossible if I didn't get help, and soon. Ashamed, I asked a friend who'd studied statistics at Boston University. Even though it was a pain in the ass taking the T from Somerville to Boston twice a week, it was worth it. With her help, I squeaked by with an A minus and maintained my dignity. An A minus wasn't a poor grade, probably better than I deserved, but I took it as a personal affront to my intelligence. I vowed to never let a subject get the best of me again.

According to medical journals, *miscarriage* is the term used for pregnancy loss before twenty weeks' gestation. After this point it's considered a stillbirth. I was technically nineteen weeks and three days when my baby died, so my paperwork reads miscarriage, even though I gave birth to a baby who was so very still. *Miscarriage.* A triggering word if there ever was one. It's like I misplaced my baby, as if he was a set of keys or an errant sock, lost in the wash. What a terrible word to describe a terrible event. To make things worse, my hospital reports labeled my loss a medical abortion. This phrasing implies something else entirely and leaves me shaking and sick every time I open an insurance bill.

Statistically, as many as half of all pregnancies might end in miscarriage. The exact number isn't known, since many happen before a woman even knows she's pregnant. A *missed* miscarriage, they call it. For the sake of statistics, the risk is calculated using only data relating to confirmed pregnancies. Based on this, ten to fifteen of every hundred pregnancies end in miscarriage before the end of the first trimester. Second-trimester losses, those that happen between thirteen and nineteen weeks, occur in one to five of every hundred pregnancies. The common average, taking into account all the different losses, is one in four. Twenty-five percent. A quarter of all pregnancies end in miscarriage.

Repeating or "recurrent" pregnancy loss is when a woman has two or more miscarriages in a row. About one in a hundred women will suffer recurrent loss. Most of these losses, about 75 percent, have no known cause. On a brighter note, 65 percent of these women will go on to

have a successful pregnancy at some point. As for the other
35 percent . . .

I consider the odds. Some of the websites give slightly
different figures, but mostly they're consistent. Intellectu-
ally, the numbers make sense. Cold, hard facts that should
be undisputable, since they've been recorded, studied, and
repeated in many different journals. Yet it's still hard to
ground these findings in reality. I've known more than
four pregnant women, and not one has mentioned miscarriage. It's possible one might've had an early unknown
loss and gone on to have healthy children, blissfully
unaware of the life that grew in her belly, over before she
ever knew it existed. It's also possible one lost a baby and
never talked about it. Having experienced my own loss, I
don't talk about it much, but it's all I think about. There
isn't a minute in the day when it's not at the forefront of
my mind.

A glutton for information, I greedily stalk the loss
forums without sharing my own story. From the safety of
my computer, I commiserate and compare my pain to that
of the women posting while holding my own loss close to
my heart. When I'm not on forums, I'm scouring medical journals and parenting blogs, absorbing every fact and
anecdote, struggling to make sense of the vast quantity of
information. Usually facts comfort me, but I feel like I'm
stuck back in statistics class, staring at a bunch of numbers
that don't add up.

Like my own loss, most miscarriages have an unknown
cause. Yet there are lists and lists of possible reasons. On
one end of the spectrum, there are the obscure genetic
disorders affecting the baby and/or mother, scary disorders that make the fetus incompatible with life. On the
other end are reasons so basic it makes me want to cry.
The age and weight of the mother, how much caffeine she
consumes, her blood pressure. All these little things might
affect the fetus negatively—or have no affect at all.

Statistics still confuse me. I'm never clear on whether the odds are good or bad. Since I'm a horse person, people always assume I'm an expert racehorse bettor. I may be able to pick a fast runner, but I have zero clue how the odds work. Is one in three good odds? If yes, good for who—the horse? The bettor? Would this be a safe bet? My inability to understand something that others intuit so easily frustrates me. Staring down at my notepad, covered in doodles and numbers underlined for emphasis, I wonder what it all means. I'm the one in a hundred who miscarried in the second trimester. Usually you *want* to be the one in a hundred, or a thousand or a million. You're a *winner* when you're the one in a billion who hits the lottery jackpot. Miscarriage odds produce only losers. In theory, my chances of having another loss are only 35 percent, which seems like a low number. But if I could be the 1 percent, 35 seems an easy number to hit.

My eyes are tired from staring at the blue light of the computer screen. The clock on the wall says 11:45 PM. Owen's been asleep for well over an hour. He tiptoed into my study to kiss me good-night, and I tried to explain the odds to him. In typical Owen fashion, he proclaimed, "Lightning doesn't strike twice." He loves stupid phrases like that. Still annoyed from our appointment earlier, I didn't feel like arguing, even though he's wrong. In fact, lightning is *more* likely to strike the same place again, since the same weather patterns are more likely to occur at the same geographical site. Using this logic, my chances of recurrent loss loom even bigger.

I sit a moment longer, the laptop warm and whirring on my lap. I should go to bed, but my hand hovers above the keyboard. *Fifteen more minutes.* Clicking open another link, this one relating to maternal disorders causing late-term loss, I take comfort in the soothing buzz of infinite information purring at my fingertips.

✦ 25 ✦

CLAIRE

After
August 19

Smug best describes the look on my sister's face as she waltzes into my kitchen, settling herself on a barstool like she owns the place. The air around her sizzles with expectation, and from years of experience, I know she's itching for me to ask her what's going on. Rather than telling me why she needed to see me at seven thirty on a Saturday morning, she sent me an ominous text declaring she had news to share.

Always dramatic, she waits for me to beg her to spill the beans. Just for fun I pretend disinterest, choosing to make pancakes instead. I've thoroughly enjoyed watching her frustration mount since she arrived. Mixing the batter, I smile to myself, allowing myself a few more moments of sisterly indulgence. Sometimes it's just too easy.

Looking up from the bowl, I sense her eyeing me. "Chocolate chip or blueberry?" I ask, savoring the little bit of steam I imagine blowing from her ears.

"Blueberry." Her shoulders sink, and she grabs a banana from the bowl in the center of the island. "So," she says, letting the word hang in the air, hoping I'll pick it up and run with it.

I've played with her long enough. Exhaustion brings out my evil side, and she's caught me before my first cup of coffee.

"So, what's the big news you couldn't tell me over the phone?" I ask, chuckling at the way she instantly brightens.

"Remember how I told you my doctor was running some tests?"

I nod my head, a vague recollection of this conversation coming to mind. Since the miscarriage, Cassidy has obsessed over every potential reason for it. I recall the results being inconclusive, which of course devastated Cassidy but didn't surprise me much.

"Turns out I have a rare autoimmune disorder." She beams. By the way she says this, you'd think she'd just told me she'd won the lottery. "Three, actually."

"Three what?"

"Disorders," she clarifies, shaking her head at me, annoyed. Still trying to wrap my head around what seems like a disproportionate amount of excitement at such a diagnosis, I wait for the punch line. But she just stares at me, waiting for a response. Exactly what response, I'm unsure.

I ladle a few globs of pancake mix onto the griddle, and they bubble as they hit the hot iron. "Congratulations, I guess?" I venture, feigning a smile.

Her eyes sparkle across the bar, and she cocks her head to the side. If I were a different type of sister, this look would have resulted in a lot of hair pulling and scratching in our younger years. Always the peacekeeper and utterly devoted to my big sister, I never let that look get to me. If anything, I envied her ability to say *I told you* so without ever opening her mouth.

"I know you hate medical mumbo jumbo," she says, causing a nerve to tic in the corner of my right eye. Again with the assumptions. "I'll keep it simple. The tests show I have markers for a few disorders which have been positively linked to second-term miscarriage. So basically, my body had a hard time maintaining a pregnancy because it was busy fighting itself. Better yet, there's medication I can take that should keep it under control if I get pregnant again."

Turning from my sister, I flip the pancakes and take a deep breath. Usually I can control my irritation, but something about the flippant way she's talking down to me snaps a fragment of my self-control.

"You know, women without medical degrees have been giving birth for thousands of years," I say without looking at her.

"Um, sure. Why is that relevant?" she snorts.

"Just wanted to remind you that us 'plebeians' also get pregnant and have babies. A doctorate isn't a prerequisite for reproduction." Turning the oven to warm, I spin to face her, resting my hip against the stove. "I understand you're happy to have your blessed *reason* for this happening. I am," I say, not wanting to completely burst her bubble. For such a smart girl, my sister can be magnificently obtuse as to how she comes across to others. "That's why you're here today, right? To gloat? Prove I was wrong and you were right, like always?"

Cassidy looks down at her hands and shrugs. Moving the pancakes to the warming rack, I ladle a few more onto the griddle. The boys will be up soon and ravenous. No such thing as too many pancakes.

"Now you can control the situation, just like you wanted. I'm happy you've gotten an answer, especially if it makes it easier for you. But I still believe there's an element to childbirth that's out of our hands, and no amount of testing or 'mumbo jumbo' will change my mind. We'll just have to agree to disagree."

Cassidy sulks. I'm sure she envisioned this conversation going differently. Maybe I should have pretended to be thrilled and apologized for ever doubting science. Too late for that now. Setting a few pancakes on a warm plate, I slide them in her direction. She dribbles syrup over the stack, still eyeing me warily. Opening her mouth to speak, she snaps it shut, a thin veil of smugness masking her face once more as though she's proud of herself for biting her tongue.

"What?" I ask, wishing I could slap her across the head with my spatula. Taking a bite of her breakfast, she gives me a thumbs-up but says nothing. "Just say it. We have like ten minutes, max, before this house turns into a zoo. Speak now or forever hold your peace."

Cassidy sighs, placing her fork at the edge of her plate. "It's nothing, really. I don't expect you to understand this," she starts. Noticing my raised brows, she backtracks, shaking her head. "Not the medical shit, the other stuff. This whole mothering thing has just been so . . . simple for you."

I snort, but before I can argue she holds up a finger and I wait, eager to hear the load of shit she's so eager to sell me.

"You've been playing with dolls since you were five years old. You always knew you wanted to me a mom," she says, gesturing around my kitchen as if it's the clearest representation of every dream I've ever held. A door slams somewhere upstairs. "Everything has always come so easy for you. School, boys, motherhood. You make it look so effortless. It's hard for someone like me to compare, and it's even harder when I've faced roadblocks at every turn. First, we can't get pregnant. Then we lose the baby. If I believed in signs, I'd be convinced a big one is trying to keep me from having children."

Sympathy is the appropriate response right now, but my patience with Cassidy has run out. I'm happy to mediate between her and Mom to keep the peace, but I refuse to coddle this self-pitying, woe-is-me attitude she's been holding on to for so long now. Especially when it's utter bullshit.

"You have got to be kidding me, right?" She looks up, surprised at my tone. "You think things have always come easy to *me*?" As I say the words out loud, my irritation quickly turns to anger. Maybe it's because I'm a Scorpio, but my mood swings tend to be swift and violent, even though they're few and far between. "Cass, you've completely reimagined things to paint yourself the victim in this story. You've never gotten less than an A in school and were the teacher's pet since kindergarten. I was *fine* in school, but nothing close to perfect, so I'm not sure where you come off saying school was easier for me. It wasn't, I promise. Being in your shadow made it even harder. Maybe I would've been extraordinary if I wasn't following in your perfect footsteps." I take a deep breath, just getting started. Another door slams upstairs. Two of the three are up. Pitter-pattering little feet roam the hallways as they use the bathroom and torment each other. I hope they find their way into my bedroom and wake up their father. That might buy us a few more minutes.

"And *boys*? You bat your eyelashes and guys fall over themselves to help you. For fuck's sake, your freaking hair color costs women hundreds of dollars to mimic." I only half joke, touching my own honey-blond highlights. "You were born with that shit. Can't get it in a bottle."

Cassidy shakes her head, her cheeks inflamed. "Never mind. I didn't explain myself correctly." Sidestepping the appropriate apology, she has the nerve to look wounded.

I grimace and raise a brow at her. "And that," I say, wagging my finger in her direction like she was one of my children. "Right there. Your aloof *who, me?* act has gotten a little old over the years," I say, trying my best to imitate her doe-eyed expression.

Biting her lip, she looks away, and I soften my tone. "I don't mean to be harsh on you. But you sit there and only see what I show you. You never ask what's really going on." My anger fades with every word. "You don't know what it's like for me, and I don't presume to know what you're going through. The difference is, I ask." Her cheeks burn pink, and I know I've hit home for her. I know what she thinks. Because I'm a stay-at-home mom, I must be just like our own mother. Even though Cassidy's done everything in her power to be the opposite of Mom, you can't fight genetics. She could run away to school and look down on domestic life, but she couldn't run away from her true nature. She is more like Mom than she'd ever admit.

"So cut the shit, Cass," I say, trying to lighten the mood. "It's time to move on. You went through something absolutely terrible. There's no denying that. I'm here for you whenever you need to talk about it. But you can't keep dwelling on it and using it as an excuse for poor behavior." Shane stumbles into the room, rubbing his eyes and missing a sock. "You might hate hearing all this, but it doesn't make it less true. You *can* get pregnant. You *can* have another baby when you're ready. You need to be thankful for what you have and all the good in your life." Derek races into the kitchen and heads straight for the orange juice, nearly knocking the pitcher to the floor. I grab it before it can slide off the counter and help him pour a glass for himself and his brother. They take them and head toward the TV room without saying a word.

"For fuck's sake, you're *not* a failure. This isn't some competition. Motherhood is lonely enough as it is. You can't isolate yourself by comparing your struggle with everyone else's. Lonely can make a heart desperate, and I'm afraid that's where you're headed." For all the love and happiness my life brings me, there have been plenty of times I've been overwhelmed. Times I've contemplated walking out the door and never coming back. Times I've locked myself in the bathroom to cry for ten minutes, just for some peace and quiet. Cassidy hasn't seen all that, but she'll know it someday. She needs to know we all go through it. Not just her. "We're in this together."

To my surprise, my normally stoic sister looks chastised. She turns her sad eyes on me and shrugs, her face contorting as she tries to hold back tears.

"I'm scared all the time," she confesses.

A loud bang, followed by Derek yelling, *"Mom!"* comes from the other room.

I close my eyes and let out a deep breath. "You will be scared forever," I say, smiling and resting my hand on her shoulder before heading toward the sound of destruction. "You're a mother. That's our job."

◆ 26 ◆

CASSIDY

After
August 25

> *It's your fault.*
> *Your body betrayed you.*
> *How can you even think of having another child this soon?*
> *You don't deserve joy. Your baby is dead.*
> *What makes you think you can even get pregnant again?*
> *What makes you think this one will live?*

"Cass," Owen murmurs from someplace far away. "Cass," he says again, his voice getting louder, like he's approaching from the other end of a tunnel.

Blinking my eyes open, I'm relieved to be lying in bed, the ceiling fan whirling overhead and Owen's warm hand on my bare shoulder.

"You're having a bad dream," he whispers.

I lie back against the cool pillow, hair spilling to either side of my face and a few strands sticking to my sweaty forehead. He strokes my cheek with his knuckle, wiping away a tear I didn't know fell.

"Want to talk about it?" He rests his chin against the crown of my head, and I lean against him. Since our doctor's visit I've been frosty, irritated he didn't take my side. But for now, I forget my anger and allow myself the small comfort of his strong body holding mine. I'll resume being pissed later.

Turning to face him, I'm thankful only his silhouette is visible in the unlit room. Much easier to talk when I can't see the pain etched on his features. "Same dream," I sigh. "If you can even call it a dream." I shudder against the image flashing to mind, the same one that plagues my dreams each night and creeps into my thoughts on the worst days.

"Tell me," he begs, not the first time he's asked me to share the reason I wake up at dawn crying and shaking. Usually I claim I can't remember, but I'm tired of carrying this alone.

Closing my eyes, I let it out. "I dream about my water breaking." My voice breaks, just like my body once did. "It's when I knew it was all over." The warmth of the liquid flowing down my legs haunts me. In my dreams, it sometimes trickles. Other times it gushes, threatening to fill the room and drown everyone. It keeps flowing and won't stop until I wake up in a pool of my own sweat and tears. "I've had it more often lately. Ever since I started thinking about another baby," I admit. Lately the shame and fear of this desire has been all consuming. "It doesn't help that both you and Dr. Julian think I'm a crazy person for wanting to try again so soon." The words spill out, more accusatory than intended.

"We don't think you're crazy," he says, pulling me toward him. I stiffen slightly but let him hold me, resting my wet cheek against his chest. The soothing swoosh of his heart steadies my breathing. "I just can't imagine something happening to you again," he says. "To both of us," he adds, quickly. "I want another baby too. But I don't know if I could handle watching you get your heart broken again if something went wrong."

The dam inside breaks, and it all comes rushing out. Loud, ugly cries erupt from deep inside my belly, racking my whole body. Owen rubs my back as I moan and heave against him. Squeezing me tight, he absorbs some of my grief. How could I have thought he didn't want a baby? Where I was worried about our son, he was worried about me. Again, I'm so wrapped up in my own pain I can't see what's right in front of me.

The sun filters in through the blinds by the time I exhaust my well of tears. "I'm like a bottomless pit," I hiccup. "Just when I think I've cried all the tears, a fresh wave comes. It's like all the tears I never cried saved up somewhere inside of me, and now the floodgates are open and I can't close it," I whimper. Maybe everyone is allotted a certain number of tears in their lifetime and after thirty years of dry eyes, I'm just catching up now.

"What can I do?" he whispers. Hesitantly, I lift onto my side to face him, his blue eyes wide and full of hope.

"I want to try again," I answer, letting our gaze meet and holding it firmly. I need him to understand this isn't like before, when I so desperately wanted a baby for all the wrong reasons. "Maybe not today, or even tomorrow, but sometime soon."

He doesn't look away, only nods. "Okay," he says, one corner of his mouth curling up in a smile, the dimple in his right cheek deepening. One of my favorite sights.

"Really?" I'm afraid he might take it back.

"Really," he says.

Taking his cheeks between my hands, I drop my mouth to his, covering his smile with a kiss.

"I love you," I whisper against his lips. He doesn't say it back, just kisses me harder.

♦ 27 ♦

CASSIDY

After
September 5

ONLY RECENTLY HAS THE irony of my choice to special-ize in equine reproduction hit me. As a fourth-year vet student, we were encouraged to pick a specialty before grad-uation. I knew for certain I would only work with horses. Nothing against cows and llamas, but other large animals didn't interest me. At first, I considered sports medicine, but seeing lame horse after lame horse quickly became depress-ing and the clients were über-demanding. It was no fun telling the owner of a five-hundred-thousand-dollar show jumper that their horse would never compete again no mat-ter how much money they invested in the sprained tendon.

When I delivered my first foal, I felt a spark and knew that was something I could look forward to each day. The advancements in reproductive technology and procedures such as cloning fascinated me, sealing my decision to focus my studies in this area. My time interning with a renowned specialist confirmed I'd made the right decision. All of this occurred well before I started on my own journey toward motherhood. I might have stuck with injured athletes had I known what was in store for me.

After months of artificial insemination and one risky attempt at live cover, the Lombardos had almost given up hope of impregnating their beloved Kitty. Our last-ditch effort involved another round of artificial insemination and hormone therapy, all of us aware that this was the last time and if it didn't take, Kitty would be turned out to pasture. The two-week wait dragged by slowly, and I related to the apprehension and impatience the owners felt. For months I had tortured myself waiting for my own positive pregnancy test, fourteen days dragging out to what felt like months. When we finally ultrasounded Kitty at the end of June, we were thrilled to see a fetus with a strong heartbeat, so strong it almost echoed. To our dismay, the effect was not a glitch on the machine and the echo was actually the faint trace of a second heartbeat. Kitty was finally pregnant. With twins.

"We knew this was a potential outcome," Dr. Ford says, carefully wiping the ultrasound wand before wrapping it in foam. Costing over two hundred thousand dollars, the machine is precious to our practice, and Doc is meticulous with its care. God help the horse owner or tech who lets a horse step near the cord. "Twins are always high risk," he reminds me, but his voice is gentle.

For two months we've monitored the mare closely and each time heard the double heartbeat. Today there's just one.

I pull the blue latex gloves from my hands and toss them in the garbage can wedged between the window and the custom drawers built into my SUV containing all the equipment essential to an ambulatory veterinarian. Dr. Ford drove with me to the farm, and I'm already dreading the lengthy trip back to the clinic. Most days I travel alone, but Doc insisted on tagging along today. On the one hand, I'm glad for his support. On the other, I won't be able to cry alone in the truck after breaking the terrible news.

"You going to be okay over there?" he asks, his thick brows furrowed together beneath the brim of his worn cowboy hat. Glancing at my longtime boss and friend, I nod. The creases on either side of his startingly blue eyes deepen as he strokes his well-kept beard, now more gray than black. I once joked he was looking more like Sean Connery every day, eliciting a hearty laugh and bashful smile. He claimed his wife had started likening him to Santa Claus, patting the little belly stretching against the khaki work shirt tucked above the silver belt buckle he wears every day.

"I'm okay," I assure him, squaring my shoulders and lifting my chin slightly to compose myself on the outside, even though I'm falling apart on the inside. "It's my case. I'll tell them." He nods once and gestures for me to lead the way.

Kitty stands in her stall, her belly just starting to show signs of swelling. She munches some alfalfa, one ear pricking forward in my direction as I pass her stall as though she's awaiting the news too.

"Joe, Cindy." They sit next to each other on a tack trunk with a large *L* monogrammed on the front next to their unique racing logo. *No good way to deliver bad news.* No use sugarcoating anything, especially to horse people. Farmers are no strangers to death and disappointment, their livelihoods dependent on fickle animals and weather. "At the last few ultrasounds we heard two heartbeats, one slightly stronger than the other, but both healthy and normal. Today's ultrasound confirms that one fetus hasn't survived."

To their credit, neither flinches at the news. This is just another reminder that despite our best attempts, we are still far from in control.

"This is not uncommon with cases of twins in horses. At our last appointment we discussed the risks of premature birth, low birth weight, and the potential for not maturing properly. We also warned that one or both fetuses might not survive to term."

Cindy nods, frowning. "You said we lost one fetus. How about the other?" Her voice betrays nothing, not a hint of either sadness or hope. A smear of horse spit is dried on the shoulder of her polo shirt, the farm logo prominent on her chest. Her jeans are faded from baling hay and cleaning stalls. From her hat down to her scuffed cowboy boots, she's a genuine farm girl. I'm sure she loves her horses, but make no mistake: this is also a business. When money is involved, there's no time to mourn.

Dr. Ford steps forward and clears his voice. "If I may?" he asks, and I gratefully let him take over. "The remaining fetus is still alive." Both Joe and Cindy let out a shared sigh of relief and exchange a small look that breaks my heart. My mind wanders back to the moments before the doctor came into the ER to tell me my own baby was gone. Those few minutes of false hope made the truth hurt so much worse. "However, the heartbeat isn't as strong as I'd hoped, and we are seeing decreased movement in the viable fetus. At this point in her pregnancy, I'd want the foal to be thriving. I don't want to get your hopes up, so I'll be honest with you. I'm not sure the second fetus will survive to term."

I watch Joe take his wife's hand and squeeze. With his other he pulls off his Lombardo Stables ball cap and wipes his brow. Never have I seen Joe without a hat, and I'm taken aback by how young he is. For some reason, I always assumed the couple was much older than me, but now I wonder if he's even over thirty. Dr. Ford told me they built their business together from the ground up, starting with only a handful of horses and expanding over time. Today they run one of the most successful racing and breeding farms in the state, each win resulting from their blood, sweat, and tears. I've noticed no children roaming the farm, very common in this industry, and realize the mare is probably like a child to them. My stomach cramps and my vision blurs at the thought.

"Are you okay?" Cindy asks me, reaching out an arm to steady me. I swallow, my tongue stuck to the roof of my mouth. "Let me get you some water," she says, rushing toward the mini fridge tucked in the corner of the tack room.

I take the water bottle, thanking her. "I'm sorry," I mutter, my cheeks hot and red. "The heat . . ."

Cindy smiles, and I can tell she knows. I'm never sure who Dr. Ford has told about the loss until I see a certain look in their eye. A cross between pity and curiosity. "No worries," she says. "Happens to me all the time. No cross breeze in this barn," she adds. I manage a smile, grateful for the grace she's showing me.

Promising to check back in a few weeks, we say our good-byes and leave them to their day, which will now be tinged with worry over Kitty. They head back toward their house, located down a stone path a few hundred feet from the main barn. Maybe they'll share a few words over lunch before heading off to the track to train or work with the youngsters in the corral. I imagine they'll throw themselves into their chores, life on the farm not stopping for anything.

Before going back to the truck, I shoot one last glance at the little mare, who still munches her hay, oblivious that her two babies are now one and might turn to none. I pray she doesn't feel the pain of the loss, but experience warns me otherwise.

"It will be okay," I whisper through the metal bars. She flicks her tail my way, barely lifting her gaze.

"Why don't I drive us back?" Dr. Ford offers as I make my way to the driver's side door. Nodding, I swing around to the other side, my feet and heart heavy.

"I'm sorry," I say again, ashamed at the unprofessional way I acted in the barn. I pride myself in never letting my emotions show, especially in front of such important customers.

"Stop saying you're sorry for something you never, ever have to be sorry about," he snaps back. "I don't want to hear another *I'm sorry* from you, you got that?" He backs out of the driveway and hits me with a fatherly stare, his faded blue eyes filled with compassion.

I laugh, unable to keep a smile from my face. "*Sorry.*"

"Wiseass," he mutters. We drive back to the clinic in companionable silence, listening to Willie Nelson croon in the background.

★   ★   ★

Hardly more than a girl herself, the woman sits across from an older lady who shares her same sky-blue eyes and platinum-blond hair. Lines crease both sides of the pretty older woman's mouth as she laughs at something her companion says. They must be mother and daughter. Even their voices are almost identical. Their joy is infectious, causing other guests to lift their eyes from their plates and smile toward the happy pair giggling over salads. The daughter eats with abandon, holding her fork in her right hand and cradling a baby bump with her left. A turquoise top stretches tight over the watermelon-sized bulge. She has to lean forward to eat, her giant bump making it necessary to sit too far from the table. Her belly button is visible against the thin fabric of the maternity shirt. Clearly the baby is due any minute now, and I can't help but stare.

"Penny for your thoughts?" Owen asks, jolting me from my reverie.

"Just thinking," I murmur, taking a bite of my sandwich. When you're pregnant, there are so many things you *can't* do. No alcohol, no deli meat, no sushi, limited caffeine. My turkey club would be off-limits because of a harmful bacterium called listeria. While pregnant I moaned of the injustices of denying a pregnant woman so many delicious things. Funny how I'd give it all up now without uttering one complaint if only it meant I could have my baby.

"It's nothing, really," I start, afraid to disclose the irrational jealousy I'm experiencing. "I feel guilty for ever complaining about my nausea or swollen ankles," I begin. The pregnant woman stands, looking even bigger on her feet, and passes our table as she heads toward the restroom. Owen catches my stare and frowns. "I know I never got a big bump like her." I gesture at the woman as she waddles away from us. "I even dreaded having such an enormous belly. But I miss it, weirdly enough." Saying the words out loud is enough to lift a little of the weight from my own shoulders.

"I miss it too," he admits. "I miss telling people we were expecting, and I miss putting my hand on your belly and knowing I was holding both you and the best parts of both of us," he says, smiling.

"You still mean what you said in bed the other morning?" I ask, afraid he's changed his mind in the light of day. "We haven't talked about it again, and I just wanted to get it out in the open."

He nods, a dollop of ketchup dribbling down his cheek. "Speaking of getting things out in the open," he says, wiping his chin with his knuckle but missing a little, "I was wondering if you still had some time off this month?"

Frowning, I wonder what he has up his sleeve and tap my phone to bring up my calendar. Months ago I asked for vacation time in mid-September for our baby-moon. In the chaos we never booked anything, but I still have the time off.

"I suppose I do," I answer, cocking my head to the side. "Why?"

"Don't be mad . . ."

"Nothing good ever comes after those words," I snort, unable to repress a smile.

"I planned a trip," he says, a devilish grin stretching across his face. "You always said you wanted to see the wild ponies from that book you loved as a kid, so I did a little research and rented us a house for a week. It's a quick ferry ride to the island where you can see the ponies up close and personal and see the channel they swim across in the book."

"*Misty of Chincoteague*," I whisper. "That's the name of the book."

He nods. "That's the one. It's all set. We need a vacation," he says, his eyes twinkling.

I smile, ignoring all the excuses that come to mind, intent on choosing us this time and relishing in the first happy tears I've cried in months. "You, Owen Morgan, are amazing."

He takes another bite of his burger. "And I haven't forgotten about the other conversation," he murmurs, mouth full. "I think I'd like to talk more about that too."

★   ★   ★

A little one is on the way! Please join us in celebrating the arrival of Baby Donohue September 30.

Stuffing the card—shaped like a baby elephant—back into the purple envelope, I let it flutter to the dining room table along with the other unopened mail. When it rains, it pours, and now it's storming pregnant women down on me, shoving their blissfully full bellies in my face. My friend from vet school, Olivia Donohue, and I discovered we were expecting babies right around the same time. Olivia was six weeks further along, but our shared pregnancy rekindled our friendship, which had mostly existed through Facebook in the last few years. We spent the early weeks of our pregnancies tagging each other in funny memes and emailing parenting articles to each other.

After the miscarriage I stopped, even though she kept reaching out. I never responded, scared to tell Olivia the ugly truth—my jealousy made me hate her.

The instructions on the card request that the recipient RSVP to Olivia's mother as soon as possible. Normally, I pin invites to the refrigerator door as a reminder. Currently there's a save-the-date for Owen's coworker's wedding and a lone shopping list from two months ago stuck to the steel door. Our social calendar has seen better days.

I hesitate, eyes darting around the kitchen as though someone is watching, but Owen's upstairs and Rosie's snoozing in the other room. With one last furtive glance around, I rip the card down the middle and then again and again, the satisfying sound of the paper tearing filling the silent kitchen. I let the pieces fall in the trash before scattering a few papers on top, hiding the evidence. A pang of guilt glues me in place for a second, and I almost pick the pieces out. Instead, I lift the bag from the can, deftly tying the heavy-duty orange strings in a double, then triple, knot. Guilt sinks deeper as I walk the trash down the hall and set it outside the front door for Owen to take to the curb. As I close the door, the guilt remains, but a greater sense of relief floods over me.

◆ 28 ◆

OWEN

After
September 23

THE LAST DAY OF vacation is always bittersweet. With the threat of reality imminent, all that's left is to hope you return to your life refreshed and with a renewed sense of purpose.

Obviously everyone loves vacation, but Cassidy and I complement each other especially well. When I travel, I like to immerse myself in the culture. My goal is to exist as a "local" instead of a tourist, to explore the off-the-grid places you can't find on Yelp. On the other hand, Cass is the typical type A planner. She thoroughly researches our locale, compiling lists in one of the notebooks she keeps in her purse—places to eat, places to hike, places to swim. Somehow we strike a balance between hitting all the "must see" attractions and doing it in a way that's authentic to the culture. All the while Cassidy records our journeys in the notebooks for us to look back on one day. I used to worry she was so busy writing things down she was missing the moment. But she loves keeping track of our travels, and this makes her happy. She's the yin to my traveling yang.

Something is different this trip. I won't say it's for the better, since I love all our adventures, but it's new. Cassidy hasn't consulted Google once, and there isn't a notebook in sight. I keep asking her where we should go next, but she's as lost as me. When I assumed she'd know the perfect spot from which to view the wild horses, she only shrugged and suggested we try the next beach, as if she didn't have a care in the world. Without a map, we just drive and let the adventures find us.

The photos didn't do justice to the magnificent house we've rented. Sitting right on the edge of the water, it has the most breathtaking views of the sunrise from the wraparound deck. Each day we sit together on one of the Adirondack chairs, Cassidy on my lap, head leaning against my shoulder, watching the pink sun dance across the horizon and slowly make its way into the hazy late-summer sky. As we sip our coffee in silence, the only sound is the small waves washing up onto the shore and the wind whistling through the high dune grasses. Much to Cassidy's delight, a few ponies graze nearby, tails poised against the slight breeze.

Leaning into her slight frame, the hood of her favorite sweatshirt pulled over her hair, I let my mind wander. Sunshine used to follow Cassidy wherever she went. She was a force of nature all in herself, and I fell in love with her gravitational pull. Her passion and vitality were infectious, and I survived and thrived off this energy for so long. At some point, sadness devoured the light surrounding her. I wish I could blame the miscarriage for the changes inside her, but I fear it began long before the loss. Losing the baby was the eclipse, but the threat of darkness existed before it ever passed the sun. In the last four days, the earth has shifted beneath us. On this little oasis off the coast of Virginia, Cassidy has come back to me.

The sun inches its way over the water, drenching the world in its golden halo. A gust of wind blows the hood off her head and she laughs, her wild hair spiraling around her face as if on fire.

"What should we do today?" I ask, pulling her closer to my chest, relishing the weight of her against me.

"Absolutely nothing," she says, closing her eyes and letting me hold all of her.

*   *   *

"Hurry up, we're going to be late if we don't leave now," I yell, glancing at my watch. "Well, we should have left five minutes ago," I mutter, knowing she can't hear me. Jingling the keys to our rented Jeep, I head toward the door. Cassidy's stomping around upstairs, probably looking for her shoes or a sweater. For someone who's almost compulsively on time for most things, she only ever misplaces things when we're running behind schedule.

"Two minutes!" she calls down the stairs before I hear the whine of the blow-dryer. I've been married long enough to know this won't be a quick fix, so I pour myself a drink.

The house rumbles as a deep roar of thunder passes over the beach. Drink in hand, I head toward the wall-to-wall windows overlooking the angry ocean. Less than an hour ago we walked the beach, not a hint of a storm touching the sand and blue skies as far as the eyes could see. Now the clouds roll in over the water, dark and heavy with the threat of rain. What's left of the sun backlights the sky so the downpour in the distance resembles tears streaked across the horizon. A bolt of lightning strikes over a vast wave, a sharp crack of a whip that sucks the gray from the sky. The tide is in and the water crashes toward the porch, white and foaming and hungry. The rain hasn't started, but it's coming. Upstairs the blow-dryer stops, and the growl of thunder fills the silence.

"Holy shit. Sounds like the apocalypse out there," Cassidy says, startling me. She's sneaked up behind me, her bare feet silent on the hardwood floors. In one hand she holds a pair of heels by the straps. "Look at that sky!" she exclaims as another bolt of lightning flashes hot and quick across the skyline, touching down at some distant point.

"We should go," I say, sipping the last of my Scotch. A wave crashes closer to our deck, the edge of the foam creeping up to the pillars supporting us.

If we want to avoid getting soaked, we need to hurry. She hates the rain, hates getting her hair wet, and I can tell she put some extra effort into styling it tonight. We've made our only reservation of the trip—a fact that still amazes me—at one of the best places on the island. Since it's fancier than the local spots we've been favoring, I've worn my dark wash jeans and a light blue button down. My navy blazer is folded over my arm in case the night cools down. It's the first time we've dressed up in a while, and Cassidy seemed so excited at the prospect of wearing something other than shorts and flip-flops. She's chosen a canary-yellow sundress, the color bringing out the copper strands in her hair, which is loose and wavy around her shoulders.

"Let's stay in," she says, looking up at me with wild eyes.

"No, you've been looking forward to the mussels all day." Unable to resist Googling the menu, Cassidy had already decided on our first course. I take a few strands of her hair between my fingers and gently twist, letting it fall against her cheek. "You look beautiful," I whisper. "I need to take you out and show you off."

She smiles and kisses me gently on the mouth. "Let's stay and watch the storm," she says more assertively. "Whenever we go to these fancy dinners, we always end up spending too much money and coming home and raiding the fridge anyway."

Laughing, I shake my head. She's not wrong. "But you're all dressed up," I say, but find myself warming to the idea of another night with just the two of us. Outside, the sky rages as the rain closes in on the shore. If we're going to leave, we need to get in the car, now.

"You get the wine and I'll get the cheese," she says, dropping her heels to the floor. Sliding in her bare feet toward the kitchen, she rummages through our limited choices. "Hurry," she squeals, "We don't want to miss it!"

"Miss what?" I laugh, pulling two wineglasses from the drying rack and hurrying despite not knowing what for. I uncork the bottle of Malbec from the night before.

"The storm." Another flash of lightning hits, this one even closer to home.

★ ★ ★

The rain starts as we settle onto the deck chairs. It comes fast and furious, the clouds dumping buckets into the water and sand as the waves churn desperately to keep up. No longer hot with the last remnants of summer, the air is chilly, holding on to the promise of the changes to come. On the dunes, the grass bends precariously against the high winds, the long strands lying parallel to the ground but refusing to break. In the morning they'll stand tall once again as they reach back up toward the sun.

Just beyond the edge of the roof, the downpour splatters against the exposed stone, and water droplets ricochet in our direction but fall just short of our chairs. Reaching under the table, I set the electric fire pit burning and watch the flames dance across Cassidy's face.

"Thanks," she says, rubbing her bare forearms and sipping her wine. "It's beautiful, isn't it?" she murmurs as her eyes roam the horizon. A wave grows, its barrel getting bigger and taller before crashing against the walkway leading up to our porch. She stands and tiptoes toward the railing, just shy of the overhang so she's barely protected from the whipping rain. A fine mist coats her face, and her eyelashes sparkle with dew. Up here we're at the edge of danger, but I feel safe and protected from the elements.

Lifting myself from the chair, I slide up behind her and guide her back toward the fire. "You're beautiful," I whisper. Spinning to face me, she raises her hand and caresses my cheek, fingers trailing through my beard. The wind howls in the eves, our very own storm soundtrack.

"Are you hungry?" The cheese board sits untouched on the side table. A devilish smile plays across her lips, and her green eyes twinkle as she dances her fingertips down my shoulder, landing on my chest.

"Starving," I answer, covering her mouth with my own, eager to chase the lightning from her eyes.

★ ★ ★

As quickly as it arrived, it's gone. Sitting together on the couch, wrapped in a cozy afghan, we watch the darkness trail north across the ocean and away down the beach. The ocean churns, but the waves are black and heavy with sleep, as though the ferocity of the storm wore them out. The sun's already far gone, leaving behind a bright-purple canvas free of any moon. A few brilliant stars fight through the haze and shine like disco balls in the sky.

In the twilight her hair is almost violet. Many years ago, I fell in love with her hair, even before I knew the girl it belonged to. For months I only ever saw her hurrying around campus, her red hair streaming behind her as she darted from class to dorm to library. Although we didn't share any classes, we crossed paths quite often and I learned her schedule. Since I was too shy to make the first move, it took an injured woodland creature and a handkerchief for me to find an excuse to actually speak to her. It took me another year of friendship before I gathered the courage to ask for more. I chuckle at the memory.

"What's so funny?" she asks, sitting up a little straighter and nibbling a piece of cheddar from our long-forgotten dinner.

"Nothing," I whisper into her ear. "That was quite the storm, wasn't it?" My body still buzzes with electricity.

Her mouth turns up in a playful smile I can't resist. "That, my dear, was a fucking hurricane."

♦ 29 ♦

CASSIDY

After
October 10

IT'S GOING TO BE one of *those days*. First, it's a Tuesday. Most people bemoan Mondays as the start of the work-week, but I'm not most people. The universal day off for those involved with the care and training of horses is Monday. After a long weekend racing or competing, the horse community—my office included—rests on what's typically the first workday for the rest of the world.

Of course, there's not really any such thing as a day off for horse people. Horses still need to eat every day. They also love getting sick on Mondays, as if they some-how know it's a sacred day for their caretakers. On the off chance I'm free from colics or lacerations, Mondays are saved for all the errands and chores I neglect the other six days. As a result, Tuesdays are my *Monday*. Today is shap-ing up into a particularly rough one, and it's not even eight AM yet.

I grimace, dumping the rest of my coffee down the drain. Once a month, coffee tastes like copper pennies in my mouth and makes me jittery and prone to migraines instead of invigorated. Eight hours of farm calls while dealing with Aunt Flow stretches before me like a bad dream, and I wish I could crawl back under the covers for a few hours. I know all women suffer the inconvenience, but my job is especially brutal this time of the month. Half the barns I visit don't have bathrooms, and the other half have only porta-potties or "restrooms" not much better than a horse's stall. In fact, peeing in a stall would be better than in some of those spider-ridden caves. Combine that with standing on my feet all day, no matter how severe the cramps or heavy the flow is, and that's why I dread my period. I throw a few tampons in my bag even though I'm not bleeding yet. I know she's coming, and there's nothing worse than being stranded and leaking in someone's barn with no backup.

"I'm leaving!" I yell up the stairs. The shower's stopped, meaning Owen will probably be on his way downstairs any second now. He takes pride in needing only seven minutes to get ready for work.

Like clockwork, the floorboards in the hallway creak under his familiar weight, announcing his arrival just before he enters the kitchen. For the hundredth time, I make a mental note to get a carpet runner for the hall. It goes to the bottom of an endless list of things I need to get for the new house—pillows, picture frames, curtains for the front room. Unfortunately, I can't really refer to it as our "new" house anymore, since we've been here for years, but it makes me feel better. Someday I'll get to it.

"Any coffee left?" he asks, rounding the corner and pulling me in for a quick hug and kiss good-bye.

"Plenty," I say, turning my head away as I'm assaulted by a potent smell. "Whoa, cologne," I laugh. "You have a hot date I don't know about?" He laughs too and makes a show of sniffing his armpits. "No cologne, just me and the soap," he says, striding across the kitchen to pour himself a cup of coffee. "Guess I'm just extra clean this morning, not surrounded by my usual cloud of sawdust and grime."

I wrinkle my nose and shrug. "I prefer you dirty," I say, swallowing the bile collecting in the back of my throat. Toast would help settle my stomach, but there's no time. The old granola bar on my desk will have to do. "Love you," I call, eager to get out the door and into the fresh air. He blows me a kiss as I leave, my stomach churning with every step.

★　★　★

"Why did you inject both coffin joints when the horse presented lame only on the right side?" Amy asks as we finally pull into the clinic at 7:14 PM. It's late, but I'm actually surprised we finished this early with the schedule we had booked for the day. Somehow my intern is still bright-eyed and bushy-tailed, despite lugging my machines around all day and jogging beside countless lame horses. When we set off this morning, I worried that her incessant cheerfulness and never-ending questions might worsen my migraine, but I'm thankful for her hustle. I'd still be on the road right now without her assistance.

"I'll go over everything tomorrow during morning rounds," I answer, cutting the engine and taking a deep breath. A heavy cramp rolls in my stomach. A hot shower and a glass of wine are all I want right now. Maybe Owen will give me a massage if I ask nicely. "I'm beat," I say, mustering a smile. "Thank you for your help. You did great," I add.

I'm ashamed to admit I complained to Dr. Ford about Amy tagging along. Usually I prefer working alone, but it's part of my job to take the interns out into the field every once in a while. A stab of guilt softens me to the inexperienced girl gazing at me with adoration. I was once an eager graduate annoying my own boss, but he had the compassion to tolerate me, never letting on what a nuisance I was.

"No, thank *you!* That was one of the best days ever."
She fumbles with the seat belt, her lap covered by a stack
of folders and my iPad. "I learned so much."

Smiling through a cramp, I grind my back teeth. "See
you tomorrow," I say, hoping she gets herself loose quickly.
Finally she's free, and she waves before slamming the door
and skipping to her own car. My brain sings angrily at
the sound. Shoving a tampon in my back pocket, I leave
the car running while I head inside to lock up and use the
bathroom. I hope I'm gushing. The pain always subsides
once the blood flows. This period has been messing with
me all day, making an already hard day even harder.

★　★　★

Owen's standing in front of the stove stirring what looks
like tomato sauce. As soon as the smell hits me, my stomach gurgles, reminding me I've survived on two granola
bars and a lot of Diet Cokes today. Sacrificing healthy eating is a reality every ambulatory veterinarian knows. Amy
didn't seem to mind missing lunch, which bodes well for
her future in the profession.

"Smells delicious," I say, kicking off my boots. The
weight of the day falls on my shoulders, and the prospect
of climbing the stairs is exhausting. "Ten minutes. I need
to shower. If I don't now, I'm definitely falling asleep
smelling like horses."

"And that's different how?" Owen calls over his shoulder, blue eyes dancing. "Go, I've got this." Rosie sits at
attention by his feet, hoping for an errant noodle or meat-
ball. I'm sure Owen "accidentally" dropped a few bites her
way already, always a sucker for her big brown eyes.

I stick my tongue out at him before starting up the
narrow staircase, every step a chore, my legs wooden and
heavy. I haven't had this kind of day in a while. Scheduling
appointments is tricky, since it's hard to estimate how long
each procedure will take. Horses have so many variables

that I usually tack on an extra fifteen minutes to each call. My office manager is amazing, but she thinks I'm superwoman, able to fly from call to call. She forgets to map the distance between barns, so I'm constantly hustling, racing my way down the Mass Pike and forgoing minor things like lunch and bathroom breaks.

The scalding water pelts my back and eases the wave of light cramps radiating from my uterus. Still no blood. As I let my head fall back, the water dissolves away the dirt and stress of the day. Normally I love my showers so hot they burn. But tonight the steam from the shower is too much to bear, and I'm desperately fumbling with the faucet to cool off. Sticking my head outside the curtains, I gasp for air, the sticky fumes from the shower choking me. Drying off quickly, I open the door to let some cold air into the room. Too lazy to fight with my hair, I run some serum through the mess. I need food and an enormous glass of wine. I'll brush my hair later.

Under the sink is a box of tampons. The light-headedness is a sure sign of blood loss, the scientific part of my brain insists. The logical part recognizes I would've seen the proof spiraling down the drain, but I ignore this nagging voice. Beside the tampons is a bag of pregnancy test strips I've neglected to hide from myself. As I close the bathroom door, the familiar guilt washes over me. I feel like I'm doing something wrong just holding the test in my hands. I have every period symptom, so I know it will be negative, but what's the harm in taking one? I pee on the strip and change the tampon—still dry. Two birds, one stone. Wrapping the test in a piece of tissue, I stuff it into the pocket of my pajama pants and head downstairs. In my experience, the most surefire way to bring about your period is to take a pregnancy test. Ask any woman trying to get pregnant—she'll agree.

★　★　★

"That's awesome," I answer automatically, my mind a million miles away. *What if we're pregnant?* The rational part of my brain rolls its eyes at the hopeful part that's come out of hiding. How many times will my body fool me? I'm definitely getting my period. The hopeful half keeps trying to twist the symptoms into pregnancy signs, but the smarter half knows the truth. I'm getting my period, just like every other time I've been through this.

"Yeah, I mean, the aliens are super excited," Owen says, sipping his beer.

I shake my head. "Wait, what?" The baby thoughts subside, and I'm confused and angry at myself for getting sucked back into the vortex so easily. It's not like I haven't thought about babies lately; I've just gotten better at tuning out the nonsense. Traveling back down the TTC path is terrifying. My obsession drove me near to insanity last time. The test burns a hole in my pocket, the temptation of madness. I wish I hadn't taken the damn thing.

"You're lost in space right now," he laughs. "Just like the alien colony I traveled to that you thought was so awesome." I stare at him. What the hell is he talking about?

"Never mind, I'm just playing with you," he says, taking a bite of the rigatoni, one of four meals Owen can cook. The other three are tuna casserole, meat loaf, and shepherd's pie. His midwestern love of comfort food followed him east.

Digging into my own plate, I wash it down with a long gulp of Pinot Noir. I've been unable to enjoy the delicious meal for all my distraction. "I'm sorry, I'm tired and feeling like shit. I have my period," I add. Like most males of the species, he thinks the female cycle is a mysterious beast best handled with care and compassion, if not outright fear. He winces and I excuse myself to the bathroom, letting my fork fall into the tomato sauce midbite.

My hands shake as I unwrap the strip and lift it toward the vanity light. Beneath the blue test line is a second, fainter blue line. As I turn the test left and right, the line remains clear and solid. I blink, afraid I'm imagining it into existence. No matter how I tilt it, the test is positive.

I take a deep breath, but it doesn't steady my nerves or slow my racing heart. In my hand I hold a positive test, and in my belly, I hold a baby. A wave of panic nearly knocks me off my feet, and I sit on the closed toilet lid, hands shaking. The taste of wine goes sour in my mouth. I've been drinking all month, completely unaware of the life inside me. Earlier today I took two sets of X-rays, and even though I wore my lead, I wonder if that's protection enough. My brain rewinds the last month like a crazy slide show, pausing and replaying all the cups of coffee I've downed, all the sushi I've eaten, and all the moments of devil-may-care attitude I've exhibited toward my own health and well-being, never mind a baby's.

"Cass?" Owen calls, tapping on the door. Pushing it open, he drops to his knees in front of me. "Are you okay?" he asks, eyeing me up and down, worry creased across his face.

Silently, I hold up the test. He looks at it, then back at me, lifting his brow.

"Is that a line?" he asks, squinting. "Cass, is that a line?"

Unable to speak, I nod. Fear. Happiness. Confusion. I'm so full of every emotion I can't find the words.

"Are we having a baby?" he murmurs, his own voice barely a whisper. I let the tears fall and nod my head. I'm not sure if they're happy tears or scared ones, most likely a mix of the two. Unable to turn off my inner calendar, I start ticking off the days, trying to calculate when this happened, how far along I might be. *October 10.* Today's date hits me with the force of a hurricane wind.

Today was my original due date.

A wave of nausea rolls over me and I swallow it back, afraid to give voice to the fear. I refuse to let it ruin this moment. Instead, I close my eyes and say a little prayer to the angel looking over my shoulder. I can read this as a good omen or a bad one. Today, I'm choosing good.

"We're having a baby," I whisper, wrapping my arms around Owen's neck. I need to take another test, confirm it's not a false positive, but in my heart, I know it's real. I feel it in my core. Today is the day I am supposed to have a baby.

♦ 30 ♦

OWEN

"**D**AD, WHAT'S THAT FOR?" *the little boy asks, peering up from behind a strand of reddish-blond hair that's a perfect blend of my own sandy-blond and his mom's copper locks. The little boy desperately needs a haircut, even though the long curls are adorably unruly.*

"It's called a protractor, it's used to help make drawings of buildings," I say. The little guy gazes up at me with curious eyes. Turquoise, unlike either parent's, a color all his own. There's a spattering of freckles across his sunburned cheeks. He should be wearing a baseball cap to protect his fair skin.

"Can I see?" He stands on his tiptoes but is nowhere near tall enough to see onto the drafting table.

"Sure, buddy." I drag a stool over and lift him up by his armpits. He's eye level with the table. He's a slight boy, but his arms and legs are compact with little muscles. Maybe he'll be a baseball player. Or play soccer. Too early to tell for sure, but if I had to guess, I'd say he won't be big enough for the football field. Just as well. All those hard hits can't be good for growing bodies.

"Cool," the boy murmurs, touching the drafting paper. I open my mouth to chastise him, afraid his little fingers might smudge the pencil, but stop myself. I can always redo it, so I let him look and touch. Something in the back of my mind tells me he'll be *interested in his daddy for only so long before video games and friends take over.*

"Here," I say, handing the boy a pencil. *The boy switches it from his right hand to his left—just like his mother. I pick up the protractor and gently place my hand over my son's and show him how to trace along the edge of the ruler. The boy purses his lips, the tip of his tongue sticking out, deep in concentration.*

"Can I do it myself, Dad?" *the little boy asks, looking up at me with his wide eyes. It's like looking at an old photograph.*

"Dad?"

★ ★ ★

"Dad?"

★ ★ ★

"Owen?" Cassidy murmurs, shaking my shoulder gently. The dream drifts away slowly. I squeeze my eyes shut, trying to catch one last glimpse before it floats away, but it's already gone.

When I open my eyes, reality settles in as dawn fades to daylight. Cassidy stares at me from where she's propped up on her pillow, her green eyes curious, framed with the same long lashes as those of the little boy in my dream.

"You okay?" she asks, brow furrowing. Her hair sticks out in every direction, an unruly halo of loose curls.

I nod, savoring the last image of the little boy looking up at me and calling my name. Soon his face will be just beyond my grasp, hovering on the horizon of my mind's eye until I dream of him again. I contemplate telling Cassidy but don't. I hate keeping things from her, but I want this small thing for myself. It may lose some of its magic if I unleash it on the waking world. For this reason, I don't begrudge her the small things I know she keeps to herself. We all have special secrets we hold dear. The dreams of my son are mine and mine alone. Normally, secrets are hard for me, but not this one.

"Just a dream," I murmur, kissing her mouth. She wrinkles her nose at my morning breath.

"Anything good?" she asks.

"I can't remember," I say. She smiles at me, unconvinced, but doesn't pressure me for more. "But I'm pretty sure it was a good one."

◆ 31 ◆

CASSIDY

After
October 20

W HEN I CALLED TO schedule my first appointment, I was told it was customary to wait until eight weeks for the first ultrasound. Waiting three more weeks filled me with such acute terror that I'm sure the receptionist could tell by the tone of my voice that I needed to be seen sooner.

She put me on a quick hold before agreeing to make an exception. She passed along a message from Dr. Julian herself, warning me that it was often difficult to hear a fetal heartbeat this early and that this was the primary reason she urged patients to wait those extra weeks. No heartbeat didn't always indicate a problem, rather that her machinery wasn't sensitive enough to pick it up.

I assured her I understood the risks but still wanted to be seen. I've no doubt many parents do panic, only to come back a few weeks later to hear a healthy heart, beating away. This doesn't scare me. I saw my baby's heart beating strong and loud plenty of times. Until I didn't. It's everything else that fills me with dread. All the unknown factors that might go wrong with this pregnancy, along with something deeper, something darker.

I'm scared to hope.

To hope this baby might be okay, only to have my world shattered when it's not. To get excited for a new life when my son never had a chance at one.

★   ★   ★

Despite Dr. Julian's warning, the internal ultrasound picks up a steady heartbeat, and the tiny dot that will be our baby is clearly visible in the sac. Owen is obviously relieved, clutching hope like a drowning man clinging to a raft. I wish it were as easy for me.

My first ultrasound with our son wasn't much different from this one, but I was a different person then. *Then* I felt nothing but pure joy at hearing a strong heartbeat. *Then* I was elated when the doctor informed us he was measuring properly and growth was on track. *Then* I was arrogant enough to expect everything to be okay. I assumed we'd have a baby in nine months. *Now* I'd never be so cavalier. This baby's strong today, but who's saying it will be tomorrow? Or the next day. If the miscarriage has taught me anything, it's that anything can happen, at any time. So, I vow to take nothing for granted. I smile along with Owen and the doctor, but my throat's dry and my own heart is anything but strong.

"Since you're considered high risk, I'll be seeing you for a few extra ultrasounds in the first two trimesters. At thirteen weeks you'll have the Ultra-Screen," Dr. Julian says, referring to the in-depth genetic panel that checks for chromosomal abnormalities. She rattles off a few more dates, and by my calculations, I'll be at the doctor's office approximately every two weeks.

"But the last baby had nothing wrong with him on the ultrasounds," Owen interrupts. The autopsy and ultrasound confirmed he had no genetic or physical deficits. I've read the report so many times, I have it memorized.

"Nope, my hostile uterus was the problem," I kid. Owen's face falls, and I wave him away. "I know. It *wasn't my fault*," I mimic, trying not to roll my eyes. "But something about my body was the problem; let's hope it was a one-off." I cling to this hope, praying that whatever happened was a fluke. An anomaly. Truly one in a million. But reality's much bleaker. We won't know if I'm prone to recurrent miscarriage until I have another. Possibly the worst catch-22 ever.

Dr. Julian clears her throat. "It's true we found nothing wrong with the fetus. Your blood work showed some autoimmune physiology that might affect the body's ability to maintain a pregnancy. We started you on a daily blood thinner, which should prevent clots. If we suspect any other problems related to this, we'll prescribe something stronger."

I nod. After my diagnosis, I researched how certain disorders are treated. Some require daily injections of a blood thinner. For now, I hope the one small pill a day is enough.

She goes over a few more details before abruptly standing and saying her good-byes. As we leave, she hands me a printed-out copy of our tiny dot baby, and I tuck it carefully into my purse. My mind instantly goes to the album folded away in my son's memory box. My son at eight weeks, then twelve, and finally at sixteen. The only photos I'll ever have.

"You okay?" Owen asks as we head back to the car.

I've been pregnant for forty days. My due date is June 16. I have about 240 days until then. Two hundred ten days—give or take—until my baby can survive outside the womb without major problems. In my heart, I know I won't be "okay" until my baby's safe in my arms.

"Sure," I mumble, my left hand falling to my stomach. It's too early to feel movement and my body hasn't rounded, but my baby's in there and my womb thrums with the electric presence of life.

★   ★   ★

I can't understand the fascination with social media that grips so many of my peers and has completely overtaken the younger generation. Facebook was founded while I was in college, and I've watched it morph into what it's become today. Instagram's a little better. I follow a few nature photographers and horse accounts, but if I scroll through my news feed a few times a week, that's a lot for me. Our clinic maintains a business account I contribute to every once in a while. According to our office manager, clients like seeing updates. I'm always surprised when I scroll upon a picture of myself standing next to a horse's head or bent over an ultrasound machine. The interns are in charge of the witty or informational captions beneath the picture. No doubt the clients enjoy seeing their vets at work in carefully curated and captioned photos, but I wonder if it actually helps garner more business. I'm pretty sure the Lombardos don't give a shit if our Instagram is updated as long as we keep their horses healthy.

Now that it's too late to go into the office, I regret taking the whole day off from work. My brain could use a distraction from all the worrying. But the schedule is already set, so I'd only be twiddling my thumbs at the clinic instead of from the comfort of my own couch. So, I put my thumbs to work and open Instagram, ready for some mindless scrolling. Most of my feed consists of animal and medical accounts, with the occasional photo of an exotic location thrown in to remind me of all the places I once wished to travel to but never got around to visiting. "Liking" the pictures on Insta is the next-best thing. Not immune to guilty pleasures, I follow a handful of celebrity accounts. Even I can appreciate the glitz and glamour and pure marketing genius of the Kardashian lifestyle as illustrated through their heavily photoshopped and purposeful pictures.

My thumb stops as I come to a lesser-known celebrity, the wife of one of my favorite comedians. I followed her after one of her pictures piqued my interest. Young and beautiful with a legend of a husband, she had a cool and down-to-earth persona I found most refreshing and compelling. Her posts comprised mostly photos of her family (they had four children), books she was reading, and some products she used (but wasn't paid to promote—according to her captions). Her account was normal, almost boring—in a good way—since it gave a glimpse into the life of a celebrity that looked very much like my own life. Her post today stops me in my virtual tracks.

We are sad to share that our angel passed away today at four months . . . The caption appears beneath a candid picture of her face, free of any makeup and staring straight at the camera, her oldest daughter leaning against her chest. The rest of her post is frank and honest, thanking God for her other healthy babies but wondering why this happened and expressing surprise at finding out such a thing could happen so late in a pregnancy. The words resonate deep within my soul. She says miscarriage happens to one in four women in the United States but is rarely talked about. The second picture in her post is a simple reminder: *I am the 1 in 4. October is Miscarriage Awareness Month.*

Staring at this woman's brave confession, I head to the comments section, where hundreds of fans have already landed. Most are condolences. Many women share their own story of loss. A few hurtful posters shame her for publicly posting something so private instead of spending the time grieving with family, accusing her of posting for attention. These comments make my blood boil. Who are these people to dictate how she grieves? I click on the profile images beside each nasty message. Two are men. One is an older woman, a grandmother of eight according to her profile. A bot with no picture exclaims, I DO NOT FEEL SORRY FOR U! U HAVE 4 BABY ALREADY AND PEOPLE CANNOT HAVE ANY BE THANKFUL AND MOVE ON! The words sting as I recognize hate born of jealousy and ignorance. Didn't a small, envious part of my soul think the same, just for a second? I'd never plaster such vitriol on someone else's pain, but it's telling how people judge each other's grief. *You have other babies, so your loss is not as great as that of someone with none.*

I take a screenshot of the second picture and crop the image until I have a square box with a simple statistic inside. Before I can change my mind, I click the plus sign at the bottom of my profile screen and add the picture without further editing. It needs none. Underneath, I type a simple caption:

I am the 1 in 4.
Rest in Peace ~Angel Baby Morgan~ <3
#miscarriagematters #miscarriageawareness
SHARE.

Locking my screen, I toss the phone on the couch beside me before shutting my eyes, my mind at ease.

◆ 32 ◆

JOAN

I PREFER FACEBOOK TO Instagram. Until recently, all I
had was Facebook until Claire set me up on Instagram,
insisting it was the "new" way to share pictures. But all
my friends still post plenty of photos on Facebook, more
than ever before. It's also great for keeping up with all the
news—like a one-stop shop for catching up on friends,
politics, and gossip. My friends and I can't get enough of
the funny pictures with witty phrases on them. "Memes."
We get a kick out of sending them to one another.

Although I consider myself proficient in navigating
the realm of Facebook and using its special messenger
system, Instagram's still a bit of a mystery. As on Facebook, you can comment and "like" people's pictures,
but there's a different vibe to what people share. On
Facebook, there's an album for every occasion. Betty's
granddaughter was baptized last week, and the next day
I clicked through at least twenty photos of the day. They
weren't all great. Sometimes family members are blinking or not looking at the camera, but the assortment
makes it *real*. These albums leave me smiling and feeling
closer to my friend, even though we haven't seen each
other in years.

Instagram, on the other hand, creates distance between the user and the follower. The pictures are clearly edited or filtered. Instead of an array of photos, there's usually just one picked for its apparent perfection. No simple album name will do, either. Instead, there's some ominous caption leaving me to wonder what the actual picture is about. Can't they just say when and where this picture was taken? For some reason, an inspirational quote seems like a better description. Facebook brings people together. Instagram keeps us apart, highlighting the divide in our lives. Claire made fun of me when I voiced this opinion, claiming I was from a different generation.

I rarely get messages on Instagram, so I don't check my account often. I follow only a handful of people, so I don't miss much. After scrolling through Facebook this morning, I open Instagram for the first time in a few days. The little arrow in the top right corner of my screen has a red circle and a number highlighted. I know enough to understand this means I have a message, maybe even quite a few, and a little rumble of excitement fills my body. It's the same way I used to feel when I received a letter in the mail. No one sends letters anymore, unfortunately. Not quite the same anticipation as ripping open an envelope and holding a handwritten page in your hand, but as good as it gets in this day and age.

When I click on the dot, my message log pops up and I see I have six messages. The first is from Helen Ember, the mother of a girl Cassidy went to high school with (but is no longer friends with, she will argue, despite what a kind girl Helen's Janice is).

Yesterday, 6:42 PM
HEmber55: Is everything okay with Cassidy? Janice and I are worried about her. Sending prayers. Call me if you need ANYTHING.

I frown, not sure what my good friend is referring to. I scroll down and see she's forwarded a post from someone else's page. I click the thumbnail and see my daughter's Instagram account, DrCassidyDMV. Quickly I scan the image and then the caption. There are over a hundred likes and dozens of comments.

I click the next message. This one from Lynn Briggs, a woman I met in a painting class a few years back.

Yesterday, 7:39 PM
BriggsyBoo3: Joan! I had no idea. My thoughts and prayers are with you and your daughter at this time. Please call me if you need someone to talk to. I can't imagine what you are going through. Give Cassidy a hug for me. <3

Cassidy's post is attached to the message again. *I am the 1 in 4.* I shake my head, confused. It's been months since she lost the baby, and she's hardly spoken about it. What a shock to see my normally reserved daughter's public business out in the world for everyone to see and comment on. I swallow back a lump of bile forming in the back of my throat.

The next four messages are mostly the same. Friends sending prayers and expressing distress at the news. I'm embarrassed that some of my friends had to find out the news over something as impersonal as Instagram. Anger replaces my initial confusion, and I scroll through the comments. Each word of sympathy infuses me with renewed irritation. I've begged Cassidy to talk to me, yet she's shut me out, choosing to parade her grief in front of perfect strangers instead. Nothing like picking a scar off an old wound.

Closing my message screen, I type Cassidy's username into the search bar, and her profile comes up. Most of her infrequent posts are of her and Owen on vacations or of work-related stuff. I click on a photo of her and Owen skiing in New Hampshire. Fifty-two likes. A photo of their dog Rosie snoozing under a maple tree, forty-seven likes. I click her newest post, added yesterday afternoon, and it already has 131 likes. Instagram is great for making you double-tap out of sympathy.

Using the skills my youngest daughter taught me, I send the post to Claire.

Today 8:42 AM:
Joaniegirl57: Did you see this? Please call me.

★ ★ ★

It's almost ten by the time Claire calls. The two extra cups of coffee I've drunk have left me jittery and irritable. This sense of unrest has only been heightened by the likes and comments Cassidy's post racks up as I stare at her feed, refreshing every few minutes. For someone who claims to hate false friends and insincere platitudes, her post is bringing up a lot of both. I'm pretty sure some commenters haven't talked to my daughter in ten years.

"Well, it's about time," I answer before Claire even says hello. "Did you see Cassidy's post?" I pace to the window and peek through the curtains. Jack's outside, puttering back and forth from the shed to the garage. When I showed him Cassidy's latest antics, he waved me away. He's made it clear he has no use for social media. Refusing to even get a smartphone, he's a man of a different era. Different century, almost. Although his stubbornness is frustrating, it's also kind of charming, like a breath of fresh air.

"Good morning, Mom," Claire mutters as I let the curtains fall back into place.

Taking a deep breath, I step back from the window and sit. "Sorry. I'm just a little worked up this morning," I say. My hips are killing me, and I shuffle from one seat bone to the other on the hard chair. Rain must be in the forecast.

"It's okay, and yes, I saw her post," she says. "I'm not sure why you're so upset over it."

My heart races and the blood rushes to my cheeks. "I don't understand why she posted such a thing," I say, flustered. "And why now? It's been months. How does she expect to move on if she keeps bringing it up every chance she can?"

Claire's silent on the other end of the line. I fear the connection's lost, but then she clears her throat. "She doesn't bring it up whenever she can. She's sharing a very real and troubling statistic," she adds. "No one talks about miscarriage, for obvious reasons. But it happens to so many women. I think she is just trying to share her story so other women might feel okay doing the same." Claire pauses, and I can hear a little voice in the background, maybe Derek, followed by the rustling of a bag. Snack time. "I actually think it's really brave of her. It couldn't have been easy."

"Brave? I expected more from your sister. Do you know how many people have messaged me about this? Worried about Cassidy and me?" I say, shaking my head. "She bit my head off for sharing this with a few close friends, yet here she is, begging for sympathy from strangers on the internet. I don't understand. Cass never struck me as an attention whore, but now I wonder."

Claire sighs down the line.

"What?"

"Cassidy can share her story with whoever she wants. It's her story to tell. She was upset you told people when the pain was still raw and new. Maybe she needed these last few months to process what happened and now she's ready?"

Considering this, I think back to the conversations I've had with Cassidy since May. They've been few and far between. Shaking my head, I stop pretending to understand the motivations of my oldest. She'll remain a mystery until the day I die, I fear. "Maybe," I reluctantly agree. "I just wish she considered how this would affect those around her. I wasn't prepared to feel all these emotions again out of the blue."

Silence again. It's not often my Claire is at a loss for words, and I worry she's taking her sister's side on this. "Well, I don't think she was thinking about that when she posted it, and I doubt she intended to hurt you."

"Maybe not," I say, my blood pressure slowly falling. Despite her odd quietness today, Claire's knack for decompressing the situation is intact.

Now the boys' voices can be heard clearly, each trying to outtalk the next. I smile, wishing I were there to help Claire wrangle the wild things. They've always acted nice for their grandma, certain a treat or two will be forthcoming. "Mom, I gotta run. Do me a favor and don't do anything rash? Give it a day or two so you can cool down before you call her, okay?" she asks.

"Sure thing," I promise. "Love you. Please say hi to the boys for me." I hit end, the quiet of the house settling over me like a heavy weight. I'm tempted to call Cassidy but fight the urge. Let her call me if she wants. Stranger things have happened.

Unable to resist the lure of Instagram, I open the app and scroll back through the comments on the photo. Mine is hidden near the bottom, not visible when you open the post. I have to click MORE to get past the first forty to find it.

Joaniegirl57: You have real family and friends who love and support you. No need to search for it here. Let's move on and look to the future. Dad and I love you. Xo
2h Reply

I hold my finger over my comment, pretty sure I can delete it by swiping left or right. Claire will be disappointed if she sees it, but I wrote it before our conversation. Two hours ago, I was still shocked and upset. By now I'm sure Cassidy and a dozen other people have already read it. It'll seem conspicuous if I erase it now. Perhaps I should've called Cassidy or messaged her privately, but the damage is done. Maybe next time she'll think twice before plastering her private life across the internet without a second thought for how it impacts others and I'll think twice about commenting out of anger. Most likely we will end up in a fight, but I can't do anything right regarding Cassidy, so I'm damned if I do, damned if I don't. Why hold back now?

◆ 33 ◆

OWEN

After
November 10

NEW ENGLAND COLONIAL ARCHITECTURE is both unique and sturdy. Houses built in the 1800s still stand tall and proud, a testament to the craftmanship and care put into their construction. The most basic style is the classic colonial, once a one-room, two-storied box with pine clapboard sides and a central fireplace. As time went by, the early settlers expanded on it to create the updated versions we see replicated today. A simple variation is the Cape Cod style, quaint and often dormered, a classic on all New England streets.

A larger staple in the northeast is the stately Georgian, bigger than its predecessors but still solid and upright with little decoration. The federal mansion was the king of the bunch, large and ornate with arches and an abundance of multipaned windows. Such houses line the famous Beacon Street in Boston and are favored in nearby Salem. But my favorite style is often unappreciated. Practical and distinctive in its sloping roof, the New England saltbox reigns supreme in my heart.

A variation on the classic square build of the colonial, it has the inimitable slanted roof off the back of the house, an early expansion to add more space for larger families at

the turn of the century. Our house was built in 1854, and
aside from twentieth-century updates, the original floor
plan is untouched. We intended to remodel while keeping the bones of the house intact, but eight years later the
house remains the same as it was the day we first fell in
love with it.

My midwestern sensibility contradicts my Yankee
desire to want *more, more, more*. Since moving east, I've
adapted to fit in with the Red Sox cap–sporting, Bruins
jersey–wearing locals I studied alongside in college and
work with every day. But I'm still considered an "other,"
no matter how often I reference my love of the Patriots
and Dunkin' Donuts. Cassidy claims my open and guile-
less face gives me away. Around here, locals are guarded
and shrewd and proud of it. On the outside, I look like any
other construction worker with my broad shoulders and
callused hands, arms strong from manual labor not hours
in the gym. But on the inside, I'm still "other." When I
pledged a fraternity, I was given the nickname Cheesehe-
ead, even though I was from Kansas and not Wisconsin.
The brothers laughed as they poured me another beer and
assured me it was all the same out there, just a lot of corn
and cheese.

Maybe my dad had a little Yankee in him too. He
pushed me to do better, to want more. More of what,
I'm not sure. Just *more*. More money, a better job, a bigger house, a nicer car. The American dream used to be
a house with a white picket fence and a family with 2.5
children nestled inside. Now success is measured by the
square footage of your home and whether your vacation "cottage" is in the mountains or on the Cape—even
better if you have both. Dad was a simple man, a history teacher at our local high school who was beloved
by everyone. Although he taught world history, he was
especially passionate about American history. When I was
little, he told me stories of brave homesteaders setting out

on the Oregon trail with dreams of a bigger, better life for their families. I loved hearing about how men got rich in gold by hitching up their wagons and heading west. I decided long ago I wanted to be like those brave pioneers and never settle for less than the best for my own family. This meant *more*. It meant forgoing the familiar and, in my case, heading east.

Once or twice a year Dad would start planning a family vacation. Mom would smile and indulge his whimsy before quietly reminding him of the leaky faucet he'd yet to call the plumber about or the new set of tires needed for the minivan. Something essential always impeded Dad's trip, and he'd declare "next year" before retreating into his study to read about great men of times past. Over the years the excuses varied—money, timing, weather. We never got around to visiting Yellowstone like Dad wanted, although with the amount he talked about it, it's almost like we did.

"My parents should go on a trip this year," I say, muting the morning news.

Looking up from her tea, Cassidy lifts her brows. "They should," she agrees. "We could invite them here to visit?" It has been a while since they traveled east, but it's not what I mean.

"No, like a proper trip." I sigh, unsure how to explain what I'm feeling inside. "My dad's talked about seeing the national parks my entire life, and they've never left Kansas except to visit us here."

Cassidy frowns, pursing her lips. She'd been trying to cut back on coffee but has never liked tea as an alternative. "Well, traveling is expensive, and they're both so busy with their clubs and committees," she says. "Your dad's basically the town mayor now that he's retired. He seems happy."

I chuckle. Dad ran for selectman of our tiny town and won by a landslide. Mom's cochair of the auxiliary club and so active in the church community you'd think she ran the place. But even so, don't they ever want to leave Cottonwood Falls?

"Maybe," I concede. "I'm sure Mom has more money squirreled away in the coffee tin above the sink than we have in our 401(k)." Each week, after her grocery shopping was done, she'd put a five-dollar bill in the jar on top of the fridge. It was her rainy-day fund, the reason she compulsively clipped coupons and shopped the circular. "They can probably afford to travel the world twice around after a lifetime of being so thrifty."

Cassidy wrinkles her brow. "If you're really concerned about them, let's buy them tickets for somewhere. How about renting an RV? Then they can take the wheel wherever their hearts desire," she says, warming to the idea. "It can be our Christmas gift to them, force them into making a move. Your mom would never turn down such a present," she says, her smile devilish. "She's way too polite for that."

I can't help but crack a smile. "You're right. Too polite for her own good. Somehow she's politely excused herself from living most of her life," I mutter, unable to hide the bitterness in my tone.

Cassidy frowns. I've never strayed from the carefully curated image of my family. In Cassidy's mind, my mom's basically June Cleaver. How could a town called Cottonwood Falls be anything but idyllic? We even had a collie growing up. Cass can't resist teasing me about falling into the wishing well whenever we visit my parent's house.

"What's this really about?" she asks. "Do you want to go on vacation again?"

Even though I'd love to take Cass somewhere exotic, like Paris or Rome, that's not it. I'm not sure what's come over me. Maybe it's not about my parents or vacations. It's about *more*. My desire for more and all the things keeping me from them. I'm tired of waiting and wanting and ready to start doing.

"I want to build the addition," I blurt out. "I don't want to wait anymore."

"Like, right now?" Her hand settles across her belly, an instinctive reaction I've noticed more and more lately.

A million reasons to wait run through my head, and I silence them. "Right now. I'm tired of waiting for more money or more time. I don't want to wait until after the baby's born," I add, knowing it'll be the next words out of her mouth. "There will always be a hundred reasons not to do it." I reach out and take her hands, keeping them close to her stomach. "We've wanted this for so long. We've planned it out so much, it almost seems real," I say, thinking about my dad's plans to go west. "But it's always been so much easier to talk about wanting things and never do them. It's time to make it real."

"Okay," she says, squeezing my fingers.

I look up, surprised. "Wait, what?"

"Okay," she repeats, laughing. "Let's do it."

"For real?" I ask, afraid I'm missing something, some part of the deal I didn't negotiate yet.

"Yes, for real," she exclaims. "Stop asking me or I might change my mind!"

Stunned, I run my hands through my hair and shake my head, overwhelmed by my own grand plans. I never expected her to say yes. Now I have no excuse to let myself off the hook.

"It will be amazing," I promise, kissing her cheek and standing from the couch, too excited to sit still.

"There's no doubt in my mind," she says. I lay my hands on her belly a beat, absorbing the promise inside. There's so much to do, so much more.

♦ 34 ♦

CASSIDY

After
November 25

Don't walk under a ladder. Never let a black cat cross your path. Find a penny, pick it up, then all day you'll have good luck. *Bad luck comes in threes.* My mother always reminded Claire and me of all the silly superstitions we should be wary of, even giving us each a rabbit's foot for our key chain when we first got our licenses. Naturally, I never paid much attention to her nonsense, assuming it was just another way my mother shirked responsibility by blaming the universe for all things—both good and bad—that happened to her. But lately I find myself fearing that the omens hold some truth. As hard as I try, I can't dodge the feeling that Kitty's loss and my own are interconnected. *Bad luck comes in threes.* When will the unlucky third strike, strike?

It's common to wait until after the first-trimester mark to announce a pregnancy to family and friends. After the first thirteen weeks, the risk of miscarriage reduces and you're considered in the "safe zone." Like a beacon of hope, doctors promise that the morning sickness, the headaches, the exhaustion, and all the other little miseries of the first few weeks will fade upon hitting this milestone, the magical second trimester. It's at this stage when your energy and libido increase and women are enveloped in the elusive pregnancy glow. Like a good pregnant woman, I waited to share the news last time. I know better now. There is no safe zone.

Owen wanted to wait again this time, but I had a different perspective. Part of me yearned to divulge my secret, to bask in people's joy over the promise of a new life—even if only for a little while. We agreed to compromise, deciding to tell anyone we would feel comfortable sharing the loss with. But even after sharing only with our closest family and friends, it's obvious that this time is different. My miscarriage has left people unsure how to react to my new pregnancy. There's the group who solidly believe *everything happens for a reason* who assure me this new baby was my plan all along. It's a nice sentiment, but it still stings, like my son had to die to make way for the life I was meant to have. These people take comfort in the promise of good things rising from the rubble of disaster. I wish I were more like them. Dr. Ford falls into this group, and for this reason I've waited to tell him. I'm not ready for the entire practice to know yet, and I want a little more distance between work and my private life this time around. If John would keep it to himself, it would be one thing. But my previous loss won't prevent him from sharing the wonderful news. He's a farmer at heart, and death won't distract him from the prospect of new life.

The most common reaction so far is to pretend my loss never happened, as though uttering the word *miscarriage* might jinx me. I never correct them about this not being my first pregnancy. Honestly, playing along is a relief. For a minute I can almost imagine a pregnancy not tarnished by fear and anxiety until I note the look of sympathy cross their face and realize it's only make-believe.

With my son, I hit thirteen weeks and thought I was safe. Now I'm only reminded how nothing is ever certain. It's hard to imagine ever feeling safe again, not for twenty-seven more weeks or until my baby is crying in my arms. I can't imagine how hard it is for women who have recurrent losses, forced to achieve each milestone while knowing it's not measuring anything. How many times would those women dare to let their hearts soar only to have everything fall out from beneath them when they lost another baby? I hope I never know that answer firsthand.

"Ready?" Dr. Ford asks, jolting me from my wandering thoughts.

I nod and crack my neck from side to side, making a mental note to Google whether joint stiffness is associated with pregnancy or if I'm just getting old.

We pull up in front of the familiar barn and start preparing the equipment. A deep twinge low on the left side of my belly stops me in my tracks. My right hand shoots toward my hip, and I lose my grip on the ultrasound case.

"Whoa there," Dr. Ford says, grabbing the machine in its stainless-steel box before it hits the gravel. "Careful there, kiddo," he says, maneuvering it the rest of the way out of the truck. "I plan to sell this thing and buy myself a sports car one day," he kids. He's laughing, but I know he would've been devastated if I'd actually dropped it. The box is pretty solid, but the machine itself is so delicate that even the smallest dent might cause a defect that would need repair. The clinic has only the one machine and can't afford for it to be out of commission with so many mares in foal.

"Sorry," I mutter, cheeks pink. "Hand cramped up." I hold up my hand and limply wag it in his direction. He nods, but from the look he shoots me from beneath the brim of his cowboy hat, I can tell he's got something to say.

"Grab the meds and her chart while I lug this sucker in," he says. After I prepare the drugs and pull up Kitty's chart on the iPad, I close my eyes and pray, asking the horse gods to watch over the little mare and keep the twin in her womb healthy. A penny shines in the sunlight, heads up, at the edge of the walkway. Without thinking, I bend and snatch it up, slipping it into my back pocket.

John's already deep in conversation with the Lombardos by the time I reach the stall. Checking on pregnant mares is a routine part of the practice, but after a few months, most experienced horsemen—like these owners—watch the progress with little additional guidance. Three of the mares we inseminated recently gave birth without any intervention at all. The owners only called to share the news that the foals were born healthy. Horse people are amazingly self-sufficient compared to other pet owners. John jokes that many horsemen deserve honorary medical degrees after working day in and day out with the animals their entire lives. Half the students that graduated vet school had never touched a horse or cow before specializing in large-animal medicine. Books can teach you anatomy and physiology, but the animals themselves are the best teachers.

"As you know, only a small percentage of twins survive in utero past fifty days," he continues, Joe and Cindy nodding intently. "Thankfully, we've passed that point, and it appears like the pregnancy is progressing normally," he finishes, smiling warmly. Always practical and calm, John's barn-side demeanor is second to none. He can deliver grave news in the most gracious of ways, a skill some human doctors could learn from this wise old horse doctor. "However, after losing the first twin, the chances of the second being born premature or with slight defects increased."

Joe, a piece of hay dangling from his lower lip like a cowboy in an old western, nods and sighs. "So, what are we checking today?"

I shift my gaze to the mother-to-be. About six months along, the mare's gained a healthy amount of weight and her coat is shiny. She stares back at me with an interested and alert expression. To the untrained eye, she's the picture of a normal pregnant horse. Shutting my eyes, I fight back the onslaught of my own memories—me at four months pregnant, happy, healthy, the perfect pregnant woman. Unfortunately, I'm all too aware that what's happening *inside* the body might tell a vastly different tale.

Wiping my sweaty hands on my chambray work shirt, I focus on my breath. Even though the morning sickness has subsided, stress exacerbates the headaches looming just on the edge of my consciousness all the time. Leaning against the bale of hay in the aisle and dropping my chin to my chest, I count to five and hope the wave of light-headedness passes.

"Cassidy?" John looks at me, face creased with concern. "You okay?" I smile and nod, hoping it's not mistaken for a grimace. I've already run from this barn in a state of despair once before. I refuse to make a fool of myself again.

"I'm good." Forcing the bile to the back of my throat, I push away from my perch on the hay. "As Dr. Ford was saying, we're simply taking some extra precautions with Kitty. It's possible the mare will spontaneously abort the remaining foal between six and eight months," I say, thankful my internal autopilot is kicking in. *Spontaneous abortion.* They plastered the same term all over my own medical charts and then the bills and insurance claims. The phrase circles in my mind over and over. "If this occurs, the mare will go into labor and pass the fetus naturally, but sometimes the body won't recognize the loss and try to continue to nourish the baby. This can lead to dangerous issues for the mare, so we'd like to mitigate those risks by checking on the status of the foal now," I finish, hoping no one can hear my voice crack. A memory of my milk-filled breasts leaking as though they cried for my dead baby almost breaks me, but I swallow it back.

"So, you're checking to see if the foal is already dead?" Cindy asks. Leave it to a cowgirl to cut to the chase.

"Yes," John answers. "On external exam, she looks just as she should for this point in her pregnancy. We can't tell the size of the foal, but we can make sure it's in the correct position and has a strong heartbeat," he adds, placing his enormous hand on my back and letting it sit there a moment. The heavy weight grounds me, and I let my thoughts spiral away.

We're greeted with some gentle nudging when we enter Kitty's stall. Reaching my stereoscope under her elbow, I listen to her steady heart rhythm and hope the baby inside is as strong as its mom. Red-haired horses, called chestnuts, are known to be tough, just like their human counterparts.

"I think she's okay with the tranquilizer," I say, standing at her head and stroking her velvet nose. I let my forehead rest against the soft fur on her cheek. Maybe my good juju will transfer.

John nods and proceeds with the exam. Humming softly under his breath, he methodically runs his hand down from spine to center and then back again with the ultrasound wand. When he reaches the midpoint on Kitty's right side, he lifts his brow, pausing for a few seconds before continuing his track. Placing the instrument back at the spot where he stopped before, he runs it back and forth in the shape of a square, putting firm pressure against the mare's skin. Kitty leans away from the pressure and I hold my hand against her left shoulder, preventing her from moving. Finding a heartbeat on the Doppler isn't easy. The wand needs to be precisely positioned to hear anything, especially as the mare's stomach grows larger. John continues to hum, his nervous tell. He only hums when he's anxious.

"And there we go," he says, cocking his ear toward the machine. Suddenly the steady whoosh-whoosh of the machine fills the stall. He clicks the screen and takes a dozen pictures, moving his hand a few inches each way to take a dozen more. All the while the foal's heartbeat sounds on, music to our ears.

"We have a fighter," he says, removing the wand and grinning ear to ear. The Lombardos let out a sigh of relief, allowing themselves a shared moment of happiness.

I press my face into Kitty's neck, my hand gripping her shoulder for support, and let the tears burning at the corners of my eyes trickle off and land on her soft coat, the color of a shiny lucky penny.

✦ 35 ✦

CLAIRE

After
December 24

CHRISTMAS IS MY FAVORITE holiday. The Thanksgiving dishes aren't even dry before I'm getting a head start on the decorating, setting the electric candles in the windows and wreaths on all the doors. If I had my way, I'd string up the lights and trim the tree the very next day. Steve insists I wait until after December 1, lest the neighbors feel pressured to rush their own setups. But I can't think of anything better than the whole street alight with festive cheer the moment those hideous cornucopias and pumpkins are gone.

Each year I spend the last week in November happily carting carefully labeled boxes up from the basement to start the painstaking process of preparing the house for the Scofield holiday extravaganza.

Every Friday before Christmas we host the neighborhood holiday cocktail party, a boozy, child-free evening for our entire street to come together to drink and be merry. Christmas Eve dinner is the highlight of the season, even though it's only my parents and sister this year. I have a feeling it should be an eventful night, despite the small gathering.

After years of decorating the house in the same greens and reds, I've decided to upgrade my old and worn-out ornaments. For months I've picked up pieces here and there, hoping inspiration would hit me once the time came to put it all together. Above our inlaid-marble fireplace, I've layered the mantel in a faux-spruce garland frosted with sparkling silver accents. Every few inches a silver-coated pine cone hangs from a branch, catching the light from the crystal chandelier. The boys and I hand dipped the cones, and despite the awful mess we made, they turned out even better than the Pinterest board that inspired them.

The side tables are covered in green tablecloths, with charming mason jars filled with spruce twigs and berries sitting atop each one. To Steve's dismay, I lightly glazed all the mirrors in the house with a thin dusting of silver glitter spray, so your reflection shines back from beneath a flurry of sparkly snow. I assured him it's washable, but I haven't tested that out yet.

"Are place cards really necessary?" Steve asks, wrapping his long arms around my waist as I stare intently at the table. I lean back against his shoulder, relishing the feeling of his warm body holding me up.

"Careful, or I'll seat you between my mother and Cassidy," I warn, only half kidding. My plan is to keep them well distanced across the table, but maybe they'd be less apt to get into trouble if I wedged my mild-mannered and jovial husband between them.

He squeezes me and kisses the crown of my head. "If you only give me one gift this Christmas, please let it be seating me far, far away from that train wreck," he kids. I take a deep breath and slouch against him. He's right. Even if it might serve my purposes, it'd be cruel and unusual punishment to force him to play the mediator. Hostile at the best of times, my sister and mother have been especially volatile these last few weeks. As far as I know, they haven't spoken since my mother's cringeworthy comment on Cassidy's Instagram post. Honestly, this only proves that Mom shouldn't be allowed on social media, but that's a topic for another day.

I moan. "This would be easier if I had ten more people to buffer in between them. Is it too late to invite your parents?"

Steve smiles and pulls away, eager to get back to the living room, where the boys are watching *The Grinch*. "If you want to start a war with *my* sister, you can try to steal them away for the night," he says, his voice light even though I know he's serious.

I wave him away, and he leaves me to my seat juggling. As great as it would be to have those seven extra bodies here now, I understand that every family has its internal struggles. Since his sister's divorce, she's stopped coming for Christmas Eve dinner. With four kids in tow, it's too hard to make the trip from Connecticut. Steve's parents stayed the first year so she wouldn't be alone, but we're heading into the third year that they've been held hostage. I'm hoping that once the kids get a little older, she'll start coming again, or at least lend us my in-laws every other year, but for now I leave it be.

Allowing myself one last scan of the table, I nod in satisfaction. The Christmas china gleams on the dark-green tablecloth. A vase full of fur branches and holly sparkles in the center against the warm glow of the candles. I top each plate with a silver napkin and a silver-dipped pine cone. The silver place cards are the final touch, each guest's name carefully calligraphed in green marker. It looks perfect. Pulling my phone out of my back pocket, I snap a few pictures, proud of my handiwork. Maybe I'll add it to my own Instagram feed later tonight.

Somehow, it's already three PM. Guests will arrive at four thirty for cocktails and appetizers. The boys are showered and as clean as little boys can get, but they still need to dress in their outfits and comb their hair. The clock is ticking.

When I peek into the living room, it fills my heart with joy to see all my boys snuggled on the couch watching Jim Carrey as the Grinch sled down the mountain. I notice Steve isn't dressed yet and hope he's at least showered and shaved, since it's the only thing he had on his to-do list today.

"I'm going to go clean up. Please just keep an ear out for the timers?" I ask, knowing it's unlikely they'll go off before I'm finished—but just in case.

"Sure," Steve murmurs, not looking away from the screen.

Taking one last look at the peaceful scene in my living room, I scurry up the stairs, giving myself exactly twenty-five minutes to get my own hair, makeup, and clothes arranged. It's the calm before the storm, and my heart races a little as I think about all the little details I have left to do before the party starts.

★ ★ ★

"It's very . . . shiny . . ." These are the first words out of Mom's mouth, before she's even slipped out of her purple peacoat. Steve winks at me as he takes the jacket, shaking off the light dusting of snow covering the shoulders.

Thankful for the pre-appetizer glass of Chardonnay I gulped in the kitchen, I bare my teeth in what I hope passes as a smile. "Thank you. I was going for something different this year," I answer. If only this would end the conversation. I know all too well it's only the beginning, thanks to Mom's newfound revelation that she can sense people's color aura. When she told me she was taking a mindful-art class at the senior center, I was thrilled she was getting out of the house and meeting like-minded people. Then she started claiming she could see peoples "true colors," and I wished she'd stayed home with Dad.

As if on cue, she clears her throat. "Did you know that a silver aura indicates creativity and fresh ideas?" she asks, stepping out of the foyer toward the kitchen.

"Well, this was a creative, fresh idea of mine, you could say," I tease, hoping to keep the tone light and cheerful. The few times I've heard Mom "read" auras, she started with a few positive traits before things took a left turn toward insulting.

"See, there is something to this," she murmurs, bee-lining straight for the wine bar. She manages to enter the room without making eye contact with my sister, who's perched on a stool at the island, nibbling from a plate of cheese. Owen's next to her, his beer mug poised at his lips as if he froze while about to take a sip.

Cassidy opens her mouth, and I shake my head. Nothing she says right now can possibly be nice and I refuse to let dinner be ruined by my unruly female family members.

"I've never noticed a silver aura around your person," Mom muses, squinting at the label of a cabernet before replacing it in favor of a merlot. "But silver in one's space has a lot of benefits." She pours herself a healthy glass and turns to face the room. Dad lumbers in and heads toward Cass, kissing her on the cheek. My mom raises a brow. "For one thing, silver is great for keeping good energy flowing and especially good at removing stagnant pools of energy from the space," she says, her eyes shifting pointedly toward my sister before glancing around at the sparkling lights in the kitchen. I've strung some dainty garland around the cupboards, and in the dim light the silver tones flashed. "Silver is great for cutting unwanted and unhealthy connections, especially psychic ones," she muses, taking a sip of the wine. My sister looks like she's on the verge of exploding, but out of deference to me—or dad's hand on her shoulder—she keeps her lips sealed.

"On a less spiritual note, an abundance of silver shows an abundance of money. Usually I would consider this much gauche and gaudy, but I like how you softened it with the dark green. Otherwise it really would have been a bit too much," she says, smiling widely.

"I'm glad you like it," I mumble, the glint in the room suddenly a little too bright and showy. Maybe the traditional red and green was the better choice after all. I've always been self-conscious about our wealth, careful not to shove Steve's success in my family's face. The red-and-green bows of Christmases past softened the crisp, modern lines in the kitchen, whereas the silver highlights them. Silver seemed classy yesterday, but tonight it only looks cheap.

"Was that your Christmas gift?" Cassidy says, her voice high and loud in the uncomfortable silence of the kitchen. "Are you going to read everyone's aura tonight? Or was that little bit reserved as an honor to our hostess, who's no doubt worked tirelessly to create such a beautiful evening for her family?"

Dad steadies his hand against Cassidy's shoulder.

"It's okay. I'm just happy we're all here to celebrate together," I say, finding Steve's eyes over the counter. He nods, taking the pass.

"Yes, thank you all for coming. Claire and I look forward to Christmas Eve all year long, and I know the boys do too," Steve says, lifting his glass of wine. "Let's have a brief cheers to family before digging into these wonderful appetizers. To family," he says.

"To family," we all say in chorus, although I'm pretty sure Cassidy is rolling her eyes at our mother while draining the sparkling cider in her champagne flute. At least she's not able to drink. I'm not sure I could handle them both drunk.

So far, Christmas Eve's off to exactly the start I expected. If nothing else, I'm sure it will be one for the record books.

★　★　★

Seating Derek across from Mom seemed like a safe choice. But I forgot how unpredictable little boys can be. Combine that with Mom, who's already three glasses of red wine deep, and it was bound to end in one way and one way only. Disaster.

"Oh, how fancy," Mom declares upon entering the dining room. The chandelier glitters and the candles on the table glow against the dim backdrop. "Should we sit anywhere?" she asks, even though I'm certain she sees the name cards at each seat. I pretend not to notice and usher the boys in front of me, pointing to their chairs.

"Actually, your names are on cards at your seat," I say, trying to sound casual but failing. Steve smiles at me as he helps Derek into his chair.

"The boys wanted to pick where everyone sat this year," Steve adds, unfolding a napkin onto Derek's lap. Our son opens his mouth to protest this little fib, but Steve catches him before he can throw me under the bus. I'll have to give them both extra desserts later. I silently send a thank-you to Steve. Sometimes he acts aloof, but he's always there for me, ready to catch me when I stumble.

"Well, then I'm extra honored that Derek wanted to sit across from his Grandma," Mom says, her words starting to slur. She needs food, quick, or things will only spiral downward even faster than they currently are.

We find our seats and say grace. We manage to pass the vegetables without incident. My dad and Owen talk about the renovations at Cassidy's house while we all chew our food, content to listen to their chatter about bathroom fixtures. Some of the tension leaves my body as I dare hope the evening might go on in this pleasant manner.

"Grandma, did you see the video I asked Mommy to send you about the Lego ninja set I really, really want for Christmas?" Derek interrupts, his mouth full of mashed potatoes.

"Derek, Uncle Owen and Grandpa are talking. It's not nice to interrupt," I chastise, hoping to steer the conversation away from this topic. "It's also gross to talk with your mouth full. You know better."

"Sorry," he says, mouth still full.

"What video?" Mom asks, looking at me from her corner of the table.

Color rushes to my cheeks. Denial or truth?

Taking this as an opportunity to share his latest obsession with both Legos and everything the child YouTube star Evan last-name-unknown has suggested for his millions of subscribers, Derek puts his fork on his plate and explains things to the table. "Evan from EvanTube is the coolest kid in the universe. Each week he plays with new toys and decides what the best new toy to buy is," he says, his words coming out so fast they stumble over one another. "The best thing he's *ever* played with, in my opinion and also his, are the new Lego Ninjago sets. You need to get Old Spinjitzu Master Wu—he's the leader— and then there are the young ninjas and their cities and cars. It's so cool, Grandma. Didn't you watch the video?"

Mom carefully places her own fork on the edge of her plate and shakes her head. "I'm sorry, honey, I must've missed the message from your mom. All that sounds really neat, though," she adds, fixing me with a scathing glare from across the table. "I'm sure you meant to send it to me, right, darling?"

"I'm sorry, Derek, it slipped my mind. I'm sure Santa Claus saw it on your list though," I mumble, my mother's stare relentless.

"What is a YouTube channel?" she asks. "It that like Facebook?"

Eager to keep the conversation focused on his favorite topic, Derek jumps in. "Not really, it's way better. It's a place where you can watch videos with other people. Evan and his family make one each week, and he makes a *ton* of money doing it *and* he gets all these free toys. I want to be like Evan when I grow up."

My mom lets out a mirthless chuckle. "Is that right? Well, I'll be darned. It seems like just anyone can be famous nowadays, doesn't it?" She asks the table. "I mean, look at all the celebrities on Instagram posting things and making all that money. It's just crazy to me. Sounds like this boy's family is really profiting off their son's celebrity," she says, her tone getting colder. "It amazes me what people will post on the internet for all the world to see, just to get attention."

Her rant is cut short by the sharp whine of a chair being pushed back too hard against the hardwood floors. Cassidy stands and tosses her napkin onto her mostly empty plate. "I'm not feeling well. I'm going to go lay down for a few minutes," she says, one hand on her belly. I rise, but she waves me back down. "Please, finish. Everything's been so good, Claire. I think I just overdid it," she says, and I sink back into my chair. Little Matty coos and slaps his high chair for good measure.

Owen pats my hand and promises to check on her in a minute. Swallowing back tears, I nod. I could've predicted one of them storming from the table middinner; I just never guessed it would be Cassidy. I'm disappointed to see the faint gleam of victory in Mom's eyes as she continues to sip her wine, ignoring the chaos she's caused.

"She's right," Mom says, draining her glass again. "Everything is delicious. I wouldn't take it personally, dear. Your sister's always been so sensitive," she says, shrugging.

Before I can stop myself, I slap my hands on the table. The candles shake, casting the room in shivering shadows, and everyone jerks their gazes from where they've been silently studying their plates. "Enough!" I hiss. "One minute she's too sensitive; the next she has no emotions. What exactly is the proper amount of feeling she should show?" I snarl, my breath coming in ragged bursts. Somewhere my big sister is crying alone into a pillow, hiding her feelings, because unless you were willing to be silent and steady—like good-girl Claire—those feelings were either too big or too small. Normally, I'd let it slide and make sure dinner ended on a cheerful note. Not this year. Maybe all the silver has put me in the mood for change. "Lay off her, for once. Not everything needs to be psychoanalyzed by you. Sometimes decorations are just for fun, and sometimes social media posts aren't meant to be dissected and taken so personally." I'm rambling but don't even care. I should've said it long ago. "Sometimes it's okay to say you like something even when you don't. Sometimes it's even better to hit 'like' on a post and move on, keeping your comments to yourself."

Everyone stares at me, mouths agape and forkfuls of food frozen midbite. The grandfather clock on the wall ticks ominously. Steve hides a small smile with his fist, and Dad bites back an impressed smirk. Mom picks up her fork and makes a show of finishing the last of her mashed potatoes. "These potatoes really are great," she says, not looking in my direction. "Maybe after dinner you can show me that video," she says, eyeing Derek from above her tortoiseshell glasses.

Clueless about the bigger problem in the room, Derek shakes his head happily. "I'll get my iPad and show you before we watch the movie!" he says, pushing his empty plate away. "May I be excused, Mom?" he asks, eager to go upstairs and get his toy to show his loving grandma.

"Sure," I say, too tired to argue.

Dinner was over, anyway.

★ ★ ★

Like our dad, Cassidy never let us see her cry. I've never seen Dad shed a tear, though Cassidy swears he did once after one of our old dogs died. Always a sucker for small things—like animals and his daughters—he's a big man with an even bigger heart. I'm not surprised some old mutt broke his heart, and I'm even less surprised to find him already comforting Cassidy.

Hovering in the doorway to the library—a lofty name for the small room, which is hardly more than a couch and a few bookshelves—I watch Dad hold my trembling sister in his embrace. She leans her tearstained cheek against the soft flannel of his shoulder as he shushes into her hair. They don't notice me at first, but I catch his eye and he smiles, urging me to come in. Tentatively, I walk across the plush carpet and sit on the daybed next to my sister. She wipes her face, now mostly dry, and sighs.

"I'm sorry," she moans, a slight smile cracking one side of her pretty mouth. "I really didn't intend on making a scene, but I was on the verge of either murdering Mom or bursting into tears. I figured running away was the least I could do to save us all," she kids.

Shaking my head, I bump my shoulder against hers. "Well, you made me lose a bet with Steve. I had fifty bucks you'd start a fight at the table, ten extra if it involved food getting thrown. Never imagined you'd be the one storming out of the room."

She rolls her eyes but grins. "Must be the hormones. I'm becoming a big softy. Didn't have it in me to make her cry in front of the boys. Even if she deserved it."

Dad lets out a long breath. "And this is my cue to leave," he says, patting us both on the head, a habit that once irritated us, especially as teens, when he found it especially fun to mess up our carefully sprayed hair. Now we both lean into it, embracing the mess. "I know your mother can be a little much sometimes," he says carefully. He stands, and his full height towers over us as we sit on the sofa. I feel like we're little kids again. "But she really loves you, and sometimes she doesn't know how to express that love." He stops, as if he's already said too much. "Anyway, don't be too hard on her. She's always done her best. You girls aren't as easy as you think you are." With that, he gives us one long last look and leaves us alone in the library.

Turning to face me, Cassidy furrows her brow. "Really, I'm sorry I messed up dinner. I just couldn't sit there any longer," she says, her slight shoulders shaking.

I laugh. "I wish you'd stayed. I finally snapped at her and you missed it," I say, amused at the surprised expression she gives me. "You would've been proud. I took a page straight out of your book and tried to put her in her place."

"How'd that go?" she asks, lifting an eyebrow.

"She basically ignored me and finished dinner." I shrug, "I don't have the same effect on her as you."

Cassidy fiddles with a thread on her sweater. "I guess we should go back out there," she mumbles, pulling the string so that the cuff unravels. "It's my year to pick the movie."

Each year we alternate who picks the holiday movie we'll watch before laying out the milk and cookies for Santa. After settling on a movie, we each open a gift— always the same thing, pajamas—and change into them before snuggling up on the couch together as a family. Last year Dad picked *Die Hard*, insisting it was a Christmas classic. A minor argument over whether the boys were old enough to watch something so violent ensued, but Dad was persistent, and we relented. It didn't matter anyway, since all three fell asleep before things got too crazy. I don't even need to ask Cassidy her pick. It's always the same.

"You know she hates that movie," I groan, shaking my head.

She grins her most wicked grin, sending me back in time to when she was fourteen and I idolized every move she made. "Exactly," she giggles. "But that's not why I'm picking it. It's undeniably the *best* Christmas movie ever made."

I groan again. "Can't you throw me a bone and pick *It's a Wonderful Life* or *Miracle on 34ᵗʰ Street*?"

"Those movies are terrible, and you know it," she says, laughing. "Love you." She stands and heads out toward the kitchen, blowing me a kiss over her shoulder.

"Love you back," I mutter, bracing myself for round two.

★ ★ ★

Kevin McCallister is ordering himself a plain pizza all to himself when Mom finally speaks up. I'm surprised it took her this long, although I'm glad for the small respite from hostility, short-lived though it may have been.

"Really, Claire, we should turn this off before the boys see any more of this nonsense," she huffs, her wineglass replaced with a small tumbler of Bailey's on ice.

Derek looks at me desperately, shaking his head against my chest. *Home Alone* is his favorite too. I gently smooth back his wavy hair, too long already even though it was just cut.

"It's fine, Mom. Derek's seen it and Shane's about five minutes from passing out," I say, nodding toward my middle son, who struggles to keep his heavy eyes open. Curled up beside Steve, he's only managed to hold out this long for fear of missing out on something his big brother is doing.

Mom harrumphs from her spot on the love seat. Dad's eyes have been half-shut since we opened presents around the tree. "I just don't understand why you like such *garbage*," she says, breathing haughtily into her glass. "What kind of mother would forget her own child at home, especially at Christmastime?" she says, the same complaint she makes each time we watch this movie. She loves lecturing about the McCallister family's poor parenting skills, the mother's in particular. Usually we nod and let her mumble under her breath until she's exhausted her grievances and resigned to watching the rest in silence, stewing in self-righteous indignation. I should've known we wouldn't get off the hook so easily this year.

"Well, Mom, you *are* the prime example of a perfect mother. Makes sense you need to criticize this fictional character to prove you are, in fact, superior," Cassidy murmurs, smiling like a fox. "While you never left us behind on your trip to Paris, you also never let us forget you weren't able to go to Paris because of us. Not sure which is more detrimental, actually." She shrugs before turning back to watch the pizza delivery boy rushing from the sound of bullets on the screen.

Mom's mouth hangs open in shock. I bite the inside of my cheek to keep myself from laughing, unsure if the sudden urge to giggle stems from the sense of discomfort in the room or the fact that I've never seen this particular look on my mom's face before. Cassidy stares ahead at the TV screen, seemingly oblivious to the reaction she's caused. I know better. Cassidy knows exactly what she's set in motion.

"Of all the things to say to me," Mom hisses, struggling to push herself up off the deep cushions of the couch. She jostles my father, who opens his eyes and looks around, blinking with confusion. "I didn't come here tonight to be abused by my own children," she huffs, shaking Dad's arm a little too hard. "It's time to go, Jack," she says, her indignation turning to something else. Something far less funny. In the dim light, she looks like an old woman whose feelings have been hurt.

"Mom, stay," I say, unable to get up under Derek's weight. Steve pauses the movie and looks to me for direction.

Mom shakes her head, the wrinkles around her mouth deepening. She looks older than ever. "Derek, we look forward to seeing you tomorrow and hearing all about the presents Santa got you," she says, quickly dropping a kiss on my son's forehead. "Thanks for having us over," she mumbles as an afterthought, not looking me in the eye.

Dad ambles after her, clearly unsure what transpired while he dozed off. "Merry Christmas, everyone," he says to the room, waving his bear paw of a hand to the rest of us, who wave back, a little stunned at how quickly the evening turned from bad to worse.

"Love you all," he says, hurrying to catch up with Mom, who's already out of sight.

Their footsteps echo down the hall, and only after the front door closes does Cassidy turn back to the rest of us.

"Was it something I said?"

◆ 36 ◆

CASSIDY

After
January 13

"NAMASTE," THE INSTRUCTOR SAYS, bowing her head and touching her lips to her fingertips raised in prayer.

"*Namaste*," I whisper in union with the rest of the class. I'm one of nine moms sitting in various formations, some propped up with pillows, depending on the size and heft of their baby bump. Closing my eyes, I breathe in, the smell of lavender mixing with someone's coconut shampoo. Even the earthy smell of sweat is not entirely unpleasant. The room smells alive.

The silence is slowly broken as I open my eyes. Glancing around, I notice the different degrees of pregnancy situated around the room, everyone reflected in the mirror at the front of the room. Most of the women are visibly showing, but none so large that yoga has become too cumbersome. My own stomach is just starting to protrude. While dressing earlier, I had a moment's pause before pulling on a formfitting top that highlights my little melon. I never saw a bump with my first pregnancy, and it still makes me feel as though my baby might never have existed at all. This time around I wear the added weight with pride, showcasing my ever-changing body.

Two mats away, a woman struggles to get to her feet. We lock eyes before I can look away, and a flash of embarrassment crosses both our faces before she collapses forward onto her hands and starts laughing, her curly brown hair falling around her cheeks and bouncing as she heaves a gigantic sigh.

"It was a lot easier getting myself down into this position," she chuckles, lifting her gaze back toward me. "Maybe I'll just stay in child's pose," she kids, letting her rear end collapse back toward her heels. She sprawls her arms out to either side and shifts to the right so her bump is awkwardly pointing in my direction.

"Here, let me help," I offer, reaching my hands toward hers and hoisting her up. We wobble together for a second, but she ends up upright, using my shoulder for balance.

"Thanks," she says, wiping a strand of tight curls out of her face. "I'm Layla," she says. "I'd offer you my hand again, but I feel like we're pretty well acquainted already." She smiles widely, a dimple in each smooth cheek.

"Cassidy," I say, noticing that Layla looks about ready to pop now that she's not on the floor.

"Third baby," Layla says, catching my surprised expression. I wince and smile sheepishly. I should know better than to stare at another pregnant woman's stomach. "It's okay. I'm huge, I know," she says, her striking sand-colored eyes sparkling. "Would you believe it if I told you I still have almost three months to go? I swear I looked three months pregnant the day I took the pregnancy test," she says, laughing and rubbing her lower back. "My ass will never be the same."

"I'm sorry," I say, flustered. "I didn't mean to stare. You look beautiful," I add. This is what the books mean by *pregnancy glow*. Layla's skin is clear and shining from a light within. Each spiral of hair is bouncy and full of life, framing her heart-shaped face like a halo. I've never seen someone so pretty in real life.

"Please, I'm huge and sweaty and starving," Layla says, bending at her knees to scoop up a red mat. "Want to go earn back the calories we just burned?" she asks, lifting one brow.

A hundred excuses come to mind. Squelching the voice screaming *no, no, no,* I refuse to let my insecurities get the best of me this time. Layla is exactly the type of woman who always intimidates me, tall and statuesque with strong features. Women like her make me feel small and less-than. I've always considered my petite frame a blessing, but when standing next to someone a foot taller than you—especially a woman—it's hard not to feel like a child. Where Layla is obviously outgoing and dynamic, I'm typically reserved. Layla is a pregnant woman who wields her belly like a goddess, matronly and proud. Here I am with my tiny bump, constantly questioning my status as mother.

"You're coming with me," she says, grabbing my free hand and leading me toward the door. Before I can open my mouth to protest, she continues. "I'll drive," she says, nodding toward a minivan parked right outside the studio doors. I can't help but smile. Even goddesses drive minivans.

★   ★   ★

"Girl, you are eating for two. Indulge!" Layla says, her voice loud and raspy and lovely. I'd ordered the scrambled eggs with yogurt and fruit. Considering most mornings I make do with a banana and a breakfast bar, I think my order is fairly indulgent. Layla has other ideas.

"I'll have the Nutella French toast, a side of bacon, and home fries please," she tells the waitress. Glancing at me, she adds, "Two sides of bacon. We're hungry." She rubs her belly and the waitress smiles.

"You can have some of my French toast," she says. "It's delicious here." Sipping her orange juice, she beams at me like we're old friends, not women who met literally an hour ago.

At times like this I wish I were better at small talk or girl talk—any kind of talk, really. The silence stretches between us, and I make myself busy looking out the window at the people passing by. Some are rushing, probably ticking errands off their never-ending list of things to do, while others enjoy a lazy Saturday stroll. I glance at Layla, afraid she's bored, but she seems perfectly content to people-watch and sip her decaf coffee. Why is it I'm always so uneasy in these moments?

"How long have you been practicing yoga?" I ask, desperate for some conversation that might make Layla not regret inviting me to breakfast.

She shrugs. "I don't really 'practice,'" she says, adding her own air quotes around the last word. "I'm definitely not a yoga mom. I started during this pregnancy to help me relax and maybe meet some other moms in the area."

I nod, happy to have found some similar ground. "Me too," I say. "I've done yoga for a few years, but I thought joining a pregnancy class might help me meet people."

"Is this your first?" Layla asks, her face open and innocent. I imagine slapping that perfect face, lashing out against this mother of three who ignorantly believes motherhood is something so simple. *Is this your first?* A question I've been asked dozens of times and will be asked a dozen more. Such a simple question, but the answer is anything but. I swallow back my irrational rage, hoping my smile isn't as monstrous as I feel.

"And here you go," the waitress announces, placing our food in front of us, the perfect buffer against more questions.

"Any other children?" Layla repeats. Almost the same, but somehow less hurtful.

I shake my head, stabbing into my eggs with one hand. "No other children," I answer, the words falling like bricks from my mouth. Every time I deny his existence, I push my unborn son a little further away, dishonoring his memory a little more. How can I reconcile not having any living children with polite society? I haven't figured it out yet, so I answer the complicated question simply. "How about you?" I ask, since this is how people converse. Even a social dummy like me knows this.

"I have a son named Henry," she says, shoveling a very large and unladylike bite of maple-syrup-drenched French toast into her mouth. She swallows, not noticing the Nutella on her lower lip. "He'll be five next month," she says, dabbing her face with a napkin. "Light of my life, the little devil."

Maybe I misheard earlier, but my memory is generally my strong suit. "I thought you said this was your third?" I ask, savoring the cheesy eggs, perfectly fluffy. Although my dish is delicious, I'm a little jealous of the decadent concoction Layla digs into. As if she's read my mind, she cuts off a big piece and plops it onto a side place before nudging it my way.

"My third pregnancy, yes," she says, not missing a beat. She pops a piece of crispy bacon into her mouth. "I miscarried my second pregnancy at eight weeks," she adds. She tells me this as if she were reciting the weather or reading off the menu. "That was a year ago. This little guy or girl is our rainbow baby," she says, placing her greasy fingers on her bump.

I've never heard someone speak so casually about miscarriage. In fact, I've never heard anyone speak about it at all aside from celebrities on social media. On the rare occurrence when someone asks about my first pregnancy, I tell them I lost the baby. End of story, no further questions. In private, I stalk miscarriage and grief blogs where other mothers openly communicate about their losses, but I've never spoken face-to-face with another woman who's experienced losing a baby.

"I'm so sorry to hear about your loss," I say, my mouth dry. A slight wave of nausea passes over me, and I lay my fork down. The smell of eggs wafts up and I push my plate away, suddenly full.

At least it was early, I think to myself. Eight weeks. Some women don't even know they're pregnant at that point. The fetus is barely more than a bunch of cells, not a fully formed baby with fingers and toes. The image of my little boy, so tiny he fit in the palm of my hand, comes to mind.

"Thank you," she says. "Are you okay? You look really pale." She stares at me with concern and slides my water glass toward me. "Take a sip," she orders, and watches me take a long guzzle. Some of the blood comes back to my head.

"I'm okay," I mumble, my tongue sticking to the roof of my mouth. Layla stares at me so intently, I swear she can see into my soul. "No, actually," I say, letting out a hurried breath. "I'm not okay. I lost my first pregnancy too."

Layla's face falls. "Oh, honey," she murmurs. "I'm so sorry. Tell me about it."

Tell me about it. No one, not even Owen or my own mother, has asked me to talk about it.

"It was a few months ago," I start, voice shaking. "I miscarried at twenty weeks, and it was horrible." It feels good to admit how terrible it was instead of trying to hide the horror, afraid I'd scare them away. This woman knows the pain and misery I feel.

"I can't imagine," she says, reaching her hands across the table. Her fingers are sticky with syrup, but I don't mind. I clutch her hand like a lifeline. "I thought I'd die of heartbreak, and my baby was only eight weeks, barely a twinkle in the womb. I don't know how I would have survived losing it later," she says. "And this was your first pregnancy? I don't know how you did it. I had my baby boy at home to help me through, and I thank God every day for my blessings," she says, squeezing my hand a little tighter.

I shake my head, not sure what to say. Layla is right. Listening to her speak about her own loss, I realize I've been so wrong in so many ways. Losing my first baby so late in pregnancy was unfair and awful and might sound worse than Layla's loss, but losing a baby at *any* stage is terrible. My first instinct was to compare my loss to her's and judge the degrees of our pain and deem my own loss *greater*. And this isn't the first time. For months I've read stories of women who miscarried at five, twelve, fourteen weeks. Only a handful lost babies past my own mark. Many of these women had other children at home. For every story, I quantified and compared the pain to my own using some sick formula I created—how many weeks along minus how many children at home plus how many additional pregnancy losses—all factors to help me deduce whose pain was greatest.

Safe behind my keyboard, I gave myself permission to think women with other live children should be thankful for the ones they had. Their pain was *less than*. Women who lost babies before a heartbeat was heard should be thankful it was only a bundle of cells and they didn't have to deliver a fetus. Their pain was *less than*. It was wrong, but it made me feel better.

I'm ashamed of myself now that I've talked to Layla, a real, live woman who has experienced loss. I've been blind. You can love your existing children and still mourn the one you lost. Women who miscarry early still deserve to grieve, since a mother's love is instant. Diminishing the pain of others made me feel better in some twisted way. For too long I've held on to the idea that *my* pain was the most painful of pains, and it's grown into a malignant tumor inside me.

So, I open up and tell Layla the complete story. I start with my water breaking and relive holding my son in my palm, his face perfect and blue. I don't stop and I let the tears fall. She doesn't interrupt, just listens and cries with me. This woman I've known less than an hour shares in my pain and doesn't compare it to her own or judge it to be greater or less than.

"It sucked," I say, finally finishing my story. I wipe my cheeks and try to smile. "But we are lucky to be pregnant again," I add, still afraid to offend the karmic gods who've blessed us both with another chance. Society insists that we be thankful for our gift, even if it's tainted with pain and grief.

"Of course I'm thankful," Layla says, picking up her fork. "But that doesn't mean I'm not terrified."

Looking into her startingly light eyes, I see my own reflection and nod. "Completely, fucking terrified," I agree. I pick up my own fork and take a bite of her French toast, relishing the way the sugar melts in my mouth.

✦ 37 ✦

CASSIDY

After
January 28

THE BABY HASN'T KICKED in a few hours, and I'm worried. Not worried enough to text Owen in a panic. Not yet, anyway. But worried enough to start down the rabbit hole of Googling and consulting the baby forums.

Today began like any other day with a small coffee and banana on my drive to the clinic. Usually the little jolt of caffeine wakes him up and I feel the familiar fluttery hiccups in my lower belly. But not today. Today he's been still, even as I bent around a horse with a swollen leg and examined the lame animal. Finished with my first patient, I sit in the truck with the radio off, hoping the silence and stillness will allow me to focus on my body and feel something. Anything.

I swallow the lump rising in the back of my throat, the first little bubble of hysteria beginning to take shape. Instead, I try to temper the panic by focusing on my next call. Letting my body run on cruise control, I make it to the second farm and find another lame horse. Different limb, same basic treatment. I prescribe icing the knee and a cold poultice to relieve the swelling. I distribute a mild anti-inflammatory and suggest a follow-up appointment if the horse is still sore in three days. Thankfully I can diagnose and treat these ailments in my sleep, and the customer doesn't even notice my mind is elsewhere.

As I close up my truck once more, the first stab of pain slices across my abdomen from left to right. After the first throb, it settles to a dull ache, almost like a hunger pang. Resting my arm on the trunk, I take a deep breath and count to five. Another pang, this one sharper and higher on my side.

My eyes water and full-blown panic sets in as I stumble to get into the driver's seat. Glancing in the rearview mirror, I notice my hair is stuck to my sweaty forehead and my hands are shaking on the wheel. From the driveway the barn owner looks toward me with a concerned face, and I hold up my fingers in a weak wave as I back out of the drive, hitting the gas a little too hard and sending gravel sailing. The owner waves back and smiles, probably assuming I'm just running late for my next call.

Without signaling, I pull out into traffic and cut off a mid-sized sedan, who slams on the brakes before laying on the horn. Flustered, I pull onto the shoulder and slide to park just in time for the car to pass me in an angry hurry but not so fast that the driver doesn't have time to hit the horn once more and flip me off with the other hand. Taking another deep breath, I lay my hands on my bump. Closing my eyes, I wish for him to kick against my touch. Last week I swear I felt him, even though Owen claimed he couldn't feel a thing. Maybe I imagined it all along. Lifting my light sweater, I press my palms firmly on my hard belly, but still nothing. Then another pang.

Fighting back tears, I scroll through my phone and dial Owen's number. The phone rings repeatedly across my Bluetooth speakers, cutting to his voice mail message. I want to scream. Why isn't he there?

"Call me as soon as you get this," I say, even though I know he never listens to his voicemail. I follow up with a text. *Call me. Going to Dr. Julian's now. Meet me there.* I worry two missed messages might frighten him but decide I don't care. It should scare him. I'm terrified. After hitting send, I pull back out into traffic and cause an SUV to swerve to avoid clipping my back bumper. The driver lays on the horn and I flip him off, answering with my own horn even though I know it's my fault.

★   ★   ★

Cutting to the front of the line while cradling my tiny bump, I demand to be seen at once. The girl at the front desk is both patient and kind, despite my terrible behavior upon entering Dr. Julian's office. For a split second, I contemplated going straight to the emergency room, but I couldn't face that trauma again, not alone. The other women waiting take a step back and look at me with pity before turning their eyes away as though my pain might be contagious.

With a practiced smile, the receptionist leads me directly to an exam room and motions for a nurse to come straight over. Embarrassed at my rude display in the waiting room, I compose myself and hope the other pregnant women understand I'm not truly a bitch, just scared. I glance down at my phone. No service and I'm not connected to Wi-Fi. Owen has no way of getting in touch with me and is probably worried sick.

This morning we both pretended this afternoon's appointment was like any other. But it's not. Today is our twenty-week ultrasound. The milestone we've been looking forward to with both excitement and trepidation. Afraid to put voice to the lingering fear, we ignored the sense of foreboding and treated it like just another day. Just another ultrasound.

The nurse takes my blood pressure and vitals before asking me to leave a urine sample, like any other visit to the OB. Afraid to look down after wiping, I spare a glance at the tissue and am relieved there isn't any blood. The cramping is gone, leaving just a tightness across my midsection. On the quick drive to the office, I convinced myself I was covered in blood and even checked my pants twice for stains before rushing into the clinic.

Walking back to the exam room, I hear him before I see him. "I'm looking for my wife?" Owen says, his voice loud and distressed. "Cassidy Morgan?" I wait in the hall as the receptionist points him in my direction and he locks eyes with me, his face dropping to my stomach. "Cass," he moans, his lower lip trembling. "Are you okay?" He pulls me into his arms for a quick embrace before letting go to inspect me. "Is the baby . . . ?"

I shrug, unable to find my voice. Any semblance of composure falls away in his presence. "I don't know. I started having pain, and I got so scared," I whisper, voice breaking. "I didn't want to go to the hospital," I say, shaking my head. "Then you didn't pick up the phone, and I didn't know what to do . . ."

He pulls me against his shoulder. The handful of women in the waiting area look down at their magazines, anyplace but at the distressed couple embracing in the hallway. "It's going to be okay," he murmurs. "Let's go into the room," he says, eyeing our audience. "I'm here now."

We head back to the exam room, leaving the door cracked. Two minutes later a new nurse heads in, clipboard in hand. It's Sarah, the same nurse I've seen at every appointment since our loss. I'm happy I won't have to repeat my terrible history again, since she already knows my story.

"You're a few hours early for your appointment," Sarah kids, her tone light but her eyes compassionate. "What's going on?" she asks.

Suddenly I feel foolish. The cramping has stopped and I feel perfectly normal again, just freaked out. I've never been an alarmist, but everything has changed. Who is this harried woman panicking on the exam table? "I had some cramps earlier while at work, and I might have overreacted. I actually feel a lot better now," I say, color rising to my cheeks. "I just wanted to come in and get checked out in case something was happening. Like before."

Sarah nods and pets my forearm. She reminds me of Owen's mom, soft in all the right places. "You did the right thing. Let's go to the sonogram room and take a look. You're lucky—the room is empty, so we can just get to all the fun stuff a few hours ahead of time." She stands and motions for us to follow to a high-tech room dedicated to specialty imaging. Two giant screens line the wall, and an exam chair is set up next to a large ultrasound machine. Today we'll get to see all the different parts of our baby boy. Because of the extra blood testing done earlier in the pregnancy, the gender won't be a surprise, but I'm still excited to see all his pieces.

Sarah asks me to lie on the chair and lift my shirt as she fills in my information on the computer screen. Rubbing some warm jelly on my stomach and on the wand, she murmurs, "Don't worry. It's all going to be okay." I wish I could take her at her word—*it's all going to be okay*—but I can't let go of the hard nugget of fear lodged in my core, in my marrow. Maybe I'll see my baby today and things will look perfect, but nothing will be okay until I hold him, crying and alive in my arms.

★ ★ ★

Owen's mesmerized by the bits and blurs moving across the screens suspended from the ceiling. His enthusiasm is contagious, and I smile along with him. It's amazing how clearly we can see his little toes, his pert nose. Holding my hand in his own, Owen squeezes each time the nurse points out another organ, proclaiming each in perfect order while methodically measuring and recording as we go. Every time the baby moves, Owen nudges me on the shoulder to make sure I'm watching. He's beaming from ear to ear.

"Do you want to know the sex?" Sarah asks, lifting the probe and squeezing more blue jelly onto my belly.

"We know . . ." Owen starts, but I shake my head playfully and put a finger to my lips.

"Yes, please," I say. Why not pretend we're a "normal" couple, excited to find out the sex of our baby? It's refreshing to feel this sense of ease and innocence, even if it might be short-lived and artificial.

"Let's see if I can get a good picture," she says, furrowing her brow as she digs the probe into my belly a little harder at a right angle. "Little bugger is being shy," she jokes, passing the wand back and forth. I arch my back and wriggle a little further up into the chair, hoping to jostle him into a better position. He's been twitching like a jumping bean the entire exam, and suddenly he's playing coy. "There we go!" She taps a few buttons, freezing the moment. I study the image, confused. I'm not a human doctor, but I'm familiar with reading ultrasounds. There must be a mistake, because if I'm seeing things correctly, something important is missing.

"It's a girl!" she exclaims, smiling at us.

Her smile fades as she sees the bewilderment on our faces. Owen drops my hand. "But the blood work said it was a boy." His eyes flit between me and Sarah before landing on the black-and-white screen. He squints, but I know it's nothing more than gibberish to his untrained eyes.

"There must be a mistake," I say as I study the image. Sarah has frozen the image on a very clear shot of our baby, and it looks like a girl. "We had the blood test done with the genetic panel a few weeks ago, and the results came back as male," I say, feeling guilty for "tricking" Sarah into thinking we didn't know the sex. "We just wanted to be surprised all over again," I mumble. Panic creeps back, sliding around my heart once again. Something's wrong.

Sarah nods and snaps a few more pictures before replacing the wand. If she has an opinion, she keeps it to herself. "I'll run and get Dr. Julian," she says. "We have multiple views of your baby here, but I want her to look." Seeing the concern on our faces, she continues, "I'm sure there's nothing to worry about. I've been doing this for twelve years and have seen a lot of babies. Yours looks like a perfectly normal and healthy baby girl. I'm sure there's a reasonable explanation for everything," she says, excusing herself from the room.

Owen turns to me. "It's okay, right?" His desperate look of hope is all too familiar. The last time an ultrasound technician left to consult the doctor, the news was anything but okay. "Maybe the blood test was wrong? Or maybe it's a bad angle?"

I frown and study the images. Sarah has to be right. There must be a perfectly logical and scientific explanation for why the blood test and the imaging don't match. Normally, science and facts calm me. Order and logic bring definition to this chaotic world. But every scientific reason that comes to mind implies a problem with the fetus, and I can't help but jump immediately to the worst-case scenario. My ability to hope for the best has been forever corrupted.

"Maybe he's just crossing his legs or something," I mutter, realizing Owen is actually waiting for a response. My answer seems to satisfy him, and he lets out an audible sigh. Whenever he's nervous, he holds his breath before letting it out in a giant whoosh, a tic I normally find endearing. Not today. Today I'm annoyed at how quickly I'm able to put his mind at ease while I'm still overcome with anxiety. Why is it I'm the one who always takes away his fears and then holds on to them, adding to my own crushing load? Why can't we both just sit and share the discomfort?

Before I can say anything else, Sarah returns with Dr. Julian on her heels. She nods a quick hello and settles onto the stool, getting straight to business. Instead of using the images Sarah froze, she takes the wand in her own hand and maneuvers it until she finds a satisfactory view. Both Sarah and the doctor study the new image. Sarah's face creases with worry and she glances at her boss, clearly afraid she's made a mistake. A pang of guilt hits me, but I brush it aside. I'll apologize after I know my baby is okay.

"Nice, strong heartbeat," Dr. Julian says, digging the probe into my stomach at an angle. "There you go," she says, motioning toward the screen. I squint in that direction, my brain acknowledging what I'm seeing but failing to make the right connections. "This is definitely a girl," she says, shaking her head. She clicks a few buttons and zooms in. An image of between our baby girl's legs looms above us.

"You're having a baby girl," she confirms, her voice clear, with no note of hesitation.

"How?" Owen asks. I'm thankful he finds his voice, since my own is lost somewhere.

Dr. Julian chuckles. "Well, for one thing, she's missing some vital pieces that would make her a boy."

"We know the difference between a girl and boy," I say, harsher than I intend. I swallow and force myself to relax, although I'm hardly in the mood for joking. I don't understand why the doctor isn't more concerned about this sudden turn of events. "The blood test came back weeks ago, and we were told we were having a boy," I say, hoping the hysteria inside isn't leaking through my voice yet. "The blood test is ninety-nine percent accurate or something. Is something wrong with the baby? Has he not developed?" Trying to imagine what could cause the discrepancy between the two tests only makes my mind spiral outward, each reason worse than the last.

Dr. Julian wheels the stool toward the foot of the exam chair and rests her palms on her knees as the nurse hands me a towel to wipe my belly.

"I'm sure you're both a little confused, especially since I was the one who told you the blood test was the most reliable," she begins, pushing her glasses up her nose with a finger. "Usually that's the case. However, there are some special instances we don't account for because they're so rare. They are anomalies, if you will."

Owen leans forward on the edge of his seat. I lean back, waiting for the bad news to drop. *Anomaly.* Not the word I want associated with my baby. Sarah said the baby looked healthy and strong, with a good heartbeat and normal growth. I try to fixate on the positive aspects of this visit. So what if there's some confusion about the sex if it's growing and alive? I steel myself for the giant *BUT* I've been waiting for since the start of the appointment. Your baby is healthy *BUT.* Everything is okay, *BUT* . . .

"The blood test doesn't quantify the amount of Y chromosome in the mother's blood, only detects the presence of the chromosome. A mother will have zero detection of Y chromosome in her blood stream if the fetus is female. If there's any Y present, the fetus is determined to be male. This is true for all basic cases," she says, speaking slowly and as simply as possible. I wish she would get to it. Even Owen knows boys have an X and Y while girls have two Xs. "Cassidy, your blood test came back male because it picked up some amount of Y chromosome in your blood," she said. I open my mouth to interrupt, but she stops me by holding up her finger. "However, I suspect the test picked up residual Y chromosome left in your body from your previous pregnancy."

I rack my brain for any instances of this happening in my experience, but veterinarians don't test for gender in horses. Our patients tend not to ask whether they are having a filly or colt. Nowhere in any of the baby forums have I read about this happening, although I've never looked for such specific cases. It never occurred to me I'd need to.

"How is that possible?" I ask.

"Studies have shown the genetic makeup of a fetus can last quite some time in the tissues of the mother. Some might argue that a mother is forever altered with every child she carries," she says, clearly getting into her own argument. "Your miscarriage was only a few months ago, and it's been shown that residual markers of pregnancy might be testable in a mother's blood for up to a year after birth." *Or after loss*, I think. "Since the test doesn't quantify how much Y material is in the blood, it could be a trace amount and still register as positive for a male fetus."

Letting the information sink in, I turn to face Owen, who's staring at the doctor with a slightly dumbfounded expression. Our baby is fine. Our baby *girl* is perfectly healthy, and that's all that matters. I squeeze Owen's shoulder, and he gives me a hesitant smile as he tries to digest the new information. I should be thrilled that everything is okay, but the results of the blood test linger. My baby son refuses to let go. Even as his sister grows in my belly, he persists. My heart tightens with the all-too-familiar twinge of grief. I want to feel joy, but sadness drifts into its rightful place.

"A girl," Owen murmurs. For months we've been imagining our life with a little boy, a mini Owen. Not once have we considered what it might be like with a daughter. "I always wanted a little girl," he says, a smile spreading across his face as his voice cracks. His eyes fill with tears and my own follow suit.

"Me too," I admit, turning to study the monitor again.

"We'll leave you guys for a few minutes." Sarah retreats and Dr. Julian pauses in the doorway, "Come by my office before you go."

We sit in silence, staring at the images of our baby girl.

"Crazy," I say, shaking my head. "What are the odds we would be the one percent whose blood test was wrong?"

Owen shrugs. "I always knew we were special," he says, his wet eyes twinkling. "It's kind of awesome, actually," he says. "He's still a part of you. Maybe he'll always be part of you."

These moments remind me why I love this man so fiercely. His innocence and ability to see the good in everything is never-ending, no matter how much tragedy we suffer. Our son will be part of me forever; I don't need a blood test to tell me this. He burrowed straight through my tissues, past my marrow, and into my soul. Owen is staring at me with pure love and adoration, and it should be easy to simply bask in his loving glow. But a voice from deep inside refuses to be silenced. It's the same voice I tried to ignore weeks ago when we first found out we were having a son and I felt a sting of disappointment, afraid of a "replacement" son. That voice mocks me now. *Are you happy now?* it taunts. Owen wraps his arms around me, and I lean into his tender embrace, hoping it might help ease the sick feeling in the pit of my stomach. All I want is to celebrate the baby girl we're having and to honor the baby boy who will always be with us. The voice quiets, but I know it's not done with me. It'll sing me to sleep later, the familiar song of guilt and loss, making sure I don't forget the words.

✦ 38 ✦

CLAIRE

I HOVER THE CURSOR above the *join discussion* button but don't press it. My fingers are paralyzed by fear, unable to do the simplest of actions. *Click.* Reality looms around me. I'm a twenty-nine-year-old stay-at-home mom. It's been almost ten years since I was a student. In another lifetime I had a promising career as a marketing executive, but I made the conscious choice to raise my children instead. I don't regret my decision. I'd choose it again and again. So what the hell am I doing? I take a sip of my Chardonnay, wondering if it's too late to back out now. It's just an online workshop, a six-week introductory course. It's hardly anything, but it feels like everything.

I've always enjoyed writing. In college, I yearned to major in English literature but recognized such a degree had limited career prospects. Also, I was more interested in writing creatively than reading others' work, so I knew I'd need to follow up my bachelor's with an MFA. But even an advanced degree didn't guarantee a paying job. In the end, I settled on marketing. This gave me an outlet for my creative energy, and my love of words came in handy for the ad copy I produced. It wasn't the same as writing poetry or prose, but it would pay the bills.

For years I've kept a journal, filled mostly with my experiences of motherhood, since I've dedicated most of my adult life to this task. But I've also jotted down my hopes and dreams and sketched the world around me with my words. Under my bed is a stack of beautifully bound notebooks filled edge to edge with my musings, each meticulously labeled and stored in chronological order. Lately, the pages call to me more often. They compel my hand to record my daydreams, stories that feel real for all the time I spend thinking of them. Stories about mothers and daughters and friendship and heartache. Stories with characters that could be me or anyone at all. These stories twirl in my head as I drift to sleep. My eyes snap open at two in the morning as a piece of dialogue or description comes to mind, and in a sleepy haze I jot down a few notes in the journal I always keep on my nightstand. One morning Steve asked why I was so tired, so I told him about my nocturnal scribbles. He suggested I write a book. Like it's that easy.

I'm no author. I'm hardly a writer at all. I keep a diary, like so many others in the world. Recording my thoughts isn't *real* writing. Writing a book is laughable, so I pushed it out of my mind at the time. But the idea keeps coming back, as though this story is trying to burst forth from me. Even my phone's notepad is filled with tidbits of prose, and I've outlined an entire novel in my head. Since Steve put the notion out into the universe, I've been writing in secret, stashing my notebook in my purse and stealing away to write in solitude, never easy in a houseful of needy boys.

Aloof though he may be, Steve noticed. Usually we exchange small gifts on Valentine's Day. Nothing extravagant, just a little something to honor the day and honor our love. Last year it was perfume and concert tickets. This year my gift was a piece of paper folded into a card, a printout of a six-week creative fiction course he'd enrolled me in. To say I was surprised is an understatement. Surprised, giddy, terrified. It's the best present he's ever gotten me.

Day one of the course and I'm frozen in place. All that stands between me and an exciting adventure is one little click. My notes are spread on the desk beside my laptop. A half-completed outline is open in a Word document. I'm eager to take the leap but scared to fall. *Who do I think I am?*

Writing a novel is an outrageous goal for a woman like me. I have no experience, no training, and no time. My calendar is booked. One look at my giant whiteboard and that much is clear. When would I write this book—in between making breakfast and story time at the library? Maybe after baseball practice or while the boys do their homework? My life is busy and full and satisfying. I feel greedy for wanting—needing—more.

Maybe this is how Mom felt. Her desire to create was so great that she couldn't focus on anything else in her life. Cassidy and I blocked her potential, squandered her talent. She painted, but not in the way she wanted, not with two kids and a house to run. Will that be my fate? Will I write, but not the way I want to write, and end up bitter with nothing to show for it? I long to talk to Cassidy but fear she'll only see this as one more way I'm like our mother. She's always questioned my decision to stay at home and hinted I should get back out in the working world. I doubt she'd qualify novel writing as real work. I could talk to Mom, but what's the point? Maybe she'd be proud, but inevitably it would become about her. For once, I want it to be about me.

I take another sip of wine. Maybe a blog would be better. A mommy blog. That way I could write about things I have some authority to speak on. Share my tips and tricks for raising three boys. How to host a great Christmas Eve dinner. How to find time to exercise and get your prepregnancy bod back. I can think of a hundred different topics, and none of them excites me. Plus, I'd need a platform and a social media following, neither of which interests me at all. No, I don't want to be a mommy blogger. I want to be a writer.

Closing my eyes, I click. I know I'm only entering a discussion, but I feel like I'm entering a whole new phase of my life.

◆ 39 ◆

CASSIDY

After
April 1

M Y PHONE BUZZES ON the nightstand, jolting me from
a deep and dreamless sleep. Desperate to quiet the
incessant hum, I nearly knock my reading lamp over before
finally grasping it in my palm. It continues to vibrate as I
fumble with my sleepy thumb and swipe the angry red
answer command. Owen barely stirs next to me, and I'm
thankful he's such a sound sleeper.

It's 2:10 AM. The witching hour. It can only be an
emergency at this ungodly hour. The familiar thrum of
adrenaline surges through my body as my senses quicken
and I go from sleep to alert at once.

"Dr. Morgan," I say, my voice betraying my exhaustion. I assume this is a veterinary emergency, not some
other type.

"Sorry to call so late, Doc," the soft but steely voice
of Cindy Lombardo drawls across the phone line. "I think
Kitty is having a wee bit of a hard time tonight. Seems like
this foal might make its entrance a little early," she says. If
Cindy weren't such an experienced horsewoman, I might
ask a few simple questions to ensure the mare was actually
in labor. But this isn't her first rodeo, so to speak, and she
wouldn't call unless there was a problem.

Swinging my legs over the side of the bed, I'm tilted off-balance by the weight of my belly. It seems to have popped overnight. I'm still getting used to my unfamiliar shape, the roundness both pleasing and annoying. At times like this I wish for my normally lithe frame back, and I fumble in my drawer for a pair of pants with enough stretch to accommodate the bump. Shopping for maternity clothes is on my list of things to do, but like most things not work related, it's low on the totem pole.

Holding the phone to my shoulder with my cheek, I whisper, "I'll be there in twenty," before dropping it to the vanity. Thankfully, my body responds to the call like it always does, and my synapses continue to fire wildly, erasing any remnants of sleep. My eyes adjust to the darkness, and I pull out a pair of worn jeans and shirt using the thin stream of moonlight illuminating the room. Owen rolls over and sighs but doesn't wake.

I tug my jeans up over my hips, bouncing up and down on the cold wooden floor in my bare feet. The jeans are at least an inch away from buttoning, no matter how hard I pull across my waist. *Awesome*, I think, letting out a frustrated breath. I pull an oversized sweater over my shirt and hope it covers my hips.

"The mare is having the baby," I murmur, reaching across the bed and brushing a dry kiss against Owen's cool cheek. "Be back soon, I hope."

He rustles against my touch and cracks an eye open. "Good luck. I love you."

I tiptoe out of the room, my heart thrumming with anxiety and excitement.

* * *

Dr. Ford is away this weekend, so I'm the only vet on call for overnight emergencies. He was hesitant to leave me alone in my "delicate condition," but I assured him (all the while rolling my eyes) I could handle three nights alone, even in such a fragile state. As exhausting as on-call shifts can be, some of my favorite memories come from such midnight adventures.

Delivering a foal is exciting no matter what time of day, but twilight deliveries are always special. Often I'm called to a barn only to find a perfectly healthy filly or colt being cared for by a perfectly happy mare. Horses gave birth without medical intervention for thousands of years and are as capable today as they were then. Horse *owners*, on the other hand, prefer the presence of a medical professional to ease their own minds. As I pull into the Lombardos' farm, I fear this might be one of the few cases where I'm actually needed.

The clock on the dash glows green in the dark: *2:45 AM*. I grab my foaling bag and head toward the barn, a beacon of light in the otherwise black setting.

"It's too soon," Joe says from inside the mare's stall as soon as I walk in. "She still has a few weeks." His shoulders fall as his eyes trail back to Kitty, who's lying in the center of the stall atop a fluffy pile of new stray, her big belly heaving. I note that her breaths are shallow and labored.

The mare's eyes roll back in her head as I enter the stall, the whites clearly visible as her natural instinct to view me as a predator and threat to herself and her baby are overridden by hundreds of years of domestication.

Foal birth in the wild is a much different experience. The stallion and the herd stand guard around the laboring mother to protect them against danger. It's the mare's job to deliver the foal quickly and efficiently. The longer the mare and foal lie on the ground, the longer the entire herd is vulnerable to attack. Once the foal is born, it's on its feet within thirty minutes and nursing not long after. Hundreds of years of instincts were put to the test when horses were placed in stalls to give birth, often surrounded by the strange two-legged creatures who resemble predators.

"It's okay, mama," I say, my voice calm and soothing. The mare tries in vain to lift her head from the floor but drops it as I crouch and reach my hand out to steady her shoulder. "How are you doing, Kitty?" I pet her sweaty neck with one hand and place my thumb and forefinger under her jaw to take her pulse. "You remember me, don't you?" The mare sniffs my palm with her soft muzzle. Sensing I'm not a threat, she relaxes her shoulders back into her bed of straw. I quickly flip up her top lip and note the mare's dry, white gums, a clear sign of dehydration. I wonder how long the mare was laboring before Cindy called. The barn is outfitted with top-of-the-line monitoring technology, but most horsemen won't interfere until absolutely necessary.

As if reading my mind, Joe clears his voice. "She's only been at it since eleven. We noticed the early signs at night check, but she settled into her hay and seemed okay, so we thought it might be false labor. Around midnight she went down and seemed a bit uncomfortable but not distressed. She's only been struggling for the last hour or so. You think the babe is breech?"

Stroking the mare's forehead, I feel her intense gaze follow me as I make my way toward the back of her body. A horse can see almost 360 degrees with its huge, wide-set eyes. However, there is a blind spot directly behind them. As I make my way out of Kitty's sight, I'm careful to keep one hand firmly against her bulging stomach to remind her I'm not a danger to her or the baby. I need her to trust me, which is a lot to ask of her in her compromised state. Her instinct is to rise to her feet or even kick at me. I need her to lie still.

Her breathing is irregular, not surprising under the current circumstances. Each labored intake keeps time with her contractions. Kitty was once a prized athlete, but all her training couldn't prepare her for the struggle of birth. From the start, this pregnancy has been difficult. It was only to be expected that labor would turn out to be hard too.

Pulling a set of elbow-length gloves from my back pocket, I slide them on in one expert motion and set aside Kitty's tail. Reaching inside, I search for the foal. Frowning, I feel a hoof and back leg where there should be a head.

"Foal is breech," I confirm to Joe, who only nods. I think we both knew this was the case but hoped we were wrong. "It needs to come out now," I murmur, biting my lip. Pushing my arm in a little farther, I struggle to find a hind leg. Contacting a hoof, I get a firm grip. "Would you mind holding her head and keeping her calm?" I ask. Sweat breaks out on my forehead despite the cool air, and I wipe it against my shoulder. Although it's unlikely Kitty can stand, if she thinks I'm trying to hurt the baby she could panic, and that's the last thing I want while positioned directly behind her powerful hind legs.

Joe nods and holds the mare's halter in both hands, resting her head on his lap. Kitty sighs as he rubs one of her ears, and her panicked eyes calm. "All set up here," he says, leaning his weight against the mare's shoulder in case she should struggle to stand.

Sliding my hand down the foal's legs, I grab a tiny ankle in either hand. I steady my own breath in time with the mare's heavy contractions. As Kitty breathes out, I brace my right leg on the floor and lean all my weight backward while tugging the foal firmly for ten seconds. The mare tries to look back at me, but Joe murmurs in her ear, coaxing her to relax. He'll make a brilliant Lamaze partner one day.

"One or two more of those and I think we'll have him," I say, my heart rate rising with exertion. Again I wait for the mare to contract and brace myself, pulling even harder this time as the foal's small hooves become visible inch by inch. "Last one, mama," I murmur. My hair is plastered to my forehead, and every muscle in my body is aching and stretching. I can't imagine how Kitty feels. She's getting tired, her breathing faster and shallower. Her last contraction was less forceful against my forearm than the ones before. "One more, girl," I say, more to myself than anything.

I grunt as Kitty contracts against my arm, and I almost lose my grip. Clutching for purchase, I find the foal's hock—the elbow of his hind leg. The mare must feel the pressure easing, because she contracts strongly again, and it's enough to push the foal all the way out, almost on top of me. Laughing with relief, I shuffle out of the way as the baby slips onto the straw, its tiny muzzle already pushing aside the remnants of the birthing sac.

"There we go!" Joe exclaims, his voice booming with pride and relief. Kitty instantly brightens as she lifts herself off her side to look back at her new baby, all long legs and big ears, lying by her back legs. Quickly taking inventory, I note the foal is a male—a colt—and has all the essential body parts and appears vibrant and healthy. Her exhaustion forgotten, Kitty rises to her feet and begins licking and cleaning her colt. Soon she will nudge him into a standing position, allowing him a few failed attempts as he gets used to his wobbly legs. Within the hour he will nurse. Wild horses didn't have the luxury of resting after birth, and even though Kitty birthed in the comfort of a well-lit and bedded barn, this afterbirth will be no different.

"Congratulations! A healthy colt," I say, peeling off the gloves. I'm sweaty and covered in blood and dirt. Horse labor is a messy affair.

"Thank you, Doc," Cindy says, appearing in the doorway of the stall. "I'm sorry I wasn't out here," she says, dropping her chin. "I was worried sick and certain we'd lose one or both of them when I called you. I was a chicken and watching on the camera," she admits. I can tell she's ashamed, but I need no explanation. I understand the desire to hide from the painful reality of death. "Looks like this little guy just couldn't wait to get out," she says, smiling as the mare cleans the colt's face and eyes. He's dark brown, nearly black, with four white markings on his legs and a long white blaze on his face. He'll grow into quite the stunning stallion.

"He's a little small, but alert and well proportioned," I say, heading toward the stall door with Joe. "If he doesn't start nursing in the next ninety minutes, call me and I can come back and help them along," I say, although I doubt it'll be necessary. The little guy is strong and has already proven himself to be a fighter these last ten months.

"Early Bird," Cindy says. Both Joe and I cock our heads at her in question. "That's what we'll call him. Birdie for short." The colt is already trying to stand, and we all laugh as he lifts his long, sticklike hind legs up but can't figure out how to make the front ones follow. He crumples forward in a pile of limbs, and his mother continues to clean him, ignoring his fall.

"I love it," I say, patting her on the arm.

"You go on home now and get some rest," Joe says, not taking his eyes off the mare and foal. "You have your own little birdie to take care of," he says, sparing me a wink out of the corner of his eye.

I cradle my belly gently. So caught up in the moment, I've almost forgotten I'm pregnant. I close my eyes and thank whatever or whoever is looking over Kitty today and pray that same luck will shine down on me when my time comes. Birdie defied all the odds and was born healthy and beautiful. As much as I try to separate my pregnancy journey from this mare's, I can't deny the relief I feel at seeing the foal born tonight. Kitty has suffered loss and hardship in this pregnancy and triumphed. I can only hope for my own happy ending.

"Good night. Call me if you need anything at all," I say, zipping up my beat-up leather bag and leaving the Lombardos by the stall door, arms around each other.

"We will," Cindy murmurs, but she doesn't take her eyes from the miracle before her. I can't blame her. Those first few minutes after a foal is born never feel real, as though if you look away—even for a second—it might all disappear or turn out to be just a magical dream.

◆ 40 ◆

CASSIDY

After
April 16

"OH MY GOSH, LOOK at these!" I exclaim, holding up a pair of booties for all to see. The small crowd of women ooh and aah as I pull a matching fur hat and mitten set from the box. Everything seems impossibly tiny but perfectly proportioned. "Thank you, Sandy," I say, my eyes skimming the room until I find the gift giver. Sandy is the receptionist at the clinic and has known me since I was an intern, fresh out of school. She's watched me grow from a timid doctor to the woman and soon-to-be mother I am today. She blows me a kiss and I beam back at her, the spotlight not so bad.

I was afraid my baby shower would be as torturous as my bridal shower but am pleasantly pleased to admit this is almost fun. I'd begged my mother to let me open my bridal shower gifts in private after the party but was told it was *tradition* and people *expected* to see their gifts opened at such an event. I'm pretty sure no one paid any attention to the toaster ovens and cutlery, more interested in the bottomless mimosa bar. I didn't bother fighting about opening gifts today, knowing it was a losing battle. However, everyone seems mesmerized by the adorable toys and frilly outfits in each carefully wrapped present. Who can resist tiny socks and stuffed animals and the gift of *life* on display at a baby shower?

My sister hands me another bag and I rest it on my lap, afraid my ever-growing belly might knock it to the floor. Although I'm carrying small, I feel huge and off-balance. For the party I decided on a pretty empire-waist dress and heels, but wish I were in my oversized sweats and slippers. Everything is hot and uncomfortable when you're pregnant, and heels are never a good idea.

The package clinks as I shift my legs, whatever's inside sounding breakable. Plucking the card out first, I skim it and force a smile. It's from Tara. Tara whom I haven't seen or talked with since our hot yoga date gone wrong. I wrestled with whether to invite her at all and assumed she wouldn't show up. *Guess the promise of free booze was too tempting to turn down.*

"This one's from Tara," I announce, my voice brittle through my cracked smile. Somehow Tara avoided me earlier while everyone mingled over appetizers and champagne. Maybe she sneaked in late on purpose. She's rarely on time for anything, so why would she show up on time for this?

Inside the gigantic gift bag are a few different-sized boxes hidden among multicolored tissue paper. Ripping the shiny wrapping paper off the first box, I pull what's inside out onto my lap. *Mama's Juice* reads the hand-painted inscription across the front of a giant wineglass. Resting this part of the present on my thigh, I rummage through the tissue paper and pull out the rest of the gifts, one by one. Next is a bottle of my favorite rosé. It's from a vineyard we visited years ago on Long Island. It's a delicious peachy-pink wine that tastes like sunshine in a bottle. She must've special-ordered it, since stores never carry it in stock. Easing the wrapping off a second box, I find a pair of luxurious sheepskin slippers with a gift card to the expensive and indulgent Lavender Farms Spa tucked inside the toe. In a sea of presents for my baby girl, Tara has gone rogue and given gifts meant only for me. It's a rebel move, and my battle-worn heart melts a little at the gesture.

Looking up, I catch Tara's eye. She's biting her lip, waiting to see if I love or hate the gift. It was a risk straying from the registry, especially considering how things were between us. "Thank you," I say, hoping she can sense the sincerity in my voice. "I'm sure going to need this in a few months."

Tara lifts her glass and clears her throat. "I didn't know what to get a baby," she says, her voice clear and high, the confident tone in her voice hiding the insecurity I saw a few moments before. "But I knew exactly what to get you."

I nod and tuck the presents back into the gift bag one by one. Claire hands me another basket overflowing with books and stuffed animals, and the moment is broken by more delight over the joys of baby toys.

★   ★   ★

By three o'clock I'm counting down the minutes until I can get the hell out of these high heels. All in all, the party was an overwhelming success. Baby Morgan was showered with so much love and affection that I'm not quite sure where it'll all go. Owen has already made his appearance, waltzing into the roomful of women with beautiful bouquets for me and both our mothers. As a surprise, his parents flew in for the shower despite telling us they couldn't make it. At the moment, Owen, his dad, and my father are outside attending to the giant array of gifts that need to get back to the house, hopefully in one trip. Thankfully, between my SUV and Owen's truck, we should get it done with some creative packing.

"One last toast before you go?" a familiar voice chirps in my ear. I turn to Tara, who's as luminous as ever, holding a champagne flute toward me. I open my mouth to protest, but she rolls her eyes. "It's mostly orange juice," she adds, before I can lecture. "A splash of champagne is good for you," she says. "Trust me, I'm a doctor."

Blame it on the hormones, but the last of my defenses crumble as I take the mimosa—a fitting olive branch— from my best friend's outstretched hand and lean in for a hug. She's taken by surprise and stiffens against my embrace before hugging me back even tighter. "I'm sorry," I whisper against her ear.

Tara bites her lip and shakes her head. "No, Cass, I'm sorry. I was a complete and utter bitch to you," she says, her beautiful face falling, making her look older than her years. "I'm truly so happy for you and Owen."

"Thank you. It means a lot to me." At one time, what Tara thought was of the utmost importance to me. But if the last few months have taught me anything, it's that although I love my friend, her approval isn't something I seek as fiercely as before. "I've missed you," I admit. "I know things won't be the same as before, but I really do love you."

Tara takes a long sip of her mimosa. She teeters in her four-inch stilettos. I fear she's bypassed silly brunch tipsy and is well on her way to sloppy drunk. Drunk Tara means sappy, overemotional Tara. She's never had an in-between. "Everything is so different now." Finding an empty chair, she falls not so gracefully into it. "It just feels like everyone around me is all grown up and settled . . . and then there's me," she says, gesturing to nowhere and no one in particular. "I'm still *Tara*, single and ready to mingle." She finishes her mimosa and wipes her mouth with the back of her hand, smudging her pretty pink lipstick. "Sometimes it's nice," she murmurs. "But mostly it's lonely." A few tears fall, and she absently brushes them away. "I'm so happy for you, but I hate you a bit too," she confesses, laughing a little. "Not really, of course. Just hate that you left me behind."

All this time I've thought Tara pitied my quaint sub-urban life. The little barbs, the snarky reminders of who

I once was—I took them as Tara viewing me as weak and lacking ambition. Never once did I attribute her actions to jealousy. Strange, since I'm all too accustomed to the familiar grip of envy. It was my mistake. I assumed Tara thought I wanted what *she* had, not the other way around.

"Friends again?" I ask, reaching out my hand to hold hers.

She shakes her head and smiles. "Stop." She closes her eyes against the tears falling unabashedly from her heavily mascaraed eyes. "Please, don't even say anything else. I'm the asshole here, not you. I just wanted to tell you again how happy I am for you. I don't want this to be about me." We both laugh for a second, recognizing how often in our years together things have revolved around Tara. It isn't something I can be mad about; it just happens. "I know I have a tendency towards the dramatic, but this really isn't about that now. I promise." She squeezes my hand. "I love you, Cass, and I'm going to love your baby girl."

All the emotions hit me at once. Love. Nostalgia. Sadness. But one shines brightest, and that's hope. "I love you too," I say, grinning. "I expect Auntie Tara to spoil the crap out of my kid," I tease.

She sniffles and the brightness returns to her eyes, even as her makeup runs down her cheeks. "Oh, don't worry," she says, a mischievous twinkle in her eye. "I will definitely be the cool aunt who sneaks her the first beer and cigarette," she jokes.

I roll my eyes. "You know how I feel about cigarettes."

"Fine, no cigs," she amends. "No promises on the beer, though," she says, and we both laugh like old times, for a few minutes.

✦ 41 ✦

OWEN

After
April 19

F OR ONCE, THE GROUNDHOG is right. In all my years
living in the Northeast, I've noticed that the promise of winter ending is dangled in front of you first by
the groundhog, then by Mother Nature herself. By the
end of February, the weather turns just enough for you to
become cautiously optimistic, wondering if this year the
fat little rodent will get it right. Mother Nature blesses
us with a few warm days as we head into March, so the
tulips and daffodils spread their buds and birds start chirp-
ing each morning, tempting us with spring. Then *bam!*
Snowstorm. The world's blanketed in ten inches of snow
and the ground freezes over again, killing all the hopeful
blossoms and sending the birds back to their nests. Spring's
a mere glimmer on the horizon again, and you end up
feeling silly for even hoping this year might be different.
But maybe this year's the year . . .

I knock on some wood. Even though April Fool's Day
has come and gone, winter's a bitch that might have a few
tricks left up her sleeve. I'm thankful she held back her
wrath until the giant hole in our roof was fixed back up.
Someone is watching over us.

Cassidy giggles as she holds her arms outstretched in front of her, allowing me to guide her by the shoulder. Lacking enough ribbon to tie the whole house up with a giant bow, I settled for a blindfold.

"You know I've been in and out of these rooms for the past two months, right?" She tries to peek, but I swat her hand away playfully.

In reality, she's hardly set foot back here since my crew started construction. Once the plumbing in the kitchen was turned off, she had no reason to enter the work zone and relied on takeout food and the makeshift kitchen (a mini fridge and coffeemaker) I'd set up in the front room. She thinks she knows what she's walking into, but I think I've finally succeeded in surprising her.

"So quiet back here without all those hammers," she muses as we make our way to the darkened kitchen.

"You ready?" I ask, eager to see her face as I unveil years' worth of dreaming, finally made into a reality.

"Yes!" she squeals. Gingerly I untie the blindfold and let it slip to the floor. I flick on the switch to my right, and like magic, our new kitchen illuminates before us.

The centerpiece of the kitchen is the huge quartz island, gleaming white and expansive below an antique cast-iron chandelier, its soft-glow bulbs highlighting the slight sparkle in the surface. Pot racks are suspended on either side of the light fixture, and a new set of copper pans gleam like new pennies. The old galley kitchen is replaced by dark-wood cabinets lining the perimeter of the room. To the left, built-in stainless-steel appliances shine beside more counter space. In the center of the wall is a twelve-paned window above a white farm sink. On either side of an arched doorway are more cabinets and the entrance to the walk-in pantry.

"Owen," Cassidy gushes, running her fingertips along the island. "I can't believe this is the same kitchen," she says, eyes darting from one thing to the next. Her gaze falls to the floor, where new stone tile has replaced the old scuffed wood.

"Ready to see the rest?" I ask, eager to show off every square inch of what I've created for her, for us.

She laughs, fixing her dazzling smile on me. "There's more?"

Suddenly bashful, I take her hand to lead her down the hallway. On our left, the old powder room has been replaced with a modern guest bath. The walls are painted a light gray and the ceilings are open and airy, unlike the old bathroom, which always made me feel like I was peeing under a staircase.

"Is it me, or is everything taller?" she asks, looking up at the ceiling.

It's like she can read my mind. "We raised the ceiling. I was sick of feeling like a giant in a Hobbit house," I kid, although it's exactly how I felt when standing in the back half of our old saltbox. "I was afraid raising the ceiling might stray too far from the original architecture, but we were able to maintain the overall shape of the house while adding a few vertical feet to the back rooms."

She nods appreciatively, looking up and noticing the ceiling. "Oh my god!" she exclaims, eyes wide. "Is that a copper tin ceiling?" The brushed surface reflects against the soft lighting.

I just smile and nod, basking in her happiness. "Close your eyes," I say, turning to face her. "Don't make me blindfold you again," I threaten. She rolls her eyes at me but lets her lids flutter down, her eyelashes almost grazing her cheeks. I steer her farther down the hall to the final reveal.

"Ta-da!" I exclaim, and she opens her eyes.

She raises her hand to her mouth before letting it fall to her heart. Although not a huge space, the last room is lined on two sides by floor-to-ceiling windows, making it appear much larger than the twelve-by-twelve listed on the blueprints. Centered in the back wall are a set of original French doors that open up to the new stone patio. On either side, picture windows are set above built-in desks and custom cabinets. Along one side is a suede sectional with an assortment of blankets and pillows. I envisioned her reading one of her novels curled in one corner when I designed the room.

"Owen," she whispers, her eyes filling with tears. "It's perfect," she says, stepping toward me and hugging me tightly. "Did you pick out all this furniture?" she asks, unable to hide the surprise from her voice.

"I know how to decorate, you know," I tease. "I just always let you handle the decor, since you enjoy it so much," I joke. "Look at the ceiling in here," I say, pointing above us. Although I'm capable of picking a paint color, I'll always be more interested in the grain of the wood or the shape of a unique doorframe. "Isn't it amazing?"

She glances up as I point to the slight slope of the ceiling and the thick wooden beams evenly spaced against the stark white ceiling.

"We tried to keep the authenticity of the original house, since we raised the ceiling so much higher in the other rooms. We pitched is back down here so from the exterior view it has the same dimensions as its original shape."

"You're a genius," she says, smiling up at me. I look for any indication she's being facetious, but there's nothing but admiration in her eyes.

"I should have done this years ago," I muse, shaking my head. "Always waiting for a better time," I say, squinting down at her. "Turned out there was never a perfect time." I shrug, trying to chase away the nagging regret threatening to ruin the moment. I reach out and rest my hand on her belly. "Obviously, doing this at the end of the winter while you're seven months pregnant was the *best* time to start," I joke. Beneath my fingers, I feel our baby girl kick. Someone agrees with me.

"Nothing like a little pressure to get things rolling," she teases, laying her hand over mine. The baby kicks a little harder.

We stand in silence a few moments, both lost in our own worlds before turning to face each other, coming back together.

"Thank you," she says, leaning into me. "Thank you for doing this for us."

I'll do anything for you, I think, and hug her tighter. "I should have done it sooner." I kiss the crown of her hair and pull away, taking her left hand in my own. "Let me show you the patio," I say, leading her out the French doors and into the bright April sunlight. "Not trying to boast, but the fire pit is fucking amazing."

✦ 42 ✦

CASSIDY

After
April 29

WHOEVER DESIGNED THE STORE layout at Beyond Babies is either a psycho or a complete genius. The diapers are nowhere near the diaper bags. The car seats are on the opposite end of the store from the strollers. The bottles aren't next to the pumps, and I've no idea where to start looking for binkies or bibs. Incredibly frustrating but guaranteed to ensure that you walk the entire store perimeter to find the one thing you came for. Along the way I've managed to pick up way more stuff than I needed, which is exactly the intent of this macabre layout. My arms are full, and I regret forgoing the cart at the front of the store.

Weaving through maternity, I find my way to customer service, the whole purpose of my journey into this maze. Sliding into line behind a young woman with an infant strapped to her chest, I shift the breast pump I need to return to my other arm and almost drop the whole lot of crap I'm holding. Thankfully, my giant belly catches the onesies before they fall to the floor. The baby in the carrier yawns before settling back to sleep just as my own little one does somersaults inside, kicking me squarely in the bladder.

Pulling my phone from my back pocket, I try to distract myself from my sudden need to pee. "Shit!" I mutter, swiping too hard and sending my phone flying from
my palm. If I hadn't been holding a three-hundred-dollar
pump in one hand, I might have been able to save the
iPhone, but now I only hope its rubber case will protect it
from shattering on the tile.

"I got it," the girl, who can't be older than twenty-three,
says brightly as she bends, hand cradling the back of her
infant's sleeping head, to scoop my phone from the floor. I
envy her flexibility.

"Thanks," I say, flashing her a quick smile while avoiding eye contact. Awkward small talk is the last thing I'm in
the mood for, and I pray the girl will turn around and follow
the unwritten code of customer service line etiquette.

"How far along are you?" she asks, her hand stroking
the peach fuzz on the back of her baby's head. "I miss
being pregnant," she says, sighing and looking down at
her own living and breathing baby wistfully. "I can't wait
until he's a bit older so I can have the next one."

Straightening the bottom of my oversized sweater, I
pull it a little tighter over my bump. For a second I contemplate frowning at the girl and denying I'm pregnant
at all. Undoubtedly, she'd double back in horror at her
blunder and apologize, maybe even turn back toward
the front of the line. I decide I can't be so mean to this
naïve girl.

"Seven months," I say. The girl cocks her head and
looks adoringly at my belly. She keeps grinning at me,
waiting for my next response. Social decorum sinks in and
I resign to the conversation, now that any chance of escape
seems slim. "How old is your little guy?" I note the boy's
tiny lips puckered around a blue binky. His head is covered
in a layer of blond hair so light it's almost white, and his
eyebrows match. "He's beautiful." This pretty young lady
has created a very attractive baby.

"Ten weeks tomorrow," she answers quickly. "Time's just flying by. I can't believe he's almost three months already!" she exclaims, her voice rising. The boy's eyes flutter at the sound of his mom's voice, but stay closed. "I'm sorry I'm such a mess," she says, gesturing toward her perfectly matching yoga pants and top. "I feel like such a slob. He hasn't been eating or sleeping well, and I've hardly had any time to get back in shape." I can't tell if she's serious. Eyeing her slim body and perfectly curled hair, I wonder what she looked like before the baby if *this* constitutes a mess.

"You look great," I reassure her. I'm sure I'm not the first and won't be the last to tell her the same thing. I doubt she realizes most normal women don't bounce back as quickly, especially when they're over thirty.

"I'm Victoria," she says, holding out a slender hand that I take gingerly in my own, painfully aware of my rough cuticles and callused fingers compared to her neat manicure. "This is Cody," she adds, beaming at her son. "He only sleeps in this carrier." She laughs, her voice high and brittle. Her eyes, though startlingly blue, are tinged with red and ringed with purple hollows beneath the lashes.

"Cassidy," I say, as the line shifts forward a few inches. I glance down at my phone. No text or calls, no clients reaching out with questions about their horses. My phone's only silent when I'm bored and eager for a distraction.

"Is this your first?" Victoria asks, her pale, unlined face turning back in my direction.

"Sorry?" I ask, pretending to be engrossed in my locked cell screen.

"Your first child?"

The air crackles between us, my senses charged and on high alert. A sharp stab of anger hits just above my temple and radiates down by body, working its way into my chest and gripping my heart, clenching it in its hot grasp and squeezing. It's been a while since someone has triggered this familiar sensation, but it settles into my bones like the cancer it is. There are only two acceptable answers to this question—*yes*, I have others, and *no*, I don't. My answer is not so black-and-white. I see red and answer with the unacceptable truth.

"I don't have any other living children, but I miscarried my son at twenty weeks last year," I say through gritted teeth. "So, no, this isn't my first pregnancy, and yes, I've had another child, although this will be my first live one." The beast inside me rages as Victoria's cheeks warm from pink to a violent red. Her lip begins to quiver, and her shoulders shake. As tears start to well in her eyes, the current in the air fizzles as the beast, victorious, retreats and my anger deflates.

Swearing under my breath, I take a step forward. "I'm sorry," I mumble. "I didn't mean to attack you." I feel my own composure slipping now that Victoria is openly crying.

She shakes her head, mascara streaming down both cheeks. "No, I'm sorry," she sobs. "I'm sorry about your baby. My mom lost two babies when I was growing up," she says, sniffling. "It destroyed my parents." She shakes her head but doesn't wipe away the tears. "I can't imagine what you're going through."

The other women in line watch us. A few children gawk while their mothers shush them and instruct them not to stare. She lets me take her hand as I struggle to find my voice. "Please, don't apologize. I don't know why I said those things," I whisper, the back of my throat threatening to close. I need water and fresh air. "I'm sorry," I mutter again, feeling light-headed. "I need to go." Handing Victoria the breast pump with the receipt taped to the top, I turn on my heels and drop the rest of my stuff on the counter.

"But—your return!" she calls out, causing baby Cody's eyes to blink open. He lets out a blood-curdling scream, letting everyone in line know exactly how he feels about being so rudely woken up.

"Keep it," I stutter, pushing past the few people in front of us in my hurry to the exit. My belly bumps up against another heavily pregnant woman, who sneers and clutches her stomach protectively.

The automatic doors slide open and I suck in the cool, spring air like a drowning woman coming up from the depths. As I stumble off the curb, a Prius squeals to a stop and I wave in their direction as I hurry to my SUV across the lot. As I open the door, my phone beeps. Pulling it out, I see all the missed calls and texts. Cleary the store was a dead zone. I resist the urge to throw the phone out the window and lean my forehead against the steering wheel, allowing the tears to finally fall.

★ ★ ★

My parents refused to buy me a pony of my own but agreed to pay for riding lessons at a local farm when I was nine years old. For two summers I rode an old pony named Ryder, a midsized gelding with long, shaggy brown hair. Ryder wasn't the most beautiful horse on the farm, but he was dependable and steady and loved to be brushed and "fixed"—something I enjoyed even more than the actual riding. Ryder obediently stood on the ties every Tuesday while I wrapped his legs in bandages, pretending to fix a broken ankle or an imaginary cut on his forearm. I'd spend hours washing the white socks on his legs until they shone and were scrubbed to surgical standards, a detail my trainer found quite odd. Ryder loved bananas and root beer popsicles and would lick my face with his fat, semidry tongue every time I gave him his favorite treats.

One Tuesday Ryder wasn't in his stall when I arrived. My trainer tried to intercept my parents before they dropped me off, but she was too late.

"Where's Ryder?" I asked, ready to fetch him from the paddock. Most of the other girls hated schlepping out to the fields to catch a pony from his muddy turnout, but I loved it. I'd rather spend my time at the barn currying a dirty pony than practicing trot drills and canter transitions.

My trainer, a leathery older woman who rarely smiled and preferred barking her orders, leaned down and put a hand on either of my shoulders. Her muscular fingers dug into my skin harder than I liked, and I remember being slightly frightened but also curious.

"Ryder got a terrible stomachache last night," she said to me, looking me square in the eye. Her wrinkled face softened, and this strange change in her face scared me worse than the words coming out of her mouth. "He passed away this morning. He was too old for surgery, and his poor stomach was twisted up really bad." So used to her furrowed brow and pursed lips, I couldn't make sense of the firm but gentle words she spoke. "Cassidy, Ryder died last night. He lived a long life here with me on the farm, and he taught a lot of little girls about horses," she said, nodding her head as she spoke. "I know you loved him a little extra special," she said, patting my shoulders before releasing me from her grasp. "And he loved you back."

I still remember her eyes watering as she told me that old lesson pony loved me back. Ryder didn't belong to me. He was owned by the stable and loved by many others, but she acknowledged my special feelings for him. She saw the impact he had on my life, and she honored Ryder's memory by reminding me how much the pony loved me, even though I only saw him every Tuesday.

For the rest of the summer, I stayed away from the barn. Tuesday afternoons I locked myself in my room and stared at the few pictures my parents had captured of me and Ryder together. I didn't have many, but I had enough to spread out on my bed, and every Tuesday I lay down across all those pictures and cried into the comforter.

One Tuesday, while I was on my way upstairs for my weekly Ryder sob-fest, the phone rang. My trainer's raspy voice echoed down the line.

"Cassidy, hon, we miss you at the barn. I know you miss Ryder, but his best friend at the stable is looking for a new girl to help take care of him," she said in her clipped Boston accent. "Big Red misses Ryder too," she said, referring to the tall red horse that lived in the stall beside Ryder and had shared a pasture with my old pony friend before he passed. "He needs someone to bandage up his legs, and you know none of the other girls do half as good a job as you," she teased. Even though she was poking fun at me, we both knew it was the truth, and I swelled with pride. I groomed and cleaned stalls better too.

I hesitated, the familiar buzz of a landline humming in my ears. "Do you know if Big Red likes bananas, or does he prefer apples?" I asked, hoping the big horse might share Ryder's affinity for weird treats.

Trainer cackled. "You know what? I haven't asked him. How about you bring one of each and ask him yourself?"

I considered the offer. I missed Ryder with all my heart and feared no other horse could replace him. But Big Red missed Ryder too. He had probably been lonely and confused since Ryder left. Maybe, just maybe, I could learn to love Big Red too.

"Okay," I agreed, the promise of a new horse to love filling me with excitement. "Oh, but first I need to stop at the store for some fruit."

Smiling at the memory, I stroke the box resting on my lap. My fingers toy with the blue ribbon holding the cover closed, keeping all my memories locked inside. Just when I think I'm finally moving on, days like today remind me how far I've still left to go. I wince at the way I treated poor Victoria, a virtual stranger only trying to make polite conversation. Like an asshole, I made a snap judgment based on nothing but the way she looked.

In a haze of anger and jealousy, I assumed she'd never felt pain or heartache because she held a beautiful baby in her arms and had asked me a question she could never have known would trigger such an outrageous reaction. For some reason I took it upon myself to use my painful story as a weapon to teach her a lesson.

Turns out I'm the one who needed to be taught something. I was wrong about Victoria, so very wrong. Maybe she was blessed with an easy pregnancy, but her own mother had known loss and Victoria had grown up with that shadow in her life, the ghosts of two siblings who never were. Instead of blaming me for my harsh assumptions, she accepted my apology and empathized with me despite my horrible behavior.

Victoria wasn't the first to ask that question; she was just the first I blasted with the truth. It's been my responsibility to protect others from the discomfort the truth elicits, even though it's hurt my heart every time. Today I snapped. Poor Victoria was simply the straw that broke the camel's back.

Untying the bow and lifting the lid, I gaze at the items inside the baby box. I've been afraid that my heart will shrink each time I accept a congratulations on my new pregnancy, the new baby taking up too much space in my chest, pushing my unborn son further from memory, where he's at risk of being forgotten entirely. But it's been over twenty years, and I still smile each time I think about Ryder and his friend Red. The heart makes room and never forgets.

"Ryder," I whisper into the empty room. I gently lay a faded Polaroid of my favorite pony into the box next to a stuffed bear before pulling out a candle I placed inside for a special occasion.

Horses have always been a central part of my life. Ryder and Red were the beginning of my lifelong love affair with the majestic animals that taught me about responsibility, duty, death, and love. Ultimately, those two animals were the reason I became an equine veterinarian. It only makes sense that they'd once again steer the course of my life.

"Apple or banana?" I chuckle, lighting the candle and watching the flames dance across the walls. Closing my eyes, I mourn for the baby I never met and welcome the love I feel for the baby I'll soon be holding. In my heart I know I'll always love my first son, but I'll love my daughter too.

◆ 43 ◆

CLAIRE

After
May 1

"Y OU'RE SURE THE BOYS are okay downstairs?"
Cassidy asks as she slides the loop of a set of purple
curtains over a stainless-steel rod.

Nodding, I lift a pale-pink sweater from the bin and
feel my uterus swell. I fasten it to a tiny velvet hanger and
add it the pile next to me. "Derek and Shane have snacks,
a movie, and an emergency iPad, so they're good for the
rest of the day. The baby's napping in the Pack 'n Play for
at least another hour, so we have some time," I say, picking
up a navy striped dress. Smoothing the little sailor collar
with my finger, I find another hanger. "Girl clothes are
just so much cuter," I muse. I pull out a pink ballerina
skirt, all tulle and ridiculousness, as proof.

"I don't know. All those little bow ties and button-downs
the boys always wore were pretty darn adorable," she says,
holding out one end of the rod for me to help hang across
the long window. "It seems like everything for girls is covered in unicorns nowadays," she adds, shrugging. "I mean,
I love unicorns as much as the next girl, but she's going to
have more clothes with unicorns on them than without."

Laughing, I pick up a sweatshirt with none other than
a wide-eyed and colorfully eyelashed unicorn on the front.

"Well, unicorns are better than dinosaurs and arrows." We step back and look approvingly at our curtain-hanging handiwork. "I don't get the arrows. Seems very hipster to me," I joke.

"Speaking of unicorns . . ." Cassidy says, picking up a wooden plaque with a whimsical unicorn painted on the front. "Keeping it on theme, anyway," she says, eyeing the walls for the perfect spot.

"There," I suggest, pointing to an empty space above the diaper table.

She nods and lifts her hammer, tapping a nail into place. "Perfecto."

I busy myself hanging clothes while Cassidy sorts the bedding. She hums quietly as she works, her shoulders relaxed and whole demeanor carefree, a departure from her normally tightly wound self. Nesting suits my sister. Usually there's more differences than similarities between us, but we share this quality. I loved setting up the nursery for each of my sons. Even though I could've left the room alone after each babe, I always changed the theme while keeping it gender neutral, since Steve and I kept the sex a surprise with all three pregnancies.

As if reading my mind, Cassidy drops heavily to the floor, cradling her ever-growing belly as she tries to twist her legs into a comfortable position. "So, are you and Steve going to try one more time for a baby girl?" She starts folding the giant pile of onesies but gives up as she realizes they're too small. "I know you said three was the magic number, but I can tell you're coveting all these little dresses."

I shrug, not sure where I stand. I love my boy family. We're happy and healthy and this is enough for me. Mostly enough. Sometimes, like now, when I'm surrounded by all this baby gear, my heart tugs me in another direction and I wonder if I won't be complete unless I have one more. Fear is the only thing stopping me. Fear of disappointment if it's another boy. I know I'll love any child, girl or boy, but the pressure for the fourth to be our magical baby girl is so great I'm afraid I'll feel more let down than I'm willing to admit.

"There's an awful lot of testosterone in my house," I agree. She looks at me expectantly. Not long ago I might've held back the truth from her, but our dynamic has shifted these last few months. "I think we might try," I say. "We both want a girl so badly, but I know there's no guarantee. Then I wonder if we're crazy for wanting four children. It seems excessive nowadays. But something's missing," I admit.

Cassidy tilts her head, one of her signature tics, as familiar to me as my own tendency to crack my knuckles or bite my nails. "It would be amazing to have baby cousins so close in age," she says, eyes twinkling at the thought.

"We're working on it," I say, watching as she winces and places a hand against her belly. "You okay?"

She nods, closing her eyes. "Fine," she says finally. "Just Braxton Hicks." Her voice wavers, and I can tell she's more nervous than she's letting on. "Promise, I'm fine. I already called my doctor in a panic earlier this week. I'm getting used to them."

"Must run in the family," I say, relieved she spoke with her OB. I remember the pains well, the tugging and pulling of false contractions, nerve-racking for a woman already on the lookout for signs of labor. "I had them for weeks with all three. Don't worry. You'll know when it's the actual thing," I add. A dark cloud passes over Cassidy's face, and my stomach twists. *Shit.* "Cass, I'm sorry. I'm an asshole," I mumble, mortified that I've forgotten the details she shared with me after her loss.

"Stop, it's not your fault," she says. Her eyes are heavy, but she manages a small smile. "What happened to me was far from normal. I have an idea of what to expect, but this is all unfamiliar territory," she says. "It's good to know you had them too. Definitely makes me feel better."

"It's normal to worry. I can't imagine being pregnant after what you went through. I'd be terrified. I'm terrified *for* you," I add, hoping this won't make her more scared. I only want her to know I'm here for her. "I've been so worried for you, I wanted to wait until your little bean was stuck for good before even thinking about having another one of my own," I say, dropping my eyes to a pair of denim stretch pants with a ruffled bottom. "I thought it might break your heart if I got pregnant again," I whisper. "I couldn't do that to you."

Cassidy is silent, and I lift my gaze back to her. "I'd never begrudge you another baby," she says, biting her lip. I know for certain she'd have been happy for me if I'd gotten pregnant. Still, she's only human.

"I know," I say. "But I needed to make sure. I love you and didn't want to add any more hurt to your heart, even if it was unintentional."

Cassidy nudges my foot with her own. It's not a hug, but we've never been huggy sisters. "God, who's acting like a silly overprotective big sister now?" she teases. "Kind of nice being the baby," she says, smiling.

"I owed you one," I say, squeezing her foot.

Downstairs, Rosie barks, and we both look toward the doorway, me straining to hear if the baby is awake and Cassidy listening for the sound of Owen's car in the driveway.

"Remember how you *just* said you loved me?" I say, glancing at her out of the corner of my eye. She lifts a brow. "I need you to remember how much you love me."

"Why?" Before I can answer, the boys yell up the stairs, *Grandma's here!*

Cassidy whips her head toward me, mouth agape.

"That's why," I say innocently, pushing myself up off the floor quickly before she can kick me.

She scowls and reaches out her hands. "Help me up, at least!" she says, through gritted teeth. Back on her feet, she levels me with a chilly stare. "Evil little genius," she mutters.

I blow a kiss over my shoulder and hustle down the stairs before she resorts to her favorite childhood punishment, the dreaded charley horse.

★ ★ ★

"Cassidy, you look so much bigger than the last time I saw you!" my mom exclaims as soon as Cassidy enters the kitchen.

"Well, it's been a while since Christmas . . ." Cassidy starts, before I catch her eye and mouth *be nice*.

Pulling two Snickers bars from her purse, she hands one to each of the boys. "Now you run along and let Grandma talk to her own kiddies," she says, ruffling Derek's hair. He grimaces but allows the intrusion, since Snickers are his favorite and rarely allowed in our house. They obediently take their treats and scamper toward the den.

Turning back toward us, Mom looks around the room. "Something's different in here."

Rolling her eyes, Cassidy rests her elbows on the kitchen island. I bite my tongue, trying not to laugh.

"Did you paint? I love this color," Mom says, eyeing the counter.

Cassidy looks to me, letting me answer. "Yes, Mom, she painted," I say, chuckling. "They also added this giant island and redid the whole room, but I'm sure it's the fresh paint color you're noticing," I add, unable to help myself. Cassidy's sass is wearing off on me.

"No need for the sarcasm," Mom chastises, clucking her tongue. "Really, Claire, I'm not sure what's gotten into you." Cassidy comes to my side and elbows me.

"Wine, anyone?" Cassidy chirps, embracing the role of golden child, even if it's only for a moment.

"Well, only if you girls will join me," Mom says, pretending to eye her watch. "It's five o'clock somewhere," she titters, as if she didn't utter the same phrase a million times in our youth.

Cassidy makes herself busy pouring two large glasses of Chianti and a glass of iced tea for herself. "So," she says, turning and sliding the drinks in front of us. "To what do I owe the pleasure of this visit?" She heads back toward the fridge and pulls out a block of cheese.

Mom glares over her wineglass. My surprise attack is quickly disintegrating before my eyes.

"I thought we should get together and talk," I say, before Mom can sputter an indignant response. "Clear the air a bit."

Cassidy drops a hunk of cheddar onto a cutting board and shoots me the same look Mom is giving me from the other side of the island. If only they'd realize how similar they are, we wouldn't be in this mess.

Half standing from the stool, Mom grabs her purse. "Clearly I wasn't invited here to receive an apology," she says, rolling her shoulders back and lifting her chin. Cassidy stares back at her. Mom turns to me, waiting for an explanation. I'm at a loss for words.

"No, Mom, I'm not apologizing," Cassidy says, sighing. "But you're welcome to stay and talk. I'd like to talk." The bravado leaves her voice, and I let out a little breath. Maybe this wasn't such a terrible idea. Cassidy heads to the pantry for some crackers, leaving Mom perched on her seat, unsure whether to stay or go. I shoot her a pleading look, hoping it'll be enough to make her stay.

She purses her lips but doesn't get up. "One drink," she concedes, taking a long sip of wine. "But I'm not sure I'll stay for dinner."

Cassidy's nostrils flare, but she bites her tongue.

Thank you, I mouth.

I hate you, she mouths back.

★   ★   ★

One drink turns into two. I try to keep up with Mom drink for drink, but before I know it, we've finished the bottle and most of a second.

"I don't understand why you're so nervous about delivery," Mom says, leaning her ample chest against the counter top while swirling the last of her wine in one hand and popping a slice of cheddar into her mouth with the other. "Women have been delivering babies since the dawn of time," she says, as though this is a novel observation. "There's nothing more natural than delivering a baby," she finishes, sliding her glass toward me for a refill. Reluctantly, I pour her a small sip, finishing off the bottle.

Cassidy and I exchange a look. After a few glasses of wine, Mom can be callous and sometimes cruel. It's not a malicious meanness but one born of ignorance and naïveté. She never knows when to shut up.

"I know, Mom," Cassidy says, shaking her head. "I'm just anxious to get her here safe and sound. It's not the actual delivery I'm worried about."

"I guess that makes sense. Considering all you've been through," she says. I wince at the offhand way my mother acknowledges Cassidy's miscarriage.

"Yeah, losing the baby did shake me up a bit," Cassidy says through gritted teeth.

Clapping my hands together a little too loudly, I hope to break the growing tension in the room. Mom hardly notices Cassidy's anger, which serves to infuriate my sister more. I'm precariously close to losing control of the already tenuous situation.

"What about names?" I ask, trying to steer the conversation into safer territory. "Planning on keeping it a secret until the end?"

Cassidy looks relieved. Fighting with Mom is tiring her out. Even the most stubborn have their breaking point.

"We narrowed it down to two," she says, instantly brightening. "Owen thinks we'll know which suits her best once we see her, so I guess we won't know until she's born."

To the surprise of both of us, Mom laughs. "It's true." She turns away, drifting back in time for a moment. Cassidy and I exchange a glance. Mom rarely reminisces. Looking back to Cassidy, she smiles. "Your father wanted to name you Katherine, after his mother. But as soon as I saw you, I knew you weren't a Katherine. Your eyes were so green and had this sparkle. Katherine seemed too . . . ordinary. You weren't a girl that would be named after someone else."

Cassidy's cheeks are flushed pink as she stares at Mom, entranced by this story we've never been told.

"I poured through this big book of baby names that listed what each one meant. As soon as I came across *Cassidy*, I fell in love. 'Clever,' that's what it means. I knew if I named my baby Cassidy, she'd grow up to be smart and curious." Mom blinks, mouth lifting into a half smile. "And I was right."

At times like this I want to both hug and strangle Mom. All our lives, Cassidy and I have begged for little anecdotes like this one. I know for certain we've both asked about the origin of our names, but we were always met with the same response. *I don't remember. We just liked the name. We must've heard it somewhere.* Boring, unsatisfactory answers that inspired nothing but disappointment. Why hasn't she shared this story before? Looking at Mom now, her auburn hair spun with more gray than not and the lines around her eyes deepening every day, I wonder how things might have been different if she'd shared these memories with us. Maybe it would have been easier to look past her shortcomings and focus on all the good times. Or maybe glimmers of this *othermom* only highlight that she was capable of being better and chose not to be.

"I guess Owen's onto something then," I murmur, looking between my sister and Mom. I glimpse the vibrant young woman Mom once was, overwhelmed by mother-hood. For a moment it's there, the past so vividly recalled, but just as quickly it disappears, leaving the three Marshall women, all grown up.

◆ 44 ◆

May 13
CASSIDY 9:17 AM

SHE HASN'T MOVED ENOUGH today. Lately it feels like she's trying to break free of her ever more constricting confines, unable to turn around and settling for karate chopping me in the bladder every few minutes. Bracing myself against the cool subway tiles, I let the scalding water beat against my aching back while firmly pressing my hand against my bulging belly. I tap two fingers above my belly button—*wake up!*

Closing my eyes, I grimace as a wave of pain radiates from my shoulders to my toes. The pain tightens its grip on my stomach and squeezes my already sore lower back so hard I see stars blur on the periphery of my vision. The contraction ebbs away and I drop my head, letting my wet hair hang limply against my back.

My baby is the size of a spaghetti squash or a pineapple, depending on the app. She's nearing her full height but only weighs around four or five pounds at this point. Hopefully she's begun her downward decent into the uterus so she'll be in position for birth in a few weeks. According to my OB, she's running out of room to turn. I hope this is why I don't feel the constant swooshing of her swimming in my belly. Maybe she's found her spot.

The Braxton Hicks started a few weeks ago. The only thing consistent about them is their inconsistency. Today they're especially bad, stronger and closer together than ever before. I rest my hand on my hip, pushing against the pressure of the ache but finding no relief. Thankfully I'm off from work. My only appointment is with the couch and television.

I open my eyes against the hot water. A sharp, knife-like pain stabs into my side, and before I can turn off the faucet, I'm doubling over, clutching the wall for support. Grabbing for the curtain, I catch myself before my disproportionate body loses its balance and slips in the tub. Swallowing back the sudden urge to vomit, I cling to the curtain, hot water pelting me in the chest as I struggle to catch my breath. The pain comes back and hits me in the same spot, but this time I'm ready and breathe out heavily through my mouth, dizziness threatening to overcome me. Gazing up at the overhead light, a pretty fixture Owen installed right after we moved in, I watch the steam rise and curl toward the exhaust fan before dancing out through the ceiling. I focus on the steam, imagining there's fresh air somewhere up there, if I can only sniff it out.

Carefully, I drop to my knees, holding the side of the claw-foot tub as I fold my enormous belly over my thighs. I remember crawling on my knees once before, desperate to make it down the stairs to my phone.

"Please, God, let my baby be okay," I whisper. I haven't prayed in years, and I'm not even sure I believe in God. But I need all the help I can get. I'm willing to make a deal with the devil if it keeps my baby safe. "Don't let me lose this baby too." I wince as my back tightens, and I see a flash of white behind my eyes.

A trail of red runs down my thighs and swirls toward the drain. Despite the scorching-hot water, I'm frozen with fear.

Forcing myself to move, I heave myself back to standing, desperate to get out of the bathroom and to the phone. I need to call Owen. My legs are wooden and heavy and refuse to listen to my screaming brain. I'm transported back to the waiting room, the hot seepage of my water breaking down my legs. I wipe at my inner thigh, horrified when my hand is covered in warm, sticky blood. Before I can stop myself, I throw up over the side of the tub. Finally, my body responds, and I force myself to continue moving. My baby needs me.

★ ★ ★

OWEN 9:42 AM

An overwhelming sense of déjà vu passes over me as I pull up to the emergency room. Well, *screech up* might be a more apt way of describing it, but to the valet's credit, he doesn't even blink as I throw him my keys and nearly knock him over as I rush inside to get a wheelchair.

I was in the lumber aisle at Home Depot when Cassidy called. It took me a few seconds to reconcile the calm way she spoke with the information she was giving me—that I needed to come home right away because the baby was coming. "It's too soon," I answered, as if that simple fact might change what she'd told me. "There's still a month to go." She didn't respond, only moaned in agony. I abandoned my cart in the middle of aisle two.

She waddled out the front door as I pulled into the drive, one hand on her back and her face twisted in pain. "The bag?" I mumbled, our perfect delivery-day plan quickly unraveling. Cassidy needed her robe and those special postpartum pajama bottoms she had insisted on ordering. Where was the damn bag? We kept meaning to pack the duffel, but we thought we had time. Plenty of time.

She shook her head and let me help her into the truck. Last time I had to drag her kicking and screaming to the hospital. I almost wished she'd fight back now. This calm demeanor was unnerving, as if she'd already lost something. In the truck she sat perched on one side, arms curled around her bump as if she could hold the baby inside by sheer force. I raced the familiar path to the hospital, catching the tail end of a yellow light and hoping the cop who loved to use it as a speed trap wasn't out this morning. Luck was on our side, and we made the sixteen-minute journey in just under twelve.

By another stroke of luck, the emergency room is almost empty and I'm able to flag down a nurse to help me fetch Cassidy from the car. We maneuver her into a chair, lifting her arms and legs like she's a doll. Her pale face barely registers anything. I don't like the look in her eyes. She stares down at her belly, blankly.

"It's going to be okay," I say, jogging behind the nurse as we rush toward the elevators. Déjà vu threatens to crush me again, but I force myself back into the present moment.

Cassidy looks up at me and shakes her head before looking back into her lap. I follow her gaze to the two dark stains on her gray sweatpants, one on either leg. I stop dead in my tracks, bile rising to my throat. *Please God, let her be okay*, I think before pushing myself forward again, into the elevator.

★ ★ ★

CASSIDY 10:22 AM

Most babies born at thirty-five weeks' gestation survive with minimal health deficits, the biggest risk being immature lungs, which might require the baby to spend some time in the NICU. I repeat these facts like a mantra, straining in the back parts of my brain for the exact statistics for survival rates. It's pretty high. Over 90 percent, I think. But my baby coming early isn't the problem. Early, I can deal with. I'm nervous that early labor combined with a lack of movement means something bad. I've no idea if she moved overnight, so she may have been still for as many as eighteen hours now. All the books agreed this is bad.

"Are you fucking kidding me?" I mumble as the orderly pushes me into the last room on the left in the labor-and-delivery unit. Owen lifts a brow. I try to suppress my annoyance that he's forgotten that this was the room. The room we were in *before*. "Anything look familiar in here?" I ask, hating the sarcasm dripping from my voice but unable to stop myself.

The color drains from his face. "Oh, shit. I'll ask for a new room," he says, looking desperately at the aide, who pretends he's not listening to our conversation.

"It's fine," I say, shrugging. "It's just a room." Owen bites his lip, torn between making a big deal or letting it be. The nurse said it was a busy day for babies, so it's possible it's the only room available. I'm not willing to delay being seen and risk irritating the staff just to get a different room.

A nurse and doctor enter and descend on me with practiced efficiency. They help me onto the bed and quickly attach monitors to my belly and arm. The nurse takes my vitals while rattling off a list of questions she'll dutifully note in my chart. I wonder if my folder lists the details of my miscarriage or if there's a fresh chart for each new baby.

"Have you given birth before?" she asks, after recording my blood pressure, temperature, and oxygen levels.

A cramp seizes my lower belly, and I squeeze my eyes shut, pursing my lips. "Yes," I manage, my voice a whistle through the pain.

"Vaginally or caesarean?"

Another cramp. I can't talk through it, which—if the books can be trusted—indicates I'm getting closer to delivery.

Owen clears his throat, my voice in the storm. "We miscarried our first child at twenty weeks. She had a natural delivery," he says, squeezing my shoulder gently.

The nurse nods. "I'm sorry," she says, scribbling in my chart. "We'll do an ultrasound and check the baby's heartbeat first, then a vaginal exam to see how far dilated and effaced you are," she says, her voice low and soothing. "It seems you're far enough along for this to be a nice, standard delivery," she adds, sensing the tension in the room. "Try to relax. We'll take good care of you." She smiles and busies herself getting materials ready to place an IV in my arm. I remember the drill. Another nurse enters and settles onto the stool next to the bed.

"All right, mama," she says, a slight southern drawl lilting her words. "Let's take a peek at the little one." As she squeezes blue jelly onto my belly, I brace myself for the worst. Instead, the beautiful sound of my baby's heartbeat fills the room. *Whoosh, whoosh, whoosh*, its rhythm steady and strong. My eyes fill with tears as another cramp coils through my insides. I smile through the pain and see Owen is grinning, tears running down his cheeks.

"Heartbeat is strong," the nurse confirms, moving the wand down. She rolls the wand left and right, pushing a little harder on the left side of my belly and clicking buttons on the machine with her free hand. I lean back into the pillows and allow myself a moment of peace while I wait for the next contraction.

The nurse furrows her brow and I lean forward. "Looks like the baby's in the posterior position," she says, resting her hands on the side of the bed. "This means she's 'sunny-side-up,' if you will. The hardest part of her head is resting against your lower back, explaining the intense back labor you're feeling. Ideally, she'll turn to the face-down position, but your water has already broken, so she's running out of room in there."

Over the years I've dealt with posterior and breech births often in equine deliveries. Many of those labors needed manual help. "I told the nurse earlier I haven't felt much movement today. Is that normal?"

The nurse nods. "Sometimes as they get closer to delivery, they simply run out of room to kick as much. It's likely she turned around into this position and that initiated labor." She wipes the ultrasound wand down and pushes the machine away as she stands. "Looks like your girl is a little impatient," she jokes.

Owen laughs, some color returning to his cheeks. "Wonder where she gets that from?" he says, nudging me lightly.

"Better early than never." I grimace against a new contraction. "Most importantly, when can I get that epidural?" I ask, the promise of some pain relief almost as good as knowing everything is okay. So far.

★　★　★

Cassidy 11:37 AM

The drugs differ from the first time. *Before* I slipped into a hazy, half-awake state. All I remember are the faded sounds of machines and nurses, a lot of background noise set against a vivid array of dancing lights that hovered just behind my eyelids. Those drugs slipped into my arm and quickly seeped through my entire body, erasing any contractions, any feelings at all. It was like I was swimming through a purple cloud that should've been pain but was soft and blurred. I didn't feel my baby leave my body. It pains me to admit I was nearly unconscious for that monumental action, but it was probably for the best. No one deserves to experience that torture awake.

Now I'm numb from my belly button to my toes but hyperaware of everything else in the room. The machines chirp every few seconds, proof my baby is still actively trying to make her way into the world. Although I can't feel the contractions, the machine by my shoulder shows they are coming fast and furious.

"How much longer?" I ask the room. Owen's sitting in the chair next to the bed, scrolling through his phone. A memory, clear as a photograph, of him cradling his head in his hands as I lay on this same bed, delivering our lost child, comes to mind. I guess part of me was conscious through the mist of drugs. I'm plagued by a stab of guilt for leaving him alone that horrible day. I was given the benefit of sedation to calm my hysteria, but poor Owen had to fend for himself, to bear witness to our son's arrival. "It must almost be time." The machine to my right bleeps in answer.

A dark-haired nurse walks in. *Click.* Another memory. I remember her walking toward my bed another time, but her eyes were sadder before. This same nurse handed me my baby boy, wrapped in a silken shroud, to say our last good-byes. I try to recall her name, but it eludes me.

"I'm sure you don't remember me," I say as she fiddles with the bag of IV fluids dripping into my arm. Owen lifts his head. Recognition flashes in his eyes. "We were here about a year ago when we lost our baby." Although it'll never be easy, it's less difficult to talk about the miscarriage each time I say it out loud. "You were our nurse then, and I just wanted to thank you again for everything you did for us."

Moira, her name card now visible, brushes back a strand of hair as she studies me a little closer. As she recognizes me, warmth fills her brown eyes and she lifts a hand to her heart. "Oh, honey, of course I remember you," she says. "I was so sorry for your loss." She shakes her head before smiling again. "But look at you now!" she exclaims. "It makes me so happy to be here, bringing your second baby into the world." She takes my hand and squeezes. "I'm sure a million people have told you everything happens for a reason," she pauses. I can't help but stiffen at the expression. I've heard it a hundred times by now, and it's still tough to hear. "And I'm sure you've bristled every time some-one says it." She chuckles knowingly. "But your angel baby paved the way for this miracle today. Your little girl is proof that even after the darkest storm, there comes a rainbow." The machine blips beside us, my contractions getting closer together. "It appears your rainbow baby hears us talking about her and wants to join the conversation," she says, winking. "Get ready, mama. I think we're ready to push."

★　★　★

OWEN 12:45 PM

The ice chips I'm fetching for Cassidy seem inadequate. Even though she's been actively pushing for only thirty minutes, her body's been laboring to get our baby out all day. She's clearly exhausted. The doctor called for a quick break to let her rest, but I'm not sure how much more she can handle. She lies on the bed, her chestnut hair plastered across her sweaty brow.

Sensing me beside her she opens her eyes and manages a weak smile before letting me pop two ice chips into her mouth. She's had nothing to eat or drink in hours.

A few minutes later Moira steps into the room. "Cassidy, you're fully effaced and dilated, but the baby hasn't moved from the negative-one position, meaning she still has a long way to go."

I rest my hand on her shoulder. "What does that mean?" I ask as Dr. Julian strides in while pulling on a new pair of gloves.

An alarm on the blood pressure machine sounds loudly, and Moira hits a few buttons. The doctor frowns and furrows her brow. "Blood pressure is spiking a bit, but the contractions are pretty intense. How do you feel otherwise?"

Cassidy tries to lift her head off the pillow but lets it fall back down. I glance at the screen and watch as the numbers rise: 130/100. 148/110. 153/120.

"She normally has really low blood pressure," I say, panic setting in despite my best efforts to stay calm. "I've never seen it that high."

Cassidy turns to look up at me, smiling reassuringly. "I'm okay, Owen, I feel . . ." Her eyes roll back in her head, the whites horrifyingly white before they slip closed. Stunned, I reach my hand to her cheek as if I might rouse her. She feels cool and clammy.

The machine chirps angrily, the pressure dropping instead of rising. It falls down to 100/70 and keeps dipping. Moira presses the call button and I stand, frozen in place, as two more nurses rush into the room. Every machine beeps at once and they growl instructions to each other.

"The fetal heartbeat is elevated . . ."

"Mom's blood pressure is dropping . . ."

"We need to take her into surgery, now . . ."

The nurses continue to talk over each other as one pulls at the machines attached to Cassidy, who lies unconscious on the bed. Time stands still as they wheel her out of the room, ignoring me completely.

"Mr. Morgan?" Moira repeats. I'm not sure how long she's been calling me from the doorway, but I can tell it's not the first time. "Cassidy's getting prepped for an emergency cesarean now. I need you to follow me," she says gently, gesturing for me to hurry up. Our possessions are scattered around the room, and I'm unsure if I'm supposed to leave them or gather them up first. Moira senses my hesitation. "Don't worry. You'll be coming back here. I'll keep your things safe," she promises. A hundred questions run through my mind as I rush to follow her down the hall.

"Cassidy's pressure dropped, and she passed out," she says, stating the obvious. "The baby is in distress. She didn't turn enough to make her way out, and it appears as if the cord might cause some flow complications. The doctors want to get her out as soon as possible to avoid any further risk to Cassidy or the baby." I nod, swallowing back the giant lump threatening to choke me. "Cassidy's getting prepped and asked for you to be there with her."

I nod, still unable to find my voice.

Moira places a hand on my arm. "I need you to buck up," she says, staring me straight in the face, her expression serious. "I don't need you passing out in there because you catch sight of a little blood. She's going to be okay. They both are. Your wife is strong and she needs you right now, so take a deep breath and stand by her side until that baby comes out. You got it?" She releases my arm but gives me one last hard look.

"Yes, ma'am," I say, some color coming back to my cheeks. Moira's right, of course. I'm not the one being cut open, even if I do feel like I'm being torn to pieces.

"All right then," she says, smiling again. "Follow me." She picks up the pace as she heads toward the surgical ward, and I have to jog to keep up.

★　★　★

OWEN 1:05 PM

I'm handed a blue gown, booties, and a cap before entering the surgical room. Watching Moira, I mimic the way she places the gown, slit facing backward, over her scrubs. The booties barely fit over my sneakers.

"You're going to stand next to Cassidy's head. She's awake but a little scared right now. It's your job to keep her calm," she says, snapping a pair of gloves onto her small hands. "Whatever you do, do *not* look behind the curtain. Too many dads peek and end up passed out on the floor. We don't need you hitting your head and getting rushed to the ER," she teases. "No looking."

I nod, my own blood pressure dropping at the thought. "No worries there. Blood and guts make me queasy." She shoots me a concerned look. "I'll be fine. Promise."

Following her through the automatic doors, I'm over-whelmed by the intense brightness of the room. White walls, white floors, white curtains, and harsh white flu-orescent bulbs cast a stark, artificial white glow on the stainless-steel counters and equipment. Dr. Julian stands above Cassidy's exposed belly with a marker in hand. Squinting, I realize she's marking the spots on my wife's body she intends to cut open. Swallowing back a wave of nausea, I avert my gaze to take in the rest of Cassidy's body, which is covered in blue drapes. Moira leads me past a white curtain spread about two feet high and two feet wide across the expanse of Cass's shoulders.

"Hi," I say, reaching down to kiss Cassidy's cool fore-head. Her hair is tucked inside a blue cap like my own. "How are you doing?"

She smiles, her teeth chattering. "I'm good," she says, voice shaking. "But I'm freezing." Her lips are tinged pur-ple. Looking around, I don't see any blankets.

Moira hears the exchange. "The epidural tends to have that affect," she says matter-of-factly. "I'll grab some hot-water bottles for around your shoulders. That should help."

Within a minute she returns with warm bottles that she places gently under Cassidy's shoulders and to either side of her rib cage. I wish I could rub some warmth into my wife, but I'm rendered helpless, watching as both her arms are stretched to the side and she's instructed not to move.

"All right, Cassidy," Dr. Julian says, popping her head in front of the curtain. Her mask is pulled down over her chin and she holds both gloved hands in front of her chest, as if in prayer. "We're ready to start. We should have your little girl out in about twenty minutes. We'll give you a few minutes to say hi. Then we'll need another half hour to stich you back up before sending you to recovery. Dad will go with baby and a nurse to the recovery room and meet you there," she says, her voice clear and worry-free. "Any questions?"

Cassidy turns to me, apprehension creasing her forehead. "Will I be able to do skin-to-skin?" she asks. For weeks, Cassidy obsessed over our birth plan, which includes her spending the first thirty minutes after birth holding our little girl against her chest for better bonding and feeding success. I fear her plan might need to be readjusted.

"Don't worry, we'll have you stitched up and ready for all the skin time you want, I promise."

Cassidy frowns, disappointed. I catch her eye and pucker my lips, blowing her a kiss. She smiles and kisses back. "I'm ready," she says, her voice small.

"You might feel a little light pulling and tugging, but that's normal," Dr. Julian says. My own stomach seizes at the thought, and I thank God he created women to give birth. I sure as hell couldn't do this.

★ ★ ★

CASSIDY 1:24 PM

Well, this is weird, I think to myself as I feel the slight tugging and pulling Dr. Julian warned about. Having not felt anything from the waist down all day, it's strange to suddenly have the ghost of sensation once again. Closing my eyes, I focus on the small movements behind the curtain. I swear I feel them removing my organs, moving them aside to make way for my baby. Maybe I'm only imagining it, but it's surreal all the same. Perhaps because I'm a science geek, I find it more fascinating than I should. I want to tell Owen what I'm experiencing but fear he'll get woozy and faint. He's never been great with the gross.

Classical music plays over the speakers, and I'm glad for the noise. The sound of the machine's bleeping was driving me crazy. Behind the curtain Dr. Julian talks about her own children with a nurse. It comforts me that this surgery is so routine that she's able to converse about the mundane while slicing into me.

"Any minute now," Moira says. She stands with one foot on either side of the curtain. "Get ready, dad; mom's arms have to stay still, but you can hold the babe up to her cheek."

My heart drops. I hoped to at least touch my baby's face with my hand. Logically, I understand I'm in the middle of abdominal surgery, but the naïve part of me wishes they'd make an exception.

The voices behind the drape fall silent, leaving only Vivaldi's *Spring Concerto* humming in the background. One last tug proceeds the best sound I've ever heard. My baby's first cry.

"Congratulation, guys, you have a perfect baby girl," Dr. Julian says, rounding the table with a squirming red bundle. Moira quickly wipes her off and wraps her in a blue-and-pink hospital swaddle, placing a tiny pink hat on her bald head.

Owen reaches out and takes our daughter, holding her to his chest as if she's breakable. No longer crying, our daughter studies him with half-opened eyes. Owen looks down at our little girl with complete adoration and my heart swells, full. He carefully bends and holds her tiny body against my cheek. She nuzzles her face against mine as tears spill from my eyes.

"She's perfect," I murmur, wishing I could hold her to my chest and feel the weight I've been carrying inside me for all these months.

"Baby Morgan was delivered at one twenty-four PM on May thirteenth. She weighs five pounds, seven ounces, and is eighteen point five inches long," Dr. Julian recites while Moira dutifully records the information. "We'll have her cleaned up and run a few tests, but from what I can tell, she's perfectly healthy. Even though she made her appearance a little early, I'd argue she came at the perfect time, just in time for Mother's Day," she says. "Now, let's get you stitched up so you can go back and hold your baby." She disappears once again behind the curtain.

"I love you," Owen says, cradling our baby on his shoulder. I smile, not surprised at how naturally he's taken to holding her.

"I love you both," I say, resting my head a little deeper into the pillow. "Lillie?" I murmur, letting my eyes flutter closed. "I want to name her Lillie," I repeat. Owen nods, kissing our little miracle before following Moira toward recovery. Vivaldi continues to twinkle in the background. Taking a deep breath, I feel myself get put back together, piece by piece.

✦ 45 ✦

JOAN

May 14

Holding the painting tucked beneath my arm, secure against my hip, I wonder if balloons or flowers would've been a more appropriate thing to bring to the hospital. I was so excited to have finished in time, it never crossed my mind to give this gift after Cassidy was home.

Of course, now I wonder if I've made a giant mistake. Knowing my ornery daughter, she'll see it as just one more thing to pack up and take home from the hospital. And where will I put it? Maybe I'll prop it on the windowsill, assuming she has a window. What if she's sharing a room with someone and there's no space? Perhaps I'll offer to take it home and bring it to her house another day. Yes. That's what I'll do. I'll show her the painting today but deliver it later this week. Gives us an excellent excuse for another visit.

Jack takes my other elbow, his gentle touch reminding me to breathe. I lean my weight against him, no words necessary after all these years. Even when we first met, so long ago I can't even tell you how many years, I never needed to fill the silent spaces that fell between us. As a child, I was described as outgoing and talkative (when one was being kind) or as dramatic and annoying (when one was less kind). My own parents were distant and forgetful, and as an only child desperate for their love and affection, I learned that the best way to get attention was by acting out, not always favorably. Although they mostly ignored me, the rare instances where I elicited a response were worth it, so I talked more and more, eager for their approval. This habit lingered past adolescence and plagues me today. Quiet makes me uncomfortable. Except with Jack. Somehow his silence is heavy with everything I've ever longed for.

"Ready?" he asks, hand poised to knock on the door. I texted Owen earlier, so they're expecting us, but Jack always knocks before entering any room. Two teenage daughters taught him a bit about privacy.

I nod, adjusting the painting in my arm, self-conscious. He knocks and Owen murmurs a hushed "Come in," and I wonder if the baby's sleeping. A stab of disappointment runs through me.

"Congratulations, sweetheart," Jack says, beaming as he strides across the private room and kisses Cassidy on the cheek.

Cassidy cradles a small bundle wrapped in a yellow receiving blanket to her chest. "Dad," she says, looking at him with the same adoring gaze she always saved for him. She glances toward me as I make my way to the side of her bed. "Hi, Mom," she says, smiling. I notice the purple circles beneath both eyes and the little wrinkles fanning out from either side. She looks tired but radiant, her wild hair frizzing around her forehead like a soft pink crown. "This is Lillie," she says, maneuvering her arms so we have a better view of our newest grandchild.

Owen reaches his hand across the bed, pumping Jack's hand in an enthusiastic show of male spirit. So much is said with that gesture. Hello, congratulations, well done. How much simpler to be a man.

"She's beautiful," I murmur, eager to hold her to my own bosom, to kiss the light dusting of sandy-blond hair on her head. Realizing I can't hold the baby while holding the painting, I lift it and prop one corner on the edge of the bed. "I made this for you," I say, overcome with a sudden shyness. Jack nods at me, urging me on. "We can take it home with us and bring it back to your house next week, if that's easier."

Cassidy tilts her head to the side, readjusting Lillie in her arms and pulling her a little closer. I shrink against her scrutiny, self-conscious of her stare. Even though I once dreamed of working in an art gallery or having my own exhibit, sharing my work has never come easily for me. Life prevented me from realizing these lofty, childish dreams, but I never stopped painting. The weight of Cassidy's judgment makes me wonder if I could've handled the pressure anyway.

Normally I favor simple landscapes, painted in watercolors and acrylic. Although I prefer to paint from a photo or while studying a scene live, my style errs toward surrealism. Jack likens it to a dreamscape, the way I *wish* something might look. So, if I'm painting a mountain scene, I play with the size ratios and colors so it looks mostly real, but there's an element of pure imagination there too.

For Cassidy I wanted something special, to signify the colossal change from woman to mother she's experiencing. At first, I considered a butterfly on a flower. Had I known she planned on naming her baby Lillie, I would have painted a Lily. But maybe not—that would have been too obvious, a simple metaphor that doesn't befit the complicated nature of Cassidy's personality or transformation.

One morning after a rough early-winter storm, I sat at my kitchen table, drinking coffee and staring out the window. The worst of the rain had stopped, but the glass was streaked with thick droplets that stuck, fat and heavy, to the surface and refused to fall. Wisps of pale-blue sky separated thick gray storm clouds, cracking through the corners and filling in the splinters as the sun tried to rise in the unwelcoming atmosphere. Ever persistent, bright-yellow rays of sunshine peaked through the darkness, radiating off my window and reflecting a hundred colors in every direction. Sipping my coffee, I watched a thin rainbow stretch across the backdrop of my yard, fading and reappearing as I moved my head from side to side. When I looked directly forward, my window resembled stained glass, catching all the colors of the rainbow in its tearstained surface.

An artist always has a notebook at hand, and I quickly sketched an idea for what I might paint Cassidy. Far from my normal landscapes, this was unlike anything I'd captured before, and I was both scared and excited at the prospect. For months I worked on the project, trying to depict the view of that rainbow stretching across the storm-ravaged sky through the lens of those last raindrops.

The final painting is more than I envisioned. I only hope it's clear I painted the scene through a window and that my use of watercolors, blending and bleeding, gives the impression of a rainy day and not of a painter who lost control of her brush.

Silence looms in the room, and I long to fill it. Jack shakes his head once and I bite my lip, waiting for Cassidy to say something. Anything.

"Mom, it's beautiful." Her brows furrow as she continues to study it. I hold my breath, waiting for the *but* that comes after any compliment from my oldest daughter. "I don't even know what to say. I can't believe you painted that for me."

Confused, I search her face for sarcasm and find none. "I just wanted something for you to hang in her room," I stammer, unable to put into words all the reasons I wanted to make something for her and why I wanted to make this piece in particular. Cassidy's never been more than passingly interested in my art. She considered it a hobby or worse, an indulgent quirk. I often sensed her thinly veiled resentment every time I worked on a piece while she was younger, as though my art offended her, made me less of a mother.

"What's it called?" she asks, lifting her gaze to me. Her eyes are shining brightly, and my heart fills with relief. Apologizing has never come easy for either of us.

Embarrassed, I look at my sneakers. It has a name, though I never thought she'd ask. *"What We Carry,"* I say. "We carry all the colors of the rainbow inside of us, if you look in the right places."

All around Cassidy, colors swirl and blend, her normally turbulent aura finally at peace. I stare at my daughter and am dazzled at the pure white light—all the colors of her own rainbow blending into one, shining from within.

Cassidy smiles at me. "Can you put it on the windowsill?" she asks, nodding toward the lone window. A bouquet is perched on one side. "Then do you want to hold her? I think she wants to meet her grandma."

♦ 46 ♦

CASSIDY

May 14

LILLIE SUCKLES GREEDILY AT my breast, her lips parted around my nipple, knowing exactly what to do. She'll eat for another fifteen minutes before dozing off, safely cradled in my arms. Maybe I'll shut my eyes too. *Sleep when the baby sleeps*, everyone says. But I can rest when I get home. Right now, I'm afraid to miss one moment. Even sleeping she's enthralling.

I'm alone with Lillie for the first time. Owen and my parents are grabbing lunch so I can have some privacy, and the nursing staff is checking in less frequently after their initial routine of hourly visits. I relish the lovely quiet after hours of beeping machines and excited chatter.

Mom's painting is propped up on the window, the bright sun a backdrop for its unsettling landscape. Although a handful of her paintings hung around our house growing up, I never looked closely at them. Art was never my strong suit, or so I said to spite my mother, refusing to admit to liking something she found such joy in. Understandable as a teenager, ridiculous for a grown woman. I always assumed she drew flowers and trees, pastel-colored pictures of our backyard to pass the time. Never did I imagine she created images so surreal and unnerving.

The colors pulsate, the edges blurring so all the shades roll together without boundaries. On the surface it's just a rainbow in a rainy sky. But it's so much more. It's turbulence and change. Beauty and fury. Calmness and distortion. Blue bleeds into purple and fades to red. Through my tears, the picture contorts beautifully. Somehow my mother, who's never understood me, captured everything inside me on a piece of canvas.

Lillie's breathing slows gradually until she's asleep, her mouth still puckered and sucking. My heart surges with love as she nestles into the nook of my shoulder. Biting back the tears, I fear my chest might explode, it's so full. My love for Lillie is absolute and without question. I'm no longer afraid of this love and realize my heart was big enough this whole time. For so long I've worried myself sick over whether it's possible to love two things at once. Now I know the expansion of your heart is infinite. There's always room for more.

I lost a baby and I still love him. I carried him inside my belly, along with all my hopes and dreams for his future. When I lost him, I let the guilt and shame weigh me down. The burden of his loss overpowered everything, even the joy he inspired with his short existence. But my grief has blossomed into something else. Something better. I carry my heart on the outside now, a six-pound piece of me and Owen that I'll love and cherish and worry over forever and always. I'm able to remember the son I mis-carried while making new memories with the daughter I hold now. I can be thankful for all I have and still respect that which I don't have any longer. Just like Claire said, things aren't always black-and-white, and some things don't make sense. This used to bother me. The part of me eager to control and understand everything insisted on a logical explanation when, in truth, some things just *are*. Claire also reminded me that Owen is there to share the load, that we carry this monumental weight of parenthood together.

What we carry is each other, our family. And *that* is everything.

Outside the sun's hidden behind a cloud, so the painting is cast in a different light than before. It's changed, just like me. I'm not the same woman I was yesterday or last year or ten years before that. My whole life I've chased some ideal image of myself, convinced if I did *this* and then *that*, I'd be one thing and not the other, when all along I could be all the things at once. I'm a changeling. It's possible to be a daughter, a sister, a wife, a professional, a student, a teacher, a mother. Just because you're one doesn't diminish another. When I lost my baby, I thought I couldn't call myself a mother until I held my child in my arms. Now I know I was a mother all along.

The sun peeks from behind the cloud, and a radiant light reflects from the corner of the picture, like a beacon shining out from the dark.

As I close my eyes, sleep threatens to pull me under, and I succumb. I'm unsettled. I'm hopeful. I'm scared. I'm changed but have never felt more myself.

"Everything happens for a reason," I whisper against Lillie's soft head. My thoughts quiet, and beautiful darkness slips over me.

DISCUSSION GUIDE QUESTIONS

1. The novel places the reader right in the middle of Cassidy experiencing a miscarriage. We don't know much about Cassidy yet, but discuss how her reaction to being told her baby is lost informs who she is as a character. How might different types of women react to this news?

2. Cassidy has a hard time when people, even her own family, try to offer her comfort. Why is this? Do you think this is reasonable, or is she being too sensitive? Overreacting?

3. After returning home from the hospital, Cassidy insists on immediately taking her wedding dress to a donation center. Why can't she wait? What do you think her state of mind is, and how does this dictate her decision-making and response to Owen's hesitancy?

4. Cassidy and her mother, Joan, often butt heads. Both of them are convinced it's because they are so different from each other, but what do you think? Maybe they are more alike than they care to admit. Discuss.

5. Cassidy takes comfort in facts and figures and relishes being in control. However, she is a veterinarian and has a soft spot for animals. As a professional, she knows there is no actual relationship between her own pregnancy struggles and those of her patient,

Kitty, but she can't help but compare the two. Discuss what this says about her as a character and how humans look to make connections to help explain the inexplicable.

6. Cassidy and Claire have a close relationship but are very different. Claire is the peacekeeper and Cassidy the fighter. Claire chose to be a stay-at-home mother—something Cassidy claims disdain for—while Cassidy chose a career. Do you think Cassidy's "disdain" stems from something deeper? Jealousy? Curiosity? Fear?

7. Cassidy and Owen take pride in their "fighting skills" compared with how their own parents and other married couples argue. What do you think about their method of giving each other time and space before talking out their differences? Does this seem to be working for them in relation to the miscarriage? What about before?

8. Cassidy doesn't understand how one in four women have had a miscarriage yet she's never met another woman who's had one . . . unless she has. She wonders whether people simply don't talk about it outside the protected spaces—marriage, with sisters, or even on internet forums. Why do you think miscarriage is something women can't talk about, even with each other? In your experience, what stigmas are associated with pregnancy loss?

9. Claire tells Cassidy that it's normal to be scared about motherhood and that she'll be scared forever. What do you think she means by this? Is this true in your own experience?

10. Cassidy shares her loss on Instagram to mixed reviews. Some famous celebrities have made the news by coming forward and sharing their own losses in the media. They have faced similar reactions, a mixture of backlash and support. What do you think?

Should more women share their stories openly, or is this something better discussed in private?

11. Common wisdom suggests that women wait until after the first trimester to share a positive pregnancy announcement. Women who've had miscarriages often disregard this advice. Cassidy's of the opinion that there's never a "safe" point in the pregnancy, so there's no reason to wait on sharing the news. Others might wait until much later in the pregnancy to be sure they're out of danger. What are your thoughts?

12. Owen loves clichés and catchphrases. How does this speak to Owen's character? Do you have any that you are especially fond of or use frequently?

13. There are many instances in the novel where a character's intentions differ from their actions. Joan is a prime example of this. She often thinks she is being helpful and supportive but is perceived much differently. Talk about this. If this intent is pure but the delivery is flawed, is it fair for Cassidy to react in the ways she does?

14. Cassidy sometimes compares her own pain to that of others and admits that she's ashamed that it makes her feel better. Why do humans do this? Are you guilty of this sometimes too?

15. Cassidy and Tara have been friends since college. In the last fifteen years, a lot has changed, but they always seem to find their way back to each other. This is true of many female friendships that stand the test of time. How do you nurture your friendships while allowing for growth in your own life? Do you think Tara and Cassidy will be able to remain friends, or have they grown too far apart?

16. Owen wants nothing more than to "fix" Cassidy but feels helpless at every turn. How is renovating their house representative of him fixing their relationship?

What does this say about how a dad reacts to miscarriage as opposed to a mom?

17. There are four points of view in the story, although the majority of space is dedicated to Cassidy's viewpoint. Discuss how the other characters help you better understand Cassidy and the story as a whole. Do you have a favorite character? Whom do you relate to the most?

18. Who do you think has the biggest transformation over the course of the story? Which relationship is most changed?

19. Discuss the title of the novel. Each character has a unique perspective on what we carry as a person, mother, father, husband. What do you think the significance of the title is?

20. There's a common expression: after every storm comes a rainbow. This theme is reflected throughout the novel. Lillie is Owen and Cassidy's rainbow baby—the baby born after a loss. But a baby wasn't the only rainbow and the miscarriage wasn't the only storm in the novel. Discuss how sometimes things need to break before they can come back together, in both the novel and in real life.

ACKNOWLEDGMENTS

Thank you to my wonderful editor, Tara Gavin. Your belief in this novel has made it what it is today. Your guidance and wisdom gave me the confidence to bring *What We Carry* into the world.

Thank you to the amazing team at Alcove Press. Melissa Rechter and Madeline Rathle—thank you for always answering my questions and putting up with my annoying type A personality. Your assistance and support throughout this process will not be forgotten.

Rachel Keith, my fantastic copy editor. If only you could sit by my side while I write and fix all my tense and comma issues! My book is better because of you.

Thank you to the members of the WFWA and the 2021 Debut Facebook group. I learned so much from all of you, and your encouragement kept me going when times got tough.

To Kenny, Lindsay, and Amelia—thank you for reading early drafts of the book. You have no idea how much it meant to me for you to even read it, and your comments and advice were invaluable.

Thank you to all the women who shared their stories with me. I see you. I hope this book makes you feel heard.

Horses. Just like Cassidy, I've always found comfort in the barn. I'm thankful for a life surrounded by these majestic creatures. Just being in their presence makes me feel better. I'm lucky enough to be able to do two things I love for a living—horseback riding and writing. It was a joy to combine my two passions in the pages of this book.

My family and friends. Thank you for your endless support. It's always a little embarrassing telling people you wrote a book, but all of you were so excited to read it and willing to help make my dreams come true. I'm blessed to have such an extensive network of amazing people surrounding me. Hopefully I've come a long way from making up stories of ponies behaving like people—but we all have to start somewhere!

Kevin and my girls. You are the reason I wrote this book. I began writing *What We Carry* a few months after my first daughter was born. After endless drafts and revisions, I sent my "final" manuscript out days before I was due with my second daughter. The rest—the publishing deal, more revisions, marketing—was all done with two under two and a full-time job running my own business. I wouldn't have had the time or resolve to follow this through without you, Kevin. You're an incredible husband and partner and your belief in me was absolute—even when I didn't believe in myself. Everything I do, I do for you three.

Angel Baby Fogarty. 10.13.17. You will never be forgotten.